Mischka's Tale

Mischka's Tale

Robert W. Griffin

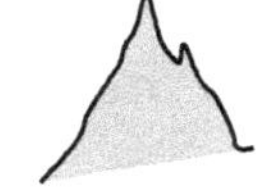

Beinn Ard Publishing

Beinn Ard Publishing
Hollis, NH 03049
www.beinnard.com

ISBN 978-1-889314-32-3 (hardcover)
ISBN 978-1-889314-33-4 (paperback)
ISBN 978-1-889314-34-X (eBook)
ISBN 978-1-889314-35-8 (ePDF)

Library of Congress Control Number: 2014906706

First edition April 2014

The Journey to Antar was published as a stand-alone volume in 2010 by Beinn Ard Publishing, Hollis NH.

For more information on the world of Mischka's Tale, including maps, see www.beinnard.com.

Printed in the United States of America.

To Garth and Luis,
who first heard this story

Contents

Wraith's Vale

Foreword

The world of Mischka's Tale is above all a world of music. The story begins in the rough northern hills, where Mischka's father is a shepherd and his mother a weaver of coarse cloth. But even in these difficult circumstances, Mischka and his siblings are drawn into a love of music, fostered by a wandering harpist who visits their holding, strengthened in the songs they sing together, by the tunes that Mischka plays on the flute that his sister makes for him.

Music becomes his livelihood and more: it is the center of his life, shared with his wife and children, with his extended family and with a world that is enriched by the music he creates. It is not just entertainment, but a force of nature and a force in nature, both beautiful and terrible. In this world, music is a power that can wound and that can heal, that can protect and that can destroy.

In this complexity, music reflects both the human and mythic dimensions of the story. Life is not simple, however beautiful it may be. Love is not simple, at once the source both of the greatest joys and of the greatest sorrows. Love for his wife, Ferenth, for his family and his friends, for the world in which he lives is the well-spring of Mischka's music. But his love for Ferenth drives Mischka to the vale of the wraiths when she dies. Love for his brother-in-law drives him to share Ferrar's exile and then to confront the powerful Baron that Ferrar antagonizes. Ferrar's love for Brethil leads to jealousy and tragedy, as well as to happiness.

The world in which Mischka lives is not just a human world, but also a world informed by other dimensions of life. It is a world in which nature is a living force, visible in the terrible storm that shipwrecks Mischka on the Island of the Forest and in the power of the Chalice of Dyùn. It is a world in which our longing for those who have died becomes the cruelest weapon of tormentors who take their forms. It is a world of transformation, in which the Beisht uses the power of her voice to turn to stone anyone who cannot answer its questions. It is the world of the Lady, creator and sustainer, at once deeply known and forever veiled, caring sustainer and terrible destroyer, celebrated in the most ancient songs of the silver-haired people of the Island of the Forest and in the newly-written songs of Mischka and his family.

The world of Mischka's Tale is not our own. But it is a world in which we may see our own, including those dimensions of meaning and mystery of which we are not always aware, dimensions that pervade our lives no less than those of Mischka and his family.

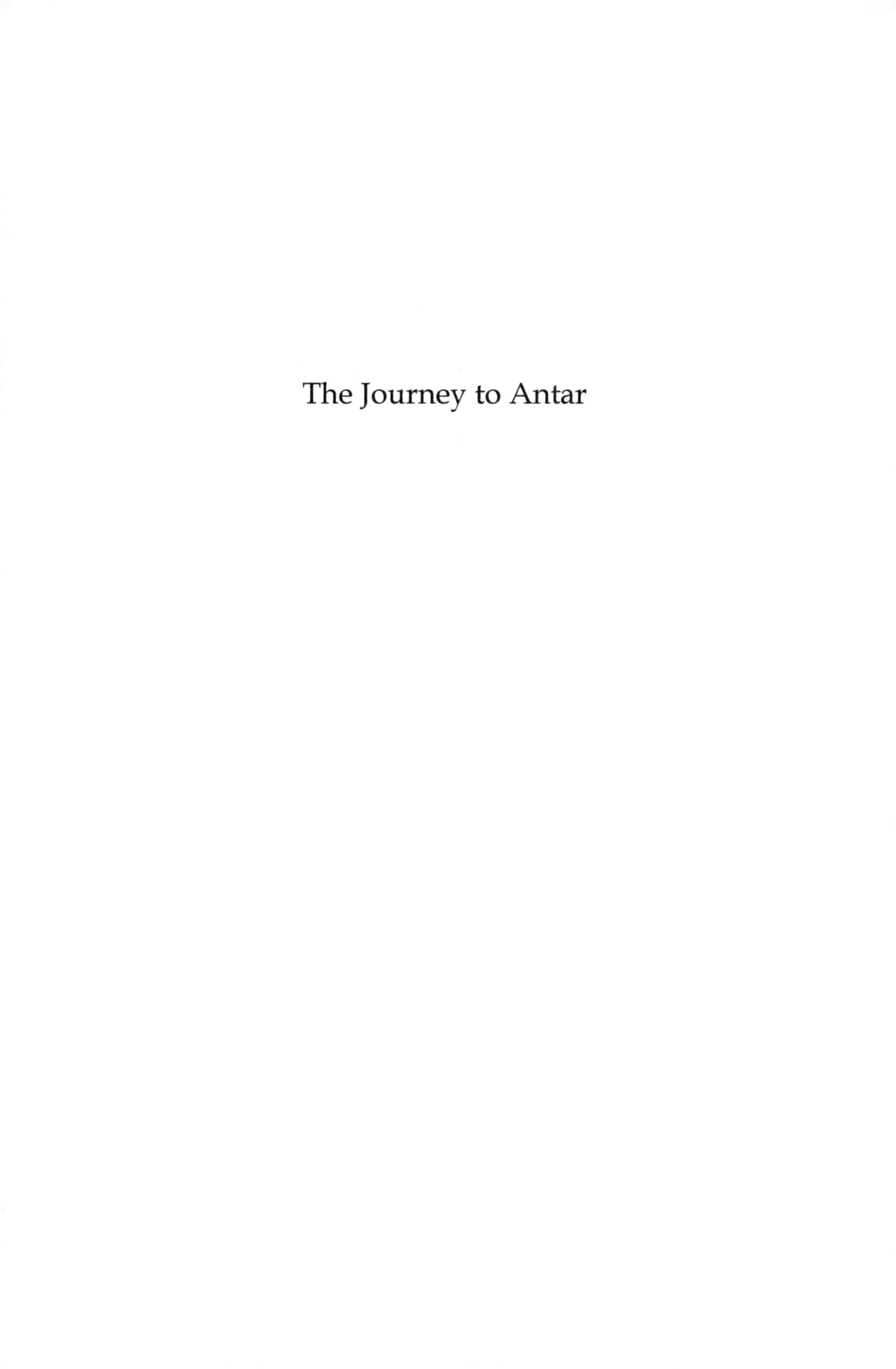

The Journey to Antar

The Singer most knows Her song,
Filling soul and heart.
But those Her music touches sense
Her grace, take their part.

Chapter 1

Mischka Leaves Home

High up on the shoulder of the Tabirnian Hills, where the rocks come up out of the ground every winter and are stacked every spring in walls that wander crazily over the fields —a better harvest than that land ever yields in grain or grass — lived a herdsman named Andor and his family.

Andor and his wife, Nimsha, had three children. Linar was the oldest and strongest. Lutha, the second, was the only daughter, as strong-willed as her father. Mischka was the youngest. From the time he was born everyone called him just Misk: the youngest and the smallest and the stubbornest too. "As stubborn as any of our goats," his father used to say. So Misk was, even as a boy. Once he got an idea in his head, he would stick to it, no matter what.

Once when he was just three, accompanying his father to where their goats grazed in the high meadows, Misk decided that he wanted to ride one of the goats. The moment his father wasn't looking, Misk climbed on the back of Strenua, the largest she-goat. She tossed him off, but Misk climbed on again. She tossed him off again and Misk climbed on again, until at last that goat out of sheer exasperation just lay down on the ground with Misk sitting on top of her. That was the way Misk was.

Misk adored Linar and Lutha, but as they were older and burdened with responsibilities they often had little time for him. Every day, Linar pastured the sheep and the goats on the hillside while Lutha worked with her mother, tending the house, weaving the yarn from the goats and sheep into homespun cloth, preparing the meals or tending the garden, singing all the while.

Sometimes Misk would sit on the stone floor of the cottage, teasing the cat with the yarn that his mother was weaving until at last Nimsha would say, "Misk, must you always be underfoot!"

Misk would reply, "But what can I do? There is nothing for me to do!"

"Then go out and work with your brother, or help your father in the fields, or go walk by yourself. But please don't bother us."

Many long walks Misk took by himself, just exploring the hills. But more often he went out across the meadows to where the goats were grazing in the high fields, where his brother Linar sat with his flocks through heat of summer and cold of autumn and spring.

"Linar, what can I do," Misk would ask.

"Come sit by me," Linar would reply, "and I'll tell you a story." Then he would tell Misk a story of snow-bound nights when the wolves howled on the hills or of brilliant summer days when the larks launched themselves high into the air and sang as though their hearts would burst.

Misk told stories too, though his were not usually as well put together as his brother's. But more often he played the flute that Lutha had made for him from a carefully bored and oiled piece of apple wood. Whenever her father let her take the time, Lutha worked on one musical instrument or another: a tambour, a sistrum, even a small kithar she strung with gut from their own sheep.

"Enough of this!" Andor often said angrily. "Get back to your weaving, girl!" But Misk loved to sit with Lutha as she worked carefully on a new flute or drum, smoothing the wood with pumice stone, polishing it with fleece. Linar was like a father to Misk and Misk loved him deeply. But Lutha he loved with all his heart.

As they walked through the hills, carrying dinner to Linar where he pastured the flocks, she often sang to him.

Oh, many's the lad will walk with me
And many's the lad will go.
Many's the lad will walk with me
And many's the lad I'll know.

Many's the lad will walk with me
And many's the lad I'll see.

But the only lad that I will love
Is the lad who's here with me.

Everywhere that I shall go,
Everywhere that I shall be,
Everywhere I walk alone,
It's you alone I'll see.

Though many's the lad that I will know,
And many's the lad I'll see,
It's he alone that I will love,
The lad who's here with me.

"Lutha, what will I be when I grow up?" Misk asked one day.

"No doubt you'll be a shepherd like Linar."

"And what will you be, Lutha?"

"What will I be, little brother? I have dreamed that someone there will be who will take my hand and walk with me beyond these fields."

"Walk as we do, you and I?"

"Yes, and talk as we do, and sing as we do. Far from these hills we'll wander, to where kestrels are flying and winds are wild. We'll speak then, he and I, of who we are and what we want to become."

"Just as we do," said Misk proudly.

"Yes," replied Lutha. "Just as we do. But whenever we talk, he and I, wherever I go and whatever I do, you'll be in my thoughts."

They walked through the fields to where Linar was that day, high up on the hillside, and the three of them sat in the late evening sun, as the larks tumbled and sang overhead and the curlews called. While they sat and talked, a tune came into Misk's head. He took his flute and started to play. Lutha and Linar smiled as they listened.

"Look, Misk," remarked Linar when the tune was done. "Do you see the eagle soaring high above us? That eagle is the queen of the birds. Her kingdom is far from here, high in the Beinnyn Gial mountains to the north. There amid the highest peaks, ancient wise ones live in a great citadel. The eagle queen is their messenger, their eyes to watch over the world. When there are deep troubles, the wise ones send some wanderer across the roads, someone you will never know, never recognize. He comes to your house and raps on the door, just as night is falling. You run to lift the latch and he says: 'I am a stranger seeking food and lodging.' If you close the door to him and turn him away, your house will never prosper. But if you open the door and let him in, give him milk and bread, a slice of cheese or a bit of fruit, in the morning he'll be gone, but your house will be blessed. You'll know that fortune will follow you for the rest of your days, for you have entertained a messenger of the wise."

"But what message do they bring, these strangers?" asked Misk, wide-eyed.

"A reminder that there is more to the world than your little part of it," replied Lutha, smiling at her brothers. "That there is other music to hear, other wonders to see, mysteries that lie just beyond the horizon. Nothing more than that and nothing less."

Lutha's greatest friend was Niëra, the daughter of their nearest neighbor. Misk often went with his sister when she visited Niëra and her parents. The three of them sat on the grass at the door of the cottage, Misk playing his flute while Lutha and Niëra talked of their dreams and hopes. As Niëra grew older her talk turned more and more to Linar: what he was doing, what he was thinking, what kind of person he was. Lutha would smile and say, "Niëra, my sister, perhaps one day you'll be my sister in truth!" Then Niëra would blush, lower her eyes, and laugh softly with Lutha.

One day they were sitting at the door of the cottage talking of Linar when Niëra's father, Ratha, came back from the fields with his sons. "And you, dear Lutha, who is the man for you?" he teased.

"I don't know yet," Lutha replied. "I only know I'll find him one day, even if he's far from here, even if he's in Antar itself."

"You trust you'll find him, no matter how where he may be?"

"Someday, somewhere. Perhaps he's one of the strangers from the far mountains who'll come with the night and knock on our door. Together we'll wander across Thallhiar, to Fossa, to Antar, from the Rhenn Varrey to the Beinnyn Ard, from the Beinnyn Gial peaks to the Southern Cities."

As she spoke of wandering, her eyes grew bright. A lilt came to her voice at the thought of the far distant lands she might see.

Misk looked up from the picture he was drawing with a piece of charcoal on the stone at the doorstep. "Lutha, don't go without me!"

"You're young, Misk. If I have to leave, what will you do?"

"I'll come and find you. Wherever you go, I'll come and find you."

"I believe you would do that," Lutha laughed.

"I will," insisted her brother.

"Where would you go if you left our fields and mountains?" asked Niëra.

"The world is wide," replied Lutha. "But above all I'd go to the great city of Antar. It's said that there the streets are stone, the houses are built of marble and strong wood. If you stand on the topmost tiers of the city you can look far out to the ocean. Just think, Niëra, to see the ocean and the harbor white with ships' sails!"

One evening in the summer of Misk's twelfth year, there came a knock on the door as the family sat at dinner. When Misk ran to open it, there stood a man in a dark cloak. "Do you have shelter for the night for a poor minstrel, wandering these hills? I am Leland, servant to no man but singer to all."

"For the stranger there is always room in our house," replied Andor. "We have little to offer. But come in and we'll share what we have."

They sat at the door of the cottage after eating, watching the sun drop beneath a horizon flaming with red and gold. "She seeks her rest," Leland remarked. "So must I, soon. For a weary traveler, this was a welcome indeed. May I offer in return music or news of the wider world?"

"First," replied Andor, "what news of Thallhiar?"

"Fair weather and gentle winds, lark song in the heights and sun warm on the fields."

"What news of the great city of Antar?" asked Lutha eagerly.

"Do you know the city?" asked the minstrel curiously. "It's far from here."

"I've never been there," Lutha replied, "but it is well known to all. There the wealth of Egeria gathers. Many are the great houses. Bejeweled lords stroll the streets, proud in their magnificence."

"It is not a place for a poor herdsman," growled Andor.

"Yet it is a place for artisans, as I see you are," replied Leland, gesturing to the hangings on the wall and Lutha's bandoret on the shelf. "In the weavers' quarter are fine rugs, blankets and gowns. In the street of the instrument makers are not only such poor instruments as mine, but also great gilded harps for the singers of the lords of Antar."

"We have no need of gild and gowns. We live here close to the earth and close to the Lady. We have need of nothing more," responded Andor sternly.

"Yet is there not a gleam in your eye, young one, when you look at this poor harp? Your fingers itch to stroke the strings. Here, try it." Leland placed the small traveling harp he was strumming in Misk's hands. Misk plucked the strings, marveling at the soft, gentle music that came from them.

"There's the touch of the harpist in your fingers," observed the minstrel.

"His fingers will get work enough as a shepherd," interrupted Andor, "tending the flocks and shearing the wool, carrying it to market. If one day when he's grown he decides that music is what he needs, then he may travel to the southern cities to find a harp that he can use. Perhaps one day he will take our fleeces to the gates of Antar itself and there he may walk the streets and find what he wishes."

"It is a dangerous journey," cautioned Leland, "and a long one. Yet one can find the way. Travel east from here and in four moons' walk you'll arrive in Antar on the shores of the great ocean, the eastern boundary of Egeria. That's a city of music! But come, let me repay your kindness with a song or two."

He sang for them old songs and new, while Misk and Lutha listened with rapt attention. For years after that, Misk dreamed of the stranger and his harp, of a voice that seemed to echo inside him with a deep and unassuageable longing for distant places and wondrous sights: waterfalls cascading down from the peaks of mountains, early sun on the snow fields of the peaks gilded with morning red. Walking over the fields, carrying dinner to Linar, or sitting at the door of the cottage, spinning and carding the wool, Lutha and Misk talked of Leland and his songs. They sang again the songs that he had sung for them, making up new words or adapting the old ones as it suited them.

Soon three years had passed and Linar was twenty-two, grown to be a man taller and broader-shouldered even than his father. Misk grew as well, but not fast enough, he thought.

"What can I do to become like you?" he asked his brother.

"Become what you are, Misk," Linar replied. "Whatever you are, inside yourself, that is what you should be."

But that was no answer for Misk, who wanted to be like Linar. So he ran and swam and lifted rocks hoping to grow as tall and strong as his brother.

"What can I do? I'll never be like Linar," Misk sobbed to his mother.

"Oh Misk," Nimsha replied. "You're already as tall as Lutha. You're still young. Your full growth will come in time." But for Misk, such an answer was no comfort.

One day Linar came home and said that he had asked Niëra to marry him.

"Are you going away then, Linar?" asked Misk.

"Not far. I'll be building a house for us, out beyond in the pastures."

"You're young yet to be married," said Andor dourly. "What will we do with another mouth to feed and barely enough for ourselves?"

"Would you rather have me leave, Father?"

Andor shook his head. "There's no good answer for things like this. Better that you should wait yet a few years. But youth will ever do what it wishes."

Misk begged and begged Linar to stay. Linar said only, "Misk, there is a time in each person's life when your life changes and what has been is no longer what will be. For me, that time has come."

Lutha went about the house with a brow like thunder, angry at her father for his selfishness even as she was glad for her brother and Niëra. What had been a family where each, if not completely happy, yet at least took pleasure in the others, grew somber and quiet. Niëra, when Linar brought her to visit, wondered at the sorrow in the family.

"Perhaps it's not the time for us to marry," she said to Linar.

"When I have finished our house, then it will be time," Linar replied.

He asked Misk to come help him on the house, but his father said no. "It is enough that you are shirking your work. Misk will take over pasturing the flocks that you have abandoned."

"Do you begrudge me the time to build my own house? What of your own father? Did you not build this house with your own hands?"

"So I did. But that didn't keep me from tending my parent's flock as well."

"Have you no good wishes," asked Linar, "no kind words to speak at this separation? Would you rather that I leave now?"

"Do what you will," shouted his father. "Do what you will."

So Linar left and the work of tending the flock fell to Misk. In the evenings he drove the goats back to the fold, then when the meal was done said to his parents, "I am going to see Linar."

His father frowned, but Misk left the house and crossed the fields to where his brother's house was slowly taking shape. Through the long evenings Misk worked with Linar and Niëra's eldest brother, Herach, raising the stones, helping to lay the cross-beams and roof tiles. At times Lutha came as well, to sing in her clear sweet voice while Misk joined in with his flute. When the sound of their song came across the field to their parents' house, Nimsha wept and Andor scowled.

Linar finished the cottage just as the Hare Moon was giving way to Harvest. Linar and Niëra invited the families and few neighbors to the ceremony of sharing the wheaten cake and marriage feast. Niëra's father had given the couple four ewes and a ram, as well as the yearling for the feast. Andor, shamed by his neighbor, had given five ewes to them as well, but grudgingly. He took the piece of wheaten cake that Niëra brought to him but continued to glower at his son. Ratha rose and gave his blessing to the couple. Then the guests looked at Andor expectantly. It was only after Nimsha's urgently whispered entreaties that he at last rose to his feet.

"I had hoped that my children would be steadfast supports for the old age that even now approaches. But they abandon us, go their headstrong way. They ask my blessing? Then may the Lady give them what blessing they deserve. I'll say no more."

Lutha's face flushed red with anger. But Nimsha laid her hand on her daughter's arm and Lutha remained silent, saying nothing until she returned to their cottage with her parents and Misk when the marriage feast was done.

She went to her room and returned clad in a set of Misk's trews and jerkin, wool cape on her shoulders and her bandoret slung at her side.

"I will not stay here any longer," she said coldly to her father. He did not reply, only looked at her just as coldly.

"Where will you go?" asked Nimsha. "Will you leave us too, like your brother?"

"You drive us away," said Lutha, "You ask of us every sacrifice and give us nothing but sorrow."

"Go then," said Andor at last, his eyes flashing under his dark brows. "Go then and do not ask to come back."

"Lutha, where will you go?" cried Misk. "Don't go," he pleaded.

"Misk," she said to her brother, "for each there is something we must do. For me it is this."

"Take me with you, Lutha! Take me!"

"Not yet. But when the time comes that you too must leave, then come and find me."

"But where will you be?"

"I don't know. Somewhere far from here."

"But what will you do?"

"Our mother is the best of weavers and I am not much less than she. I'll follow that trade, if I can find a place. Look for me in Antar, in the quarter of the weavers. Look for me there."

Then she was gone and there was no laughter in the house. When Misk came home from tending the flocks, the table was cold. The meals were poor, his parents silent.

It was a long and silent winter. Misk worked beside his father milking, shearing and lambing. He gathered nuts and wood in the forests beyond the downs, stopping by his brother's cottage with the last berries of autumn and the first greens of spring. But at last on the eve of Lark Moon, when the may bloomed in the forests, he too stood before his parents, with all the determination of his sixteen years.

"I cannot stay any longer. I must go and find Lutha. I must go to Antar and find her."

"What of us?" pleaded his mother.

"Linar is just beyond the fields, yet you say nothing to him. Lutha has left, yet you have not gone after her. If I leave, is it any surprise?"

"Go then," said Andor bitterly. "There is no place here for those who will not stay."

"Nor place for those who would," retorted Misk as he walked from the house.

He stopped first at Linar's cottage. Niëra, heavy with child, gave him a strong hug. "Are you on your way then?" she asked.

"I'm going to find Lutha."

"May you succeed in your search," said Niëra.

"When you do," added Linar, "tell her that you and she must bring music back to these fields. Tell her that when she comes back, we will be here to welcome her."

"I'll tell her," promised Misk. "I'll tell her that, Linar."

"Oh Misk," said Niëra. "What will you do, my little brother?"

"What I've always done: walk and sing. Don't worry for me."

Then Misk was out the door, across the fields and away to find his sister.

Chapter 2

Firfal's Players

By the next day, Misk was far from his parents' house. He was still among the fields, on the broad expanse of the downs, and he still followed the same path that he had walked on other days, pasturing his flocks in upland meadows. He wondered what his father would do now, with no one to tend the sheep while he was working in the fields, growing the few crops they did. His mother Nimsha, what was she doing? Stirring her dyes? Cooking the noon meal on the fireplace hearth? Or sitting in the doorway, looking to the east where he had gone? He thought of Linar and Niëra, alone in their cottage with a baby on the way and so little to support themselves. He could hardly bear to think of leaving them. But then Lutha his sister came to his mind, perhaps by now in Antar, a city that was only a rumor to those who lived high on the western downs of Egeria, and he felt a stir of excitement.

To the east of Andor's pastures, the mountains came in, forming a cradle around the farmstead there, the holding of Niëra's parents. Misk stopped at the cottage to bid them goodbye.

"Why, it's young Misk!" exclaimed Ratha. "Have you come for a visit?"

"Not a visit, but a farewell. I'm on my way to Antar, to find my sister Lutha."

"All the way to Antar! Well, it's not so long since Lutha came this same way. And as we did for her, we'll send you off with what we can that might help you on your journey."

"What's that?" asked Misk.

"There are three things that one needs for the long journey," replied Ratha. "A light heart, a full stomach, and a strong leg."

"Strong legs I have," declared Misk. Misk had grown over the winter, though his face was still smooth and beardless, and his limbs had the gangly looseness of the growing boy.

"That you do. Yet something to protect your feet would not come amiss. Perhaps these will fit you."

He held out a pair of strong boots to Misk.

"But don't you need them?" asked Misk hesitantly.

"I can always make another. You'll need them more than I. Take them, with our good wishes."

"A full stomach you'll need as well," added Nirin, his wife. She packed a leather sack with bread, fruit and cheese and gave it to Misk.

"A light heart you'll need, most of all," continued Ratha. "Without it, the road will be long and weary."

"What can you give me for that?" asked Misk with a rueful smile.

"Just this," replied Ratha. "When you think the way is longest and the troubles are most grim, hold fast to the thought of these fields: the sun warm on your face, the wind tossing your hair. Hold fast to the thought of the good that's here. Even when most you feel despair at what you've left behind and seemingly lost, still your heart will grow lighter to know these things are always yours, that the world is a place of beauty and strength, and that it is there always for those with eyes to see it."

Nirin embraced the boy, then held him at arms' length, looking up into his eyes. "As you think of this, young Misk, listen to the songs that rise in your heart. Tune your music to these melodies and everyone who hears you will welcome you as we always have."

"But one who undertakes a journey such as yours must take his full name," declared Ratha. "From now on, you must be Mischka, not Misk!!"

So it was as Mischka that he went on his way. His heart was heavy at the thought of leaving the hills, friends and family he had always known. But each time he thought of finding Lutha, he rejoiced once again at the stone under his feet and the grass in the distance, the mountains behind him and the unknown path ahead.

Two days' walk southeast of his parents' house was the small village Sheltring. It sat on the banks of the Greveling and through it passed the road leading from the mountains east to Antar. When Mischka arrived, the preparations were underway for the dance that they held every sevennight in the village square. As Mischka walked through the streets, smiling at people, they greeted and welcomed him. When he smiled back, they asked, "Are you come for the dance, stranger?"

"I'm on my way to Antar," Mischka replied.

"Antar!" they exclaimed. "Well then, you have many miles to go. But for tonight come and dance with us."

"Thank you," Mischka answered with a shake of his head. "But I must be on my way."

He went to the banks of the river and sat there, watching the current coursing away to the south, and thought of turning in that direction rather than to the east. Yet his heart was pulled toward Antar, for Lutha had said that that was where she would be. As he sat by the river, he took out his pipe and added a descant to the rippling murmur of the water as it coursed along the bank.

When he stopped his playing he looked up. A young girl was standing in front of him.

"That was a good tune. Play it again!" she demanded.

"It was nothing," laughed Mischka, "just a little twiddling I made up."

"It was nice," insisted the girl. "Play again and let me dance to it."

So Mischka played. The girl began to dance, one arm above her head, her feet under her skirts lifting as she whirled and stepped. She laughed and smiled as she danced. When at last she stopped, breathless, she insisted once more: "You must come to the dance tonight, and play for us!"

"Play for you?" repeated Mischka

"Yes! Although our musicians are good, none of them play like you."

"I don't know that I can stay," replied Mischka. "I have a long journey ahead."

"Stay just for tonight, then," interrupted the girl. "Come and have supper with us and then you can go on your way tomorrow."

"Where do you live?"

"I'll show you. What's your name?" she asked.

"I'm called Mischka."

"I'm Zelah. Where are you from?"

"I'm from the mountains. I've been a shepherd, but now I'm on my way to Antar."

As they walked through the streets, the vendors hawking fruit and bread and cheese called to them, "Come buy of me. A warm cloak for the night, woven in Antar itself."

"Not for me," laughed Mischka, his hands raised in friendly refusal. "I'm on my way there."

"It is a long way to travel. The Lady smile on your road," replied the merchant.

The girl led him to her house, a small wood frame on one of the quiet streets of the village.

"Father! Father, come and see! This is Mischka. He plays the flute and will play for us tonight."

"A stranger is it? Come in. Where are you from?"

"A small steading to the north. I'm on my way to Antar."

"Your feet must be weary from the miles. Come and join us." He took Mischka to the table where Zelah's two brothers and mother were already sitting. There on the table was thick lentil soup, hearty bread, and greens from their own garden.

"I have a little I can share," offered Mischka, taking out some of the cheese that Nirin had given him. "This is from my neighbors. They made it themselves."

"We will try a little," agreed Zelah's father, cutting a small piece. "This is good farm cheese. There's nothing wrong with that. So you've come for the dance?"

"I hadn't intended to," replied Mischka, "But Zelah thought that I might join in the playing tonight."

"Yes Father, he plays the flute. It's wonderful!"

"There's always room for another musician. When you get tired of playing, take a turn with the dancers."

"All our musicians are from the village," remarked Zelah's older brother, Reshak. "Now and then a wanderer comes to join them, as we hope you will."

"Have you ever met the minstrel, Leland?" asked Mischka.

"He's passed through Sheltring several times," replied Zelah's younger brother, Narthek. "He's plays the harp, does he not?"

"Yes," Mischka agreed. "Once he stopped at our house."

"So far out of the way! You are lucky that he visited you," responded Reshak,

"Is he here tonight?" asked Mischka.

"No, but perhaps you'll find him in your travels. I've heard he crosses the land from the western mountains to the sea, from the southern cities to the great northern peaks and Antar itself," continued Reshak.

At last Zelah's father said, "Come, it's time for the dance." Her two brothers shouted, "We'll see you there!" and went off to find their friends in the town who would join them at the dance.

The whole village, it seemed, came to the square, the grassy sward under the trees, where lanterns hung from the boughs, torches flickered in the late spring evening air. At one end of the green were gathered a small group of musicians: one with a kithar, another with a drum. Zelah's father led Mischka up to the group. "We have a visitor with us tonight," he told them.

"Welcome, stranger. Are you a musician too?" asked the kithar player.

"I can play the flute," replied Mischka doubtfully.

"Then welcome! We'll be glad to have your flute join in our music."

"I've never played except with my brother and sister," protested Mischka.

"Then think of us as your brother and sister," the drum player answered. "Do you know this one?" They began a lilting tune, playing it through once and then inviting Mischka to join in.

As they played, onto the grassy sward came the people of the town. Joining hands together they began to dance, in couples for this, leaping and whirling among the trees, laughing.

One of the village boys stepped to the center and began to dance alone. He pranced and whirled, then another stepped to the center and a great circle formed around the dancers. Together they leapt and twirled, while everyone laughed and shouted encouragement, until at last the musicians stopped to catch their breath. Laughter and applause rang out.

"Well done, stranger," they shouted to Mischka, "well done!"

Then the musicians began a slower tune, a tune of longing and hope. Young and old formed again a great circle. They wove to the left and to the right, then one led them in a great chain. Beyond the circle, couples danced together, arms around each other. The music rose into the night sky, seeming to wash the stars until they were brighter than Mischka had ever seen before.

When morning came, Mischka went on his way, heading east along the great road, traveling again towards Antar.

That night he lay on cool grass, his cloak wrapped about him. He had bread and cheese that Zelah's mother had given him, and a flask of water. But for a boy of seventeen, after a long day of walking, it was a hungry night. So he took his flute from his pocket and began playing. The wind whistling across the high meadow played a counterpoint to his song, a burden beneath his tune. His music rode the wind, ringing clear and sweet into the darkness.

The next morning when he woke up, he saw a plume of smoke beyond the ridge north of the road. "This may be travelers like me," he thought. "At least I can see who it is and perhaps find company for my journey." So he set off across the field to the fire that he saw.

As he approached over the rim of the hill, he saw below him beside a stream a brightly painted wagon, a piebald horse and, seated around a fire, three people. One was the largest, fattest man he'd ever seen; in his hands was a harp he played quietly and deftly. The other two were young, not much older or bigger than Mischka himself.

"Who is this then," shouted the man who sat by the fire. "What little wisp is this that comes to our hearth? Ferenth, go and greet him and bring him forward."

One of the two smaller figures by the fire rose and came towards Mischka, who saw that it was a girl of his own age.

"You're welcome, stranger," she said quietly, her light blue eyes looking confidently into his. "Would you join us?"

"I have not much to offer," replied Mischka, holding out empty hands.

"We have enough to share. Come join us by the fire. I am Ferenth. My brother Ferrar, our master Firfal and I welcome you."

Mischka nodded and Ferenth led him to the fire. As Mischka approached he could see that in fact the big man was even bigger than he had thought, a giant of a man in girth. He sat on a little stool. Surely if he'd sat on the ground it would have been impossible for him to stand up!

Near the fire knelt a boy, very much like the girl. Their faces were similar and their gestures also much the same. The boy looked up quickly with a suspicious glance that darkened his eyes and then continued with his cooking.

Well, well!" roared Firfal. "What, I wonder, is this little smidgen, this little wisp, this little scrap of a person?"

"I am Mischka."

"Mischka! A good name. And where are you from, Mischka the wanderer?"

"Across the fields to the western hills, several days' journey."

"Do you play the flute?" Ferenth asked.

"Somewhat," replied Mischka, turning to her.

"Were you playing last night?"

"Did you hear me?"

"We did and wondered who might be out so late, entertaining the wind and the grass."

"Where are you off to, my young reed?" interrupted Firfal.

"I am going to Antar, to find my sister."

"On a quest are you?" inquired Firfal again.

"I promised my sister that I would find her and she planned to travel to Antar. So I am going there as well."

"It is a long way to Antar." Firfal stroked his triple chin ruminatively, looking at Mischka. "How do you mean to get there?"

"By my own feet. It is not so far but that I can walk there, if Lutha did."

"Ah, but are you sure that she arrived?" demanded Firfal, wagging his finger at Mischka. "There are many stories of those who searched for Antar and lost their way."

"She said she would meet me there and so she will."

"Is it long since she went?" asked Ferenth.

"Almost a year," Mischka replied sadly.

"Many things change even in that time, my young sparrow," warned Firfal. "Many dreams will be forgotten and many promises will be broken."

"Lutha will not break her promise to me. She told me she would wait for me in Antar. She told me I would find her there, if I came to look for her. She will be there."

"So she may," agreed Firfal. "But it is a long and dangerous way. For such a small sprat as you, doubly dangerous. There are bandits and fierce animals. What will you do when you meet them?"

"Run away!" replied Mischka, laughing.

"Can you run as fast as a bandit on his mount? Can you run as fast as the wraiths if you stray into their silver valley? Can you do these things, my little parsnip?"

"I am not afraid," protested Mischka. "If I must face these things to find my sister, I will."

"Firfal," said Ferenth, placing her hand on the fat man's shoulder, "since he plays the flute, wouldn't he be a good addition to our troupe?"

"Perhaps, perhaps. Tell me, wisp, have you any desire to be a player?"

"To play what?" asked Mischka dubiously.

"We are a troupe of storytellers and musicians, myself and my two young companions here. Ferenth is a singer. No bird has a lovelier voice than she. As for her brother, Ferrar, no one is more skilled than he at acrobatics, tumbling and juggling. Though his voice is rough, his hands make a music of their own with spheres of crystal and torches flaming. I have no rival on a multitude of instruments, to make you the sweetest songs or the most stirring melodies. I am Firfal, and Firfal is fearful of nothing."

Mischka looked at the fat man and at his two companions, the young girl Ferenth and her brother Ferrar who glared at him still with angry and scornful eyes.

"Come now, my little owlet. Show us that you are really a sparrow, or perhaps even a nightingale. Let us hear what music you can bring to our troupe."

Mischka took the flute from his pack. He thought for a moment, then began again the slow melody he had played the night before, as he sat looking up at the stars: a quiet melody, a serious melody, winding its way as it had the night before across the landscape.

Firfal pursed his lips, his head tilted to one side, while Ferenth stood quietly, her eyes on Mischka's face. Ferrar looked up from the cooking pot, glaring at Mischka with animosity. When Mischka finished, Firfal nodded his head once and said slowly, "So, perhaps you are a sparrow, if not a nightingale. Such little tunings are well enough."

"It is a song my sister made. She said it reminded her of me, of the yearning she said was in me."

"Yearning for what?" asked Ferenth.

"For now, above all to find her and find that she is well."

"Is that all you wish for? To find your sister? Will you stay with her, once you find her?" demanded Ferrar.

Mischka turned to Ferrar, where he knelt by the fire stirring the pot containing their breakfast. "If your sister were gone, would you look for her?"

"We will never be parted, my sister and I," retorted Ferrar.

"But if you were, wouldn't you look for her?"

"You ask what is impossible," replied Ferrar angrily. "We are twins, born from the same mother in the same birth. Nothing will separate us." He went back to cooking the meal.

"You see," added Firfal, "many are the reasons that we travel and many are the friendships that we form. Who knows what you may learn if you join us and make one with our company."

Mischka looked at Ferrar sitting by the fire, the mistrust still in his eyes. He looked back at Firfal, the great fat man, his face shrewd and yet honest and welcoming enough. Finally he looked at Ferenth, who returned his look with confidence and welcome.

"I'll join you, on two conditions."

"What are they my little sparrow?"

"First, that whatever path we take, it must lead to Antar."

"All paths lead to Antar," laughed Firfal. "Where else should they lead? And what is your second demand?"

"That you teach me to play your harp."

"If you have the talent for it, then you are welcome to learn. Ferenth, my nightingale, bring my smaller harp from the caravan for our sparrow to try. And bring a bowl for our new comrade so that he can join us for this excellent meal that Ferrar has prepared."

Ferenth ran to the wagon and brought another bowl and the lap harp in its leather case. Together the four players sat down to eat, while overhead the swallows flew, calling to one another in the bright voice of spring.

Chapter 3

Mischka the Singer

So Firfal's troupe, with Mischka now among them, resumed their journey across the country, following a path that led eastward across the downs. It was an old stony track, at times barely distinguishable from the rock that peered up from the grass. Occasionally they stopped in a small village where Mischka played his flute, Ferenth sang, and Ferrar tumbled and juggled. Then Firfal brought out one or another of his instruments, most often his harp with its many strings, and played lovely old melodies or lively tunes with it cradled in his lap. At times he told stories of strange far-off places or great adventures.

So they went from place to place, and each night Mischka asked, "Are we on the road to Antar, Firfal?" Each night Firfal replied, "We are always on the road to Antar, my young sparrow, always on the road to Antar."

From town to town Firfal and his players went, singing and telling stories as spring turned to summer, here joining in a dance or there sitting in a corner of the marketplace, where Firfal waited for the ring of the coins in the bowl before he told the climax of his tale.

One of the villages they reached just as the day was coming to its end was big enough to boast an inn, uncommon in that part of the world. Here in the north of Egeria such villages as Rockford, where a river coursing through the town provided a way into the northern mountains and forest, were the only place inns could be found. There trappers and miners of the north brought furs from the forest or jewels from the mountains to trade.

The inn was called the White Hart. On the board outside was painted the head of a stag, a white stag with golden antlers.

"That is an interesting sign you have, innkeeper," remarked Firfal as they sat around the table at the inn door, drinking cans of sour ale. "It must be the white stag of King Terrant depicted there."

"I know no white stag except my own inn," grumbled the innkeeper dourly.

"Ah, but there is a story in that," replied Firfal. "Do you not know how the great white stag traversed these very mountains?"

"This inn I have from my father, and he from his father before him," retorted the innkeeper. "They knew nothing of legends. The white hart is but the name of the inn."

"Of course, of course," agreed Firfal soothingly. "This is a good supper, innkeeper. Here is your payment for it. Such was the worth of your food that a little additional payment in the form of a story for your patrons may not come amiss."

"We have no need here for story-tellers," warned the innkeeper,

"Then think of us as servants of the Lady," replied Firfal, "here to instruct you in the great stories of the past, present and future."

"We have no need for priests nor stories neither," declared the innkeeper.

"No stories at all? Oh my good friend, you deny yourself one of the great pleasures of life. But though you do not wish to listen, my young friends here would not mind hearing a story. Those who chance to overhear may listen as well."

"What story is this?" asked Mischka.

"A great and wondrous story. For you see, it is told that in these very mountains, in years long past, Terrant, king of Antar, was on a journey from his palace to the great western ranges of Ardmoar. As they rode along the great western road, one of the courtiers shouted 'Look, sire!' and pointed off into the forest that bounded the road. There they caught a glimpse of a flash of white that disappeared into the trees.

"'We will follow him,' said the king. 'It was a great white stag of noble proportions and I would hunt it.'

"The king's word was law, so the courtiers pitched their pavilions by the side of the road. The servants stayed to prepare the supper for the king and his entourage, who rode into the forest to find the great white stag. The forest was thick and the trees were close together. As the king rode through the forest at a great gallop in the direction the stag had disappeared, he became separated from the others. Soon the whole party was lost in the forest, each one separated from the next. They shouted and called, but through the deceits of echoes they found themselves ever farther from each other.

"Night came on. One by one the courtiers straggled back to the road and then rode along it until they found the camp and the servants. But the king didn't return and there was great consternation. So again the party rode out, with trumpeters and flaring torches, searching through the forest for the king. All that night they searched, and the next, and the next, but not a sign of the king could they find. Then on the fourth day, as the courtiers straggled back, despairing of ever finding the king again, the king rode into the camp. His horse was sleek and glossy. His eyes were bright as the stars that blazed in the night sky.

"'My king!' the courtiers cried, 'where have you been?'

"'I have had the most wonderful adventure. As I followed the white stag, with all of you far behind, the trees led me one way, deeper and deeper into the forest. Now and then I would find a trace of his passage, leading me still onward, deeper and deeper into the glen. I came at last to a mountain wall that rose sheer in front of me. Before the wall stood the white stag. It turned and looked at me with a challenging eye, then disappeared. In its place stood a man whom I knew to be a king, dressed in white robes with a golden crown on his head. Behind him the wall of the cliff had opened. A great entrance hall led into the mountainside. The stag-king called out to me, 'Greetings, King Terrant. Will you try our hospitality?'

"'I dismounted from my stallion. Two men came out from the hall, took my horse from my hands and led him aside. Then the stag-king with his crown of gold placed his hand on his heart and said, 'I pledge you that if you will enter with me, no sorrow will befall you.'

"'So I went in. The cavern was full of light and music. Great tapestries draped the walls. In the center of the hall was a round table laden with delicacies, and before it sat a goodly company. They came forward, greeted me and led me to the table.'

"'The stag-king seated himself at the head of the table and gestured to me to sit next to him. The musicians played, the wine flowed. Then a woman, the fairest of them all, came to me, put out her hand and led me forward into the dance. As we danced, all things were changed: we were among trees and stars and we danced to lyres and harps, to horns and flutes. My thoughts spun until I knew no longer where I was. I danced, danced and danced. When the dance was done, the king came to me again.'

"'"You must leave," he announced.'

"'"Did you not promise me all would be well if I followed you?"'

"'"So I did," averred the king. "So it is."'

"'"But this one night was short, and my heart is sore that I must leave."'

"'The king looked at me and his eyes were dark. "Say that you will return and this sorrow will be mended," he promised.'

"'"I will return,' I said."

"'Then the hall vanished: the table and the tapestries, the brilliant light of the fire. There was nothing there but the dim light of the pale moon, the soft sound of wind in the trees. At the cliff wall my horse stood, rested and newly saddled.'

"'As I promised,' continued King Terrant, 'I will return, I who alone have seen the home of the white stag.' With that, he wheeled his horse and rode back into the forest, nor has he been seen from that day to this."

In the silence that followed the story, the innkeeper and rough patrons of the tavern looked at Firfal with wonder in their eyes. "We must make a song of this story," Firfal remarked casually to Ferenth, breaking the spell he had woven, "a song of the king and the white stag, of magic and enchantments, of the stars in the evening when the king rode back to his camp."

"Master," begged the innkeeper, his hands clasped before him, "will you not tell us another story?"

"Not tonight," laughed Firfal, "Stories are better when they are set alone like the jewels they are. Yet music we will gladly share with you."

"More wine all around, more wine," shouted the innkeeper. While the maid brought out the wine and served it around, the innkeeper himself filled a great silver goblet and held it out to Firfal. As the patrons shouted and applauded, Firfal drank the vessel dry.

"Now, my good friends," announced Firfal, "as our patron has been so gracious, my troupe and I will entertain you."

He bid Ferenth, Mischka and Ferrar take up their instruments. In the light of the torches at the inn door, the people of the town crowded to the tavern while Firfal led his troupe in tune after tune.

At last, when the night had grown late, Firfal laid down his harp. "That is all, my friends. And as we began with a story of the white stag, so here is the song that Berneth the king's bard sang, when he returned at last to Antar."

Deep in the forest stands a cavern
Deep in the forest dark.
Where towering trees keep close their shade,
A cliff stands sheer and stark.

There burn in velvet darkness
Torches blazing bright.
There music of enchantment rises
On the wings of night.

There in darkness and in light,
A door stands waiting wide.
Who will find it? Who will dare
The secret that it hides?

"There has been no king in Antar since, only the ruling council," added Firfal. "Though many have sought the cavern and king and company, none has ever found them." With that he bid the company good night, and the musicians retired to their rooms.

As they traveled, Ferenth often talked with Mischka, telling him of the things she and Ferrar had seen or done. But she never talked of their parents, nor of where she and her brother had been born, nor of how they had met Firfal. When Mischka asked, Ferenth fell silent, turning to look at her brother. The only reply was a black look from Ferrar. Ferrar was still mistrustful of Mischka and wouldn't let him talk long with Ferenth, but would push him aside and insist, "You must go and talk to Firfal. My sister and I have things to discuss." Then Mischka would turn away, while Ferenth's eyes followed him with a sad look.

She told him of their travels with Firfal, of how they watched the crowd grow rapt, drawing closer as he told a story. She told him of Ferrar's talent as an acrobat, his handsprings and handstands and back flips, his lean wiry form making magic in the air. She told him how Firfal turned to her, just as he did now, and asked gently, "Little nightingale, will you sing for us?" Then Ferenth held her brother's hand and sang old songs of love and loss.

The three of them had traveled back and forth across the northern plains and hills of Egeria, among the small villages, through the countryside, earning food and shelter, perhaps a few coppers here or silvers there, depending on the whim of the audience. So they had come at last to that narrow track high among the hills where they had met Mischka.

They traveled in the same way now. On nights when they sat alone in the dark by the fire, Firfal with his harp, Mischka with his pipe and Ferenth with her tabor, Firfal would ask, "Do you know this tune?" Then Mischka, listening, would feel it inside him and find it in his fingers, traversing the wood of his flute.

One night, as the heat of the summer day was giving way to the cool winds from the mountains, Firfal asked, "Ferenth, do you remember this old tune?"

As he played it, Ferrar looked up with anger in his eyes and shouted, "Firfal, what are you doing! You promised you would never play that again."

"But on such a night?" protested Firfal, "when the stars are so bright, and the air so warm? Would you not sing that song again, Ferenth?"

"Don't sing it, Ferenth, don't sing it!" insisted Ferrar.

"If you wish," agreed Ferenth sadly.

"You promised you would never sing it again," insisted Ferrar again.

"I know a song about stars," suggested Mischka. "I can sing you this one instead, that my sister taught to me." He looked up into the sky, into the silence, and began to sing. It was a lilting, haunting tune, with few words, but it was as though the sky was suddenly bright and the air even warmer.

His voice had changed. No longer the high sweet voice of boyhood, it had grown and changed, a little rough from Mischka's singing so rarely since Lutha had left. But as he sang, it was as though a bond was lifted from his voice, as though things that had been dormant in him for too long came to life again at last. As Mischka continued, Firfal drew a soft accompaniment from his harp. Then Ferenth added a counterpoint to what Mischka was singing. The tenor and soprano voices rose and filled the night with the lovely old music.

Upon the loom of night is woven
Cloth of stars, moth-wing soft.
Who the weft and warp has strung?
Who the weaver? Whose the cloth?

"There," said Firfal softly, "there's your voice, my sparrow".

Ferrar sat by the fire, a dark look in his eyes. "That's enough for tonight," he said angrily. "Ferenth, come, I want to talk to you."

Ferenth rose up, gave a smile to Mischka, and went to sit by Ferrar, her head bent to his, their light hair visible even in the dark. Now and again a dark look from Ferrar's eyes flashed in Mischka's direction.

"Well, my young sparrow, I thought there might be a song inside you, if not one of mine or one of my stories, then one of your own. Would you sing that song tomorrow with Ferenth?"

"Yes," Mischka concurred. "But I do not think that Ferrar will like it."

"Ferrar will like the coppers we receive, for with the two of you singing, my playing on the harp, and Ferrar juggling, we will win such silver from the townspeople of Rybridge and such gold from the people of Antar that none will be richer than we."

"Antar? Then we will go there?"

"Of course," Firfal assured him. "We have only to prepare ourselves, to make our music as perfect as it can be."

"Then we will," agreed Mischka, thinking of what it would be like to be in Antar. He was glad that he was with Ferenth and Firfal. Even Ferrar could be good company, and Mischka was amazed by the skill and poetry of the boy's movement. But still he hoped to find his sister.

The next day they reached the small town of Rybridge. There, Firfal again told the great story of how Sorast had led people from the south to where the Rhenvore Mountains of northeast Egeria met the Searidge of the coast. He drove the light-eyed strangers from their city there between the mountains and the sea, above the great harbor, and renamed it Antar. From there, people had spread across the north of Egeria, each town living under the leadership of Antar and yet free to itself, free to govern as it wished.

Then Ferenth sang, Mischka played, and Ferrar juggled. At last Firfal said, "My friends, I bring you a wonder. Listen. Listen to the song of the stars." Firfal lightly played a melody on his harp as Ferenth and Mischka stepped forward. Ferrar took up his crystal spheres. Then Ferenth and Mischka sang and in the bright sunlight of the village square it was as though stars had come to earth and flashed in Ferrar's hands.

Chapter 4

The Horse Fair

At the end of the performance, a stranger stepped from the crowd. He was tall, taller than Firfal, but very lean. His face was carved in deep lines, as though he'd seen many places and traveled far in wind and the rain. He had a staff in his hand, slung across his shoulder a leather satchel. The hood of his cloak lay back so that his light hair glinted in the afternoon sun. His eyes so were so light a blue that they seemed almost silver.

"You sing well," the stranger remarked to Ferenth, looking intently at her face and then at her brother as he tossed a silver denar into their copper bowl. "Do you stay here long?"

"No, stranger," replied Firfal, grinning. "We journey from town to town to bring what we may of pleasure and beauty to these small villages."

"It is a great gift you bring."

"We could wish it were more warmly appreciated," hinted Firfal, gesturing at the copper bowl and its few coins.

The stranger laughed, took another coin from the purse at his belt and tossed it into the bowl. "Do you travel far?"

"We are on our way to Antar," declared Mischka, stepping forward to stand beside Firfal.

"Antar," mused the stranger. "A great distance from here and many empty miles lie between. Would you care for company on your travels? I can offer you a staff and a strong arm to wield it. There are many dangers on the road between here and Antar."

"We thank you for your concern," interrupted Ferrar, "but we can defend ourselves."

"Yet there are many dangers, as you, a traveler, should know: bandits and worse. One may find danger anywhere and most often where you least expect it."

"We have taken care of ourselves for many years. Firfal, we have no need of his company. Tell him so!" demanded Ferrar.

"Perhaps you will change your mind," replied the stranger calmly. "Perhaps what I have to offer may be welcome at another time. If you change your mind, I am staying at the Briarbush. It is not hard to find, the only inn Rybridge can boast. Ask for Imrach."

The stranger looked again at each of them, his gaze lingering on Ferrar. Then he turned and walked unhurriedly away.

Ferrar's eyes followed him, their light blue darkened with suspicion. "What did he want?" he demanded of Firfal.

"To join us, that's all, to be our companion and protector."

"Should you have sent him away?" Ferenth asked her brother.

"We have no need of him," insisted Ferrar, scowling. "I will take care of you. You have nothing to fear."

"Then all is well," agreed Firfal. "Come, let us be on our way and find someplace to camp for the night. We will save the Briarbush and the company of strangers for another time."

Several days later, they had made their way to the next small town, a village called Birchwood. It had only a dozen houses and a well where all the families drew their water and traders set out their wares when they came to the village. Each Restday, the families from the village gathered at the well and sang songs of praise and supplication to the Lady.

Firfal and his friends went to the largest house in the village and asked there for shelter for the night. The man who came to the door had a great grizzled beard and his eyes were keen and questioning.

"We have no room in our village for beggars," he warned.

"We are not beggars," Firfal answered. "If you will not offer shelter out of compassion for those who travel, then we have money to pay."

"We will not take your money," replied the householder. "If you mean no ill then you are welcome. But if you have deceit in your heart, then beware of those you would deceive."

"Good neighbor, we have no deceit in heart or mind. We're but poor travelers and entertainers. We would join you for your Restday celebration tomorrow, if you will let us."

"Then come in and be welcome. We will give you as good as we have. I am Tevadh. This is my wife Leva. Tevar!" he shouted. "Go and tend our guests' animal."

"I will help you," offered Mischka, as the boy came to the door. Tevar and Mischka led Fortia, the piebald mare, behind the inn to the small byre where the farmer kept a cow, a red shaggy-haired longhorn, and a pair of oxen to plow the fields to the west of town.

"You can keep your horse here," Tevar suggested. "I can help you rub her down, if you want."

Mischka and Tevar each grabbed a wisp of straw and began to rub down the mare. When they were done, they gave her a handful of oats and a manger of hay.

"Have you come far?" asked Tevar.

"Very far. My home is more than two months' walk to the west. We've been in twenty villages since I joined up with Firfal."

"What do you do? Where are you going?"

"We're on our way to Antar."

"I know of Antar. It's far to the East, they say. Why are you traveling so far?"

"To find something I've lost."

"But how do you support yourselves?"

"We'll show you tomorrow," promised Mischka.

That night at supper, their host leaned across the table and asked, "What news of the country at large?"

"No news but as always," Firfal replied. "The villages are quiet and the great city Antar seethes with trouble."

"So it always is," agreed their host. "Thus we stay here in our village, where we may be at peace with our neighbors and not trouble about power and wealth."

"You do well enough, it seems," remarked Firfal.

"Well enough. Yet one drought, one year when summer doesn't come and we are no better off than you."

"We too do well enough," retorted Ferrar.

"What do you do then, you strangers who travel the road with your brightly colored wagon?" asked the householder.

"We are musicians and story-tellers," explained Firfal. "We bring into the lives of those we pass something of the great wisdom of the past, something of the great beauty of this moment, something of the great insight of the future."

"I see you have a silver tongue in your head, at least. Nor do you seem to be stinting yourselves, with your great girth."

"We do well enough," Firfal grinned.

"Will you join us in our worship tomorrow?"

"That we will indeed. If you will allow us, we would add something of our own to your celebration."

"We'll give you no payment," cautioned their host.

"Nor do we seek any," replied Firfal. "We too are grateful to the Lady and offer what we have out of gratitude."

"Then sleep well this evening and join us in the morning in the village square."

Leva took them upstairs. "You may use this room. Our son Tevar will sleep in the main room tonight."

"Take care to keep your door closed," warned Tevadh. "Our dog guards the house at night. Do not seek to leave your room until we are up in the morning."

"So little trust?" commented Firfal. "We are grateful for the shelter and will do as you wish."

Soon morning was there. The house was astir, the air filled with the smell of freshly baked bread.

"Come down and eat," shouted Tevadh. "Breakfast is on the table."

Down to the flagged kitchen they returned. When they had eaten, Tevadh took a two-handed wooden goblet and a flask from the cupboard and led them outside. The village was gathered in a circle around the well.

Tevadh gestured to the visitors to join the circle. Then he drew a bucket of clear water from the well. He poured it into the wooden chalice and lifted it up to the sky. Then he began walking around the circle, from person to person, offering each a drink from the goblet as all the people of the village raised their voices in a morning prayer.

Mischka was surprised to see Imrach in the circle across from them, still wearing his travel-stained cloak. When the host, walking from person to person in the circle, reached the newcomer he greeted him soberly. "Welcome stranger," he said. Imrach bowed his head in reply, took the offered cup and drank.

When Tevadh had gone the round and all had drunk from the chalice, he poured what remained back into the well. Then he unstoppered the flask and poured wine into the chalice. As he raised the chalice, the townspeople sang a hymn of gratitude to the Lady that protected and sustained them.

Lady of light,
We raise to you this cup
Celebrating what you give us.

Your sun runs swift
Across the arc of sky
Too bright for us to look upon.

We cannot bear its splendor
But view it, sparkling, in the wine
That you have given us.

Then Firfal said, "My friends, in gratitude for the welcome you have shown us, we wish to offer you one more gift."

Their host looked around at his neighbors and asked: "What say you, people of Birchwood? Shall we accept the gift these strangers have to offer?"

"We accept," came from the voices of one and all. So Firfal began the story of the creation, of how the great Dyùn had stood alone and out of the fullness of her being brought forth all that is. First had come wisdom, the source and foundation of all creation. Then Dyùn created light, and stars shone in the darkness, then her moon to grace the night and her sun to bring the day. Rain gathered in the clouds, earth rose from the sea, plants sprang from the soil, and at last animals and humankind walked amid the creation.

When the story was done, Ferenth stepped forward and began a third hymn. Mischka found himself again drawn to take part. As their two voices rose in duet, across the circle Mischka saw a glint of admiration in Imrach's eyes. But when the song was done, the stranger disappeared and Mischka didn't see him again for many days.

They set out again along the eastern road, traveling from village to village. The Dry Moon had come and gone, when Firfal said, "There is a village to the north that I have a mind to visit. Though it lies off the path to Antar, yet it is not so great a distance. The town is worth seeing for the fair they have at this time of year."

The valley of Berghowe was a fourday's journey to the north. Long ago it had been settled by horsemen of the plains and it was said that the finest horses in all the land were bred and raised in that valley. Every year at harvest there was a fair to which the villagers brought what they chose of their stock, to sell or trade. For three days Berghowe suddenly grew to a much greater size, filled with the many merchants, entertainers, and travelers who journeyed to Berghowe for the horse fair.

As they approached the small village, the road began to be lined with booths, tents and corrals. Suddenly a man with a crooked back called out to them.

"Firfal, you old thief! Have you come to trade?"

"To sing, Bentam, as always! And you, crooked lump of flesh, are you still the Baron's servant?"

"I work where I can," admitted the hunchback. "Though I serve the Baron, yet the Baron serves me."

"Serves you?" laughed Firfal. "Does he wait on you at table?"

"At table and at the door," affirmed the hunchback. "When he needs the horses that I bring, I've heard the Baron rage against those he waits on. He is always impatient. But who is this stranger with you?"

"A thrush whose voice sings through the vale in the evening," replied Firfal.

"I see you have your other two apprentices, your nightingale and your clown."

"I am no clown! I have not your back," jeered Ferrar.

"As you get older, you may yet suffer as I do," replied Bentam calmly. "Where are you staying?" he asked, turning to Firfal.

"Wherever there may be room for us," replied Firfal.

"Then stay with us. There is plenty of hay for pallets and room enough in the pavilions."

"It is too close to the Baron," apologized Firfal. "I would prefer not to trespass on his hospitality."

"Then when you have settled in, come and find me. We're just this side of the village."

"And the Baron?"

"He stays in the grandest house in Berghowe for the duration of the fair. You will undoubtedly see him, if you stay for any time at all."

Firfal led the way into the city, to an old inn that lay just inside the city limits. The Silverfish it was called, the sign old and faded.

They took a single room, all that was left, barely large enough for the four of them. Then they went out to see the fair.

As it was the first day of the fair, many horse trades were being made. There were many people: merchants in rich clothes, borderers in furs and leather, nomads of the plains in short kirtles and vests. The wonder for Mischka was the horses themselves, with proud arched necks and flaring nostrils. Ferrar went from horse to horse, patting their flanks, rubbing their forelocks, speaking to them caressingly. Mischka could see in his touch the love that Ferrar had for these horses.

Ferrar loved Firfal's old piebald mare, tending her carefully as they made their way along the road. But these were splendid beasts, the best of their kind, and the love in Ferrar's eyes troubled Ferenth as she watched him.

In front of the horse stalls stood a richly dressed man. When he saw them, he cried out, "Ha, the great fat singer is come! What do you seek here, Firfal? Do you seek to find a horse that can carry you?"

"My lord Baron," acknowledged Firfal. "The horse is not sired that can carry me. Yet my old gray horse draws the cart well enough and a bench bears me best of all. These proud animals are a touch far beyond my wealth."

"These are your apprentices?" asked the Baron. "I thought you had but two."

"The third has just joined us."

"When next you're in Antar you must come and sing for me. You, boy, you seem to know these horses?"

Ferrar turned to the Baron, anger in his eyes. "I am no boy, nor servant of yours!"

"Ah, there is fire in you," exclaimed the Baron. "But you are no man yet, and to those in power, all are boys."

"I have things I must do," Ferrar said to Firfal and walked away.

"He's a lad of temper, Baron," said Firfal soothingly as the Baron's face flushed red with anger. "No one is lighter on his feet, or better with his hands. But youth is always hasty, unlike we men of sober years. What have you planned to buy during this fair?"

So the Baron turned back to Firfal and the trader and discussed the horses, while Mischka and Ferenth followed Ferrar.

"Is your brother always so angry?" asked Mischka.

"Too often. But it is dangerous to talk as he does to the Baron, who is powerful and arrogant. Those who oppose him do not fare well."

They saw Ferrar talking with one of the horse traders. Catching sight of them, he waved and came over to them.

"That man says that there are more bandits than ever in the mountains. They have even taken to trying to steal the horses in the mountain pastures east of Berghowe."

"Perhaps we should join with others going to Antar?" asked Ferenth. "Or we could go back to the great road. That would surely be safe."

"I'm not afraid of any bandits," Ferrar replied. "We'll be safe enough on the roads we take through the mountains. I'll be glad when we leave this village and don't have any chance of running into the Baron again."

As they walked along through the market, suddenly a mastiff bounded out from one of the booths, snapping at their heels. Mischka, startled, bumped into the stand of a fruit vendor, tipping it over. Pears and apricots cascaded over the cobbles. Mischka slipped and fell among them, while the vendor shouted, "Watch what you're doing, boy! Oh, my fruit!"

As the mastiff snarled at Mischka's heels, Ferrar, laughing, reached down to grab the dog. The mastiff snapped at him, threatening to lodge his teeth in Ferrar's ankle or arm. But Ferrar's hand was as quick as an otter. He grasped the brute around the neck and held it firmly.

"Why all this bother and noise?" he asked the dog calmly, looking it in the eye. "One might think we were stealing your master's wares."

"Who will pay for my fruit?" shouted the vendor, stepping forward to Ferrar and shaking his fist.

"Is this your animal?" Ferrar replied, turning deliberately to the burly man.

"My watchdog, that he is."

"Then it is your watchdog you must ask to pay for your fruit. Had it not tried to bite us, your fruit would not have ended on the ground.." Ferrar set the dog on the ground, where it crouched at his feet. He stood and pointed to the shadow under the cart that Ferenth and Mischka had righted. The dog slunk into it, ears drooping, tail between its legs. Then Ferrar looked into the vendor's face, his hand on the hilt of the dagger at his waist. "Do you wish to press your claim against us?"

"There is no damage to your goods," interrupted Ferenth, putting a last pear back on the righted cart. "Or at least nothing but a little dust, not much more than they already had. But if we have bruised one or two, this will repay your loss." She gave him a copper coin from her purse.

Ferrar picked up three apricots that had rolled to his feet and began juggling them.

"I will take this as payment for schooling your dog, who needs better training than you have provided." With his left hand he ate one of the apricots while with his right hand he juggled the others. "These two," he said, tossing them back to the vendor, "you may have again. I advise you to see to your dog. He is not as poorly trained as his master. But if he bites the ankles of one of the fair ladies at the market, the damage might be greater than you could pay."

Restored to humor by his own deftness and by Mischka's clumsiness, Ferrar led the way back to the inn where they were staying.

Chapter 5

The Beggar

The fair resumed the next morning. Firfal, Ferrar, Ferenth and Mischka strolled through the village until, in the late morning, they came to the eastern edge of Berghowe. There, where the road led off into the mountains, sat an old man. His clothes were ragged and his eyes were clouded with white cauls. But as Firfal and the three apprentices drew close, the beggar seemed to sense them passing by. His voice was strong as he called out, "Alms, oh masters, alms for a poor blind man. Alms, masters, for the grace of the the Lady, alms!"

Firfal reached into his pouch and pulled out a silver coin. "There, my old friend. Would that coins were like frogs to breed in the mud, that this one might grow to a multitude."

"Blessings on you, master Firfal," cried the beggar. "Though my eyes cannot see, the Lady will look lightly on your path, for your generosity."

"If they do, we shall be grateful. We each of us have need of their favor."

"I am only a beggar and do not know the ways of the Lady. But their hands may reach out to any."

"Their hands have been closed to you, it seems." Ferrar looked down at the beggar with a troubled face, torn between compassion and disdain.

"Not so," replied the beggar. "Their hands are the hands of all who are generous, as you have been."

"There is gratitude for you," retorted Ferrar bitterly. "Even the coin we give to a beggar is taken for granted."

"Say rather that he has given thanks to the ones from whom all we have comes, as he should," admonished the beggar.

"They have given us hunger," laughed Firfal, "and the means to stay it. We are all of us hungry, including our wise friend. Go to the vendors' stalls," he said to Ferrar, "and bring us something we might share with this philosopher."

Ferrar, Ferenth and Mischka went off to the stalls and bought bread, wine, meat, and cheese. When they brought them back to the gate, they found Firfal and the beggar sitting together, Firfal on a small stone by the road side, the beggar sitting in the dirt. Whenever someone passed by, the beggar broke off his conversation with Firfal to call out, "Alms, for the mercy of the Lady, alms for a poor blind beggar."

The two men continued their conversation. "The finest of gifts of the Lady is surely that of the voice," asserted the beggar. "If I could be a singer, I would gladly have traded my eyes for that. One who has a voice need never be a beggar."

"And yet," interrupted Ferrar, "even entertainers like us are held as little better than beggars. Vagrants and beggars we have been called, often enough."

"None but those of no soul would speak so," the beggar protested, "for the Lady has made the world full of beauty. As I sit here at the gate in my blindness, I hear the birds in the heavens, especially at the dawning or just before, when they wake and fill the darkness with the sound of rejoicing. Then surely one cannot doubt that the Lady made the world to be a place of beauty. At night the wind rises and curves about the corners of the buildings, making its hollow singing, stirring leaves that whisper in a voice dry and light. Then surely one cannot doubt that the voice of the Lady speaks in these murmurs."

"We do not all have a poet's soul, such as you," said Firfal sadly. "Some hear nothing in the wind but a coming storm or the voice of unseen fears. Some hear nothing in the song of the birds but the call to another day of labor: for some a labor of joy, but for many only a labor of great weariness."

"Then a beggar may be richer than the richest," acknowledged the poor man in his ragged clothes. "For I have this at least, each day: to sit here by the road and listen to what music there is. The music of nature is sweet. Yet sweetest of all is the voice of one who passes by me singing or even just speaking in a voice soft and melodious."

"Here are bread, cheese and meat for you," Ferenth said. She placed it in the beggar's hands as he held them out. He chewed it delightedly with stumps of teeth barely adequate to the crusts.

"This is music indeed," mumbled the old man with satisfaction, "music that I rarely get enough of, besides."

"I expect not, in such a small village as this. Have you no children to tend you? No home?" asked Ferenth as she handed food to Firfal as well.

"I have been blind my life long. When my parents died, I was only a boy and had no trade. So I learned to beg and so have I done all these long years."

"It is a cruel world for the crippled," Ferenth sympathized.

"Not a cruel world," contradicted the beggar. "People may be cruel. Life may be difficult, but the world remains a place of beauty and generosity. Though my eyes may be closed, my heart is open."

"You deserve better than this," Mischka protested.

"What one deserves bears little relation to what one has," retorted Ferrar.

"True enough," added Firfal. "In Antar, those who have the most and live the best are often the worst and the least deserving."

Ferenth and Mischka had sat down next to the beggar to eat. Ferrar remained standing in front of them, wiping the crumbs from his hands. "I want to see what else there is in the town. Ferenth, will you come with me?"

"If you wish, my brother, "

"Go," agreed Firfal, "see what the town may have to offer. You make me nervous, hovering over me like a great stork over a frog pond. You go too, Mischka."

So off the three apprentices went, while Firfal and the beggar sat together and talked. They continued through the town, back to the small market in the central square where they had gotten the bread they shared with the beggar.

"Why didn't you sit and join us?" asked Mischka.

"I don't want to be taken for a beggar," answered Ferrar.

"To sit with a beggar is not to be one."

"It is to be taken for one, nonetheless. What chance do we have to become something better if we sit in the dust, scorned by those who pass by?"

"None looked at us with scorn," replied Ferenth calmly. "In a village such as this, even the richest is only a step above the beggar. Even a beggar can live well enough here, where none forgets what it is like to be hungry."

"I have had enough of this village," muttered Ferrar. "The townspeople can keep their coins, for all I care."

"Are you anxious to get to Antar as well?" asked Mischka.

"Antar is no better than this village, as full of beggars and dust. What does it matter where we go or what we do? But I'll be something more than a vagabond someday, I promise you."

As they were talking, suddenly there were shouts and the sound of galloping horses. Through the narrow paths between the pavilions came a tall black stallion of seventeen hands, crashing into pavilions, thrusting aside the people who reached for his halter. Shouts rang out, "Grab him! Stop him! Stop that horse!" As Mischka and Ferenth stepped back to be out of the way, Ferrar strode forward, took a great leap, and catapulted himself onto the horse's back.

The stallion reared and tossed, but Ferrar clamped his legs around him and wrapped his hands in the mane. He leaned over, his head close to the horse's ear, and began talking to it. Slowly the horse began to quiet, until it stood with legs trembling and head drooping. Out of the throng of onlookers came the trader. He looked up at Ferrar, extending a hand to him. Ferrar slid down from the horse's back.

A man dressed in the leather clothes of the horsemen of Berghowe took hold of the rough halter around the horses' head. "The blood of the brothers is in your debt," he said to Ferrar, placing his fist upon his heart. Then he led the stallion away through the crowd.

"What was that about?" asked Mischka.

"The people of the plains speak of horses as their brothers. But I don't know what he meant," replied Ferrar in a puzzled voice and shrugged his shoulders. Together Ferrar, Ferenth and Mischka returned to the Silverfish to wait for Firfal.

The next day was the last of the fair. No sooner was breakfast done than Firfal led them outside and they took their place in one corner of the square. He took his harp from the leather case, Ferrar began to limber up, Ferenth and Mischka to warm up their voices and flute.

At last Firfal called out to the passersby, "My friends! You are privileged to have among you the great entertainer Firfal and his troupe. We bring you stories and songs, music and amazing acrobatics. Come! See what we have to offer!"

He began a sprightly dance tune on the harp, while Mischka played a high descant and Ferrar juggled. Fascinated, the crowd drew nearer. Mischka noticed that among them was Imrach, the stranger they had met before, in his dark cloak, his hood thrown back so that his light hair was easily seen among the more common dark heads.

Then Ferenth sang, while Firfal played a soft accompaniment. When the song was done, Firfal called out again. "My friends, I will tell you an amazing story." He began the story of Amerach and how he had fled from Antar with his beloved Larenth to escape his father's anger and the exile declared by the council at his father's insistence. Firfal paused at each climax in the story, to wait for the clink of coins into the brass bowl before he went on.

When he was done, Imrach stepped forward with the rest of the crowd to drop a coin yet again in the copper bowl.

"A good story," he remarked to Firfal. "But you're wrong when you say Amerach and Larenth were unhappy in their exile deep in the mountains. I have heard that they never regretted what they had left behind."

"Many are the forms of the story," agreed Firfal. "I but tell you the one I know. If some know another, then let them tell it."

"I see you have pride in your craft. Still, a wise man may always learn from others."

"So a wise man does, yet will not set aside what he knows."

"You speak well and truly. We will speak again another day."

As Imrach turned to walk away, Ferrar stepped forward and grabbed his arm. "You are following us! What do you want?"

Imrach turned to face Ferrar. His eyes calmly scanned the face of the angry young man, more than a head shorter than he.

"I but follow the same path, as I said before. Many people travel the roads to Antar."

"But only you dog our steps, when the well-traveled road lies to the south."

"I too had a desire to see the horse fair of Berghowe. The mountain path you follow is a common road to Antar."

"It is our road. I warn you not to follow us or it will go the worse for you."

Imrach's voice became softer, yet somehow more compelling. "You have nothing to fear from me. Whatever dangers you face, they will not be from me. I have offered you my protection. I do not betray what I have promised to protect." He gently took Ferrar's hand from his arm and walked away, disappearing into the crowded market.

Mischka stared after the stranger, mouth agape, while Ferrar glowered. Ferenth looked at Firfal with bewilderment, for there seemed to be a gleam of recognition in Firfal's eyes. But Firfal said nothing, only beginning another story. Then they played another lively tune while Ferrar juggled. At last Firfal said, "Now my friends, I offer you something which cannot be bettered even in the great city of Antar itself. Listen, my friends, to the loveliest voices in all Thallhiar"

Once again Ferenth and Mischka sang and coins rang in the copper bowl like the bells of Restday in Antar.

If I could call the silver stars
And bid them fall and linger there,
A gleaming net I'd weave of them
To shine amid his sable hair.

Their radiance would dim amid
A loveliness more bright than theirs.
Far lovelier than stars themselves
Is he I love, more sweet and fair.

I love him more than words can hope
To say or life could e'er express,
The Northern Crown itself too small
A treasure, him to grace and dress.

Though I sought across the world
No jewel I'd find could e'er suffice,
For only stars could grace the light
Within his hair, within his eyes.

By the next morning, the fairground outside the village walls was deserted of all but a few last carts and the wooden paddocks where the grass was beaten to dust by the horses' hooves. They packed the caravan and set off on their way along the road that led east through the mountains, through the outlying pastures of Berghowe. There were hoof prints in the dust from the horses that had been brought to the fair. Occasionally they heard the whinny and gallop of the herds that were left to pasture in the mountains until the onset of winter. There was even a small herd led by a shaggy brown stallion that they glimpsed several times as they traveled east.

The Corn Moon waxed and began its wane as they traveled; the Huntsman rose in the east. They spent the feast of Vinalia singing and telling stories for the townsfolk of a small village on the Greyrive that carries the snow water of the mountains to the Vesperan Plain. They crossed the bridge over the Greyrive in its narrow gorge, white-foamed even at the onset of autumn. A fourday later found them deep in the Dagger Mountains.

The night was dark as they set up camp where a small stream crossed the road, flowing south. They found a stand of poplars, quivering in the northwest wind. As Mischka brought the water from the stream back to the camp, he heard rustlings among the trees. Slowly and carefully he walked back to the camp. "I think there may be others in the woods," he whispered to Ferrar as he knelt by the fire to set the buckets of water on the ground.

"Have you seen them?"

"Not clearly. But I heard movement in the shadows."

"We had best tell Firfal."

"Who did you see?" asked Firfal when they told him of Mischka's suspicions.

"I couldn't tell."

"Then let us not be afraid," said Firfal. "But deal with them as friends if we can." He called out. "Come join us, if you will."

Out of the dark stepped Imrach, in his dark cloak. "I take you at your word."

"Why are you following us?" shouted Ferrar in anger, drawing his dagger.

"Our ways lie together. I came to this grove first. It is you who follow me."

"But you knew that we are traveling this way. What do you want of us?"

"I do want anything. If I am not welcome, then I will go on my way."

"Come, Ferrar, Imrach," laughed Firfal. "No need for fighting among ourselves. We do not begrudge anyone the comfort of our fire and supper from our pots. Since your silver has paid for what we cook, it seems only fair that we share it with you."

"Then I'm glad to join you. Nor do I think you foolish to welcome another. Even as stout a company as you may find reason to welcome another arm."

"Trouble comes to those who seek it," retorted Ferrar, his eyes still dark with suspicion, still confronting the stranger. "We seek none. We'll see none."

"So it may be. But there are times when trouble comes unsought and even the wisest may be hard-pressed to avoid it."

"You are the only trouble we have seen. We do not need you. Go your way! You offered to do so. Do as you say!"

"My young bantam," soothed Firfal. "The stranger means us no harm, and we have food enough."

"No harm perhaps, but no good either. How do we know that he is not one of these very dangers that he warns us against?"

"So he may be," agreed Firfal. "But I think it best tonight to trust him. "

They sat down together to share the meal. Afterwards, Mischka practiced harp by the light of the fire, the plangent notes of an old ballad ringing in the darkness while Firfal and Imrach talked quietly of the rumors from Antar.

"The Baron grows too greedy, too strong. He who has most is not content with what he has. Nor does he view his wealth as responsibility, but only as privilege," said Imrach. Though he spoke calmly, there was anger in his voice.

"Why do you return there then?" asked Firfal. "For you do return, if I am not mistaken. After so many years away, what good will it do to go back?"

"I have been away many years," agreed Imrach. "I have had a long journey. But it is time to return what has long been missing."

"Did you lose something?" interrupted Mischka.

"Not that I have lost, but which was lost nonetheless," Imrach replied. "There are houses that stand empty, betrayed in the great game that they play of power and prestige. Some have lost much, some all."

"Do you seek to play the game as well?" asked Firfal.

"Not I," Imrach said firmly, "not I, not ever."

Mischka, Ferenth and Ferrar laid their bedding out. The stranger wrapped himself in his cloak to sit by the fire and take the first watch of the night. "The mountains are dangerous," he said. "It is best that at least one of us stay awake." Firfal mounted to his bed in the wagon, which as always creaked protestingly at his weight as he climbed in.

Mischka woke suddenly to sounds of fighting. All around him were shadows, dim forms only just visible in the light of early dawn. "Wake up!!" shouted Imrach. "Defend yourselves!"

Chapter 6

The Bandits

As Mischka threw aside his cloak and stood up, in the light of the early dawn he saw Imrach and Ferrar with their knives drawn, facing three bandits: rough-looking men in rough clothes, scarred boots on their feet, knives in their hands. Their leader, with a notched and battered sword, had engaged Firfal, who was standing on the steps of the caravan wielding a staff. "Come on, you misbegotten spawn of a weasel!" Firfal shouted at the bandit confronting him. "Step closer and I'll make your ears ring!" The staff whistled through the air as he swung at the bandit, who quickly dodged out of the way.

Mischka grabbed a branch from the ground near the smoldering fire and ran forward to help Firfal as Ferenth ran to help her brother and Imrach, pulling her knife from the sheath at her belt. When the bandit saw Mischka running towards him, he ducked under Firfal's cudgel and leapt for the caravan's stairs, pushing Firfal off them. Firfal hit the ground heavily as the bandit disappeared inside the caravan.

Just as Mischka reached the steps, the bandit began throwing pots and dishes and instruments out of the caravan. Firfal's harp flew from the caravan, hitting Mischka in the shoulder and knocking him to the ground. A sack of flour burst as it hit the ground, covering the grass with white. Clothes fluttered to the ground, so that old Fortia snorted and reared against the rope tethering her to the wagon. The bandit jumped down the steps, holding the leather sack with Firfal's coins that he tucked quickly inside his bearskin vest.

The bandit ran to the fire and pulled a brand from it. The end of the log flamed and sparked as he ran back to the caravan and threw it inside. He turned to face Firfal again, who had risen slowly to his feet, unsteady from his fall. The bandit feinted, then leapt forward under the swing of the staff, driving his sword into Firfal's chest. Mischka ran to Firfal as he crumpled to the ground.

The bandit slashed as the rope that held the mare to the wagon and leapt to her back just as Ferenth screamed. One of the three bandits fighting Ferrar, Imrach and Ferenth had slashed her arm, cutting deeply into the flesh.

As she gasped and fell back, dropping her knife, they heard the drumming of hooves on the ground. Down from the forest charged a brown stallion, whinnying fiercely. It ran straight for the bandit captain on Fortia, who was bucking and stamping as the bandit, hand grasping her mane, cursed and hit her with the flat of his sword. The stallion reared, its hooves nearly striking the bandit's head as he fell from the mare to the ground. He rose quickly and shouted to the rest of the bandits. All four ran to the forest and disappeared into it, while the caravan blazed and Ferrar dropped to his knees beside Ferenth.

"Damn them!" he shouted. "Damn them all!" He tore open the sleeve of her shirt, pulled his own over his head and pressed it against the wound with his hand as he held her with his other arm. The blood welling from the wound soaked quickly into the cloth. Ferrar pressed as hard as he could, while Ferenth lay in his arms with eyes closed, breathing raggedly with pain. Slowly the bleeding grew less.

Imrach brought a shirt from those scattered across the ground and tore it into strips. "Let me help," he said to Ferrar.

He took the blood-soaked rag away and bound Ferenth's arm with the clean fabric, Ferrar's eyes watching each move with fierce attention. Then he stood and walked to where Mischka knelt next to Firfal, his arm cradling the old man's head. The brown stallion stood nearby, Fortia pressed up against him. He whickered softly as Imrach approached, then his eyes went back to Firfal.

The harpist lay on his back. A thin trickle of blood came from the side of his mouth. Imrach knelt beside him.

"Are the others alright?" whispered Firfal.

"Ferrar is tending to Ferenth" Imrach replied. She will be fine, though she has lost a great deal of blood. Mischka and I are well."

"That is good," Firfal coughed, blood spitting from his mouth as a spasm of pain knotted his face. "I fear these wolves have done for me. You must take care of them, Imrach. You must see them home."

"You know who they are, then?"

"I have always known. I should have known you, too, but that it's been so long."

"We've all changed in our long journeys."

"I have begun my last journey. I'll be glad of the rest." Firfal closed his eyes and drew a hoarse breath. Mischka looked at Imrach with fear in his eyes. Imrach could only shake his head.

Then Firfal spoke again. "I only regret leaving these three young ones behind."

"I promise you, I'll take care of them."

"Trust him, my young sparrow," Firfal said to Mischka, opening his eyes. A smile flickered in his eyes. Then he shuddered, gasped, and lay still.

Imrach drew the lids down over his eyes, then rested his hand on Firfal's forehead. "Mother of all," he prayed quietly, "take him to your arms. Welcome him with love and joy." Mischka, nub with disbelief and grief, slowly laid Firfal's head on the earth. Imrach stood, laid his hand on Mischka's shoulder for a moment, then returned to Ferrar, who was still holding Ferenth in his arms.

"How is your sister?" he asked.

"I will have my revenge on those wolves," said Ferrar grimly. "They've hurt Ferenth. I'll have my revenge on them."

"How is Firfal?" asked Ferenth, opening her eyes again. "I saw them stab him. Will he recover?"

"Firfal is dead," Imrach replied, stooping down to lay his hand on Ferenth's wrist.

"No," she shouted, struggling to stand, grasping Imrach's shoulder so tightly that he felt her nails through the cloth of his shirt. Ferrar stood with her, helped her to walk to where Firfal lay, Mischka still beside him. Ferenth knelt down next to Mischka, took one of Firfal's hands in her own, her face white with the shock of her own wound and Firfal's death, unable even to cry.

"Be glad your sister is alive," said Imrach to Ferrar. "She will recover if we take care of her. We must decide what to do, whether to go on or go back. If we stay here, the bandits may return. We have little for them to take, but even the little we have may tempt them."

"I don't trust you," said Ferrar to Imrach. "Maybe this is what you wanted all along. Maybe you're part of this cursed band of thieves and are playing along with them."

"I promise you that is not so, even if I have proved of little help to you and your comrades so far. I will go with you wherever you go and defend and guide you as well as I can."

If Firfal is dead, where can we go? What can we do?"

"We could return to Rybridge," replied Imrach. "But it's a poor town. We couldn't stay there for the winter. My counsel is that it's best we go on as quickly as we can to Antar. We take what we can carry and go swiftly on our way by the fastest route. There are dangers that we must face if we go that way, but even they are less dangerous than being caught in the mountains in winter."

"I will not go without my revenge," Ferrar insisted with grim determination. "They have burnt our caravan. They have taken our money and our food. They have killed Firfal and injured my sister. I will not leave unrevenged on them."

"Food we can still find," said Imrach. "There's no time for revenge."

"There is time enough," insisted Ferrar. "If no one will help me, then I'll go alone. I'll find their lair and I'll take my revenge on them."

"We can find them, if we must, though what we will do when we find them I don't know. First let's tend to Firfal."

Mischka, Imrach and Ferrar carried Firfal to the river, Ferenth walking behind them, her right arm swathed in blood-soaked bandages. She sat next to Firfal's body while the others took stones from the riverbank until they had covered him. Then the four of them stood about the mound, Ferenth held in her brother's arms, Mischka carrying the small lap harp, its sound box cracked. He played slowly one of the ballads that Firfal had taught him. As the notes rang out above the rushing of the river, they all remembered Firfal, his great love of life and the laughter that came so easily to him.

"We have always gone where Firfal has taken us," Ferenth said when Mischka had finished. "He is the only family we've known ."

"Little family enough," muttered Ferrar bitterly. "We were his apprentices and servants, not his son and daughter."

"Why did you stay with him, then?" Imrach asked, his silver-gray eyes untroubled by the anger that Mischka could see in Ferrar.

"How else were we to live?" Ferrar demanded. "But once we're Antar it will be different. I'll find real work there. We won't be beggars any longer, sitting in the market and holding out our hands for coins."

"We're not beggars," protested Ferenth.

"Not beggars, but little better," retorted her brother. "To be scorned by those who pass by has always been torture for me. You know that. I won't bear it any longer."

"We're not scorned, but welcomed, praised for the beauty of the music we create."

I will never be satisfied with that," insisted Ferrar. "What goal have we had, traveling the roads?"

"What goal do we need," replied Ferenth, taking her brother's hand, "more than to make music and see what the world has to offer? Haven't you been glad to see the western mountains? The Greyrive and the Maienrive? What would you have done instead?"

"I'm not sure," admitted Ferrar. "I am tired of this wandering from town to town. At least Mischka gave some goal and purpose to our aimless travels. But now that Firfal is dead, I don't know what we will do."

"We must still go with Mischka to Antar, to help him find his sister."

"If you wish, once we have killed these bandits."

"Your destiny lies east in Antar," said Imrach quietly.

"What would you know of it!" retorted Ferrar.

"I know something of destiny."

"Do you read lines in hands, like the charlatans in the marketplace? At least we do not practice deceits on the gullible, like those who claim to read the future."

"No, I'm no reader of palms. But there is a line of destiny that determines who we are and what we may be, a path to follow if your feet can but find it. Then difficulties fall away and you find yourself heart and soul in agreement with the road you walk."

"How can we know whether we follow our destiny or follow self-delusion?" asked Ferenth in a troubled voice. "Who can tell us what the path is?"

"No one. You will know your path only if you know yourself. Only by looking at what holds true for you do you know whether the way you follow is the truth. Have you never had that feeling, that sudden confidence that you are following your fate?"

"The night that Mischka came," replied Ferenth. "That night I felt something like this."

"I too," agreed Mischka. "And sometimes when we sing or when I play the flute I feel that this is what I was meant to do."

"Then perhaps your destiny lies in your music. Yours, Ferrar, perhaps yours is to make such poetry in movement as none have ever seen."

"Perhaps. Perhaps I'll never be anything but a juggler and a tumbler. You said to look in your heart and see there what I want to do. If I look in my heart, all I see there is anger."

"Anger?" asked Ferenth sympathetically. "Anger at what, at whom?"

"I don't know. At those who pass by without watching, at those who give us scorn with every coin that they give, at those clad in rich clothes who look at us with disdain and derision."

"Perhaps there is something in your heart that tells you that you are the equal of any, including the Baron of Egeria himself," suggested Imrach.

"I am the equal of any! Even if I am but a juggler in the marketplace, I am the equal of any! Especially of these bandits!" Ferrar turned to the brown stallion. "My friend, thank you for your aid."

The stallion whickered and tossed its head. It turned and ran back into the forest, the sound of its gallop echoing back to them.

Gently Ferrar lifted Ferenth to the back of the piebald mare, while Mischka and Imrach bundled what remained of their clothes and belongings and put them on Fortia's back.

"The bandits took everything," Mischka replied regretfully. "What are we going to do?"

"There are fish in the river. But we can't stop here to catch them. We have to go hungry for now and hope we can find something tonight when we're safe."

"We have to take Firfal's harp with us." Ferenth held out the instrument she had pulled from under the wagon.

"Weigh ourselves down with a harp? Why would we do that??"

"We can use it to earn our living. We're on our own now."

"None of us can play it."

"Then we'll learn." Ferenth turned to Mischka and held out the harp. "Here. Even if your flute is gone, you can still make music."

"It isn't lost. I found it by the wagon. It doesn't seem to be damaged. I put it in a pack, along with a few of the clothes that looked like they might still be useful."

"Then take the harp too." Ferenth put it in his hands. "Even if it's not perfect, it's still playable. Firfal isn't with us anymore, but we can still have his music."

Mischka swung his pack to the ground. He wrapped the harp in the clothes he had collected and put it inside the pack. Then he slung the pack back to his shoulders and nodded to Ferrar. "I'm ready," he said.

They headed off into the forest at the northern edge of the meadow, where the bandits' tracks plunged back into the shadow of the woods, Imrach in the lead, scanning for the ground for signs of the bandits. In their haste, the bandits had run quickly and signs of their passage were everywhere, up through the forest into another hidden valley. Imrach followed the tracks until they were lost on the stony banks of the stream.

They camped that night by the stream, eating what little meat they had left. Ferenth washed her wound in the cold water of the stream, while Mischka scrubbed the bandages and spread them on bushes to dry. Ferrar bound fresh strips of cloth about Ferenth's arm, which bled again when the bandages were taken off. The bleeding subsided quickly when the new bandages were in place.

The next morning, Ferrar led on again. They stopped to rest as often as Ferenth needed, tired by the loss of blood and sleeping poorly from the pain. As evening drew near, they came to a boulder-filled pass leading from one valley to the next. Below them, the valley narrowed rapidly to the north until it ended in the wall of rock pierced by a cave entrance.

Directly above the cave, the vertical cliff face gave way to a slope strewn with rocks fallen from the mountain peak above them. In front of the cavern sat the four bandits. From what Mischka could see of their features behind the beards and grime, they were hard men with violence written in their coarse faces. All of them bore the marks of many cold winters when they fed only on anger and hunger. All of them bore the marks of their calling: here, one with only a single arm; there, one with only a single eye; and on all of them, scars and ill-healed wounds.

"The mountains are steep and rocky above that hole. If we wait until they go inside for the night, we could drop the mountainside down on them, seal that cavern so well that they cannot escape." Ferrar pointed to a boulder balanced at the very top of the scree. "If we can move that, it will bring down the whole hillside."

Leaving Ferenth and the horse in the shelter of the pass, Ferrar, Mischka and Imrach moved through the gathering darkness, picking their way carefully along the edge of the ridge, from stone to stone until they reached the boulder. It was even more precarious than they had seen from below. They slowly began to lever up the rock. Little by little its balance shifted, until just a hand's weight would bring it over.

"Bandits!" shouted Ferrar, his voice echoing off the walls of the valley. "Come face us if you dare!"

The rock teetered and shifted, then began to roll, at first slowly, then faster and faster. The slope of loose rock shifted and began to slide down as well, as out from the cave came the bandits. The rocks began to pour over the edge of the cliff, a hail of stones that struck one bandit and then the next. The dust rose in a cloud, glinting in the moonlight, then slowly fell back to earth.

Ferrar dropped the stones that he had picked up, intending to strike down the bandits if they escaped the fall of rock. Without speaking, Imrach led the way back along the valley rim and down to the valley floor. Turning their backs to the cliff face, where the thieves and their lair were now hidden beneath the tumbled stones, they followed the stream back down the valley, along the path that the bandits had made but would walk no longer.

In the darkness, Imrach turned to Ferrar. "Have you satisfied your thirst for revenge?"

Ferrar 's eyes were dark in dim light of the setting moon. "The taste of revenge is not as sweet as I thought it would be."

"It never is," said Imrach soberly. "It is a poison, and like all poisons, it is as bitter to those who use it as to those who suffer its venom."

"What do you know of poison?" asked Ferenth.

"I've suffered vengeance, just as you have. It was always as bitter a draft as the one you have taken tonight."

"Would it have been better to have gone our way without bringing justice to these bandits?"

"Even justice exacts a price. The price that revenge exacts is even greater."

Ferrar did not reply. Overhead the stars wheeled in silence, far distant from the struggles of those living on earth.

Chapter 7

The Beisht

When they awoke next morning, Imrach was missing. When at last he reappeared through the trees, Ferrar called out suspiciously, "Where have you been?"

"I've just been getting our breakfast," Imrach replied, holding up two fish he had caught in the river. "You have nothing to fear from me. Everything I can do to help, I will. You will need my help now that you have lost Firfal, who was an even better friend than you know."

"What do you mean by that?"

"You have come a long journey with him, you and Ferenth especially."

"And?" demanded Ferrar.

"Haven't you been surprised at how few dangers you've encountered? There are many dangers, not just the bandits we have just escaped. But you have met very few of them, under the care of Firfal. I asked once before. Now I ask again: will you let me travel with you? Though I didn't protect or rescue you from the bandits, yet I can be of help. There will be other dangers."

"Ferrar," said Ferenth. "I think we should let him come with us, since we no longer have Firfal."

"We can always tie him up at night," added Mischka, laughing.

"I'll take that as agreement," Imrach replied with a smile as he began cooking the fish over their fire. "Where do we go from here? Are you going on to Antar? What route will you take?"

"Whatever is the shortest," replied Mischka. "Antar lies in the mountains, in a great valley opening down to the sea. Coming from the west, there are but two routes to follow. One comes up from the plains, south of the mountains. To follow that, we have to go west to where the Great South Road leads through the Dagger Mountains, then north through the plain of Egeria. The other continues east from here, crosses through the valley of the Beisht, over the high pass of Silverhorn and down through the valley of the wraiths."

"Would it not be better for us to go back to the great road?" asked Ferenth.

"It would be best perhaps," replied Imrach. "Yet we have come a long way through the mountains already. From here we have a long journey back to the southern road. Though the Beisht is dangerous and its valley filled with the statues of those who didn't pass, the dangers of the mountains are as great. With winter drawing so near, we have little time to get through them before all ways are snowed shut. So I urge that we take the Silverhorn gate, past the Beisht and its questions, dangerous as that may be."

"What is the Beisht?" asked Ferrar

"In a valley before the Silverhorn pass, there's a high stone pillar. On it stands what appears to be a statue of the Beisht, half animal, half human. But as you approach it, the Beisht stops you and will not let you pass unless you answer the question that it asks. There in the valley of the Beisht you'll see many standing stones of granite. Each one of those, it's said, is a traveler who could not give the Beisht the answer it sought."

"And what are the wraiths?" Ferenth asked, as Imrach took the pan of fish from the fire and gave some to each of his comrades.

"No one knows exactly what they are. They are gathered in a deep valley through which one has to pass to get to Antar. Each person must give them a gift. It's said that unless the gift is acceptable to them, you'll be condemned to join those who linger in the valley, preying on those who enter. Only those with the power to charm the wraiths' despair can walk that valley from its western end to the black pillar that marks the limit of the wraiths' power."

"But what can charm them?" asked Ferenth, troubled with the thought of encountering these creatures.

"A story, perhaps, or a song or dance. Only the wraiths know what they will accept from anyone."

"Have you passed that way before? How did you get though" asked Ferrar suspiciously.

"I too am a singer, like all of you. This proved sufficient to pacify the wraiths so that they allowed me to pass."

"I don't fear either Beisht or wraiths," Ferrar declared. "If that's the way we must go, then we will. We go to the east?"

"To the east, always to the east, to the uttermost edge of the land."

"Then lead on and we'll follow."

"You trust me so far then?"

"I trust you no farther than the hand at the end of my arm" Ferrar replied angrily. "But for now we will follow where you lead."

So the four travelers set off. As the days passed, the landscape grew increasingly rocky and forbidding. Far behind them now were gentle hills and villages. Here there was nothing but rock and ice. Above them the ice shifted in the sunlight, and occasionally there was the rumble of a far distant avalanche as rocks that had been forced apart and held by the action of the ice tumbled to the valley far below.

For two week they journeyed, finding here a solitary house where they received a bit of bread and cheese, or there a field of marsh cattails whose roots they could dig. But for Imrach they would have been hungry indeed; he seemed especially wise in the ways of wilderness, knew where to find food or how to catch a hare. There were goats high above them on the rocks, and wild sheep, but nothing could they capture other than the small animals they could snare.

At last one night Imrach said, "tomorrow we'll reach the valley of the Beisht."

"Are we so close, then?" asked Ferenth.

"Close indeed."

"What shall we do when we arrive tomorrow?" asked Mischka.

"Each of us must go through alone," said Imrach. "Of each of us the Beisht will ask a question. It will judge whether what we answer is enough. I will go first, and each of the three of you may follow after. Sleep well, and the Lady be with you tomorrow."

So morning came. They ate what little they had left of bread and cheese from the last farmstead they had passed, then approached the entrance to the broad, stony valley. The sides were sheer, and on either side towered tall peaks, sheer sides gleaming coldly in the sunlight.

In front of them they could see a pillar and on it a stone statue, a figure with raptor wings and lion's paws. It was the Beisht.

It looked down at them with eyes of glass, as fierce as fire: not the blue of flame, but the hot red of coals burning on a hearth. Its voice was honey and ash, sweet and bitter, irresistible and terrifying as it spoke to them.

"Do you think to pass by me? Stay, strangers, and hear my questions."

Imrach stepped forward and said: "Speak, then. Twice I have passed this way before. Twice you have questioned me and twice I have answered."

"I am what I am. You will answer," said the Beisht, "and your friends with you, or stay here as stone."

"I will answer," said Imrach. "Ask your question."

"Who is it," said the Beisht, "that lives a lie, that lies in death, and dies in life?"

"What question is this?" demanded Imrach.

"I ask what I will," replied the Beisht.

Imrach looked at Ferenth and Ferrar. "I will not answer," .

"You may not pass," said the Beisht. Then it turned to Ferrar.

'Two of one, one of two, what do you seek and where do you go to find it?"

"I do not seek anything," said Ferrar.

"You are wrong, or you lie," said the Beisht. "The question is the same for you," it said to Ferenth. "Two of one, and one of two, what do you seek and where do you go to find it?"

"I too seek nothing," said Ferenth.

"My question is not answered," said the Beisht, anger burning in its eyes. "You, the third of this three," it continued, turning to Mischka, "what do you seek?"

"That I can answer," said Mischka, "I seek my sister."

"My question is not answered," said the Beisht coldly. "So little any of you know. None of you shall leave this place."

"We shall pass!" cried Imrach. "Sing with me, my friends!" Imrach began to sing, with a strong, clear voice, a song of life and hope, of the strength of love and longing. A high keening rose from the Beisht, but still Imrach sang, joined first by Ferenth, then Mischka and at last Ferrar. Still singing, Imrach began to lead the three friends through the valley, past the Beisht, whose eyes glared malevolently.

"You shall not pass!" it cried, its voice thunderous and grim. Imrach's song rose stronger still, battling with the icy cry of the Beisht. The walls of the valley seemed to shimmer with the force of the conflict between the shriek of the Beisht and the song of the four friends. Louder and stronger their song grew, as though the earth and sky joined the battle on their behalf. As the four friends reached the end of the valley, the Beisht gave a final great cry that echoed and re-echoed from the valley walls.

Then suddenly the valley lay still and eerie, faintly echoing the shrill cry of the Beisht, where the stone statues that stood along the path testified to the power the Beisht had wielded.

"We would not have come through that valley without you," said Mischka.

"We have passed through this danger," replied Imrach. "But we have one more peril still before us."

Chapter 8

The Vale of the Wraiths

Beyond the valley of the Beisht, the path led to the pass of Silverhorn. It curved along the shoulder of the mountain, on one side a vertical wall, on the other a sheer fall.

At times the path narrowed until no more than a single person's width. Both Mischka and Ferenth had to stop and hold onto the rock wall, feeling dizzy. Their legs were limp from the climb. But still they went on. At last they could see the top of the pass, yet over the mountains hung deep black clouds.

Imrach, looking up, studying them, shook his head. "That storm will be here before evening, and then this path will be a torrent. We must find someplace to shelter, or be washed from the mountain."

They began looking carefully at everything they passed, hoping that it might be at least a little shelter from the coming storm. The rock wall was sheer and the path narrow; and now above them they could hear the rumble of thunder and could see the flickering in the sky above them, behind and above the dark clouds. Then the rain began, first just a few large drops, pounding into the dust, and then heavily, a great mass of water pouring from the sky. As though they had stepped under a river's fall, they were instantly drenched and blinded by the rain; they could see it now, moving down the mountain behind them, while the water ran down the path.

They set their backs against the wall, with their blankets over them. It was at least a little wider here than on the rest of the path, and a low ridge of rock directed the water away from them as the rain came down. Around them the lightning blazed and the thunder roared, doubled and redoubled by the stone walls of the mountains. Mischka hid his eyes from the lightning, but Ferrar reveled in the storm and its fury.

Now larger stones washed down the path towards them. Waterfalls sprang up all along the sides of the valley where torrents flooded over the cliffs, crashed over the rim and plunged to the depths below. One such waterfall suddenly cascaded over the cliff above them, only a few yards from where Ferrar was backed against the wall; the force of its fall washed away all the stones and dirt, leaving only a sheer rock face.

Still the storm continued. Lightning bolts reached down toward the peaks, as though probing for any who dared to cross the ridge, and shattered on the path. The air was sharp with the tang of the lightning and their ears rang and their hearts beat loudly with fear and exhilaration. In the boom and the roar of the thunder, it was as though they could hear giant voices calling back and forth across the valley, laughter and songs and boasts. Great rocks were cast into the depths, as though stone giants were playing as boys play over a deep valley, seeing how long a stone would take to reach the bottom.

Ferenth hid her face on Ferrar's shoulder and he held her tightly. Mischka sat huddled in misery and awe as well. Only Imrach appeared unmoved by the storm, untroubled alike by lightning and rain. It was an hour later when the storm passed away, the rain slackened off, the wind shredded the mist; and above them the moon appeared in a clearing sky. The four friends, damp and miserable as they were, fell asleep there at the side of the precipice

It was early morning when they awoke, the sun just cresting the pass before them. Each of them stirred and looked around. Behind them they could see the path washed completely away by the violence of the storm. Before them there were places in the path where the water had fallen in such force that the path was gone. They took off the wet blankets, wringing the water from them, set their packs on their shoulders, and continued up the path.

Another two hours it took them to the pass. One large gap sprawled across their path. Imrach sought a way around it, but at last they had to inch their way across the face of the cliff, Ferrar first, Imrach last, holding Ferenth and Mischka by the hand to ensure they didn't tumble to the valley floor thousands of feet be-

low. So they came to the top of the pass, and there on a shoulder of Silverhorn they looked east and they could see, below them, the two pillars that marked the entrance to the vale of the wraiths.

It took the rest of the day for them to reach the pillars. "I advise that we pass through this vale today, delay no longer," said Imrach. The others agreed. They stepped between the pillars. As they did so, the air shimmered. Before him there appeared a host of flickering shapes and the valley was filled with the hollow sound of their voice.

"What gift do you bring?" they asked.

"This," said Imrach. He began to sing. His song shaped a vision of the valley as it might have been, once, before the wraiths were there. Grass grew on the stony ground, sheep pastured, a small house in the center of the valley hosted a family where children played together. The sky above was clear, the clouds drifting above the distant peaks.

The wraiths, dew closer as Imrach began to walk through the valley. "Show us more," they cried, "show us more." Consumed by the terrible hunger in their voice, the scene began to change. The colors drained away. The family sickened and died. Soon there was nothing there but the empty valley. But Imrach had reached the end of the valley, past the black stone pillar, and his song was done. A great moan went up from the wraiths.

Then Mischka stepped forward. "What is your gift?" demanded the wraiths, their voices troubled and tormented.

This," said Mischka, as he took his flute and played it to them. As he played, it seemed that once again the valley floor was carpeted with flowers, the sides of the valley grew less steep, and the heights where ice glinted turned green and soft with grass. Mischka too walked the length of the valley, and the wraiths parted before him, until at last he reached the other end of the valley where Imrach waited. Again the wraiths gave a great cry of anger and despair.

Then Ferenth stood forward.

"What is your gift?" moaned the wraiths, in voices more terrible yet.

"This," replied Ferenth. She began to sing, a song of the sun and the moon and the stars, of life bursting forth in the spring, of hope conquering fear. A shudder went through the wraiths and they drew back, and still singing, Ferenth passed through them to join Mischka and Imrach.

Last stepped forward Ferrar. "What is your gift?" demanded the wraiths in a voice more terrifying than any voice anyone had ever heard.

"This," said Ferrar. Picking up three crystal shards from the ground, he began to juggle. The sun flashing on the shards made them burn like fire as they tossed in the air. The wraiths drew forward around Ferrar in fascination, closer and closer still. "Faster," they cried. The shards spun faster though the sky. "Faster" they cried again and the shards spun still faster, and the blood flowed from Ferrar's hands as the sharp-edged crystals cut his skin to ribbons. "Faster", they cried, "faster!" Still they flashed, still they flashed. But suddenly the spinning circle of light collapsed, as Ferrar stumbled and fell to the ground.

With a hungry and tormented cry, the wraiths pressed forward on Ferrar, who cried out in pain as he struggled to regain his feet and run through them toward the safety of the valley's end. But the wraiths reached out with their chill arms and cold voices. "You are ours!" they cried and again Ferrar stumbled and fell. But Imrach ran forward and lifted Ferrar to his shoulder, his song again sounding in the stony valley, pushing back the wraiths, tormented by the music and their terrible hunger. Imrach turned and ran from the wraiths until he reached the end of the valley and fell to the dusty ground.

"Come back!" cried the wraiths, and the power of their voices tore at the four friends like cruel talons. "Come back to us. You are ours!"

But Imrach led them through a tunnel in the face of the cliff at the eastern end of the valley, and the voice of the wraiths fell to silence behind them.

At the other end of the tunnel, they found themselves in a narrow, deep canyon. They stumbled down the path until, just before darkness fell, they saw far ahead the towers of Antar, and beyond the great eastern ocean that stretched east and south. There, as night fell, they found a place of shelter among the rocks and fell to the ground in weariness and horror.

Chapter 9

In Antar

When they woke in the morning, far below them they could see the city of Antar. It was carved into the side of the tall mountain ridge that encircled it, and from the city you could see the great eastern ocean that lay curving northward along the shore until it passed beyond the reaches known to any traveler and into the lands of ice.

As the four travelers entered the city, Mischka felt overwhelmed by the noise and cries of the peddlers who abounded, by the rattle of carts, by the traffic, foot and horse. All about him, as they came though the great western gate, were the rich houses of those who had prospered in Antar, the great families who owned estates on the plain of Egeria, or whose ships rode at anchor in the harbor below. The stone streets echoed with the cries of vendors selling fruit, silver, clothes, and all manner of goods.

"We have arrived in Antar," said Imrach. "What do you seek now?"

"I know what I seek," said Mischka. "What I have sought ever since I left home: my sister Lutha."

"And how do you think to find her here, in this town?"

"She told me she would be a weaver. I'll find those who weave, and they will surely know her."

"Then let us go to the quarter of the weavers."

Imrach led them through the streets, Mischka, Ferenth and Ferrar all marveling at his knowledge of the city.

"How do you know this city so well?" asked Ferenth.

"It is many years since I was last here," replied Imrach, "but some things have remained the same."

"And do you know where to find the quarter of the weavers?" asked Mischka.

"If I do not, if it has moved since I was last here, we will find it readily enough," said Imrach. "There will be one who knows."

He led them on, past the jewelers' quarter and the iron-mongers' quarter, past the quarter of the artists, over the great stone bridge where the river came sweeping down from the cold, ice-bound peaks above, its force captured in a series of wheels that drove the industry of the town. Great trains of animals climbed the steep streets or were hauled up in the great elevation devices whose cables ran through channels carved in the rock.

At last they came to the weavers' quarter.

"We are here," said Imrach. "Go and ask where your sister may be found."

"I'll come with you," offered Ferenth.

"And I," said Ferrar.

The three of them entered one of the shops, followed by Imrach. "I am Mischka," the boy told the shopkeeper. "I have come to find my sister Lutha, who is here in Antar, a weaver."

"Lutha?" said the shopkeeper. "I know of no such name. There is no weaver of that name in our town, at least none who is a member of our guild."

"But she must be here!" exclaimed Mischka.

"Perhaps she is, but I do not know her. Now if you are here to buy, buy; if not, I must speak to my customers."

Imrach stepped forward. "You are sure of this?" he asked. "There is no weaver named Lutha?"

"I am sure of it," said the shopkeeper impatiently. "I am the guild master, how should I not know this? Ask at other shops if you wish, but there is no Lutha who is a weaver in our city."

They went to the next shop, and the next, and the answer was the same: there was no Lutha who was a weaver in Antar.

"Mischka, there's no use asking another weaver," said Ferenth. "Lutha's not here."

"She must be here. She must have come. She said she would come," insisted Mischka.

"A night's rest will not hurt us," replied Imrach. "Come, let us find lodging for the night, and then we'll see what counsel the morning may bring."

He led the way to a small inn near the central square. "The Stag's Head", the signboard said, attested by the branched antlers painted beneath the words. Inside, the inn was filled with both men and women. As the innkeeper stepped forward to welcome them, Imrach greeted him and asked for rooms.

"Rooms I have," replied the innkeeper, "for those who can pay for them."

"Pay we can," said Imrach, "and more than pay. My friends here are entertainers of no mean quality."

"If they do well and entertain my guests, a meal they may have for free. But for the room you must still pay twenty coppers."

"A fair price," agreed Imrach. "Let us see the room and if it suits us, put our things there."

The host led the way upstairs. "There you are," he said, opening the door to a small chamber under the eaves. "You may all four sleep here, and need not worry about sharing the room with another."

"It will do," replied Imrach.

"Then come down when you are ready and we will see if your music suits my guests as well as the room suits you."

As they unpacked a change of clothes, Mischka set the harp down at the side of the bed. "You have carried the harp a long way," said Imrach. "Let me see it."

He ran his fingers across the wood. "The damage is not so bad. Tomorrow, if you wish, we will take it to an instrument maker in town and see if he might not repair it."

"Do you know of such? Do you know how to play it?"

"Yes, I can play it a little," said Imrach, as he touched his fingers to the strings. "But for tonight, we will give the guests a more frugal entertainment, as befits our welcome."

Imrach led the way downstairs, where the innkeeper met them once again.

"Now, you songbirds," demanded the innkeeper, "if you wish for supper, let us hear you sing."

"Only one of us will sing," replied Imrach. "Come Ferenth, sing for them. Mischka, let them hear your flute."

While Mischka's flute wove a gentle descant, Ferenth began to sing, words of forest and flowers that grow out of the cold stones on the heights, a song of hope when the year is new on the mountain peaks above Antar.

Through silver-clad beech of Lady Grove,
Beneath snow-silvered Beinn Ven height,
From Logh Ben's mirror silver-bright
In dawn light Ynsheant rippling silver flows.

When they were finished, there was silence; then a storm of applause. Amid the applause someone shouted, "Well done, well done, children!"

There at the table, with Imrach, was a man with a gold earring in one ear, and a cast to one eye. "So," he said, "these are the young ones that you mentioned?"

"That they are," replied Imrach. "A long journey they've had from the western mountains. My friends, this is Rakal, as great a rascal as the sea has known."

"And what have they to show for their long journey?"

"Much," replied Ferrar scornfully. "We have dealt with wraith and bandits and Beisht. Can you say as much?"

"A proud bantam!" laughed Rakal. "I tell you , my fiery one, there are more wonders than that in the wide world, and those who sail the sea find them."

"What wonders?" asked Mischka.

"There are the Far Southern Lands," replied the sea captain, "where the trees bear fruit the year round and where woodsmen live alone among the trees' deep shadows. There are the great southern cities, and islands where none has gone, for they wreck any ship that seeks to land."

"One day we'll see even that," replied Ferrar.

So they ate, and all night long they talked of their adventures. As it grew late, Rakal tuned to Imrach and said, "My friend, you have come back to where it all began. Have you found what you were looking for?"

"I have found what I sought."

"And do they know you?"

"Not yet."

"You hesitate still, my old friend?"

"For reasons of my own," Imrach replied.

"Caution was never your fault!" laughed Rakal.

Imrach laughed too. "But a quiet life is all I ever sought. And now all I seek is bed. Tomorrow will be here soon, and our one last quest."

"So they will," agreed Rakal, "indeed, tomorrow will be here all too soon. Sleep well, children."

The next day, Imrach led them to the great square in the center of Antar, so that Ferrar could do his tumbling and acrobatics. There he told the story of Amerach and Larenth, for the story began here in Antar. Each of one of the great houses of Antar, they had loved each other, though her parents had forbidden the match and had succeeded in having Amerach exiled.

"But Larenth had stolen away with him and they had fled to the western mountains, never to return to Antar. Amerach's house fell silent as his brother left Antar to search for them; the house has remained empty ever since. But some say that Amerach and Larenth had two children. When Larenth died in childbirth, Amerach died of grief. The children disappeared."

"You know this story well, my friend," Rakal called out to Imrach, stepping forward from the crowd.

"A story that all should know well", replied Imrach. Then, there in the great square, they sang this song of the exile of Amerach and Larenth.

Cold blows the wind, the wind of the sea
Cold are the mountains high.
Far from the land where I was born,
It blows across the sky.

Over the land the cold wind blows,
Over the troubled land.
Over the land the cold wind blows,
Over rock and sand.

Follow the wind, wherever it leads,
Follow the mountain path,
Far to the west we'll find a home
Where we'll rest at last

As the crowd shouted its approval, a pock-faced man stepped forward and said, his voice full of the hauteur of wealth and position, "The Baron invites the singer Imrach and his troupe to serve his pleasure through their music and artistry."

"Tell the Baron that we will never be his servants, nor sing at his house," replied Ferrar angrily. The Baron's man turned away with a sardonic smile and ironic bow.

Chapter 10

The Harp Restored

So Mischka arrived at last in Antar, his long journey ending in the city he had long sought. But the quest was not yet over. That which had drawn him to the city, he had yet to find.

Mischka was up early the next morning. But when he came downstairs he found Imrach already standing at the door of the tavern, looking out at the street.

"It's a hopeless task, isn't it?" asked Mischka.

"Not hopeless," replied Imrach.

"But if she is not a weaver, then how shall we find her?"

"There are other places we can try," Imrach reassured him. "We'll go out to the city this morning. Bring the harp with you and we'll look for a shop to repair it. But first, we have another house to visit."

After they had breakfasted, Imrach led them again into the town, to the portal of a great house, where Imrach called out, "Bethor, open the gate. I've come back."

Beyond the gate, the door of a small cottage swung open. An old man shuffled forward.

"Now don't be troubling an old man," he complained. "Leave off your fooling and let an old man be."

"Am I so changed," asked Imrach, "that you do not recognize me?"

The old man peered at Imrach. "Master Imrach?" he said in a quavering voice. "Have you come back then?"

"I have come back," Imrach assured him. "Let me in, old friend."

The old man opened the gate with a trembling hand. "Oh master," he said in a troubled voice, his eyes on Imrach's face, "though the house is not as you or your brother would wish, there is little that one old couple could do, nor did we expect you would be back."

"Yet I am back," laughed Imrach, "and you are still here. Show us inside."

"You'll not be disappointed in the gardens at least," said the old man. "I tended those through the years, and sold the produce in the market to buy ourselves clothes."

Indeed the gardens were still well-tended, perhaps even among the best in Antar. But the house itself was damp and the air still, thick with dust from long years of neglect. Cobwebs hung from the ceiling. The walls and ceilings were damaged here and there by water melting from the long snows of winter. Still, it was solidly built, as were all the old houses in Antar. Even in its decay, it was still a noble house.

"Is this your house?" asked Ferenth.

"It was Amerach's house. I am his brother, and have been its guardian since he died, though a poor guardian at best. It is now yours."

"What do you mean?" asked Ferrar.

"Haven't you guessed? You are Amerach's son. You and your sister are the children of Amerach and Larenth. I too have been on a long quest; my quest ends here."

Ferrar looked at Imrach in amazement. "The son of Amerach?" he said. "The children of Amerach and Larenth?"

"Yes," said Imrach. "Come, let me show you your house."

They went from room to room, pushing back the curtains from the windows, opening the casements to look down across the slopes of Antar to the harbor, far beneath them. Here there were the holes in the carpet; there a bird had come down the chimney and left feathers scattered about the room. Yet as they went from room to room, the house seemed to stir and take on life again.

Imrach led the way to the back of the house. There, in a grand chamber looking out onto the gardens, was a picture of a young couple, painted perhaps from life, perhaps from memory.

"Are they our parents?" asked Ferrar.

"Yes, they are Amerach and Larenth," replied Imrach. "I had hoped that they might return. But at least you are here. I had been looking for you for a long time, until at last I found you in the company of my old friend, once the master singer of Antar."

"So you did know Firfal?" asked Ferenth.

"Not so well as you came to know him. But I was glad to call him a friend."

"I miss him still," said Ferenth.

"As do I," said Imrach sadly.

When they had walked from one end of the house to the other, Ferrar turned to Imrach. With a fierce smile on his face he said, "This is mine, and it will be again a living place, a place of beauty."

"That will be well," agreed Imrach. "To me it seems a still, empty house."

"My sister and I are here at last," replied Ferrar. "It will no longer be empty. Will it, Ferenth?"

Ferenth looked at Mischka. "Will you stay too?"

"If you will let me stay. I am no child of Antar. I know my parents and they are but shepherds of the western mountains."

"And as good as any," Ferrar said, a challenge in his eyes. "Stay with us and make Antar your home."

"I can't until I find Lutha. That must come first."

"So it must," agreed Ferrar. "We will find her together."

Ferrar led the way from the room and back through the house to the streets. As they reached the marketplace, they noticed a great crowd gathered in the center of the square. They could hear a voice raised in lovely song, and there, his voice still rare and true, was the minstrel Leland, who had come to Andor's farm so many years before.

Shadows lengthen.
The sun sinks beneath the western hills.
Beneath the forest canopy darkness gathers.

Darkness strengthens.
The evening wind has come from western heights
To sweep aside the gauze of daylight veils.

Embraced in night,
Your voice I hear, Lady of the Grove,
In the gentle wind and light of stars.

"So my friend," Imrach called to him when the song was done. "Have you too made your way to Antar again?"

"So I have," replied Leland. "It is good to see you."

"I know you," said Mischka. "You are the traveler who sang at our house."

"Many the house I've sung at," acknowledged the minstrel, "all across the land."

"Ours was far to the west, in the western mountains, and there you came one night and sang for us."

"You remember it so well then?" asked Leland.

"Very well. I've never forgotten!"

"Then we must speak of this. My friends," called the minstrel to the crowd that had gathered, "I must rest my voice and take some time to let it recover. Save your coin, and I will return later to entertain you again."

As the crowd dispersed, the minstrel led the way to a wine shop that sat just off the square.

"Are you a traveler too?" he asked Mischka as they sat at the shop.

"Yes," replied Mischka, "for I've come to Antar to look for my sister."

"Why do you seek here her in Antar?"

"She said she would be here."

"And have you found her?"

"Not yet," said Mischka sadly.

"What is this instrument that you carry?"

"This harp was Firfal's and now it is mine."

"Have you learned from him how to play it?"

"He taught me a little, before the harp was broken."

"Then," said the minstrel, "your apprenticeship, whatever may be the end of your search, was well begun."

"Whatever may be the end," agreed Mischka, "nothing but good has this journey given me."

"As you have given nothing but good to us," said Ferrar.

Ferenth looked at her brother. Though the remnant of anger still showed in him, still there was something more there, some sense of rightness, some sense of joy. Of the earlier suspicion he had of Mischka, there was no longer any trace.

"And such gifts must be repaid in kind and kindness," continued Ferrar, "freely given. So here's my hand, my young sprat, and a promise that we will find Lutha."

"A sprat!" protested Mischka

"Even the smallest fish may grow up to be the largest in the pond," replied Ferrar, grinning.

"Come," laughed Imrach. "Let us see if we can find a craftsman to fix this harp."

He led the way back through the city to the shop of an instrument maker. The door was open, and Imrach led the way inside.

"Mistress," he announced as they entered, "I have brought something you have lost."

The instrument maker looked up from her bench, startled, and then cried out in amazement as Mischka rushed forward shouting, "Lutha, I'm here in Antar!"

"Where have you come from?" she asked, wonder in her voice.

"All the way from our parents' home in the western mountains. We have escaped bandits, and the Beisht, and the wraiths. But what are you doing here, in this shop?"

"There was no employment for me as a weaver in Antar," explained Lutha. "But as I went from shop to shop, one of the merchants suggested that I ask for the shop of Tameren, a lutemaker, and that there I would find work. And so it was."

Tameren came forward from his workbench as well. "It has been a good arrangement for me, too. We have done enough work for today. Take yourselves off to dinner. We can work again tomorrow."

So they all went off together to a tavern, where Mischka introduced his friends to Lutha, and they told each other their adventures. At last, when the meal was done, Imrach asked, "Mischka, now that you have found you sister, what will you do?"

Mischka turned to look at Ferrar and Ferenth. "I think," he said slowly, "that there are still other places to see. Ferenth, are you of a mind to see more of the world?"

"I don't know," she replied, her eyes turning to Ferrar.

"I will stay here," he said." I have had enough of being a traveling player. But our house will always be open to you, to both of you."

"I thought my journey was to find my sister," said Mischka. "But now that I've found her, I don't think my traveling is done. This time, I think my journey may be to find myself."

"You will have much to discover," agreed Imrach. "Let Lutha repair the harp. Then you may see what the world has to offer those who offer story and song."

As Mischka, Ferrar and Ferenth walked through the town later that afternoon, a dog suddenly appeared from one of the houses and ran at them, barking loudly. Ferrar reached down and grabbed the dog by the scruff of the neck, then lifted it up laughing.

"A scoundrel of a dog it is," he said, "to jump out so at strangers." While Mischka and Ferenth laughed, Ferrar looked the dog in the eye. "Go home, little friend. Save your barking for those who mean mischief!"

At the door of the house stood the pock-faced man, the messenger for the Baron.

"So you are the children of Amerach? And restored to your house? Is it again a habitable place?

"Not yet," said Ferrar coldly, "but it will be in time. Tell your master that the children of Amerach will dwell there. I'm not inclined to let our ancient privileges lapse."

"I'll carry the word to the Baron, who bid me ask again if you will not come and entertain him and his guests."

"Never! Tell the Baron that the children of Amerach will never sing for him."

With these words, Ferrar turned and walked away, while the pock-faced man scowled and his back.

Ferenth and Mischka set forth on their travels while Ferrar, Imrach and Lutha remained in Antar. And throughout the width and breadth of Egeria there were stories of these two musicians, who could charm the birds from the trees and fill the skies with stars.

The Island of the Forest

The firs grow high
On Rhenn-ein and Rhenn-ny-steigh.
Deep the shadows, eve and noon,
In the depths of Logh Dyùn.

Chapter 11

The Return to Antar

It was spring once again and Ferenth, Mischka and their two children were returning in their caravan to Antar. They had spent the long winter traveling in the southern lands. Now that the roads were passable again, the fields dry and the snow gone from the fields, they set their course towards Antar and toward Ferenth's brother Ferrar in their great ancestral home.

Ferrar and Ferenth were the children of Amerach and Larenth, who had long ago left Antar. Now Ferrar lived in the old house with their uncle Imrach and Imrach's wife, Lutha, who was Mischka's sister. For much of the year Ferenth and Mischka traveled throughout Egeria. Ferenth, with her clear, high voice, and Mischka, with his command of the harp and other instruments, went from village to village and household to household, welcomed everywhere they went.

They avoided the haunts of bandits and did not again suffer the tragedy that they had experienced in their first trip across Thallhiar from Mischka's home to Antar. They were especially careful in their travel now because of their two children, who had inherited their parents' voices and talents. Mirath and Saschka had also inherited something of their uncle Ferrar's skill at acrobatics, at least judging from the tumbling and tricks they did in the taverns and market squares where their parents performed.

The wandering life suited the family. Saschka and Mirath were growing well and strong. Mischka and Ferenth had often taken them to visit his parents, his older brother Linar and Linar's wife Niëra, who lived in the far west of the land. His father Andor had mellowed as the years went past, especially since the death of his wife. Andor welcomed the friendship of his sons and the care that Linar gave to their flocks, now given over to the younger man. Niëra and her children visited the old man in his small stone cabin every day to prepare the meal that he would otherwise forget to prepare for himself. The old man told stories to his grandchildren as he never had to Linar, Lutha and Mischka: stories of years long past, of tending his flocks out in the open fields, of watching the antics of his own children as they grew.

One summer night, when Saschka was just twelve years old and Mirath ten, the family had arrived in a small village high in the Beinn Giall, carved deep into the rock of those tall mountains. The village looked down upon a stony valley where the villagers pastured goats and sheep. Though open to the south so that the even in winter the sun shone between the peaks that rose steep and sheer on all sides, the valley was narrow and the village deeply shadowed most of the time.

As Mischka and Ferenth walked into the village, the children who had been playing outside disappeared into the cottages that lined the dusty track and peered out of the windows at them. Few strangers came to the valley, mainly peddlers, or now and then a soldier. So the townspeople were wary, though eager to see these strangers with their gaily painted wagon.

Mischka, his hand on Greyleg's bridle, led the way into the center of the village and stopped in front of the largest house. He went up and knocked on the door. "What is it then you want?" asked the gruff, grizzled man who came to the door.

"We are singers," Mischka replied, "strangers from far to the east. The great city of Antar is our home. We have come a long way, to bring you news of the rest of the world."

"We have no need of the rest of the world," said the man. "Our valley's enough for us. Nothing touches us here and we touch none."

Ferenth stepped forward to Mischka's side. "Yet, now and again, for the sake of a broader view, a little news may be welcome. Have you heard the stories of the great wonders of these mountains in which you live? We have traveled in them and have seen their great wonders -- and terrors too!"

"We know all we need of wonders and terrors," replied the old man brusquely. "Still, you are strangers. The Lady bids us welcome all those who are come to our homes. So share a meal with us tonight and tell us what you will."

"What shall we do with our horse for the night?" asked Mischka.

"Danner!" the man shouted to his son, who appeared around the corner of the cottage. "Take care of the strangers' horse!"

"I'll help you if I may," offered Saschka, stepping forward. "Greyleg is very dear to us and we like to tend him ourselves."

"Come then and welcome," replied Danner. "I don't mind sharing the work."

"It will go faster if we curry Greyleg together," Saschka suggested.

"Go with him then," said Mischka

"You, Danner, do not dally over the work," his father admonished. "Your mother will have supper ready soon.""

The old man, introducing himself as Garach, led them into the house. It was not a large. There was one room with table and fireplace, and a second where Garach and his wife slept. Danner and three younger children bedded down by the fire at night, where the family burned the wood carted down the mountainside from the deep green forests that surrounded them. The air of the cottage was sweet with the resinous smell of fir, pine and spruce.

Garach bade them sit at table and rest, while he gave them cups of water and his wife brought in a loaf of bread and some cheese. "We've had our main meal of the day already," he explained. "But you can share the light supper that we have at this time."

"Gladly!" said Ferenth. "And let us add what we can. We have a few jars of preserved fruit. Shall I get one of those to share?"

"That would be welcome," Garach replied.

Mischka went to the door and called out to Saschka to bring a jar of cherries from the wagon to share with their hosts.

I will," shouted Saschka in reply. "We'll be done with Greyleg soon."

Mischka returned to the table and sat down with the host and his family.

"So you travel the countryside, do you?" asked Garach.

"Yes," said Mischka. "We're singers and news-carriers, especially to these places far off in the hills, which would otherwise know nothing of what passes in the world beyond their valleys."

"As I said," replied Garach, "we have no need here of news from the outside world. Nothing touches us but the wind and the rain, the snows of winter and the heat of summer. We live happily in our valley and seek nothing of the world at large."

"Yet the world may come and knock on your door," laughed Ferenth, "as we have. Then it's good to know something of what is happening. Even better, on such a summer night as this, is sharing laughter and music. I'm sure that your children would welcome a song or two." She smiled at the three children hiding behind their mother.

"We have no time for laughter," replied Garach. "Our summer is too short to waste."

"But when the winter is so long," asked Mirath, who had sat down next to Ferenth, "don't you need songs and stories to while away the nights?"

"What stories have families such as we?" Garach's wife, Flera, stepped forward to sit down at the table. "We know only pain and sorrow, deep winter snows and bitter cold, children lost and parents dying."

"Even these can be sung of with joy," replied Ferenth quietly. "What song is greater than one that celebrates the love of parents and children, even in the sorrow of loss? What song better than one that tells the love we have for each other, even in the face of the most bitter suffering?"

"If you have such songs, then we will gladly hear them," Flera replied. "But finish your bread and cheese first. Let me pour you more of this water."

"We are grateful for it," said Mischka. "You do not brew ale or bottle wine?"

"Wine and ale we have none," Garach answered. "It is too cold here for fruit. What grain we grow must feed ourselves and animals, not be turned to drink."

"Yet it may lighten the heart on long winter nights," Ferenth suggested, "whether it be honey mead or barley brew or brant wine."

"Not for us," Garach replied. "Clear water from mountain springs is all we offer you and all we have ourselves. Milk from the goats we have when we've bred them, but most of that we use for our cheese, which must also last us through the winter. We'll gather hay tomorrow. Join us in that work, if you wish."

"That we will gladly," agreed Mischka. "I too was a shepherd as a boy and long tended flocks in mountains not so unlike these, although less stark and steep. So I would gladly share in your labor for a while."

"And my daughter and I," Ferenth added, "will gladly visit those in the village who are not well and give them what comfort we may in herbs or a simple song."

"Are you a wise woman, then?" asked Flera.

"Only wise as all women are wise," Ferenth replied, "as all women must be on whom the burden of family and health rests."

"You speak the truth in this," Flera said. "The men may pride themselves that they are masters of the house, but it is women who are its soul and life."

"Let us not begin that topic," protested Mischka, laughing, "or we'll be arguing all the night long about who is the more important."

"Neither can be the more important," Ferenth replied. "We each give what we may. The strength men offer is only part of what is needed, especially when one lives so far from ease."

"So it is in music, where each plays a part and the whole is more than the individuals," Mischka agreed. "May we sing for you now? Saschka and Mirath, let us go and get the instruments. Have you brought the preserved fruit for these friends?"

"I have it here," replied Saschka, as he set a small jar of preserved figs on the table. "We brought this from Antar," he said to Garach and Flera. "Our uncle has a fig tree in his garden there. I picked the figs myself! They are sweet and taste still of the summer days in Antar. We've carried it a long way, all across the country, and it's our last jar. But you should have it and share it with others."

"This is a welcome gift," Garach said, taking up the jar and turning it slowly in his hands. "We have little fruit here in these cold mountains. Such treasures as these figs I've heard of but never tasted."

"Then taste some now," offered Mischka. He took the jar from Garach. With his knife, he carefully pried the wax seal from the top of the glass, then offered it to Flera. She dipped a knife into the preserves and spread a small amount on the crust of bread before her. Then Garach did the same.

"This is princely!" exclaimed Garach as he tasted the sweet preserves.

"No prince has better than this," Mischka agreed, laughing. "Nothing can match the taste of figs, preserved as Ferenth has these."

The children tried some too. Their grins and delighted "Oh! This is so good!" brought a smile to Garach's and Flera's faces.

"I'll go to the wagon and get the instruments," offered Mischka. "Then perhaps we may sing a song or two before the sun sets."

"If your songs are as sweet as this fruit, then you bring a greater gift to all of us here in the village than any other has ever brought," Flera replied.

So Mischka, Ferenth, Saschka and Mirath brought their instruments from the cart. As they took their seats on the stone bench in front of the cottage, Mischka suggested, "Call your neighbors, if you will. We would share this music with them, too."

So Garach sent his children from cottage to cottage. At each one, they called out, "Come hear the songs these strangers will sing for us!"

They began with a song for the children, about a girl and her doll.

There was a girl lived in a dale,
In a valley green.
She had a poppet that she loved,
Loved so dearly.
And one day as she walked with him
Beneath the spring-time leaves,
Her poppet said, "Come, dance with me!
Dance with me!"

They waltzed along the forest paths;
The poppet led the dance.
The girl danced fast and faster still,
By the doll entranced.
Through the woods they sped and as they
Dashed along the way,
Her poppet said "Dance with me!
My dear one, dance today!"

So they danced and spun and whirled
As the sun grew brighter still,
Shining through the branches
While music echoed in the rill.
But as they danced along the brook,
The poppet said to her:
"Our day of dance is nearly done.
We must return, return."

So the paths they followed home
And there the daughter sang
Of how she danced the day along,
And how the woodland rang
And how the poppet danced with her;
And all her parents said
Was "Yes, yes, that is a lovely tale,

But now it's time for bed."

So my child, if one day
You hear a poppet speak,
And if you hear it say to you,
"A dance is what I seek!"
Then take his hand and let him lead
Through forests fair and deep,
And dance with him, and laugh, and sing,
And then come home to sleep.

They sang many other songs too. They sang of forests and fields, of loss and love. They sang of the stars, as Mischka and Ferenth had sung so many times, for so many people,. At last when night had fallen, Mischka stood and said, "Before we bid you all good night, there is one more song to sing." Then he began, in his clear, strong voice, a song of thanks for the bread and cheese they had eaten, for the clear water that quenched their thirst, for the love that filled their lives.

I live among mountains
Whose slopes are steep and hard.
I live among mountains
Whose winds are cold and sharp.
But oh! My love, though you and I
Have but the little that we share,
Yet what we have is good and true,
And life is rich and fair.
All the paths that I have walked,
My life was ever blest
With laughter and with music,
With grace of peaceful rest.
When at night I lift my eyes
To stars above my head,
My heart is filled with thanks
For the life that I have led.

My heart is filled with joy
For all I have been given.
My heart is filled with love
For the life that I am living,
For those I love walk with me
Where paths are fair or rough
And share with me the songs I sing
Of thanks, of joy, of love.

In the silence of the night, amid the deep blessing of the stars and the cool mountain air, Flera and her family led Mischka, Ferenth and the children back to the house. She and Garach put them to bed in their own room that night, in gratitude for the laughter and blessing of their songs.

Life was good for Mischka and his family as the traveled the roads of Thallhiar. There was only one cloud on the horizon. In Antar, the struggle for power was ever more fierce and cruel and Ferenth's brother, Ferrar, was caught up in the game. His uncle Imrach urged him to stay apart, cautioned him against putting his heart into the politics of Antar. But as a member of one of the great houses, it was Ferrar's right to attend the assembly. He could not help but rail passionately against those who were amassing wealth at the expense of others. He bitterly condemned their greed, their abuse of power.

Antar's wealthiest and most powerful man was the one who called himself the Baron of Egeria. He was the owner of the greatest house, the richest lands. Many were the servants he had, and even more the men-at-arms, who intimidated any who opposed him. Greater even than his wealth and power were his pride and his contempt of others poorer than himself.

When Ferrar spoke angrily in the council against the Baron and his injustices, the Baron retorted derisively, sneering at those who "were nothing better than vagabonds and beggars." Each time they saw Ferrar, it seemed to Mischka and Ferenth that he spoke more angrily against the Baron. More and more, there were rumors of open conflict between Ferrar's supporters and the Baron's, and of those who sided with Ferrar being threatened or beaten by the Baron's men. Ferrar would repeat with bitter laughter the latest songs from the taverns, deriding the Baron and his followers. But those followers included many of the richest and most powerful families.

So as Mischka and Ferenth approached Antar, the thought of what new conflicts Ferrar might have gotten into weighed heavily in their thoughts. When the children were asleep, the two adults spoke in lowered voices of the rumors they had heard of the Baron's latest excesses and of Ferrar's latest protests. Little else was talked of, at least among those who concerned themselves with what happened in Antar.

Antar was the greatest and wealthiest city in the North. It exercised only a nominal authority over other towns and villages. But even the poorest homestead was anxious for news of Antar, and thought of itself as belonging to Antar.

Many people spoke of one day journeying to the city, of seeing the great waterfall that cascaded from the peaks north of the town into the great lake from which the city drew it water. Even more spoke of the great palace the Baron was building at the top of the town. They spoke of him as a spider sitting above Antar, his webs entangling all in the city.

Yet when they spoke of Ferrar, it was as a helpless gnat struggling vainly against the Baron. Too often they laughed with derision at his hopeless protests.

When Ferenth, Mischka and their family reached Ferrar's house, Lutha was there at the door to welcome them, her daughter Raëla with her. A quiet girl of sixteen years, Raëla looked at them with her mother's eyes as Lutha welcomed her brother and his family. Mirath no sooner saw her cousin than she ran to her and threw her arms around her. Raëla's face broke into a smile as she held her young cousin with a fierce protectiveness.

"Come in!" Lutha exclaimed. "We're so glad to see you, Mischka, and Ferenth! And your children, how they have grown! Can this be young Saschka? Come stand next to me. Why you are as tall as my shoulder, nearly as tall as Raëla, and you only fourteen years old! And you, Mirath, how you have grown as well!

How old are you now? Twelve, is it? Come in, come in. Do you still have that old caravan."

"We do indeed," replied Mischka, smiling. "It's carried us many a mile."

"And that old piebald horse as well?"

"No, Fortis has gone to pasture at last. We have a new one now, Greyleg."

Imrach, Lutha's husband, joined her in the doorway. "Ah, my cousins, welcome! You must be weary from traveling."

"Weary enough," agreed Mischka. "But troubled more by the rumors we have heard of Ferrar and the Baron. Are things so out of hand here in the city?"

"Out of hand? Perhaps." replied Imrach. "The Baron grows great and few can oppose him. I counsel Ferrar to be patient and guard his tongue so that he can win support. It is true, as Ferrar says, that this man who styles himself a Baron is a great danger to Antar and to all of us. He wields great power and amasses more all the time. Such power is dangerous in one man. But there are those who see him as a great leader and his money as evidence of greatness rather than greed. But we'll talk more of this later. Come, come inside!"

And so Mischka, Ferenth and their family returned to Antar.

Chapter 12

The Banishment

It was late that night, long after supper was done and the children were in bed, when at last Ferrar came in. There were lines graven in his brow and set into the corners of his mouth: lines of anger and impatience that Ferenth didn't remember being there before. Her brother had always had a hot temper, especially in his protectiveness for her. But this simmering anger and bitterness was different, it seemed to her. Nonetheless, when Ferrar saw his sister, his face lit with a deep, loving smile. He gathered her to him and held her tightly.

"Are you well, my sister?" he asked.

"Well indeed," Ferenth replied gently. "We had a very good season of traveling, but now are above all glad to be here in Antar again, here again with you."

Ferrar turned to Mischka then and grasped him warmly by the shoulders. "And you, my brother, have you taken good care of my sister?"

"As well as I can," replied Mischka, smiling. "She has always been strong-willed! Is all well with you?"

"Well enough," Ferrar answered. "There are struggles brewing in this town and many are the things I must do. But I am well enough, all the better for seeing all of you here. They look well, do they not Lutha?"

"Well indeed! I am glad we are to have them with us for a while."

"Do you still keep up your skills?" Mischka asked Ferrar.

"You mean my juggling and acrobatics? No, there is no need for those in the role I take now. It is an agile tongue that serves me best now. Have you learned a good satire or two that I can employ against this Baron who threatens to beggar and enslave us all?"

"Satire was never my strength," Mischka replied seriously. "It was always you and Rakal who were the best in that vein."

"We miss him greatly,' said Lutha. "It has been a long winter, without his jests and laughter."

"His voice is much missed," agreed Ferrar. "His tavern satires were the best defense we had against this Baron. Everyone laughed when Rakal sang, however rough his voice. There was a magic in his words that none could withstand. I need such weapons for our struggles."

'Has it come to conflict, then?" asked Mischka.

"It has always been a conflict between the Baron and me, one that you knew little of in your wanderings," replied Ferrar bitterly.

"Yet I've heard of this conflict with the Baron. Everyone in Egeria has heard of it!"

"And do they know what he threatens? Many speak of him with admiration, the more fools they. Will they speak with admiration still when he owns their farms, turns them out to walk the roads and starve?"

"Is this what he does?" asked Ferenth, troubled by the news.

"To some. Others he keeps on, little better than slaves on the farms they once owned. The houses they once had fall to his greed, the stones that had sheltered them he carts away to build the grim pile of rock that looms over the city, built on the spur at the very rim of Falls Lake."

"We could hardly miss it as we came into the valley," admitted Mischka.

"Soon it will crush us all, unless others will speak up against it with me. Why do you not speak up, uncle?"

"I have no skill in this," Imrach replied.

"You had skill enough to silence the Beisht," argued Ferrar. "Surely you have skill enough to stop this Baron. You must do more, skill or none! All of us must do more."

"It grows late, Ferrar," interrupted Lutha calmly. "Mischka and Ferenth have had a long journey. For this one night, can we not set aside the anger of this bitter conflict and enjoy their company?"

"For this one night I'll do that, for their sake," agreed Ferrar. "I beg your pardon, Imrach. The fight seems hopeless and the threat so great."

"I understand," Imrach replied. "You have reason for your anger. We hear nothing good of the Baron."

"But we hear only good from far and wide of the music of Ferenth, Mischka and their two children," said Lutha, smiling as she turned to her brother. "Will you share your music with us tonight?"

"If you will join us too!" replied Mischka laughing.

"My voice is very rusty!" Lutha protested.

"Do you no longer sing to Raëla as once you did?"

"She is too old for that now. She has grown so silent that that my voice falters when I would sing to her. But though I do not join you, sing still."

Mischka went to the hearth were he had set his harp. He carefully took it from its leather case, patched and worn from years of travel. The old harp showed evidence of having once been battered and broken. Yet in Mischka's hands, as he plucked a chord, there rose from it such a clear and singing tone that the hearts of everyone in the room lifted in joy at the simple beauty of the sound.

Then Ferenth's voice rose above the music of the harp, singing of the hopes and fears of a young woman weaving at her loom, waiting for her lover.

Long the weaving, warp and weft,
Fly my shuttle, fly!
Long the wishing he would come,
He I would were nigh.

Long I've waited here for him.
Fly my shuttle, fly!
Long I've wished that he were here,
Nights and nights gone by.

Long and long I've waited here.
Fly my shuttle, fly!
Bring my love to me again,
Ere day to night dies.

When she finished, the room was silent. Raëla's eyes were fixed on Ferenth with a fierce intensity. "Sing again!" she demanded.

"Raëla!" protested Lutha. "Come my dear one, it is time we all were in bed."

"One more song, Raëla?" asked Ferenth quietly.

Raëla nodded her head.

This time Saschka and Mirath joined their parents to sing of a young man who has found the woman that he loves. As he walks behind the plow, larks swoop and dive overhead, the sun is warm on his back and the love in his heart is warmer still than the sun that quickens seed in the furrow.

In the sky the stars have faded.
Day has turned to dawn.
In the east the light has grown.
There my love dreams on.

Deep the earth turned by the plow,
Dark in ridge and furrow.
High the lark that sings above,
Calling to her lover.

So in love with her am I!
Like the lark a-wing,
Fly my songs, fly to her,
Within her dream to sing.

Raëla sat with her dark eyes fixed on Ferenth's face. In the light of the candle, her face seemed to glow with the intensity of her concentration, her absorption in the music.

Mischka stilled the strings of the harp, then stretched his arms and yawned so widely that everyone laughed. "It grows late!" he protested. "I must to bed."

"So must we all," agreed Lutha, the smile still lingering in her eyes. "After songs such as these, we will sleep well."

But Ferenth and Mischka lay awake for a long time that night, long after everyone else had gone to sleep. They were troubled by the change in Ferrar. He had always been a bitter man, as Mischka remembered well. But never had he been so angry. Never had he shown such bitterness as it seemed that he now felt.

"I remember when I first joined Firfal's troupe," Mischka murmured to his wife. "Ferrar would hardly let you talk to me."

"I remember that too," Ferenth replied softly. "But I remember equally well how he loved me. His anger was out of love for me, out of care for me that led him to mistrust you and any other young man. Though why he should ever have mistrusted you, my love, I can't say!"

"Neither can I," agreed Mischka, laughter rippling under his words. "Have you even seen such an open and confiding countenance as this?"

"If that innocent expression is what you mean by open and confiding, then it is so. But I think there is some shrewdness in you still, my love."

"Yes, as shrewd as they come!" laughed Mischka. Then his voice again grew more serious. "But indeed, what shall we do for Ferrar?"

"We must help him," replied Ferenth. "Without our help, I fear he will not survive this conflict with the Baron."

"What do you mean?"

"Look what the Baron has done to others. All those who oppose him are exiled or cast into poverty. Ferrar has little moderation in his anger. What will he do when the Baron retaliates at last, as he surely will?"

Mischka was silent for a moment, thinking of his brother-in-law. When they first met, Ferrar had seemed nearly to hate Mischka. But they were as close now as Mischka was to his own brother and sister. Only his wife and children were dearer to him.

"I'll go with him to the city," said Mischka at last. "Perhaps we underestimate the resentment against the Baron and overestimate the danger in which Ferrar places himself."

"I wish we had Firfal with us. He was always a true friend to us. Few could see as well what goes on in others' hearts and minds."

"Do you miss him still?"

"He was father to me," replied Ferenth, "the only father I ever knew. What I learned of laughter, I learned from him. What I learned of love, I learned from him. Yes, I miss him. I always will."

"Then tomorrow," said Mischka, "as Firfal used to do, I'll frequent the taverns."

"As we often do ourselves!"

"Yes, that is often where we sing. But tomorrow I'll listen to others' singing."

So next day, when Ferrar said, "Will you come with me to see the town and hear the news?" Mischka replied, "I will gladly! I look forward to seeing how others feel about what you have to say."

"No one cares what I say," said Ferrar coldly. "They close their ears. They turn away from me. But still I'll say what I have to, in hopes that someday they may wake up out of their stupor and banish this Baron as he deserves. But come with me! See what a web the Baron has woven over Antar."

The first tavern they came to was called the Silver Lion. It was not far from the council chambers and so frequented by many of the council members and wealthy people of the city. They drank their ale and spoke in important voices of what was happening. Yet none spoke of the Baron. That topic alone seemed to be avoided by all who were there.

"Good evening, my friends," Ferrar called out as they entered. "Host, cans of ale for me and my brother."

The innkeeper turned the spigot on the great cask of ale behind him and filled flagons for each man. Ferrar led the way to a table where several of the council members were sitting. "So," he said to them, "have you heard the latest news of the Baron? "

"What news is that, gadfly?" replied one of the men. "Why must you always rail against the Baron when we seek nothing more than to rest from the labor of the day and enjoy the company of our friends?"

"Why? Because news of the Baron is more important than your gossip and stale jokes. Today the Baron bought yet more land near the docks. Have you not heard this?"

"Why should I care what the Baron does with his money?"

"Even when he buys not just land, but power? Why do you call him Baron, but for his money and land? We have never had princes, nor Barons. Why should we now? Have you heard the latest song about this Baron?"

The council members looked at each other with pained expressions. But the younger men in the tavern shouted, "Sing us your song! We hope it's a good one!"

"It is good," replied Ferrar. "Listen!"

The Baron sits atop the city,
Spinning out his webs,
He sits there like a spider,
Drawing in the threads

'Come to me my little ones,
Come my little flies!
Come to me, my gnats and bugs
And I will dine and dine.

All night I dream of eating.
All day I stuff my craw.
My webs are strong and many.
My threads th' unwary draw.

When at night I lie abed,
I think of all that I
Will eat until at last I am
As great as the great sky.

And when at last I've eaten up
All there is to see,
There'll be nothing left of you.
There'll be only me!

"That is a scandalous song!" shouted one of the councilors sitting at the table. "The Baron is no spider!"

"He spins webs enough," replied Ferrar scornfully. "All of you are caught in his snares."

"Then why do you stay in Antar?" shouted the councilor angrily. "If you cannot stand the Baron, then leave!"

"Antar needs someone to speak against him. Else he will poison us all!"

Mischka stepped forward to Ferrar's side. "I am Ferrar's brother-in-law. My wife and I have traveled far in this land. It is true what he says, fear and mistrust of the Baron grow everywhere."

"Always the little people fear those who have more than they, and envy them too," replied the councilor arrogantly. "If Ferrar had his way, none of us would have wealth at all. You are infected with the same madness as he. It must run in the family!

"What runs in our family is truth!" shouted Ferrar, "What runs in yours is cowardice! The Baron is poison, poison that will sicken all of us. We are all of us tangled already in his webs. If we do not cut yourselves loose, all of us will soon be swallowed by this spider!"

"We have less cause to fear the Baron than your rabble-rousing. What is wrong with being wealthy?"

"There is no end to greed," replied Ferrar angrily. "The more power the Baron has, the more power he wishes for himself; the more wealth he has, the more wealth he seeks. You see no need to stop him. But soon you will not be able to stop him, even if you want to! Come, my brother. We'll leave these fools to their drinking."

Ferrar was silent for a long time as they walked through the streets back to the house. Then abruptly he stopped and turned to Mischka. "Tomorrow, will you come with me to the assembly?" he asked.

"I have no voice there," Mischka replied.

"Nor have I, not a voice to which anyone pays heed. But I would be grateful of your company. I must speak out once again. This cannot go on."

"Then I will come," Mischka agreed.

The next morning Ferrar, Ferenth, Mischka and Imrach together set off early for the council meeting. Lutha stayed with Raëla and the two younger children, but before the others left she took Ferrar by the arm. "Have a care!" she warned. "I fear that there is a crisis coming and that for all of us, today is the fatal day."

"What is it, Lutha?" asked Imrach.

"I do not know," said Lutha. "But I am afraid today, as I have not been before. Be careful!"

"So I will be," said Ferrar with a voice of iron. "But I will not be silent!"

They spoke little as they walked through the streets to the council chamber next to the Lady River. As he took his place, Mischka noticed angry and hateful glances directed towards them. The Baron sat across the chamber from them, his face expressionless. As the chief counselor stood to call the meeting to order, the Baron nodded to a thin, hawk-nosed man near him.

"I declare treason against Antar!" the man shouted, jumping up from his seat.

"What treason, Preyth?" intoned the chief counselor. "What do you mean?"

"I accuse Ferrar, Amerach's son, of treason against Antar!"

"How have I committed treason?" shouted Ferrar incredulously.

"I have here the proof," replied Preyth, waving a sheaf of papers. "You are seeking to lead a great uprising against the freedom of Antar."

"This accusation is outrageous!" protested Ferrar.

"Outrageous indeed!" mocked the thin man. "I have letters from those who have confessed their part in this treason. I demand that this traitor be condemned to exile, if not indeed to death!""

He handed his papers to the chief councilor, who glanced through them. then looked around the chamber, searching for those whose names were on the letters

"You, Jarman! Do you swear that Ferrar has spoken to you of this treasonous plan?"

"I swear to it," replied a jowly man, standing up from his place on the council benches. "Night after night, Ferrar son of Amerach has urged that the only way to protect ourselves is to overthrow the council and seize control of Antar."

"I said no such thing!" shouted Ferrar. "I have said that this self-styled Baron is a great danger and that the council is failing to restrain him. But never have I said that I would overthrow it, only that we must not allow this man to continue his extortion and robbery. He must surrender his wealth to those who have need of it!"

"Like yourself?" accused Preyth scornfully.

"I need none of it! I speak for the poor who clamor for justice, growing more numerous each day as this man takes all that they have."

"And you would strip his wealth from him?"

"Yes, I would strip him of his wealth to return it to those to whom it belongs. If you on this council will not do it, you do not deserve to lead the city."

"Is this not treason that I hear," shouted the thin man, "to threaten the council that protects the citizens and the city! You have heard him, fellow councilors. Is this treason or not?"

The Baron's face twisted in a grimly satisfied smile as cries rang out from all around the chamber. "Treason! Treason! Banish him! Banish him from Antar!"

Ferrar shouted against the din. "You fools, are you blind to what this spider is doing? Are you so besotted with his wealth that you cannot see the threat he is to you? What will you do when he drives you to exile as well? "

The shouts rang out louder still. "Exile him! Exile him!"

Then Imrach stood. Such was the respect in which he was held that all grew silent. "It is the right of the council to declare banishment. You declared banishment against my brother for going against the will of his father, at my father's own urging. Bitter was the punishment he suffered in that banishment. Now you seek to drive away his son as well, and for what? For speaking the truth? If you drive him forth, then you drive me forth as well. Antar will see us never again while I live."

Guilty looks passed among some of the councilors. But in the Baron's eyes there was a flash of triumph. He nodded once again to the thin, hawk-faced man.

"Then leave with him!" shouted Preyth scornfully. "We have no need of traitors!"

"There are no traitors except this Baron!" shouted Ferrar in reply. "Mischka, Mischka, say something!"

Again the crowd fell silent as Mischka stood up.

"We have traveled the length and breadth of the land and everywhere we hear rumors of this conflict. It troubles everyone, not just those in Antar. Set aside this accusation of treason! Think of what you do, lest you rip apart not just Antar but Egeria, perhaps even all of Thallhiar."

"It is not we who cause this conflict," Preyth interrupted, shouting Mischka down. "You have heard how Ferrar has conspired against the council! You have heard how he seeks to plunge Antar into chaos!"

"I have committed no treason!" declared Ferrar hotly. "I only demand of the council that it do what must be done to protect us all from the greed and deceit of the Baron!"

"And if it does not do what you demand, you will destroy the council and Antar!" Preyth interrupted again. "What say you, fellow councilors? Shall we not banish this serpent, this traitor?"

"Banish him, banish him!" rose the cry from all sides of the chamber.

The Baron rose from his chair. "Chief councilor, I call the question: shall Ferrar be banished?"

The chief councilor, his face as white as his hair, looked at Ferrar. "The rules of our council constrain me. We must consider this question. "

"If you do this," warned Ferrar, "you seal your own fate!"

"If we do not do this," shouted Preyth, "you bring disaster on us all!"

"Those who would banish Ferrar?" asked the chief councilor.

"Banish him, banish him!" shouted every voice in the chamber, but one.

Imrach, standing beside Mischka and Ferrar still, raised his hand, commanding silence. "I oppose this ruling," he said firmly.

In the sudden silence, one person after another turned to look in fear or triumph at the Baron. Silently he regarded first Imrach, then Mischka and lastly Ferrar as they stood alone in the center of the council chamber. Then he nodded to the chief councilor.

"It is the ruling of this council," said the chief councilor, "that Ferrar son of Amerach be banished from Antar until such time as this exile may be revoked. So be it."

"So be it!" shouted the council as the Baron rose and strode from the chamber.

Chapter 13

Leaving Antar

Ferrar looked scornfully around the council.

"Are you all creatures of this spider, walking of your own will into his webs? I fear for you and all of Antar. You have banished me this day. But it is you who are truly banished. You have sold yourselves in your fear for what you might lose. He who already so exercises his power over you cannot now be restrained. How will he be restrained when he has yet more power and your fear is even greater? If you have no courage now to stand against him, where will you find courage when you are driven from your homes? Where will you find courage when you yourselves are banished from Antar? "

"You have no voice here now!" said Preyth in scorn. "You are no longer a member of this council!"

"Then I will say no more. I will not retract my words, but they will no longer be heard in this chamber."

"Nor elsewhere in Antar, unless you wish to lose all you have!"

"My rights and my goods may not be sequestered."

"That is indeed the rule," advised the chief councilor. "None may take your home and possessions, unless you defy the ruling of this council. So it was even with Amerach when he was banished. Let none desire it."

"Yet the ruling is clear," argued the hawk-faced man. "Ferrar must be gone from Antar within three days or his life and goods are forfeit."

"So be it," said Ferrar. "I will be gone in three days. But you will remain and your lives will have little that I shall envy. The time will come when you will find yourselves wishing to change places with me."

With that he turned and strode from the chamber, Ferenth, Mischka and Imrach by his side.

They walked home in silence. Already the rumor had flown through the streets. People looked at them with eyes askance, as though in fear that the banishment might be catching and they as well forced to leave the city. Mischka thought longingly of his caravan and of the open road far from the city, but with regret, too, that this lovely city should turn out to have been so virulently poisoned.

Lutha and the children were waiting for them at the door when they reached their house. "What is it, Imrach? What has happened?" she cried, running to her husband.

"My love, we are banished," replied Imrach.

"Not you," Ferrar contradicted. "I alone am forced to walk this road."

"Where you go, my brother, I go," said Ferenth.

"And I, too," Mischka added.

"And I" said Imrach as well. "If you are banished, then so are we."

"We will not let you endure this alone," agreed Lutha. "Though this house fall and its very stones crumble away, they will cry out against the injustice that has been done to you."

"They may cry out, but none will listen," replied Ferrar. "They stop their ears. Antar is deaf. But I'll not be here to endure that deafness any longer."

"Where shall we go then?" asked Ferenth.

"We have two choices," suggested Imrach. "We can go west, as Amerach did, and find a safe haven in the Beinn Ard mountains beyond the Tabirnian Hills, far from the reach of Antar."

"Is it far enough?" asked Ferenth. "Might the Baron's arm reach even there?"

"Then we go the other way," replied Imrach. "We take ship and set sail for the southern lands, if can find any to take us."

"Rakal would take us, if he were here," Ferenth said. "But we can surely find another ship and captain, if we pay him enough. Let us sell the house and all that we cannot take with us.

That will be enough for our passage and to build a new life in another land."

Imrach shook his head. "I do not wish to give up this house that has been in our family for so many years. Though this time is a bitter one, yet someday it too will pass. If not we, then perhaps our children may one day return."

"Where do we sail to?" asked Mischka.

"Some say there are islands to the east of Antar," replied Imrach. "But no one knows if that is true. We should sail to the south. The trading route to the southern cities is well-known and many ships travel from Antar to the markets there. It is a dangerous time of year, when storms fierce and unexpected can drive ships onto rocks and shoals. But this seems to me the best choice."

"What do you know of these southern cities?" asked Lutha of her husband. "I have heard only rumor. Are they not dangerous?"

"There is no place, no road without danger," Imrach replied.

"None of you should come with me," protested Ferrar. "You are not exiled, as I am."

"There you are wrong." Ferenth took her brother's hands in her own. "This at least is certain. If you are exiled, then so are we."

"Perhaps it is time again for those skills and sleights of hand that you once practiced, if they have not grown too rusty!" laughed Mischka. "We have missed them, in our travels! This time, we'll entrust our fates to your hands, for you to juggle as skillfully as you once did shards of crystal in the valley of the wraiths."

"You have little reason to trust any skill of mine, in voice or hand," replied Ferrar bitterly.

"We have every reason," Ferenth replied. "What better reason can we have than our faith in your truth and honor?"

"What honor is there in exile? What truth in a voice that is silenced?"

"A ruling so unjust will not stand. Someday we may return."

"Never!" Ferrar looked at each member of his family in turn, his face serious and determined. "I shall never, never return!"

"Let us leave our return to the future," said Imrach, "and look to our departure. Tomorrow we will see what ship we may find to take us to the south."

So it was decided. The next morning Imrach and Ferrar set forth to the docks while Lutha and Ferenth, with the help of their serving-man Bethor, prepared the house for departure. They needed to decide what to sell, what things to move to one of the great storehouses of the city. Mischka wrote a letter to his brother Linar, then went to the market to find someone to take the letter to him. He met a band of musicians and players who agreed to carry it with them on the journey west that they would begin in just a few days. Life had grown chancy in Antar, they said. It was safer to be away from the great city, beautiful though it might be and great though the wealth it contained.

"I only hope Ferrar doesn't antagonize everyone," Lutha said to Ferenth as they and the children worked on closing the house, waiting for Mischka to return. "He has such a temper! Now when we must leave the city is no time to berate those who cannot help."

"He knows when to curb his tongue," Ferenth replied. "He and Imrach will find a ship. I'm sure of it. But
I wish you and Imrach would consider staying here, where you and Raëla will be safe."

"We will not stay here without you!" protested Raëla softly, but in a voice that brooked no disagreement.

Lutha smiled at her daughter, then turned again to Ferenth. "Who knows where your exile may lead? Who knows when it may end? We were always glad to see you after each of your wanderings, your arrival here at our house always matter for joy. But there may be no return from this exile. If you never return again to Antar, we would be parted from you forever. That, none of us could bear. So we will come with you, bear what you bear, see what you see. Where you live, we shall live. What you suffer, we shall suffer."

As that moment there was a knock on the door. Saschka ran to open it and led an older man into the room.

"What do you want?" asked Lutha angrily, recognizing Riman, one of the members of the council who had voted for Ferrar's exile.

"I have come to say farewell."

"You already said farewell in council, you and all the others that have exiled Ferrar and with him all of us who love him. I am amazed that you are not too ashamed of what you have done to face us here in our home!"

"I am ashamed, ashamed that neither I nor another spoke in the council against this exile. But your brother condemned himself from his own mouth, in his anger and his intemperance. I regret that this has happened, for I think he spoke the truth and we will face difficult times under the rule of the Baron of Egeria."

"You will face more difficult times than you know," said Ferenth quietly. "He is a cruel man, this Baron, as you know well. It will not be long before Ferrar's words come back to haunt you. This man is a spider who spins his webs to ensnare all Antar. You will see the truth of what Ferrar has said."

"I know the truth of what he has said. I strive to work against this Baron, though I fear it may cost me my home as it has cost you yours." Riman looked around the room, at the shrouded furniture and shuttered windows. "Where will you go?"

"Imrach and Ferrar are even now at the docks," replied Lutha, "trying to find someone who will take us to the southern cities."

"You will not travel overland, then?"

"That is a long way, with three children. Nor do we trust the Baron and his men. We'll be safer on the sea, far from the Baron's reach, far from his greed and wrath."

"If I can do nothing else, I will preserve this house against your return and protect your servant, as well as I can."

"For this at least we thank you." Lutha was about to turn away, when another thought occurred to her. "I would ask you one thing more."

"What is it?"

"Only this: that you send word to my brother Linar in the Tabirnian Hills to let him know what has happened here. I fear that the letter we have sent by other messengers will never reach him."

"There are few who travel that direction. But I promise that somehow, even if I myself must make the journey, I will get word to your brother and tell him what has happened. Is there anything else I can do?"

"Not unless you can reverse this ruling of the council."

"That I cannot. But I wish you fair weather and fair fortune."

"Fair fortune to you as well," replied Ferenth gently. "For your visit and help we are grateful, however much we may be angry at what has happened."

"In your leaving, Antar has lost more than you have. I pray that one day you may return and find here a better city than the one you leave behind."

As the door closed behind Riman, Ferenth turned to Lutha. "You were hard on him, my sister."

"He has been hard on us. He and his fellow councilmen are cowards. He would not speak against the Baron even though he knew Ferrar spoke the truth. Men such as this, whose conscience lives in their pockets, these are no less to be blamed than the Baron himself."

Mischka soon returned to the house. "Is there any news from Ferrar and Imrach?" he asked Ferenth.

"Not yet." She looked at her husband with troubled eyes. "Do you regret the decision we have made on behalf of my brother?"

"Love songs are treasured anywhere," Mischka replied, smiling, "and songs of love are what we have always sung best.

There will be strangers who will welcome us as family. There will be a new place that we will call home, of this I'm certain.

"With you, my love," said Ferenth, "wherever I am, I am at home. I have no regrets, however long we must travel, as long as you travel with me."

"Then let us finish getting ready for this journey!" laughed Mischka.

At the harbor, Ferrar and Imrach went from ship to ship, asking each captain if he would sail to the southern cities. But none would agree. At last they came to the Grey Dolphin, the largest ship they had seen that morning. Once again Ferrar made his request of the captain.

"None will leave the port now," replied the captain, "not when the weather has grown so uncertain and the great winter storms have begun. The risk is too great. One might never arrive, driven before the wind until the ship, stressed beyond endurance, shatters and sinks into the sea. No, you'll find none to take you, none who will dare to make this trip."

"None will dare to make this trip," argued Ferrar, "because of the Baron! It is his power that you fear and his gold you seek to hold onto. It is not the storms of the sea, but the storms of the Baron's wrath that you fear!"

"I fear no man's wrath!" retorted the captain angrily. "My ship is my own. I'm beholden to no man. But the sea is wide and deep. What need I fear any man when wave and the wind alone are danger enough."

"It is his goods you carry, his warehouses that you stock, his wealth that you increase with your voyages."

"This may be true. But if I do not carry you, it is not the Baron's doing. Only a fool would brave the coming storms. You would do better to go overland to one of the southern cities. You'll find no one to risk their life, their crew and their ship for you."

"Rakal is not such a craven! He fears neither wind nor water!"

"It is true that he sails even at this time of year. But who can say where he is? Can you wait for his return to Antar? My counsel is that you ride horses, not the waves, if you must leave! "

The early winter sun had already set when Ferrar and Imrach returned to the house. They were surprised to see that the rest of the family had nearly everything ready for departure.

"Did you find us a ship?" asked Lutha.

"A ship?" replied Ferrar bitterly. "No one would dare to take us."

"Why, what was wrong?" asked Ferenth.

"The captains are poisoned by the same fear that rules the council," replied Imrach, "if not fear of the Baron, then fear of the weather. None will set sail, however much gold we offer."

"All I do goes awry!" said Ferrar bitterly. "You should stay here. I will leave alone early tomorrow, to ride for the western mountains."

"Wherever you go," Ferenth said, taking his hands in hers, "west or east, north or south, we will go with you."

"And I will take you there!" boomed a voice as the door crashed back against the wall.

"Rakal!" shouted Raëla, running to throw her arms around the big, bearded man who stood smiling in the doorway.

"None other!" replied the captain, striding into the room. "I have missed you, my little one! But what's this that I be hearing? No sooner do I tie up my ship, my sea-eel the Astan to the dock than the shore men rush to tell me that Ferrar's exiled! You been tweaking the nose of the Baron, my young cockerel?"

"More than tweaked his nose, if his response is any indication," Ferrar replied. "His toadies voted to banish me from Antar."

"We will go with him!" said Saschka excitedly.

"And you wait not for your old friend?"

"We have to leave tomorrow," said Ferrar angrily. "The council gives us no time to prepare."

"Then well I be arrived in time! Tomorrow is soon to take ship again. But tomorrow it be! I'll lay in supplies and we weigh anchor with flood tide."

"What of the storms?" asked Imrach. "Are you not concerned about them, as the other captains seem to be?"

"Not one of them is Rakal!" said Raëla fiercely.

"'S truth, little one!" chuckled the burly captain. "We'll brave storm and shoal to see you all safely away from this spider's lair! Be at dock in the morning and we'll put Antar behind us before sun rises above the Astan's rail!"

But it was late afternoon before they were finally under way. The dock was crowded with the Baron's men as the Astan cast off and pulled out into the harbor. Only Bethor waved goodbye while the cries of the gulls wheeling overhead seemed to lament the departure of these who left Antar so unwillingly.

Ferrar stood at the rail, looking back towards the city as it grew smaller behind him. The setting sun rested on the southwestern ridge of the mountains that encircled Antar. Its last rays turned the white stone of the city houses to red.

"Well may you blush," said Ferrar bitterly, "for what you have done. I hope that is not blood that stains your walls. Yet I fear what you inflicted on us is but a tithe of what you yourself will face one day."

He turned away and looked out to the east, beyond the mountain arms enclosing the harbor of Antar, to where clouds brooded dark and heavy above the restless waves.

Chapter 14

The Voyage

When the ship had cleared the harbor, Rakal had his passengers take the children and retire to the cabin at the rear of the vessel.

"There be many stormy days ahead. Best you settle yourselves now and get used to the waves. This time of year, storms far out in the ocean trouble the seas. Even if we see no storm ourselves, waves be rough."

So Ferenth and Mischka, Imrach and Lutha, Ferrar and the children retired to the cabin to talk and decide what to do. They had only the one cabin for the eight of them, and though the hammocks slung along the walls would accommodate them all, yet there was reason to fear that they might weigh on each other's nerves.

"I will never forgive the Baron for this," muttered Ferrar, looking around their cramped quarters from the rear of the cabin. "If one day I return, it will be he who suffers."

Ferenth took his arm, leaning her head on his shoulder as Ferrar turned to look out through the small-paned windows toward Antar, disappearing into shadow. "My brother, have no regrets that we are leaving Antar. That we're all together is solace enough for all of us."

"The Baron must suffer for this. Somehow, some way, the Baron must suffer. My brother Mischka, I charge you in this: if I cannot return, then you must."

"What can a singer do against a Baron?" asked Mischka. "Can I raise storms against him or cause his house to fall to rubble?"

"Do you not remember when we faced the Beisht and our songs withstood her spells? Then we had strength in our voices."

"Yes, I remember well, though it's fifteen years since that adventure."

"Do you remember too the bandits and how we destroyed them? What is this Baron but a bandit who can be destroyed like them? Will you promise me?"

"I don't know how I can fight him. But I promise you," replied Mischka firmly, taking Ferrar's hands in his, "that I will return to Antar, with or without you. I will find a way to visit upon the Baron what he has visited upon us."

Imrach shook his head. "You are my brother's son in this passion of spirit," he said to Ferrar. "Perhaps like him you too will one day find a woman who will mean more to you than revenge."

"It may be. But if this should happen, it will be because my heart is wholly changed, taken from me and replaced with one less true and strong."

"Or perhaps you may find," replied Imrach, "that this part of you that is so wild and fierce is indeed only a part, that there are within you other parts, other rooms that will open to another's voice, another's touch."

Ferrar turned away to look out the window again in silence. Ferenth once again took his arm, their faces shadowed by the darkness falling on the city behind them.

"How long must we travel," Mischka asked Imrach, "before we reach the southern cities?"

"In twenty days, if all goes well, we reach the southern cities. Then another forty days past that we will come to the Far Southern Lands."

"Is that, then, where we are going?" asked Lutha.

"Yes," Imrach replied. "Rakal felt it would be of little use to go to the southern cities. The Baron's influence may reach even there and Ferrar, perhaps all of us, might be in danger. We will go to the Far Southern Lands and raise our families there, free of the stratagems of the Baron."

"What is it like, the Far Southern Lands?" Raëla asked her father.

"Rakal said there are great mountains far to the south that shelter the land from cold winds that would otherwise sweep across it, mountains as tall as any in Egeria and taller. What settlements there are cluster along the northern shore, where the weather is like ours, if not warmer, and the wind sweeter. But I know only what Rakal has said."

"Some stories we have heard," added Mischka. "As we wandered through Egeria, it was said that in the south the fruit grows larger and sweeter than any we know. If a way could but be found to bring it from the Far Southern Lands, those who bring it would be richer than the Baron."

"Why can they not?" asked Saschka.

"Because it is a long way, two months and more by sail," replied Imrach

"Is it certain we'll come there safely?"

"Nothing is certain," replied his uncle. "Rakal is an able captain. The Astan is sound and we have ample provisions. We can only hope and trust in his skill. Nonetheless, any number of evils may happen."

"Then we had best prepare ourselves," said Ferrar.

"And we should begin with a good night's sleep," scolded Lutha, "while the sea is calm and the night is quiet!"

When they woke the next morning, it already seemed as though they'd been on their way for weeks. Imrach was the first to be on deck, with Ferrar not far behind. The sun lay quartered off the port bow as the boat headed to the south. Rakal was talking on the aft deck with his pilot Santor who manned the great tiller arm.

"How stands the weather?" asked Imrach.

"Unsettled," answered Rakal. "Stays the wind true behind us, we'll make good way. But storms be fierce at this time of year, when season changes and water cools."

As always, Rakal's crew was a scruffy lot, only eight of them to tend the sails and steering oar, for the ship was a small one. They were friendly enough, grumbling good-naturedly about the work, though they often cast wary glances at the sky and waves. Rakal himself would often pause in his labors to speak to Raëla. "Little raven," he had taken to calling her, for Raëla had deep black hair that flew in the wind like wings of a bird.

"Have you children?" Raëla asked him one day.

"None," he replied. "It is ill done, to bring children and wife on shipboard, nor would I have them stay in port to wonder where I be and whether I be returning. Perhaps one day I'll find a place where I'll have a mind to bide and raise a family. If the day comes that I give such a pledge, I will give it with all my heart."

"As you did when you promised to take us safely to the Far Southern Lands?" asked Raëla.

"Rakal keeps his promises and will keep you safe, little raven. I promised that I would do my best to take you all from Antar to another land. The Far Southern Lands be what your father and uncle have asked for and I have set course for there. But enough of this, I have ship to sail. Cast lines over the stern and catch us fish for supper."

When Ferenth or Mischka, Ferrar or Imrach wished to talk with him, Rakal often sent them away. "I have no time for idle talk," he would say. But when Raëla alone or with the other two children asked for a story, then he would tell her marvelous tales of the sea and worlds beyond the sea, of the many places he had known: strange lands, full of strange wonders.

He told her, too, of a boy who longed to see the ocean but was born a serf on a nobleman's estate. He had run away, drawn by the white sails at the docks of Antar. There he had stowed away on a ship, crawling up the hawser that held the boat to the dock. He'd been discovered and beaten, but the ship was already underway. So they kept him on and he joined the crew, struggling with ropes and shrouds, swabbing the decks, patching leaks with tar and oakum when rough seas sprung the seams. He'd fought pirates and storms, burned under the sun and shivered in ice and snow. He'd become mate, then at last master of his own ship, unafraid of storms and shoals, of any man on sea or shore.

There Rakal ended his story, his face hard and grim. Raëla knew that he was that boy, that man who had killed and would do so again if need arose. Yet she felt comfort and safety with him. Just as her father Imrach cared for and protected her, so did this captain Rakal.

As the days passed, the waves began to grow rougher and winds stronger. One morning Rakal said, "Little raven, see you these white-crested waves before us?"

"Yes, of course," Raëla answered, where she, Saschka and Mirath sat together at the stern of the ship.

"They roll cross-wards, against the wind, driven by a storm that bears against us. When one has sailed the seas as I have, wave and wind and cloud say more than any book. They tell me now that there be a great tumult ahead."

He called to his crew. "Within the hour the tempest be upon us. Reef the sails, lash everything in place! Get you to the cabin, little raven, and keep yourself there. Close and bar the windows, bolt the door. This storm be cruel and fierce."

So it was. For two days, raging waves, fierce winds, blinding lightning and deafening thunder lashed the boat while Rakal and his crew struggled to keep it heading into the wind and athwart the waves. Raëla and all her family were sick from the pitching and tossing of the ship, unable to leave the cabin lest they lose their footing and tumble into the sea. One night Raëla heard a terrible cry and knew that one of the sailors had fallen from the shrouds and was lost, left behind and drowned as the boat was thrust inexorably onward by the tempest.

At last the storm was done. They unbolted the door and crept out on deck. Rakal was still at the tiller, his face gray and crusted with salt. "Look there!" he said hoarsely, pointing forward.

There, just off the bow, they saw an island.

"We must get ready to leave the ship," continued Rakal.

"What do you mean?" asked Imrach. "We are nowhere near the Far Southern Lands."

"We have no choice. My ship can go no farther. That be our destination, if we can reach it."

"What do you know of this island?" asked Mischka.

"Nothing. It be on no chart that I know, nor are there tales of any who has landed there. I see but one place where we can harbor and it full of rocks. It be naught but sheer cliffs pocked with shallow caves, nothing more, unless there be forest above that we cannot see. But more and fiercer tempests be on their way, too much for my Astan, brave-hearted though she be. We have no choice but to land, wait out the storms, repair the ship and resume our voyage when we may. I will bring the Astan as close as may be, but be you ready to take to the longboats should she founder."

"Is there nowhere safer to land?" asked Imrach.

"Nowhere we have seen. We wait no longer. Gather what you can take in the longboats and we will make toward shore. The Lady protect us!"

They put clothes and food, canvas and fishing line, rope and tools into the longboats while the crew climbed the shrouds to stand ready to the sails. At first the Astan moved slowly towards the shore. But then the winds and currents grew more treacherous, pushing the ship faster and faster towards sharp-edged, sea-blackened rocks that suddenly appeared in the troughs of the waves and then as suddenly disappeared in the surge and crash of the surf. Rakal swore, cursing the crew and the sea equally, shouting orders to the men wrestling with the sails while he fought the tiller.

"Lower the longboats!" he shouted to Imrach and Ferrar. "Pull for shore!"

"We'll wait for you and your men!" shouted Imrach in reply as the children and Ferenth scrambled into the longboat, Ferenth taking the tiller while the children huddled amid the bundles and baggage.

"Leave the one for us, but wait no longer! Go now!"

Mischka and Ferrar paid out one line through the block and tackle as Imrach and Lutha took the other. The longboat settled quickly into the water, banging against the side of the Astan, rocking wildly in the cross-currents. Mischka and Lutha scrambled down the into the boat, unshipping the first of the two sets of oars as Imrach and Ferrar scrambled down after them, sliced through the knots in the thick ropes to free the boat and took the other oars. The blades cut into the water and the boat swung away from the Astan. Waves splashed over the side of the boat, over its bow, across the stern, coming from every direction at once. The wind-driven salt spray stung their eyes as they looked over their shoulders, straining to see the shoreline, jolted by sudden collisions against rocks that thrust out of the sea to slam against the side of the boat. The four oars dug again and again into the water while Ferenth steered as best she could between whirlpools and wave crests, the children calling out "There's a rock! And there!"

Behind them, the Astan keeled slowly to its side, unable to make headway against the wind and current pushing it inexorably toward a cluster of jagged shoals that surfaced and disappeared repeatedly in the tumultuous waves. The ship drew closer and closer to them. Rakal's voice sounded hoarsely about the crash of waves, but there was nothing his men could do. With a splintering crash, the Astan drove onto the rocks, shuddering with the force of the collision. The crew and Rakal jumped into the foam-covered water, unable to get to the remaining longboat to free it. As Mischka and the rest of the family watched in horror, wave after wave crashed into the Astan and swept over the men struggling in the surf.

"We have to help them!" Raëla shouted, pounding on the gunwale of the longboat with her fist. "Turn around! We have to save them!"

"We can't!" shouted her father. "Ferenth, steer toward shore! It's our only hope!"

The four oars again thrust against the water and the longboat moved slowly forward. It cleared the rocks. The keel scraped on the stones of the beach. Ferrar and Imrach leapt into the water to pull the boat out of the surf while Mischka and Lutha pulled again as strongly as they could on the oars. The bow came up onto the shore, plowing into the shingle. The boat ground to a stop. They were safe! But behind them, the Astan had disappeared, shattered and sunken beneath the surface of the waves.

Chapter 15

The Island River

"Look!" shouted Raëla, pointing to the shoals where the ship had foundered. A single figure pulled himself from the water and climbed onto one of the rocks.

"It's Rakal!" she shouted.

The captain waved to them, then dove into the water and began to swim towards them.

"We have to get him!" Raëla said fiercely.

"Children, out of the boat," said Ferenth calmly. "Lutha and Imrach, stay with the children. Mischka, Ferrar, take the oars."

Lutha, Imrach and the children pushed the boat back into the water as Mischka and Ferrar clambered in and started back-rowing. Ferenth pushed the tiller hard about and the bow of the longboat swung towards the sea and Rakal. Waves crashed over his head, but he re-appeared after each one, swimming doggedly while Mischka and Ferrar rowed as hard as they could.

At last they were alongside him. Mischka and Ferrar reached out, the boat tipping dangerously as Rakal scrambled in, coughing. Once again they drove it toward shore. Imrach waded into the surf as it drew near and together with Mischka and Ferrar dragged the boat up onto the beach, out of reach of the waves.

"Poor day for a swim!" Rakal coughed, even more hoarse than before. "I be grateful for your help."

"We wouldn't let you drown!" declared Raëla fiercely.

"But I fear your crew has not survived," said Imrach sadly.

"Sailors be not swimmers." Rakal stood to climb out of the boat, staggering with weariness. "The Lady knows they were good men, but not a swimmer among them. The sea will have taken them, as it took the Astan. She were a good ship, but no match for those rocks." They carried the food and other supplies to a cave that the sea had carved into the cliffs. There they built a driftwood fire and cooked a meager supper. Ferrar was silent until the meal was done, then he could no longer restrain his bitterness, anger and guilt. "I am a curse on all of you! We will never get off this rock."

"We are at least alive," replied Ferenth, from where she sat with her arm around her daughter.

"Alive!" replied her brother. "Alive to starve here. Or if not to starve, then to live on naught but barnacles and seaweed!"

"What of the boat?" Ferenth asked Rakal. "Can we not take it and sail on to the Far Southern Lands?"

"The Far Southern Lands!" laughed Rakal. "We be farther than ever from them. I be a master sailor, but it be a fool's hope to think to sail to the Far Southern Lands."

Raëla came and sat beside him. "You will find a way for us, whatever that may be."

"You ask too much, child," replied Rakal. "I know the sea and the waves, I know the winds and the sky. I know nothing of this island."

"Are there no stories of it?" asked Mischka, "no tales that seamen tell of this place?"

"I have heard a tale," said Ferenth. "Ferrar, do you remember? Firfal told us, when we first were with him.".

"What tale is that?" asked her brother.

"You remember," urged Ferenth. "He told of a towering island, far out in the sea, ringed with sheer cliffs and tall mountains snow-capped even in summer. That must be where we are. And he said that above the cliffs there was a cleft through the close-set peaks, leading to the heart of the island where a deep, clear river runs through a great forest."

"No river comes down these cliffs.".

"Yet perhaps the story is true and we just haven't seen the river yet. Perhaps there is a forest, protected by the mountains. Do you remember that song that Firfal sang to us? It must have been about this island!"

"I remember no such song,"

"Then it is well that I remember it," said Ferenth and she began to sing.

Over the sea, an island rises
Sharp the rocks, steep the cliffs
Lashed by wind and storm.

Deep in its mountains, a forest grows,
Deep in the mountains, a river flows
Through meadows green and warm

Who has gained its shore,
Watched its sea in calm and storm?
Who has seen the forest?

Who has braved the cliffs?
Who walks the forest paths?
Whose song wakes the echo?

"I never heard this," said Mischka. "Is it indeed one that Firfal sang?"

"I remember it now," replied Ferrar. "Only once he sang it, that I recall."

"Only once to you, then," said Ferenth. "But to me, several times. He said that this song I should remember, that someday I should need it."

"What good is it to us? What help can it give? We are stranded on a deserted island with no hope of ever leaving it."

"Then tomorrow," Mischka urged, "let us find what there is on this island."

But the rain set in hard, forcing them to remain in the cave that day and the next. Their fate seemed dismal indeed. The children were fretful, but Raëla tended Saschka and Mirath with a fierce protectiveness as they played for hours, drawing pictures in the sandy floor. When all three grew tired, Mischka and Ferenth would sing marvelous songs, or Ferrar take stones and teach them how to juggle, or Lutha and Imrach entertain them with stories..

So the days passed quickly enough, and there was driftwood enough for the fire and provisions enough that they needn't fear hunger, at last for the moment.

At last the sky cleared and they could leave the cavern. The boat, though full of water, was still safe. But nothing remained of the Astan. Not a single remnant of it been cast ashore: no food, no stores, no timber, no bodies of the crew. It had been swept from the rocks that had destroyed it, its shattered hull and masts carried far out to sea.

"What shall we do, then?" asked Imrach as they looked out across the ocean that lay vast and empty before them. "Shall we try to scale this cliff, find our way through the mountains to whatever lies behind them?"

"The cave is meager shelter," replied Lutha. "It is better than nothing, but soon we will have nothing but the cave: our food is already nearly gone. We grew up among the mountains. I say that we climb this cliff if we can and find what lies beyond."

"Should we all go?" asked Mischka. "Or should some stay with the children?"

"We will not leave anyone behind," replied Imrach. "We can take better care of them if we are all together."

"First bring the boat to the cave and secure it there," advised Rakal. "It be safe so far, but another storm may wash this beach clean as when we first arrived."

"I agree with you," said Imrach. "It will be no easy task, but together we can bring it up beyond the tideline and into the cave."

"Can we not use some of this driftwood as rails or wheels?" suggested Lutha. "Would that not be easier?"

"Indeed it would," replied her husband. So together they stripped the branches from some of the larger pieces of driftwood and set them as rollers. Then, with even the children helping, they hauled the boat across the shingle and into the cave. From their provisions they made five larger bundles and three smaller ones, leaving nothing behind that might be of use. The little that was left they stacked in the boat, covered with oilcloth.

The next morning they set out from the cave, walking along the foot of the cliff as they scanned the wall of rock above them.

"It's even steeper than the one we climbed when we followed the bandits. Do you remember, Mischka?" asked Ferrar.

"I remember well," said Mischka.

"Can we climb there?" asked Ferenth, pointing to a cleft that seemed to go all the way to the top of the rock face. "Can you get to the top, Ferrar?"

"If not as lithe as once I was, yet Ferrar am I still. I will climb."

He tied a rope about his waist, and began the ascent. Slowly he went forward, inching his way up the sheer face of the cliff. Though there were handholds, they were few and shallow. Often he paused, scanning left and right, searching for a finger hold or toe hold. An hour passed and still he climbed. The wind began to blow more strongly, as though to pluck Ferrar from the face of the cliff. A second hour passed and Ferrar still had not reached the top. Only as the third hour was nearly done did Ferrar reach the top of the cliff and throw himself over. He rested a moment or two, and then called out to those below.

"Give me a moment or two while I fasten the rope, and then each of you must come up. Imrach, you next, that you may help me pull up the others."

Ferrar tied the rope around an outcropping of rock, then dropped the free end to Imrach, who tied it about him and began the climb. Slowly he made his way up the cliff face, using rope as well as hand-holds to pull himself higher and higher. At last he too had reached the top. Once more the rope was lowered and Rakal made the climb.

"Now the children, one by one," shouted Ferrar. Raëla watched with fierce concentration as her young cousins were pulled upwards by the three men above. Then again the rope was thrown down and she tied it about her waist.

"Up you come, little raven!" shouted Rakal to her.

"I am ready!" see called as her mother checked the knots once again. Soon she too was at the top of the cliff.

"Ferenth," said Mischka, "you next." So she too and then Lutha made their way to the top of the cliff, half pulled and half climbing.

"Now the provisions," he called to those above. Bundle after bundle was hauled to the top of the cliff. At last Mischka alone stood at the bottom.

"Mischka, be careful!" Ferenth shouted as the rope uncoiled once more down the cliff face. "The rope has frayed and grows weak."

"Can you climb?" Imrach shouted to him as well. "We should not risk pulling the rope again over the lip of the cliff."

Mischka began the climb, relying, as Ferrar had, on pulling himself from handhold to handhold rather than trusting himself to the frayed line. His hands grew tired and slippery from sweat as the sun, settling to the west, broke free from the clouds and shone full against his back. Suddenly his foot slipped and his hands were dragged down the rock. Only the rope around his waist saved him from falling to the rocks below.

"Mischka!" shouted Ferenth. "Hold tight, my love!"

"We'll pull you up the rest of the way!" shouted Imrach. "Hold on where you can!"

Slowly Mischka moved up the cliff, sometimes finding a ledge for his foot, sometimes a cleft from his hand, sometimes finding neither as he swung from the frayed rope. Then he was at the top! Hands reached down to grasp his and pull him over the lip of the cliff. Ferenth, Saschka and Mirath threw their arms around him, as he smiled his thanks to Imrach, Ferrar and Rakal.

Then his eyes widened amazement. In front of him rose massive snow-covered peaks. But between him, sheer as a knifecut, a deep and narrow valley led forward.

"That is the way we must go," said Ferenth. "I feel sure of it."

"So do we all," agreed Imrach.

One by one they entered the cleft, so narrow that even Mirath could touch the sides with her outstretched arms. It angled upwards steeply, winding through the rock, the walls on either side rising sheer and stark above them, shutting out the sun and sky. Then it began to descend, and a stream began to flow at their feet as water sheeted down the rocks on either side of them. The cleft broadened as the stream became a river, a small rocky strand alongside it just wide enough for them to use. The river grew loud in their ears, echoing and re-echoing from the sheer walls of the canyon

Suddenly the rocky path disappeared. There was no way forward but to walk in the water that rushed past them with a surly roar. Rakal, Imrach and Mischka took the children on their backs and waded into the river, while Ferrar, Ferenth and Lutha managed what they could of the packs. The current grew stronger as the cleft narrowed again and the water rose to their waists.

"Brace yourselves on the walls," Rakal shouted. "Careful of the rocks underfoot!"

On the rock walls above him, Mischka could see where the stream at other times had risen high above his head. He hoped that no storms in the mountains above him would suddenly send torrents of water into the ravine and sweep them all to their deaths. He stumbled into a hole he could not see and nearly fell, Mirath crying out as her hand scraped along the rocks.

"Mischka!" shouted Ferenth.

"We're alright," he shouted in reply. "Hold tight, Mirath! We'll be out of this cleft soon!"

No sooner had he said so than the ravine suddenly widened, emerging into a quiet thicket of trees, green with the new leaves of an early Spring.. The river broadened and slowed, flowing away from them along the side of the mountain and then cascading down into a deep, broad valley ringed by white-peaked mountains, dark with early evening shadows, filled with a forest of tall trees. Amid the trees they glimpsed the river, glinting here and there like silver.

"The song was true," said Ferenth softly.

It was warmer here, but the children were cold and hungry. So they made a fire, cooked some food and spread their blankets on the ground. As night fell and the fire burned down to coals, they lay down to sleep, beneath stars that glittered among the branches and softly rustling leaves above them.

Ferrar suddenly sat up, his eyes searching the darkness around him. "Do you hear that?" he whispered, his hand raised to silence the others. "I thought for a moment I heard singing."

"I hear nothing but the wind in the trees," his sister replied.

"The silence plays tricks on you," added Lutha.

"I heard something, too," said Raëla softly.

Her father rose from his blanket and knelt down by her, smoothing her dark hair as Raëla lay down again. "In the morning we will see what we find. Tonight, we must all sleep."

"I will watch," said Rakal.

"Wake me when you are weary" Imrach replied. "It will do no harm to have one awake when we are in this place we do not know. Yet I feel no threat or danger here, strange though it be to us."

"Nor do I," agreed Lutha. "Almost I feel that we have been here before, not strangers at all."

"We are welcomed," Ferenth said softly. "But by what or who, I cannot tell."

"Lady protect us all this night," Rakal murmured.

"And always," agreed Imrach as he lay down again. One by one, all but Rakal fell asleep.

They woke in the morning to bright sun just cresting the mountains far to the eastern side of the valley. A warm wind played around them, fragrant with early flowers and unfurling leaves. Ferenth began to sing, her heart filled with the beauty around her.

The sun upon my face
Your loving touch.

The wind in my hair
Your gentle breath.

Is not the joy I feel Your joy?
The love I feel Your love?

As her voice fell silent, it seemed to all of them that the song continued around them, as though echoed in the rustling of the leaves, but somehow more than any music the wind might make. Again Ferrar looked around sharply, but there was no one visible, nothing except the river behind them, the trees around them, the forested valley below them, ringed by mountains.

Ferenth smiled. "I think we are welcome here."

"Then let us go on," Lutha agreed.

Together they walked down through the trees, toward the valley below them. They said little to each other, listening to the sounds of the forest, enjoying the warmth of the sun as it filtered through the leaves. At the sun reached noon, they came out of the trees into a broad meadow. The children laughed and ran ahead of them toward the river. The meadow grass was soft and the ground firm under their feet. The sat down beside the river and shared again what food they had.

"I feel such peace here," said Ferenth, watching the children as they skipped rocks across the river. "It's as though we're inside a song, joyful, yearning, full of love and happiness. It's as though we are the song, or part of it."

"All of us?" asked Mischka.

"All of us. Perhaps the children especially so, but nonetheless all of us. Even Rakal."

"I be no singer like you," laughed Rakal. "Tell the truth, I be not altogether willing to be part of any such song. There be secrets in this forest. Time will tell if there be dangers."

"We will see," agreed Mischka. But he too felt the peace that his wife had spoken of. Whatever the troubles they might face in this new land, they were safe. They were welcome. They would find shelter and food, he was sure. As for what else they might encounter, he was content to wait for what might come.

Chapter 16

The People of the Forest

When Mischka woke in the morning, the sun was still hidden behind the mountains to the east. The grass around them was wet and the blankets drawn about them were damp with the morning dew. Everyone else was still asleep except Rakal, standing alone by the river.

"It had been a difficult time," he thought. "The children must be exhausted."

He lay there watching Rakal, whose gaze was fixed on the mountains to the west as though through them to see to the ocean beyond, filled with longing and determination to return to the ocean again.

"Perhaps he's afraid of what we may find," Mischka said to himself. "Perhaps he's afraid of something that we too should fear."

Then he saw Raëla rise and walk over to Rakal. She stood beside him, and put her hand into his.

"All my life were spent on the ocean," Mischka heard him say. "Never since I were a boy have I been so closed in by mountains as here. The ocean has its mountains too, waves that may seem as tall as these peaks. But they pass by quickly and then are gone. These mountains around us be here forever. We can never be free of them while we live in this land."

"I think they're beautiful," Raëla replied. "Look how the rays of the sun set the snow glistening on the peaks above us."

The band of brightness cast by the sun was slowly moving down the mountainside. As it did, the mountain turned from gray and white to gold and rose, a morning red that glowed as if the world were full of some inner light and radiance only glimpsed now and then.

"You are more used to the mountains than I," said Rakal. "These mountains be like home to you. To me they're not and never will. I'll not be home again until I'm again on the sea and far from this island."

"How is your head this morning?" asked Raëla.

Rakal gingerly touched his temple, where he had hit himself on a rock as he jumped into the water from the sinking boat, then grinned at his friend. "Sore, but it will do. The rock be more damaged than I. We old pirates have hard heads."

Ferenth had risen and was sharing out the bread and cheese again, what little they had left of what they had salvaged from the boat. "Do you see anything that we can eat?" she asked Rakal as he and Raëla walked over to her.

"There be fish in the stream," he said. "It be early for fruit and nut, but roots we might dig, if it be that you know what to look for. Until we know who lives here and whether they be friendly, we best eat of our own food and that sparingly."

"Why do you think there are people here?" asked Mischka.

"I have seen no sign, but nonetheless they be here, somewhere."

"I have that feeling too," said Ferrar, who had now risen as well. "There, under the eaves of the forest, they are watching us.."

"Might it be just animals in the forest?" asked Ferenth.

"Not these," replied her brother. "I feel their eyes, their thoughts."

"Perhaps it's just the forest itself," said Ferenth. "Or perhaps the stress of our journey, that we would see threat in any unknown."

"Do you feel nothing?" asked her brother.

"Nothing but a sense of welcome and of peace."

"That's what I feel too," said Lutha, "as though whoever is here is not threatened by us, or angry, but waits to see who we are and what we will do. And if we speak well to them, then they'll welcome us, let us stay."

Raëla nodded in agreement. She too felt welcome, that someone standing within the shadow of the forest was waiting to greet them.

Rakal shook his head. "This island has us all bewitched."

"Perhaps it is enchantment," said Imrach.

As they sat at breakfast together, the world of Egeria seemed far away, the island with its mysterious presence occupying their thoughts.

When they finished eating , Mischka asked "What shall we do now?"

"I say we follow the river farther into the heart of the island," replied Imrach, "to see what the forest brings and what it brings us to."

"Before we go," said Ferenth quietly, "I feel we should sing something."

"Then sing my sister," Ferrar replied. "We have nowhere we must be, no one waits for us, and perhaps your singing may soften the hearts of those who live in this forest."

Mischka and Ferenth and the two children, Raëla and Lutha also, began this song, a childhood song that they all had known for many years and often had sung together.

Morning comes. Night is past,
Brought us safely to this day,
Brought us safely here at last.

For these blessings that we share,
For the music on our way,
Praise Her who holds us in Her care.

Rakal listened as they sang, his stern and lined face smoothed and softened by the song, his eyes less stern as they rested on the face of first this singer, then that, most often returning to Raëla. When the song was done, he said: "You have much to be grateful for, you who sing like this."

As he spoke, out of the forest stepped a boy. He was dressed in a simple brown shirt and leggings, but the band holding back his long, silver hair was bright in the morning sun. He was not much taller than Raëla, slim like her, his face longer and leaner. His eyes, silver as well. watched them with an unblinking stare, not threatening but puzzled by these strangers before him.

"What do you want with us, friend?" Mischka called out.

The boy said nothing. His gaze, focused on Mischka, did not seem alarmed or frightened.

"What do you wish of us?" Mischka repeated. But the boy remained silent.

"This must be the presence I felt," replied Ferenth. "He has something to tell us, I think. We must not scare him away, but find out what it wants."

The boy turned his eyes to Ferenth as she spoke. Then he began to sing, a short, lilting, wordless melody. The boy stopped and looked at each of them in turn. At first none of them responded. Then Raëla began to sing, echoing the same subtle melody.

When she finished, the boy nodded, then turned quickly and ran into the forest.

"Where is he going? Stop him!" shouted Ferrar.

"Wait!" cautioned Imrach. "Let's do nothing rash."

"We have to follow him," declared Ferrar impatiently, "and find out who these people are and what they intend."

"We'll find out soon enough," Imrach replied. "Raëla, what did the boy say? What did you respond?"

"I don't know. I felt he was waiting for us. Singing what he had sung was the only way I could think of to assure him of our being friends."

"You were right, my daughter," Lutha agreed. "Your heart is as true as your voice."

"But the boy didn't stay," argued Ferrar. "How do we know what he is going to do?"

"We don't," Lutha replied, "but I think he intends us no ill."

"Perhaps he does not. But what of the others of his kind? "

"This is but one more thing that asks our trust."

"I'm little inclined to give trust to a stranger who speaks in music I can't understand. You are too trusting. I'll be more wary."

They waited to see what would happen. Mischka took from his pack his wooden flute and began a sprightly tune that seemed to echo the music of the river and trees. As he played,

Ferenth drew Mirath and Saschka into a dance. Raëla joined them as well, laughing as they stepped and circled together. Imrach and Lutha, looking on, laughed too, lighter in heart despite their exile and shipwreck. Rakal smiled as well, only Ferrar holding himself apart, never ceasing to scan the edge of the forest for the boy's return.

Suddenly he realized that a group of people, or whatever they might be, stood in the shadows at the edge of the forest. These were as tall as Imrach, their faces lean and sharp-angled. Dressed like the boy in tunic and leggings, their silver hair falling to their shoulders, they looked at the exiles from Antar with cool dispassion in their light eyes.

"Welcome," said Imrach, as Mischka set down his pipe. "Would you come and sit with us?"

The three strangers stepped out of the forest and walked towards the nine travelers where they stood together, Raëla with her arms around Saschka and Mirath.. As they came closer, Mischka and the others could see that there were subtle variations among them, both in face and in garb, remarkably similar to one another though they were.

"We have nothing to offer you," Imrach apologized. "We were shipwrecked on your island and barely saved ourselves, losing comrades and provisions to the sea. But we greet you in friendship and peace."

The boy they had seen earlier came running from the eaves of the wood to join the other strangers. He stood before Raëla and again sang the lilting music he had sung earlier. This time there was a hint of challenge in it, urging Raëla to respond once again.

Raëla repeated the phrase the boy had sung. The boy smiled at her and sang once again, this time to the elders who stood next to him, as if to say "See! Didn't I tell you that they are singers too?"

The elders stepped forward, each one approaching one of the adults who stood before them. Holding out their hands, each offered a single leaf, first to Imrach and Lutha, then Ferenth and Mischka, the Rakal and Ferrar. The boy approached Raëla, Mirath and Saschka and gave them leaves as well. Each leaf, shaped like a heart, had painted on it, in the center, an unfamiliar symbol.

Puzzled, each one took the leaf offered to them, Ferrar with mistrust, but the others smiling, murmuring their thanks. The three strangers nodded, then began sing, a deeper, more complex song than what the boy had sung. As they sang, something stirred in each of the listeners: something of joy, something of sadness. One by one, first Ferenth, then Mischka, Lutha and Imrach joined in the song, echoing its harmonies, repeating its wordless melodies.

The boy began to sing as well, and Raëla, Mirath and Saschka joined him, wrapped in the magic of the music. Their voices and music were lighter, laughing, but filled with the same sense of familiarity with these people that they did not recognize, but somehow understood, these people of the forest.

Chapter 17

Brethil

The music ended as first the exiles and then the strangers from the forest fell silent.

"Who are these people?" demanded Ferrar of the others. "Did you understand what they want of us?"

"Not yet," replied his sister. "But I know that they are friends now."

"Friends?" Ferrar scoffed. "Who knows what they intend, when we can't understand their language! What does this symbol mean? What do they want of us?"

"We do understand something," replied Mischka. "We understand they mean us no harm. Surely you heard this in their music too, though there is meaning there beyond what we can understand?"

"Don't you hear, Uncle," added Raëla, "that they are speaking in music, just as we do in words?"

The people of the forest observed this conversation with interest but in silence, calm and unmoved, either untroubled that they could not understand or divining the sense of what was being said.

"What do you advise that we do, Imrach?" asked Ferenth.

"We have two choices. We can ignore their welcome and stay here by the river, build shelters, see what we can find to eat."

"If they will let us!" objected Ferrar.

"They do not threaten us. I am sure of that. But even more, I feel we are invited to join them, to follow them."

"I feel this too," Ferenth quietly affirmed.

"As do I!" Raëla said confidently.

"Then follow them we will," declared Rakal. "If songs be their tongue, then I will have little to say! You shall speak for me, little raven."

"She speaks for all of us already," laughed Mischka. "Lead on, Raëla!"

They picked up their packs and Raëla stepped forward to bow to the three strangers. The boy smiled and laughed, taking her hand to pull her after him towards the forest. "Wait for us!" shouted Saschka as he and his sister ran after Raëla. One of the strangers sang again briefly, then turned, and led the way into the forest.

Deeper and deeper they went, as trees grew tall around them, dappling the path with the morning light that filtered through the young leaves above them. As they walked, the boy sang and when Raëla answered him with song, laughed and smiled. The other strangers were most often silent, singing only occasionally to each other. But when they did Mischka and his comrades listened carefully to the complex melodies, always with the feeling that they almost understood what the music conveyed.

Mischka found himself wishing for the instruments he had lost when the Astan was sank. He longed to capture the harmonies he heard, to sound out the melodies on his harp or kithar. These songs he heard, not so much songs as phrases within some larger conversation that went beyond what these strangers might be communicating in the moment, were more complex than any he knew. The tuning was subtler than he had encountered or used in music he created. It employed notes between the notes he knew, as though the strangers heard finer distinctions than he did and crafted their phrases from a richer vocabulary. It was strange to his ears, but yet touched him, spoke to him even though he was not yet sure what it meant and how to respond.

The forest was alive with music. All around them was not just the whispering of the wind in the trees and the call of birds above them, but other voices as well that together wove a subtle music welcoming them, sorrowing over what they had lost, rejoicing they were safe after their long voyage and the dangers they had passed.

After an hour of walking, they came again to the river that flowed still from the east, curving away from them and back towards them now and again as they followed the path. The strangers gestured to them to sit and other strangers appeared on a path that branched off from theirs, carrying baskets and earthenware flasks. Together they ate bread, dried fruits, a kind of cheese. They drank cool water from stoneware cups, filled from the flasks the strangers brought.

When the meal was done they walked on, deeper and deeper into the forest. At last, as afternoon was giving way to evening, they came to a great clearing circled by majestic trees. High up in each tree were wooden platforms, on some of which they could just make out partitions or walls, woven like the baskets the strangers carried. In the center of the clearing a fire burned, its flames dancing white and yellow, its coals glowing red and blue in the twilight.

All those who had led them through the forest disappeared except the boy and one of the men, who led them to the fire. He gestured to the log benches that circled the fire, bidding them sit. They set their packs on the ground and took places on the benches, the boy sitting down with Raëla, while other children appeared from among their trees, shyly curious, their voices calling out to their friend in soft queries. Other strangers descended from the shelters in the trees, carrying down from the flets their food and drink, weavings to sit on and to place about the shoulders of the exiles. Roots were placed in the fire to roast, clay pots with soup to simmer and bread to bake were set amid the coals. The benches filled as more and more people came, some bringing rugs to spread on the ground near the fire for the cooks and the children.

Then the meal was ready, shared out among all those who gathered. Mischka and the others were given bowls of stew, thick with vegetables and savory with herbs, newly baked bread fresh from the clay ovens and cups of fragrant tea. The music of the conversation around them seemed friendly and welcoming, though curious. Only Raëla seemed to be able to understand and reply as the young boy who ate with her, Mirath and Saschka laughed and talked in this strange language.

When they all had finished eating and the food was cleared away, a different kind of music began, with flutes and strung instruments as well as voices. People young and old rose from the benches to clear away the rugs near the fire and then to dance, circling with joined hands, whirling so that their silver hair glinted in the firelight, spinning stories with gesture and movement before the eyes of the amazed visitors. The children were swept into the dance, then the others as well, even Rakal and Ferrar, hands joined with each other and with the strangers in great circles and chains as the music filled them with its complex rhythms and subtle harmonies, welcoming them all.

When the dance was done, Mischka, Ferenth and the children stood before the fire, facing out into the dark, toward familiar and unfamiliar faces lit by the flames behind them. Though they didn't have Mischka's harp to accompany them, they wove the song of the stars, the song Ferenth had first sung alone when she and Ferrar traveled with Firfal so many years before. Above them, one by one, the stars appeared in the deep black velvet of the sky, as the song filled the night with its familiar harmony.

The man who led them to the village gestured toward one of the trees and they followed him to a ladder that climbed high into the branches. There they came up into a flet big enough for all nine of them, with blankets spread for sleeping. Ferenth and Lutha tucked the children in, while the others talked quietly. Ferrar sat apart from the others, silent, his eyes on the fire below them and the people who still sat around it, the music of their conversation muted and meditative.

Ferenth rose from the children's and came to sit beside her brother. "What is it, Ferrar? Why are you troubled?"

"I mean to be wary, sparing of my trust among these strangers. But I find myself drawn to them, strangely comforted by them."

"Do you not feel they are friendly, perhaps even friends?"

"Friends? They are strangers to me still. But there is something that makes me wish to know them better."

The moon rose above the trees on the east of the clearing, glinting on the river as it flowed out of the forest, turning it to quicksilver, sprinkling it with sparkling jewels. Ferenth leaned her head on her brother's shoulder. Together they listened to the music of the people beneath them, the music of the voices of their family behind them, the music of the trees around them, at last joining the others in sleep.

When dawn came, the young boy was there again. beckoning to Raëla to come and join him.

"May I, Father?" she asked. Imrach smiled and nodded. Raëla and her cousins climbed down the rope ladder, disappearing into the group of young people and children who were running about the great clearing as tables were set up under the trees. The adults climbed down as well, looking at the ashes of the fire from the night before and wondering what the day would bring. From one of the other flets, the man who had led them to the clearing descended and approached them. Next to him was a girl who had taken Ferrar's hand in the dance the night before, with her a woman who, in the similarity of their features, surely was mother of the girl.

They man bowed and trilled a querying note, as if to ask "Did you sleep well? Are you more at ease with us now?"

Ferenth smiled and the man and woman smiled back. The man touched his hand to his breast and sang a short phrase. The woman and girl did the same. Ferenth echoed back the phrases, understanding that these must be their names, similar enough to indicate their relationship, yet different enough to be unique to each one.

The young girl reached out her hand to Ferenth and Lutha, asking them to go with her. Though Ferrar frowned, Ferenth nodded her head and allowed the girl to lead them to one of the tables.

The man similarly led the men another table and offered them warm bread, stewed fruit and glass vessels of hot, fragrant tea. Although the bread had a flavor they did not recognize, compounded of herbs and some unfamiliar grain, it was nonetheless delicious and satisfying. As they ate, the man pointed at each thing in front them and sang a just a few notes, as though to say, "This is how we say bread. This is how we say fruit."

Mischka and Imrach sang back each time the man voiced one of the phrases, pointing to whatever he had pointed to. Sometimes the man smiled, sometimes shook his head and repeated the phrase. Ferrar and Rakal listened intently too, but the sea captain finally shook his head. "This is no tongue for Rakal. My little raven must learn it for me!"

The man led them to the table where Ferenth and Lutha sat, then took them through the village, showing them the weaving that was being done by both men and women, a kiln still warm from a recent firing of earthenware pots, gardens of vegetables and herbs.

As the morning went on, Mischka began to hear the subtle differences between the phrases, the beauty and complexity of the language. At times, he recognized dim echoes of a few songs in an ancient language that Firfal had sung on their journey to Antar. The words had been transformed, dropping consonants to free an inner heart of meaning expressed in music. But the words that they had once been existed as echoes still, echoes that grew stronger as Mischka listened to his teacher.

Occasionally they glimpsed the tall mountains beyond the forest, encircling the valley. Clouds caught on the mountain peaks fed the waterfalls that cascaded down into the valley on all sides. The mountains appeared impassable, impossibly high and steep. Perhaps the only way in - and the only way out - was the narrow cleft they had traversed

But as the days passed, they felt little inclination to leave. Even Ferrar seemed to relax, smiling more than he had in many years. Only Rakal, isolated in his inability to understand or frame responses in the strange language of the island, grew more silent and withdrawn. All the others quickly picked up words and phrases, the three children most rapidly but even Ferrar soon speaking, or rather, singing the language of the island, especially with the young woman he had danced with on that first evening.

They felt themselves to be part of this village, these people of the island of the forest. The certainty grew that these people meant them no harm, different though they were in their narrow faces and slim figures, their silver eyes and silver hair, their language unlike any they had ever heard. Many of the adults seemed stern and unsmiling, but even they smiled at the sound of the games in which Raëla and her cousins joined the few children of the village. Mischka was grateful for the restfulness that most of them seemed to feel, glad to see Ferrar setting aside the anger and bitterness that had tormented him in Antar.

Only Rakal was impatient to be gone, even talking about building a second boat. "There be plenty of wood here," he said to Mischka one evening as they sat over supper. "We have skill enough and tools. Best be doing something to get ourselves off this island."

Rakal often went off into the forest alone, walking back along the river to the mountains on the west side of the valley, even climbing back up to the cleft that led to the cliffs above the sea. Mischka was troubled by Rakal's restlessness, but did not know what to do. Surely he too would come to accept that they had no choice but to stay.

Ferrar felt himself more and more at home on the island. Sometimes he was angry at himself for this change of heart. But his heart had changed and he felt at home among these people as he never had before. One day, as he sat by the side of the river, idly tossing stones into it, one of the girls of the forest people came and stood beside him.

He didn't need to look up to know who it was. She was the girl he had danced with, the girl he spent more and more time with, the daughter of the leader of the people of the forest. Her name, beautiful in the music of their language, Ferrar felt must be "Brethil" in his own.

Ferrar picked up another of the stones from around him and flung across the water: five, six, seven times it skipped before it sank.

"Stone," said Brethil in her language of music. Ferrar repeated the phrase, picking up another stone and weighing it in his hand. He looked up the girl and began to speak to her in his own language, conscious that the girl could not understand him, but needing to speak of what he felt and unable to do so in her language.

"You see how I skip these stones across the surface of the river? I have been like them. They skim across the river, skip from one place to the next. I too touched only the surface of life, despite all my anger and bitterness. My sister Ferenth knew better, embraced life in love and hope. She has husband and children. I had nothing but empty speeches, futile actions and now even those are gone."

Brethil stood without speaking, her eyes fixed upon Ferrar's face. "You have no idea what I'm saying, I know," he continued. "I might as well be silent, for all that you understand."

She reached out and touched her finger to his chest.

"Who am I, you want to know?" asked Ferrar. "Who am I, indeed?"

The girl looked at him still, the silver of her irises all but gone, so wide her dark pupils, so intense her focus on him.

"I don't know who I am any longer." Ferrar placed his hand on his chest, his hand open above his heart. "But I have been Ferrar."

"Ferrar," repeated the girl, singing it not with the bitterness that Ferrar had voiced, but with hope and love.

"Yes," he replied, amazed by the beauty of the word as the girl said it. "Yes, I am he."

Again the girl sang "Ferrar" and reached out to him with both her hands, drawing him up and into her arms.

They walked all that day through the forest. Ferrar felt as though a knot long tied in his chest had loosened. Songs from long years before, from his journeys with Firfal and Ferenth and Mischka, came back to his thoughts, songs of love and loneliness, songs of hope and happiness. Sometimes he sang them to Brethil. Sometimes she sang to him, or pointed to things in the forest around them: a bird, a tree, a cloud, a small squirrel that scampered along a branch above them, chattering noisily. She laughed when he repeated the names she sang, delighted to hear him speak her language. All the words now seemed somehow familiar to him, heard and understood so quickly, as though this country, this language were something he knew already and was just remembering, so deeply was he stirred by the woman he was with, by the touch of her hand, by the wonder he felt when she spoke his name: "Ferrar! Ferrar!"

That night, when they returned to the village and Brethil went to her own flet to sleep, Ferrar felt a great sense of loss.. He was quiet over their meal that night, the others supposing that he was thinking again of Antar, of his unforgotten revenge on the Baron. But for the first night in a long time, Ferrar's thoughts had no revenge in them. They were filled with indecision and confusion, but also with joy. A spring coiled too tightly inside him had been released. All the energy flooded through him, like early spring sunshine after a long, cold winter, when the air is warm and the sunlight on your face is as palpable as gentle hands touching your cheeks and forehead and eyes.

Listening to the others around him, it was as though he saw them for the first time. Mischka and Ferenth, laughing over some story of the children, filled with love for each other. Lutha and Imrach, the depth of their love for each other and their daughter shining in their eyes. But even as he looked at them, even as he listened to the laughter of Mischka and Ferenth and the children, he could see Brethil's face and once again hear her voice as she called his name, as she told him the names of each thing they passed as they walked through the forest.

Each day they walked together through the forest and along the river, catching glimpses of the snow-capped peaks, of the cascades like veils on the steep mountains high above, resting on deep grassy swards shaded by the tallest trees that Ferrar had ever seen or on stony outcrops where thyme grew wild, filling the air with a heady fragrance even at this early time of year.

So Ferrar came to love the daughter of the forest, came to love her language, came to love the island on which at last he felt himself at home.

Chapter 18

The Council

But Rakal remained apart from the rest, even while all the others began to learn the language and to speak with the people of the forest they had come to know. Sometimes he'd be gone overnight, sleeping in the cave where they had left the boat, and when he came back Raëla would ask, "Rakal, must you go away like this?"

Rakal would reply, "Little raven, I don't belong here. The sea be where I belong and I must go and be there."

He spent long hours scouring ithe boat with sand and checking it for soundness. He gathered pitch from the fir trees in the forest, where it oozed from wounds in the bark, and carried it back to the boat to wedge between the planking and make the boat more watertight.

"What do you plan to do?" Mischka asked once when he went with Rakal to the cave..

"I don't know, only that the day will come when I cannot stay any longer here."

Spring turned to summer. At times Raëla went with Rakal down to the boat and sat there with him. At times Mischka as well left behind the rest of the family and went with Rakal. They sat and talked as they looked out over the ocean, or worked together on the boat. Mischka found himself still stirred by the thought of what he had left behind: his brother, his parents, Egeria itself that he had come to know in the long days of wandering with Firfal. He liked to hear Rakal's stories of the lands that he'd seen, and the journeys that he'd traveled. Sometimes as they sat there, Mischka would find that a song had come to his thoughts. He brought these songs back to sing to the people of the forest; for that was one thing which the people seemed never to tire of: the music which Mischka and Ferenth gave them.

At first they had only their voices and the wooden flute that Mischka had brought among his things when the Astan foundered. But Mischka longed for his harp, lost now in the sea. Speaking one day with Brethil's father, the friend that Mischka thought of as Thirlin, of the music that he used to play, he mentioned the "maker of music" he had once had, not having heard anyone speak of a harp or other instrument except his flute. "Come with me," said Thirlin, and took him to a flet filled with chests and bundles. Thirlin opened one of the chests and brought out a small wire-strung harp.

"Is this a maker of music?" he asked, handing the harp to Mischka.

Mischka was astonished. It was a beautiful instrument, with inlaid sound box and silver strings, tarnished but still clear and sweet as he plucked them, turning the pegs to bring them back into tune. It was as though his voice had been given back to him, as though some part of himself had been restored to him.

"Where is this from?" he asked.

"We brought few things with us," replied Thirlin. "I had forgotten that we once used makers of music such as this. You are welcome to it. We have no need of it."

Mischka played it often from then on, sometimes a dance tune, sometimes a wordless lament for other days and other places, now a love song, now a chantey that would make Rakal roar with laughter and burst into rough but energetic singing.

Mischka composed a new song for his friend, of the longing he felt to be once again sailing across the ocean.

Carry me far over the sea,
Carry me far, to distant lands.
Carry me far, my boat, bring me
To wondrous, unknown strands.

Carry me far over the sea,
Carry me far, my boat , wherever
The wind in the sails will lead us on,
On and on forever.

Land is long and hopes beguile,
The sea alone my wandering track,
I seek the sea, lead me there,
I leave the land at my back.

Carry me far over the sea
Carry me, my boat, alone.
The wind and the stars will sail with me
And there I'll be at home.

"That be but the smallest part," said Rakal, when Mischka sang him the song. "The sea be a wilder place. I miss the storm and surge of the waves, the bluster and blast of the wind."

"And that may destroy you," Mischka reminded him, "as it destroyed your ship and drowned all but yourself and us."

"So it may," Rakal admitted. "But that be a small price to pay. Even to die be a small price to pay for a life on the waves. There be wonders in the ocean, things that no one who stays on land may see. This island itself be a wonder and none but we have seen it."

"Or perhaps one other," said Mischka, "the one who wrote the song that Firfal sang. Perhaps songs can bring something of these wonders to those who will never see them."

"They'll never know the wonders I know, naught but the pale shadow of them. How can you tell of the great islands of ice that sail down from the north when the winter is ending, that ride high in the water and gleam in the sun like jagged teeth on which an unwary ship might founder. How would you tell of these?"

"As you have," replied Mischka, "as you have told me of them. There is beauty in what you've said, as there's beauty in this island, and the splendor of sun on the sea."

Far out on the sea the sun was setting, burning a golden track across the waves and setting the clouds ablaze with crimson fire.

"Are you determined to leave?" Mischka continued. "Would you go alone, if none goes with you?"

"Be you ready to stay?"

"The children are happy."

"What of Ferrar?"

"He's little inclined to leave now. He and Brethil have grown close. I do not think he will leave unless she goes with him, and I cannot think he would ask her to do that."

"If I must go alone, then I alone will go."

"And leave us, even Raëla?" asked Mischka. He had seen how Rakal loved Imrach's daughter, though she spent most of her time with the people of the forest and rarely came with Rakal to the cave and boat.

"She has father and mother who will protect her and care for her. She has no need for me."

"Yet it would be a hard parting," said Mischka.

But Rakal did not reply.

So the days passed, and Rakal grew more and more alone. More and more he spent his nights at the cave. More and more he spent his days searching the island for supplies. One day Mischka noticed a small pile of blue crystalline stones on the bench of the longboat.

"What are these that you've gathered?" he asked.

As Rakal picked up one the stones and held it out to his friend, Mischka saw that it was a sapphire, large and perfect, not yet cut or polished, but nonetheless beautiful.

"The glitter of the mountain walls be not just feldspar and quartz. It be jewels as well. I found these sapphires and many lesser stones. If I must leave, then I will take these to buy me a second Astan."

"I'm sure you're welcome to them. If they ease your journey and aid you in your new life, wherever it may be, who could grudge that you take them with you? But I would speak of this to the elders of the forest people."

"Speak if you will. But I will take them with me, whether they will or no."

Mischka talked with the elders of the people of the discontent that Rakal felt. "If he is so anxious to be gone," they said, "then it is best that he goes."

"And these jewels?"

"They are nothing to us. He is welcome to all he can carry. Our treasures are far different from those: the treasures of friendship and song, the treasures of laughter and of living of this place, the one place in the world where we are safe. Tell your friend he is free to leave. The currents are treacherous around the island and he will find it difficult to win free. But that is no doing nor malice of ours, nor any wish to hold him here against his will. We wish only that he may somewhere find such peace as we have found here."

"We too," Mischka assured them. Yet he was troubled as well, that friends might be called upon to part in this way, and troubled that Rakal would sail alone such a long distance. But still, the evening talks, the long stories that the people of the village told, and the very music of their voices, filled Mischka with a longing to stay with them.

Summer passed and the days grew shorter once again. On the night of Mabon, when the light and dark were balanced, the people of the village gathered for celebration, as they did at those times in spring and fall, as well as those times when day and night were at their longest. There was food and fellowship, singing and dancing that lasted the night through.

When the night was its darkest, an old man rose from his bench by the fire. The villagers grew quiet. His voice was strong despite his age, as he sang not in the language of music but in these ancient words:

Rhien tauron, Rhien talf,
Ennin randin thar aear.
Rhien duin, Rhien lin,
Gard i band, gard o tath.

Mischka remembered the melody from a song that Firfal had taught him and the words in the common tongue that went with it.

Queen of the forest, Queen of the lea,
Long we have wandered, far over the sea.
Lady of river, Lady of tarn,
Keep us in safety, keep us from harm.

"This I learned from the oldest of all peoples," Firfal had said to Mischka and Ferenth when he taught them the song, "rarely seen now in our lands. They left long years ago, it is said, to dwell in the west, all but a few, a very few." Then he sang again to them, framing the melody in just such words as the old man of the forest had used, though changed now and again as though the language on the island, shaped by time and distance, had first drifted from that Firfal had heard, long before it had transformed to music.

"Have you wandered far?" Mischka asked the old man when the song was done and he had resumed his seat by the fire.

"So the stories say. Long ago we came to this island, raised up for us that we might rest here and be content." And so they were, and so were the new friends who stayed there with them and listened to their songs.

There were still many subtleties in their language that Mischka and the others couldn't grasp. But they had mastered it sufficiently to be able to hold such conversations as these and to begin to understand how they might live among these people of the forest. They were welcomed, especially their children whose laughter mingled so easily with that of the few children of their hosts. Raëla's dark tresses and Mirath's and Saschka's brown hair stood out among the silver-headed children of the forest. But they were welcomed, as were their parents, different though they were. In their turn, Mischka and the others became more and more a part of the village, joining them in gathering food and tending the gardens, joining them in shared meals and music.

Ferrar had changed most of all. He still laughed only rarely, his face still more serious than smiling. But the bitterness and anger that has possessed him for so many years, even as a boy, had faded, as the autumn mists that cloaked the river in the morning thinned and vanished in the sunlight. Ferenth, when she saw him with Brethil, understood that it was his love for her that had changed him, given him happiness as nothing else, even his love for his sister, ever could.

One night as they sat together for supper, Ferrar said: "Brethil has told me of a beautiful lake high in the mountains. I would to go see it. They call it the Chalice of the Lady, the Chalice of Dyùn."

"No one else has spoken of this lake," Imrach replied. "Do you think they will let us see it? Is it sacred to them?"

"Brethil says that is the heart of the island to them, where the Lady once rested when she blessed their refuge. Even now the water retains the memory of her hands as they dipped into the pool, and so it is called her chalice, she said. But it is not forbidden, to them or to us."

Brethil, who sat next to Ferrar as she often did now, her hand in his and her eyes on his face as he spoke, looked at the others and nodded. "It is most beautiful there," she said.

"Then let us ask the others in the morning," said Imrach,. "Perhaps we may all go."

When the morning came they sought again Brethil's father, whom they called Thirlin, to ask if they might journey to the lake and what it was. Thirlin looked carefully at each of them. Then, slowly, as if to ensure that they all understood, he told them of the lake. What he said confirmed what Ferrar had learned from Brethil: of the Lady and how she had scooped the rock as if it were clay, lifted water to her lips in her hand, breathed upon it to bless it. They journeyed there each year when the sun was most dim and the winds that blow over the mountains ice-laden. When they approached the lake then, the trees were hung with crystal drops, ornaments to honor the Lady. But it wasn't yet time for that journey.

"Is it forbidden that one visit at another time?" asked Imrach.

"Not forbidden. But the water is powerful and the valley mysterious. It is not good for anyone to see too much of the valley and Chalice of the Lady."

"My nephew especially wishes to see this place. It has been much in his thoughts since your daughter told him of it."

'Then I will call the village together in council, that all may weigh your request."

Although Ferenth and Lutha had thought to stay with the children, when Raëla, Mirath and Saschka heard of the plan to visit the lake high in the mountains, they pleaded to be allowed to go too. To this their parents agreed, as long as there was no objection from the others in village.

The council, indeed all the adults of the village, gathered the next afternoon, seating themselves on the benches around the fire. There were troubled, even angry glances among them when Thirlin announced Ferrar and his family wanted to visit the Chalice of the Lady.

Ferrar stood and said quietly, "It is not just curiosity that leads me to seek this place, though it is not yet the turn of the year. You are what you are, your daughter told me, because of the waters of in the Chalice."

"I would find a place among you," he continued, "become one of your people, no longer a stranger. I ask that I be allowed to go to this place and to drink of its water."

Brethil came and stood by Ferrar. He took her hand in his as together they faced the council

"My daughter," asked her father, "do you wish to take this man to be your own?"

"He is dear to me, Father, I ask that he may drink at the Lady's hand and be one with us."

"Then for the sake of my daughter, I ask that this be allowed. There is naught to gainsay and all to gain from it."

As Thirlin looked from one to the next, they nodded their heads in agreement. Only one, a young man, refused to give his consent. He stood and spoke.

"We know nothing of this man, yet we are willing to change our ways for him? Willing to humor his impatience, rather than honor what we have always done?"

"There is no covenant that we break in visiting the Chalice at another time, though it is many years since any has done so," Thirlin replied. "This is neither dishonor nor disrespect. We rather welcome one among us who has taken his place in the heart of my daughter."

The young man's music grew harsh and strident, a tone Mischka had never heard from any in the village. "She gives her heart to one who can hardly speak our tongue, who will never be one of us! The Lady will refuse him, as we should. You would allow him to dip his hand into her Chalice. So be it. But the water will shrink from him, will flow through his fingers rather than touch his lips. When it does, when the Lady shows that she rejects him, then we must reject him as well. He and all who came with him must be exiled when the Lady makes her will clear in this, as She will."

"Even the children?" asked Thirlin.

"Even the children," the young man replied, his lean face even more sharply etched in his bitterness. "As with the young scorpions of the rocks high up in the mountains, they will grow soon into adults whose poison none may evade. They too must go."

Brethil stepped forward, next to Ferrar. "You are the one who seeks to poison these people, spitting this venom against the one on whom I set my heart, thinking that if it were not for him, you might be the one I would choose. I tell you, that will never be. Should the Lady reject him and he be forced to leave our island, then I will leave with him."

The young man looked at her coldly, his silver eyes narrowed in anger. "This I demand: if this one of the strangers be allowed to dip his hand in the water and attempt to drink of the Chalice, then all the strangers must make the attempt. They must all submit themselves to the judgment and justice of Dyùn."

Once again Thirlin looked from one person to the next. Again each one nodded, though some with reluctance, acknowledging that this was a right and fair request from one of their members.

"So it is agreed. Go you shall to the Chalice of Dyùn," Thirlin said to Ferrar, "and your family with you. You will endure the testing of the Lady and abide by Her decision. So be it."

That night, as they lay in their flet high above the council clearing, Imrach, Lutha, Ferenth and Mischka talked among themselves of what the judgment of the council meant. Perhaps there were dangers that Thirlin had not mentioned or that they had not understood in the language, difficult as it still was for them to fully understand.

"Is there danger in this water, do you think?" asked Ferenth. "Some poison that may hurt the children?"

"Thirlin would have warned us if that we so," replied Imrach. "But there must be some danger, or our adversary in the council would not have made the demand he did. We must be wary as we travel and when we reach this lake."

"Perhaps we should forego this trial? Or at least not ask it of the children."

"We have no choice. Ferrar forced a decision. We must do as the council requires, or leave."

"I fear we will regret this decision," said Lutha.

"What is it you fear?" asked Mischka.

"There is more mystery here than just that of the Chalice. I do not trust this man who spoke. Jealousy drives him, a jealousy is cruel and cold."

"Then we must be all the more careful as we travel," replied her husband.

"It will be good to have Rakal with us," Mischka suggested.

"If he will come," Lutha replied.

"He must," Imrach declared. "So the council has ruled. We all must go."

"I do not think he would let Raëla go without him," Ferenth said, smiling.

Mischka dreamed that night that he and the family stood at the top of a mountain pass high in the mountains. Below them lay a pool of water, so clear that it might have been air rather than liquid. From it came a fragrance so sweet and heady that it made dizzy even where he stood. He and Ferenth, alone, walked down the slope to the pool and knelt by it. They reached down to dip their hands in the water, and a figure, a woman robed in sky and veiled in wind rose from it before them. She touched their outstretched hands, that suddenly burned with the cold of the water that in that moment filled them. They raised their hands to their lips, but could neither drink nor set the water aside, searching the face of the figure before them in doubt of what they should do. But her face was distant and told them nothing. They knelt there, unable to move, as the sky drew dark around them and the wind turned to storm.

When they woke in the morning, each of them except the children and Rakal admitted that they too had had a dream like this. But when they had climbed down from the flet with their packs and provisions, and Thirlin asked if they were ready to go, no one stepped away. So Brethil led them forth from the council clearing, along a northern path up into the mountains, to find the Chalice of Dyùn.

Chapter 19

The Chalice of Dyùn

For a week they traveled, guided by Brethil first across the river and northward through the forest, then higher and higher up into the mountains on narrow and rocky paths. The trees had already lost their leaves, here among the snow-clad peaks, and were fewer and smaller as the ground grew rockier.

They saw no one else, though at times Mischka felt eyes upon him. He supposed it must just be the small deer-like animals that they occasionally glimpsed in pockets of woodland, looking at them with wary eyes, ears flicking forward in alarm.

"Strange we've seen no sign of these animals at the fires of these people," remarked Rakal.

"The deer wouldn't come near the fires," replied Ferrar. "They're much too timid for that."

"I didn't mean visiting," laughed Rakal. "I mean, strange that they don't eat them!"

"Eat them?" Brethil said uncertainly, not sure she had understood him. Ferrar's language was still unfamiliar to her, though she tried to learn it, as he tried to learn hers. "These are our brothers of the forest. No more would we eat them than we would eat the eagle that nests among these peaks."

"Forgive me," replied Rakal, raising his hands in apology. "I meant not to offend you."

Brethil lowered her eyes and turned away to lead them forward again, still farther into the mountains, over passes higher and higher still. At last, as they came over yet another ridge, a massive wall of rock rose in the distance, the northern wall of the island, from which rose three towering peaks sharply etched against a cold sky.

"There," she said, "in the lap of those mountains, lies the Chalice of the Lady."

"How soon will we arrive there?" asked Ferenth.

"It is not much farther. But beyond the valley below us, the path rises steeply. We must be careful as we walk. Countless years we have passed this way and know this path well. But each year there is some change to the track as earth shifts or rocks roll down the mountainside."

Soon they were climbing again, following the rocky and winding path. That night a sudden flurry of snow fell while they were sleeping.. When they woke in the morning, their blankets were covered with it.

Brethil was not worried. "The Lady prepares for us, sending us the feathers of the snow birds to welcome us."

They climbed higher than they had ever been. The air was thin from the height and sharp from the cold; it grew hard to breathe, only Brethil seeming to have no difficulty. They stopped more often to rest, spent another night in the cold, huddled together under a ledge that provided the only shelter they could find.

The next morning they reached the top of the long path upwards. Below them, a small valley lay at the foot of the three peaks, at its center a lake whose surface was silvered with the reflection of the rock faces around it that rose sheer and swiftly up to the peaks of the mountains high and brightly lit above them.

Brethil again led the way forward, down to the edge of the lake, an arc of stone holding the water in a nearly perfect circle.

Ferrar stepped forward next to her. He knelt down on the stone lip of the chalice, dipped his hand into the water, raised it to his mouth and drank.

For a moment he did not move. Ferenth took Mischka's hand, suddenly afraid for her brother, calling out to him: "Ferrar!" Then Ferrar slowly raised his head, turning to look up at Brethil. Mischka could see, in his brother's spare, lined face, a joy that he had never seen there, a reflection of some vision or dream new and strange.

Ferrar rose. He took Brethil's hands in his, bent his head and kissed her. Hand in hand they turned to the rest of the family, smiling. Imrach and Lutha stepped forward and knelt at the water. Each dipped a hand in the water and lifted it to drink. A deep and quiet joy shone in their faces as they rose, stepping back as the three children took their places. Each of them, Raëla, Saschka and Mirath, dipped a hand in the water and drank, to rise singing, even Mirath, the quiet Mirath, who laughed and sang as her parents had never heard her do before.

Mischka and Ferenth knelt down then on the stone verge. He reached down and scooped water from the pool, cupping it in two hands to hold it out to Ferenth. She bent her head, drank, then slowly lifted her eyes to his, eyes filled not only with the love that so often shone in them, but with a wonder and joy beyond anything he had ever known. Ferenth dipped her hands in the water, then, holding it out to her husband as he had to her.

When the water touched his lips, he felt a moment of dizziness, a momentary shock as if something inside him had been broken open. But there was no pain, only the wonder and joy he had seen in his wife, his brother, his children. He saw the veins of mineral in the rock on which he knelt in sharp sudden clarity. He saw the thread of silver in Ferenth's hair, the deep clarity and depth of her eyes. As they stood and took each other's hand, their ears were filled with a music they had always known yet somehow rarely heard, a glorious symphony in which the children's laughter was even clearer than before, the voices of their loved ones more present and full in their hearing than those voices had ever been. Around them all the earth was singing in the most glorious of voices and the song was one which they had always known and yet never heard.

But as he glanced up the path they had come, the laughter and smile died on Mischka's lips. There, outlined against the empty sky, stood the man who had spoken in council against them. He held a staff in front of him with both hands, gripping it so tightly that his knuckles were white with the strain. He advanced on Ferrar, stalking forward as though barely able to restrain himself. He started to sing, not with the gentle melodies of the forest people but with a harsh grinding that they all knew was a string of curses, so violent and fierce that their ears hurt and heads ached.

Brethil fell to her knees, her hands over her ears and Ferrar knelt beside her. The man stopped in front of Ferrar, his curses still torturing them all, his face twisted in hate and jealousy. He raised the staff over his head.

But then Mischka began to sing, with a force and desperation he had not known since Ferrar was trapped in Wraith's Vale so many years before. His music fought the fierce discords of the curses, struggled to transform them, to create a larger harmony in which their power would dissipate. But the man sang more loudly, more bitterly, with even more hate and will to hurt, brandishing the staff now at Mischka, who threatened to disarm the music that was his most powerful weapon.

But Ferenth's voice joined Mischka, then Imrach's too, and Lutha's, and Raëla's. The terrible music rose to a paralyzing shriek, fighting against the harmonies that sought to contain it, to transform.

His face contorted by hate to nothing human, the man swung his staff down at Ferrar. But Rakal leapt forward. He grabbed the staff, twisting it out of the other's hands.

"You scum! I'll take that twig of yours!" he snarled.

With a terrible cry, the man turned to run from them. Mischka, beaten to his knees by the terrible struggle, watched as Rakal raced after him and the two men disappeared over the rim of the valley.

All of them were shaken, bruised by the terrible hate they had been forced to fight. Brethil was weeping while Ferrar held her in his arms, as were the two younger children who clung to Raëla.

Mischka stood up slowly and painfully. "Ferenth, I must follow Rakal!" he said.

"Go!" she said urgently. "Don't let anything happen to them."

As Mischka reached the top of the ridge, he could see the two men scrambling up the narrow ridge on the west side of the pass, Rakal close behind the other. "Rakal, stop!" Mischka called, but Rakal seemed possessed by rage, deaf and blind to anything but the man ahead of him.

Rakal suddenly leapt forward, hands outstretched. The other man stumbled and lurched sideways, arms whirling. With a terrible scream, he fell over the edge of the cliff, tumbling to the rocks below. In the sudden silence, Mischka could hear Rakal, on his hands and knees, gasping for breath as he cursed.

Mischka slowly climbed down to where the man lay, filled with the horror of what had happened. The man lay broken on the rocks, head twisted at an impossible angle, blood on his face. His eyes stared straight up into the sky, empty now of the hate and jealousy that had so driven him. He was young, Mischka realized, really hardly more than a boy.

Mischka looked up the cliff to where Rakal now stood, looking down at him with dark, bitter eyes.

"Be he dead?" asked Rakal

Mischka nodded then knelt and closed the boy's eyes.

It took a long time for Rakal to climb down to them.

"Are you alright?" Mischka asked his friend.

"Not hurt, no. Nor be this the first time that someone met death at my hands. But I wish this had not happened."

"As do I," said Mischka.

Rakal picked up the boy and they climbed back up to the ridge. The others were still gathered at the edge of the lake. When Brethil saw the boy in Rakal's arms, she cried out with a terrible grief, her heart rent in two. She buried her face in Ferrar's shoulder sobbing.

"Oh Rakal!" said Ferenth. "How could this have happened?"

"We struggled and he fell. I would not have had this happen. But it has. Ask her what we should do. Do we bring him back with us or bury him here?

Ferrar lifted Brethil lightly away from his shoulder. "My love, the boy is dead now. Should we build a cairn here, near the Chalice?"

"We must bring him back with us," Brethil sobbed.. "We must bring him back so that he may be buried in the grove with all who die."

"Brethil," said Ferenth gently. "Are you sure we should bring him back?"

"We must. His family must bid him farewell and we must do the rites to lay him to rest in the earth."

"Let be, Ferenth," said Rakal. "I'll carry the boy."

They wrapped the body in a cloak and Rakal took him again in his arms. All that long journey back to the village, Rakal bore the burden of the boy he'd killed.

At last they reached the forest again. That night Mischka rose from Ferenth's side and sat down next to Rakal, who stared into the fire as he had every night.

"Why were you so angry?" Mischka asked.

Rakal's eyes were deeply shadowed in the firelight, his brow lined and heavy above them, scarred by the struggles of the week and the burden that he carried not only in his arms but in his heart.

"When he attacked Ferrar, all the anger of being kept here, away from the sea, stormed through my blood. He was everything I hated here. He was the hate I tried to overcome these last months. But it overcame me. It wasn't I who wrestled with him on that cliff's edge. It wasn't I who saw him fall. It wasn't I whose heart was glad to see him lie crumpled at the foot of the cliff. It was some other, named Rakal perhaps, but crueler than I. It could not have been me."

"There are in each of us other selves, strangers to us, who in such a moment can overwhelm who we truly are. What is past may not undone. But we will stand staunchly by you, even if it means leaving this land."

"Raëla has found happiness here. Whatever happens to me, she must not be torn from this place."

"My friend, it is a hard fate that you suffer. May you find rest from it someday, as Ferrar has found rest from his."

Mischka returned to Ferenth, lay down beside her and soon was asleep. But Rakal sat at the fire until morning came, his thoughts dark as the forest around him.

Chapter 20

Those Who Stay and Those Who Leave

When morning came, they set off again through the forest, each one carrying some measure of the burden of what had happened. For Mischka, that memory left him more and more distant from what he saw around him as they walked, as though the island was turning away from him, or he from it. If ever he had been, he was no longer a part of it.

But for Lutha, Imrach and Raëla, their sorrow brought them grow closer to this island and its people. They spoke more often to each other now, not just to Brethil, in the language that they were learning here. They had been changed by the water of the Chalice, their eyes open now as they had not been before. They saw the life in the forest around them gathering in upon itself to prepare for winter. They saw mysteries in the flight of birds, in the movement of clouds. The wind seemed now almost to have figure and form.

Ferrar never left Brethil's side, nor she his. They grew closer and closer to each other, changed by the Chalice and by death. Lines of anger and mistrust that had marred Ferrar's countenance for so long receded. His eyes, his darkly shadowed eyes that had held anger ever since Mischka had first met him so many years before, now reflected the warmth and radiance in Brethil's eyes, bright with the love she felt.

When they reached the clearing in the heart of the forest, all the villagers were gathered. They looked on in silence as Rakal laid down before them the burden that he carried.

Thirlin, stepped forward. He took Ferrar's face gently between his hands and looked deeply into his eyes.

"Now my son, you are truly one of us."

"I feel that I am," Ferrar replied. "I ask that Brethil and I may now live together, from this day forward."

"Is this well with you, my daughter?" asked her father.

"With all my heart," Brethil replied. She turned to Ferrar and said: "My heart has been in your hands since I first saw you, and now your heart is in mine. We shall never be separated, one from the other."

"Such is my wish," Ferrar affirmed. "May our hearts be ever open to what the other may feel, our hands ever open to what the other may give."

"You have been changed as well," Thirlin said, turning to Imrach and Lutha.

"Yes, to our great joy," Imrach replied.

"The Chalice shows you more clearly the world as the place of spirit that it truly is," the old man replied. "It shows you no less clearly your own heart and the joy that is truly yours."

Then Thirlin turned to Mischka and Ferenth. "We heard what the son of our people sang at the Chalice. The island trembled at his hate. Only the song you sang turned aside the curse that he threatened to bring on all of us. You are truly children of this island."

Mischka raised his eyes slowly to the old man's. "And what of this son of your people who lies here before you, carried home to you in the arms of the man who caused his death?"

"He is our child, to be gathered once again with his family. We are grateful that you return him to us. You need feel no fault in his fate. There is no guilt, least of all to you who strove to prevent the ill that he would have caused. But there is sorrow, sorrow that you feel, and we feel too. "

Mischka looked at Rakal, who still stood next to the body he had carried, set apart from everyone. "What of our friend?" he said Thirlin.

"He bears no guilt for what happened. Though anger is rare among us, we know what destruction it can cause, above all to the one who feels such anger. He may stay with us. But is that what he wishes?"

"Do you wish to stay?" Mischka asked his friend.

"My heart will not let me be at peace here," Rakal replied. "I'll take the boat and sail to the Far Southern Lands."

"You cannot row all that way," Mischka protested.

"Nor would I try," Rakal replied. "I'll be needing but a few days to set a mast and trim cloth for a sail."

"The people here will surely give you whatever they have," said Ferenth, "wood, cloth and food."

"Then I'll return to go back to the boat tonight and return when it is ready, to gather my things."

For three days he was gone. When he returned, the villagers had gathered food and water for him. Four packs stood there among the food and water.

"What be these, then?" he asked.

"You will not sail alone," Mischka answered. "Ferenth, Saschka, Mirath and I sail with you."

Rakal looked at them doubtfully. "You understand that we may not survive, that we may drown in the seas between here and the Far Southern Lands?"

"We understand that," replied Ferenth. "But we will not let you sail alone."

Raëla stepped forward. She was still much smaller than the sea captain, though in the six months they had been on the island she had grown rapidly and now stood nearly as tall as Ferenth.

"Farewell, my dear friend," she said, standing on tip-toes to kiss his cheek. "I cannot go with you. I have found my home here and here I must stay. "

Imrach and Lutha stepped forward to put their arms around Raëla. "We too will stay here, with our daughter."

Lutha held Mischka tightly, tears in her eyes. "My little brother, will you someday again come to look for me, as you did once before?"

"Perhaps," said Mischka. "But I know now that whatever the journeys I take, we will never truly be apart."

"Go well, my brother. Take care of these we love."

Ferenth held out her arms to Ferrar. "Oh my sister," said Ferrar, holding her tightly, "long years ago I swore I would never be parted from you, yet here I find myself swearing other oaths."

"So you should," Ferenth replied "But though our ways be separate now, one day we'll be together again, perhaps here, perhaps in the Far Southern Lands, perhaps some place we do not yet know."

She kissed him on each cheek, wet with tears, smiled into his eyes, and at last turned away to take Mischka's arm..

Raëla held out her arms to Saschka and Mirath. They ran to her and she held them tightly. She was their sister. Now they would never see her again. Raëla smiled as she held them, a sad and confiding smile.

"Farewell, my young sprats!" she said, as Firfal had once called their mother and father, in the many stories that Ferenth and Mischka had told of him. "We will see each other again, never fear!" She kissed each of them one last time.

"Come," said Ferenth.

So the four of them left the village, turning again and again to wave to family and friends, until at last the forest closed in behind them and the village was lost to sight.

But as Raëla, Imrach, Lutha, Ferrar and Brethil stood together, hoping for one last glimpse of the other, they heard from far away this song.

Leaves fall, gold, red. The year must end.
Wind blows more strongly from the sea.
High on the mountains whiteness descends
To clothe them with majesty.

Far to the east, storms arise,
Far to the west, winds blow,
Far to the north, snow flies,
South the waves will grow.

Though you sail far from here,
You are with us still.
Speak one word and we will hear.
Your thoughts our thoughts will fill.

Farewell! you must seek the sea
That we have long forsaken.
Yet this longing will we always feel
That in our hearts you waken.

The song was with them long after they could no longer hear it. "Farewell!" the music called to them with the whisper of an ancient word: "Namariё!"

Late that day, Mischka and his family came to the shore where they had landed many months before. They stowed the packs and provisions, untied the ropes that held the sail furled to the boom and pushed the boat down to the water. Everyone climbed in except for Rakal, who then gave a last push to the boat and climbed in after them.

As Rakal set course to west and south, the sun set before them. Behind them, the snowy peaks of the tall mountains of the island of the forest blazed red and gold. Mischka, Ferenth, Saschka and Mirath greeted the evening with the song of the stars they had sung so many times before. For a moment, their song returned to them once again, an echo from the cliffs. Then they were alone upon the sea.

The Baron of Egeria

What strength we have to challenge greed and power
We will bring
And neither chains nor prison silence
The truth we sing.

Chapter 21

The Return to Egeria

The winter storms were over. The port of Ravas lay quiet in the sun. Early Spring shipping was just getting underway, bringing ships from the Far Southern Lands and the cities of the eastern coast. So the dock wasn't yet busy, when the little party of four stepped off the boat. They looked around, glad to be on land again, then turned to say goodbye once more to their friends on board the ship. The two younger ones, now in early twenties, waved energetically to the grizzled and gray bearded captain who leaned over the rail to see them on their way.

"Now then, you young rapscallions," he shouted, "you do as your parents tell you and don't be getting into mischief. No more climbing on the ropes for you!"

"But Rakal, weren't you glad that we were on the ship?" asked Mirath.

"Glad to have two such monkeys as you on my ship?" he said. "Sooner take along an utan than have the two of you aboard again!" But the laugh in his eye belied his words.

Rakal had brought Mischka and his family back from the Far Southern Lands. It had been a long trip, nearly two months of sailing, for even though it was far to the south of Egeria that they had landed, in this port of Ravas, nevertheless it was still a long journey from the Far Southern Lands. Though they had skirted the worst of the storms that cross southern seas even so early in the year, it was still a difficult journey, with contrary winds and high waves that slowed their progress.

Even Rakal, who had undertaken this journey on behalf of his friends, was glad to be in port. Many a time he had come to Ravas, many a time he had sailed along the coast, even as far as Antar. Ten years before, he had taken Mischka, Ferenth and their children on a longer journey, from the port of Antar to the island of the forest far to the east. Together they had sailed from the island back to Thallhiar, making landfall on the eastern coast. There he had found a new ship and crew, then sailed south to the Far Southern Lands. Mischka and his family had settled there, once more earning great fame as singers.

But Mischka missed the family he had left behind in the Tabirnian Hills. So when Rakal returned to visit them, they had decided to set sail once more. and at last had earned money sufficient to buy their way back to Egeria.

It was a difficult parting for all of them, but especially for Saschka and Mirath, who had known nothing except for the Far Southern Lands for much of their lives, and for whom the strange country of Egeria held no allure except that which strange countries always hold for the young. But still, they had looked forward to the travel with their old friend, who each time he came to the port where they lived on the Far Southern Lands would find them and bring some wondrous treasure from his travels: a talking bird perhaps, or a rich shell, or some piece of bone carved in exotic designs. He had come back every year. Only this year Mischka had said that it was time for them to return to Egeria, and Ferenth had agreed.

"You don't want to go back there," protested Rakal. "It's all given over to the Baron now. There's no place for freedom at all in that country"

"All the more reason for us to return," said Mischka. "There's little time in any life, little enough time, and ours has but a few years to run."

"Oh my friend," said Rakal, his grizzled beard shaking in the wind as he wagged his head. "You have years before you. But you're right, death may come unawares. If there be that you must do, then you must do it while you have the strength and the will, and not wait until age robs you of both. But why go back? You've built your life here, you're known and respected. There's no need for you to seek out an old life."

"Perhaps, yet I would see my brother once more, and his wife, see where my parents are, if they are still alive after so many years. Though it may be that we must leave again once we have done that, or perhaps only live as my brother does, as a shepherd far in the west, yet at least we must go and see them, bring our children there."

'If you must go, then I will take you there -- provided, of course, that you can pay the passage."

"You will not take us there for free, old friend?"

"Ah, friends be one thing, and passengers be another," laughed Rakal. "No, if all must go, then I must have passage money to pay my crew, and not indulge such fancies as friendship might imagine. Yet this I'll say: if once you're there and you want to come back and not remain, then for friendship's sake I'll bring you home."

"Ah Rakal," laughed Mischka in turn, "what is the price of friendship? We'll bank with you what we have. If we don't need to return voyage, then perhaps we'll call on you at some other time to retrieve what we leave with you."

"The first I've heard of a pirate being a banker," said Rakal. "More often, the bankers are pirates. Yet I'll agree." So they struck the bargain. Mischka and Ferenth, Saschka and Mirath took ship with their old friend and headed north along the trade lanes, back to Egeria.

When they bid farewell to Rakal, he was, it can be said, loath to see them go and thought, for the better part of a minute, that he might go with them, entrust his ship to the second in command for what time it took to get to their home far in the west of Egeria, there where the mountains soared at the end of the world. But then the thought of being so many miles away from the sea, and of his ship in the hands of someone else who might or might not sail her well, led him to reconsider. To salve his conscience he bought them the wagon and horses with which they would set forth from the city on their way to Mischka's brother Linar, far to the west.

Mischka was little known now in his own country and his wife Ferenth as well, though she had traveled for years with Firfal, that great singer. Ferenth and her brother Ferrar had made their home with Firfal before they had at last come back to Antar and their ancestral home. From Antar, Ferrar, Ferenth and Mischka had set sail for the Far Southern Lands, in exile. But perhaps there were some who still remembered them and the wondrous songs they sang..

They resolved that once again they would pay for their travel by singing. With Saschka and Mirath, they might be once again a troupe of four, as they were so many years before with Ferrar and Firfal.

They found an inn for the night, and while Mischka and Ferenth prepared for their travels, Saschka and Mirath went out to see something the city. Saschka was a tall, thin boy, his eyes dark like his mother's and his hair brown like his father's. He had a knife loose in the sheath at his side, though little expecting any trouble in the city. Mirath saw herself as the indispensable companion of her brother, as she had been throughout the years in the Far Southern Lands.

They walked out into the city. It was even older than Antar and, unlike Antar, it had an air of leisure about it, enforced in the summer by the hot sun. Even now, before the summer had quite begun, the sun was hot overhead as they left the inn behind and wandered off into the town. Unlike some of the smaller villages which sat perched on the hillside and gleamed with whitewash in the sun, this city had houses of all kinds: some made of stone from the far hills to the west, others of wood, others still like forest cottages of whitewashed daub and wattle.

Saschka and his sister wandered through the streets, past taverns where people sat at their beer, past shops where tailors squatted in the windows, past leather workings and once, a musician's shop whose window held instruments that Saschka looked at longingly. "Let's go inside and try some of these," he suggested to Mirath.

"Do you think theirs will be as good as ours?" asked his sister.

"I don't' see how they can be, but still, let's go and try them."

Inside the shop there were all sorts of instruments, though not many of each. A harp stood in one corner, a row of kithars along one wall; and hanging on the wall, a vielle, an instrument like a very small kithar but played by holding it against your chest. Saschka and Mirath walked around the shop, marveling at the instruments. Mirath lifted down a kithar and played a few notes, and then they sang one of their laughing songs.

There was an old man who lived alone.
He had a cat that moaned and groaned.
There was an old man, he lived alone.
He had a cat.
There was an old man who lived alone.
His cat was named Frick and Frone.
Tol de redo rido rum, Tol de redo day.

There was an old man who lived alone.
He had a dog that gnawed a bone.
There was an old man, he lived alone,
He had a dog.
There was an old man who lived alone.
His dog it juggled bricks and stone.
Tol de redo rido rum, Tol de redo day.

There was an old man who lived alone.
He had a cow with a horn that shone.
There was an old man, he lived alone.
He had a cow.
There was an old man who lived alone.
His cow ran away when he came home.
Tol de redo rido rum, Tol de redo day.

"You sing well," remarked the instrument maker, Wearen. "Where did you learn this song?"

"It is one of my father's," replied Mirath. "We've come from the Far Southern Lands and are here to see the city."

"It is a grand city to see. What do you plan to do here? Will you be singers here?"

"Perhaps. But I think we are going to travel back to see my uncle and my family who live far to the west, in the mountains."

"Ah! Travelers are you?"

"Musicians always are," said Saschka. "That's what my parents were for years, before my sister and I were born. When we were young, we would travel, the four of us together. We saw many places, not many I remember after all these years, but enough."

"What is your name?" asked Wearen.

"My father's name is Mischka, my mother's Ferenth, and we are Saschka and Mirath."

"Mischka! I remember long years ago when he and his family visited here in this very city."

"So we did. We came together to Ravas."

"What brings you back?"

"I don't quite know," replied Saschka consideringly. "To see family, I think"

"After so many years? How many is it now."

"Nearly ten. Seventeen years old I am, and I was seven when we left Egeria."

"Ten years! It is strange that your father should suddenly want to come back."

"Not so suddenly," replied Mirath. "We had talked about it for years, but our friend Rakal was long away at sea."

"Rakal the pirate?" said the instrument maker in surprise.

"Yes, it's he that brought us back."

"It's said," the instrument maker remarked, "that Rakal landed on a miraculous island and that there he fought with dragons and giants."

"That sounds like a story Rakal would tell, alright," Saschka laughed. "We did have an adventure before we arrived at the Far Southern Lands, when we were banished from Antar. We were wrecked on a wondrous island. But we couldn't stay there and sailed on until they came to the Far Southern Lands."

"For young lad and lass, you've had many adventures! So, are you going to buy something?"

"I don't think so," said Saschka.

"Well, I don't mind a bit of music, if you want to go on playing. Do you know all these instruments?"

"All but that one," said Saschka, pointing to the vielle that hung from the wall in the back of the shop.

"This was given to me long ago by one of the great musicians of our city. It came, he said from other lands, far to the west. I'll show you how to play it. Take it like this, hold it against you, and then draw this, he called it the bow, across the strings."

The sound that filled the shop was far different from the kithar and harp: low, like a voice singing, with a complex and warm resonance.

"It's beautiful!" Mirath exclaimed.

"Try it!" urged the instrument maker.

Saschka took it from him, his fingers quickly finding the intervals on the fingerboard. He nestled his cheek against the wood, then drew the bow across the strings. Again the lovely sound filled the shop.

"Saschka," begged Mirath, "let me try too!"

Mirath took the vielle and placed it under her chin, placed her fingers on the fingerboard, drew the bow across the strings, at first lightly, and gently so that it squeaked and groaned, and then more confidently.

"Well done, Mirath!" said Saschka. "Would you sell this?" he asked the shopkeeper.

"To your father I would. If you wish, bring him here. He and I can discuss the price."

"We'll be back in just a moment," said Saschka and Mirath as they ran from the door. "You won't sell it to anyone else, will you?"

"No," the instrument maker laughed. "I'm hardly likely to sell this to anyone else after all these years."

Saschka and Mirath ran back to the inn. "You must come and hear, Mother!" Mirath called out excitedly as they entered. "Father, we've found an instrument maker's shop, and in it he has the most marvelous instrument that you've ever heard!"

"Well , we must come and hear it then ," agreed Mischka, rising from the table. "We'll see you later. innkeeper, and do our best to entertain your guests."

"I'll be glad to have you come," said the innkeeper, "and hope that they will welcome what you have to offer."

As Mischka and Ferenth and their children walked back through the streets, the sun was high overhead. The town lay somnolent, many of the windows closely shuttered. But still, unlike the heat of the summer when everything would cease for a time, at this time of the year there were still cool winds off the water and down from the hills to the north, and the air was not yet dense with moisture. They enjoyed the smell of the air and the cool of the breeze as they walked along, talking and laughing. They came to the instrument maker's shop and went inside.

"I hear that you have some treasure that my son wants to buy," said Mischka to Wearen.

"Treasure it is, an instrument the like of which you have not seen, nor will see again, I think."

He took down the vielle and showed it to Mischka. "Yes, I remember," said Mischka. "Firfal talked of these."

"Let me show you," said Mirath to her father. The instrument maker handed it to her and she played a simple tune as Ferenth and Mischka watched.

"It is a beautiful instrument," said Mischka. "But I don't have much money."

"Then pay me in news," said the instrument maker.

"In news?" asked Mischka.

"Was it not you who long years ago was exiled by the Baron?"

"So it was," Mischka acknowledged, "or at least it was my brother-in-law, Ferrar."

"Have you come back to revenge yourself on this Baron?"

Mischka looked at the instrument maker assessingly for a moment. Though the years had treated him well, yet they had taught him to be less trusting than he might have been.

"I've come back to see my brother," said Mischka, "to see again the land where I grew up, to go with my wife and children to the city of Antar, that the children may see what their parents once knew. That is what I have come for, and all that I seek."

The instrument maker also looked at Mischka for a long time. "Yet they say that rebellion has begun in Egeria."

"Rebellion? Against the council?"

"Against the Baron, who is now the council and leads everyone down whatever path he chooses. As one servant of music to another, I warn you, my friend, stay clear of those rebellions."

"I will. They are nothing to me, as long as the Baron sees me as nothing to him. Now, this is what gold I have," said Mischka, drawing from his pocket two gold pieces, the price of a week's lodging, or perhaps two in one of the smaller inns.

"I'll take one of these," said the instrument maker, "in token of the value of this small bit of wood. Take it with you, use it well. If ever you need help, send word here to the shop of Wearen."

The next day they began their travels, heading west from Ravas on the road to the great mountains of the north. As they journeyed, they practiced their songs. That night, when they came to a small village, Mischka went to the inn and offered the owner that for their room and their meal for the night they would entertain the patrons of the inn.

"Entertainers!" scoffed the inn-keeper. "What need have I of those! People come to drink, not to sing."

"But if they sing, then will their throats be the more dry, and they will order wine the more freely. If there is something to keep them, will they not buy more than their one glass of ale and stay to listen? May you not have yet a larger crowd?"

"Perhaps, perhaps. I am willing to try. But I tell you this, stranger. If my patrons do not like your songs, then neither room nor board will you get this night."

"Fair enough," Mischka replied. He went to the cart and from it drew an old harp, wrapped in a canvas case. It bore signs of many years of playing. The strings were black in the afternoon sunlight. He took as well an old kithar that he handed to Ferenth, and tabor and cymbal that he handed to his children.

As they waited for evening to come and the innkeeper to begin to serve his patrons, they practiced by the door of the inn, singing wonderful songs of faraway places, not least the songs of the forest people, whom they had met on the far away isle of the forest. As they sang, people stopped and came closer. When they finished, one person after another asked, "Who are you and where are you from?"

"My friends, we are singers newly arrived from the Far Southern Lands."

"The Far Southern Lands!"

"Yes, we lived there for many years and now have come home, back to our own country. We hope to entertain you this evening, here in this humble establishment, with the songs we've learned: songs of strange and faraway places, and songs of this our homeland."

So they sang, and the crowd gathered,. When at last dinner time came the innkeeper said: "Well, if the crowd you've gathered this afternoon is any indication of what you will do this evening, then I am willing to take a chance. Come, and have something to eat before the evening gets started."

They went in, and there was the innkeeper and his two children, each of whom served in the inn. His wife prepared the meals that were served. There was one other, a stranger as well.

"Good evening, stranger. Where do you come from?" asked Mischka.

"I too am a traveler," said the stranger. "Long on the road and many miles yet to go. It is strange to find any from the Far Southern Lands here, any who would return from that land of reputed plenty to live in this barren place."

'Barren?" asked Mischka.

"Barren enough," said the stranger, "with all that we have subject to tax."

"No talk of sedition here," urged the innkeeper. "I will not hear any talk of politics."

"Afraid, are you?" scoffed the stranger.

"Not afraid, but I will not have politics talked here," declared the innkeeper stoutly.

"Then tell us of the Far Southern Lands," said the stranger to Mischka.

"What is there to tell. It is all you've heard, a land of many wonders, of tall mountains and green fields, of great herds of game that wander the open prairies, of great waterfalls and of great gardens blossoming like the world in its youth. There are but few people yet, who establish a foothold there upon the shores and who venture now and then into the interior to see what may be seen. We lived there and were happy for many years."

"You see its trade in the market, taxed beyond what most people can afford."

"But the true riches of the Far Southern Lands are things that may not be brought here," said Mischka.

"Yes that's true," continued Ferenth. "Not just the wonders of the continent, for those we sing of tonight and perhaps catch in some form, but even more the treasures that grow there and cannot survive the long journey to Egeria. Fruits larger than any you've seen and sweeter than any you've tasted. And grain, heavy in the head."

"From what you say," said the stranger, "all people should travel there and leave behind this poor country."

"Not so poor," Mischka disagreed.

"Poor except for those few who amass all they can."

"Then it is not the fault of the country."

"I didn't say it was," replied the stranger. "But come, what else do you hear, strangers from the Far Southern Lands?"

"From the Far Southern Lands, but not just from there. Many years ago we too were of Egeria and have returned to see this country which we left so many years ago, and to which we gladly return," said Mischka.

"From where in Egeria?"

"I grew up far to the west, where the mountains reach high, and there tended sheep owned by my family. My brother lives there still, and perhaps my parents if they are still alive."

"And you, lady? Where are you from?"

"From the roads of Egeria," replied Ferenth. "I long traveled them singing, until I met my husband and with him journeyed to the Far Southern Lands."

"And left years ago, you said? Egeria has changed since you left, and not I think for the better. You've heard of the Baron. Even before you left perhaps he was a power to be reckoned with?"

"We've heard of him," Mischka replied. "Even then he was strong and powerful and had amassed great land and riches."

"He has amassed more still. All the power of the country lies in his hands now. The web he spins from his seat in Antar enwraps all of the country."

"No more politics, I say!" objected the innkeeper. "Stranger, if you would stay here you must cease this talk."

"I but tell these strangers what they must know if they would live in Egeria."

"You tell them more than one should know and you tell them not aright. True it is that the Baron has great wealth. But is there not peace and plenty in the land?"

"Peace?" said the stranger thoughtfully. "For those who live as the Baron wills and pay his taxes with no complaint. But for those who stand in his way or whose way he wants, is there peace for them? For those who have been displaced from their homes, for those who live on the streets of the city, is there peace for them? You innkeeper, when you give half of what you earn to swell the coffers of the Baron and your children are dressed in cast-offs, is there peace for you?"

"Peace enough," declared the innkeeper angrily. "Enough talk! It is time for you to try singing and see what patrons you bring to my door this evening."

They took their places along the long wall while the stranger sat at one of the tables. As they sang, the evening custom began and many people came to listen to them. Sometimes their songs were joyful and sometimes full of great sadness. Sometimes they spoke of great wonders, and sometimes of horrors; of great sea-journeys where the waves towered above the ship, or of a quiet evening with the children.

Then Saschka brought out his flute, a flute that like his parents' instruments had seen long years of use. The supple, subtle sounds of the instrument filled the small room of the tavern and the patrons grew quiet. Even the innkeeper stopped in his custom to hear the haunting melody that the stranger boy played.

Chapter 22

The Road North and West

The next morning, as the host gave their breakfast, he offered them advice regarding the road they should take.

"Take the great road – it's easy enough to follow -- northward across the great plain of Egeria until you come to the mountains. Then follow the road to the west. But surely if you have lived here you know these roads?"

"The northern and western roads I know well," replied Mischka, "and that from many years of travel. But though I have been to this part of Egeria many times, yet it has been ten years since we were here and things may change."

"May and do," agreed the innkeeper thoughtfully. "Yet these roads are the same. There's not been such change in this country as the stranger implied."

"Change enough," said the stranger, who came in as they sat talking, having been outside after a very early breakfast. "My friends, if you are ready to leave, I'll see you on your way and perhaps travel with you for a while."

"I do not know that I would travel with this one," advised the innkeeper. "We know nothing of him, he's a stranger here. Though he's courteous enough, he speaks treason often. The Baron's soldiers are many and his ears more still. If you would stay out of trouble, I counsel you stay away from this man."

"One may avoid trouble," replied the stranger, "by closing one's eyes -- or one may fall into a pit. I counsel it is better to walk with your eyes open, that you may see the snares."

"And if you yourself are one of those snares?" said the innkeeper.

"Then all the more reason that you should keep me in your sight, if you would not have me at your back."

"I do not think that we will be troubled by this stranger," said Mischka. "If you wish to travel with us, then do. Yet we go slowly, and for such as you, perhaps our journey may be over long."

"For a while," replied the stranger, "our paths lie together. Then I must go my own way. I have errands there that call me."

"Into the northern mountains?" warned the innkeeper. "Naught lives there but brigands."

"So they say," agreed the stranger. "Perhaps my errand is to them."

"Perhaps you are one of them," said the innkeeper suspiciously.

"Perhaps I am. But I tell you truly, these travelers have nothing to fear from me."

"Then travel with us as long as you wish," said Mischka. "To you, innkeeper, thanks for the meals and shelter."

"Thanks to you, the custom last night was more than I have ever had. If luck is with me, they'll come back tonight to talk over what they heard. If ever you come this way again, gladly would I see you here, and give you room and board once more."

"In exchange for an evening of songs?"

"Even singers such as you must pay in your own way."

"We hope we can return some day," said Ferenth. "But for now our way must lie to the north and west. Farewell."

Saschka and Mirath were talking with the two children of the innkeeper. When their father called them, they turned away and came to the wagon. They all climbed inside and set forth. They had rigged a cover over the top of the wagon, so that if they encountered spring storms, as well they might, at least they would have a dry place to bed, though their horses would have none. But Mischka hoped that, the next village lying not far ahead, only a matter of some fifteen miles, they would be there long before nightfall, and find again an inn. The innkeeper directed them to the sign of the Red Raven.

"Red Raven?" asked Ferenth.. "What can that signify?"

'None knows," replied the innkeeper. "It's an old sign, has been there for a long time."

So they went on their way and the stranger went with them, beguiling them with tales of the changes in the country, which were many and few of them good. The Baron's wealth had grown, more and more gathered in Antar, far to the north and east. The Baron's influence spread like the long drop lines of a spider and the wealth flowed up those lines, drawn by a great force at the center impossible to resist, or so it seemed.

"I've heard," said Mischka, "there are those who would resist, if they had the strength and a leader."

"Such a leader there is," replied the stranger. "His symbol is a hawk, a red hawk. If I find him, I will give him your greetings. I see our ways part here. I bid you farewell,"

"A good journey may you have, and misfortune lie far from your way," said Ferenth.

So the stranger went off.

"Father," Saschka asked, "is this true what the stranger was saying about the Baron?"

"I believe it is," replied Mischka. "Even when we were here years ago, the Baron was a greedy man and gathered to himself as much as he could. Your uncle, Ferrar, was bitter against him and it was this that led to our being exiled from Antar so many years ago: that, or see your uncle be put to death. Neither your mother nor I would stay behind when he was forced into exile at the Baron's behest."

"As we were leaving," said Mirath, "the innkeeper's daughter and son were talking with us.

"As I saw," replied Ferenth. "You were deeply engrossed in conversation with them."

"So we were," Saschka agreed. "They told us that the soldiers of the Baron travel this road, and that they have stopped travelers and demanded toll of them."

"We have nothing to give them," said Mischka. "They may demand all they like."

"Then the soldiers will take what we have: our instruments, our small bit of food. But the innkeepers' children said there was another road we could travel."

"And where is that?" asked Mischka.

"If you take a small road to the side, it will lead to a small cart track that runs to the west of this road. There we may escape the soldiers of the Baron."

"If your friends thought it well for us to take that road, then we will take their advice," When they came to the road, they turned off onto to the small, rutted track. As they passed along, they saw many farms, some empty and abandoned, and others poor. The few people they saw looked at them silently as they passed.

"The country is in great poverty," said Mischka.

"Is this the Baron's doing?" asked Saschka.

"I fear that it is," replied Mischka,. "I fear what it means. I hope my brother, and his family are safe."

So they came by rougher ways to the next town, a small village. They made their way to the sign of the Red Raven, a bird as red as any cardinal, and yet with the long rough shape of a raven. As they drew close, the innkeeper came to the door.

"Ah, travelers," he said, "have you come a long way today, are you looking for shelter? You'll find no better place than at the sign of the Red Raven."

`He was a big man, and his broad face gleamed redly, his light, sandy hair cut short on top of his head.

"We do indeed look for a place to stay," said Mischka. "We ask only that you let us pay for it by entertaining your patrons."

The innkeeper's face closed in a scowl, the broad grin wiped from it as quickly as a cloud passes across the sun.

"Pay for your stay by singing?" he said dubiously and angrily. "You trespass far on my courtesy, strangers. This is an inn, not a place for concerts. If you have not money to pay, then go your way."

"Money we have," Mischka assured him, "but it may be better for both of us if we welcome those who might wish to hear us."

"Pay me first. Then if your songs do well, perhaps I may give you the money back."

"If you don't trust us," Mischka replied, "why should we trust you? After all, we will sing before we have need of your beds. You can always lock the door against us."

The innkeeper, still scowling, looked suspiciously at Mischka. "Very well, if you wish, I will try. But for the meal..."

"For that we'll pay, if you insist," said Mischka, for already it was drawing on towards evening and they felt hungry after their long walk. Young Mirath, though strong enough for her fifteen years, was leaning heavily against her mother .

The innkeeper led them inside. There a young girl was working, wiping the tables to prepare them for the evening guests.

"Go and bring these travelers bread and cheese," the innkeeper said, "and a plate each of the stew that cooks on the hearth."

"Yes sir," replied the girl, nodding to him, and leaving the room.

"Is she your daughter?" asked Ferenth.

"No, she's an orphan of the town. She but works for me. There's little enough help she gives. Now, for the meal it will be two coppers apiece, and another copper if you want ale or wine.:

"You have wine?" asked Mischka, surprised to find it so far from the city.

"Good wine, from the western vineyards."

Mischka took out his purse and drew from it the eight coppers for the meal. "I think that tonight water will suffice for us all. We will go and draw if from the well."

Shortly the girl came back with bread, cheese, and four plates of stew that was more broth than vegetables and meat. The girl hung close by the table until Ferenth said, "What is it, child?"

"Is everything alright?" asked the girl.

"You've done well, said Ferenth. "Do you wish to talk with us?"

"Are you travelers? Where are you going?" she said, her eyes on Saschka. She too was sixteen or seventeen, though thin and perhaps less grown than she might have been had she seen less hard usage and better food.

"We travel to the north," Saschka replied. "We go to see my uncle."

"I've never seen the north, but it is where I'm from."

"What are you doing here," demanded the innkeeper angrily. "Return to the kitchen, finish preparing the supper in there."

She turned, but said softly to Ferenth. "Can I talk to you later?" she asked.

"Come and find us in our room," Ferenth replied.

"She is a good for nothing girl," said the innkeeper. "I don't know why I keep her here. She doesn't do all that I need done, and is constantly straying off, more trouble than she's worth, and that's the truth."

"And yet you feed her, clothe her?" asked Ferenth.

"What clothes she has, she must buy out of the wages that I pay. But still, more trouble than she's worth."

That night, as they sat in their room, talking by the window, for the night was still warm, though not as hot as during the day, there was a timid knock on the door. Mischka rose and opened it, and there was the girl of the tavern.

"May I come in and talk?" she asked.

"You're welcome," Mischka replied. "Come in." He closed the door behind her. "Are you done with your work for the night?"

"If he had his way, I would never be done. But for tonight at least I am finished."

"He said that you're an orphan of the town?" asked Ferenth.

"Yes," she replied. "I've lived here all my life. My parents died two years ago."

"What is your name?"

"I'm called Silvren."

"Have you no relatives here?"

"None. My parents came from the north. They were weavers, and often talked of going back."

"The north?" Mischka asked.

"Yes. They had a homestead far to the north and west."

"That is where my brother lives and where I am from."

"Would you take me there? I don't want to stay in this village."

"You know nothing of us," said Ferenth.

"I heard the songs you sang and I see your faces. What more do I need to know?"

"Many a kind face may hold a darker heart," Mischka cautioned.

"That is not so in yours," said the girl, looking from one to the next.

"Mischka, we should take her with us," said Ferenth.

"We have trouble already," Mischka replied, "a long way to go, and four of us to feed. If the reception from this inn is any indication, though people may listen they have little wealth to share." For that night, as they sang in the tavern, though many had gathered as word had spread through the village that the singers had come, yet there was little money that any had to give them. Though they had gathered a number of coppers, there was no silver and no gold from the people of the village.

"Nonetheless," said Ferenth, "we cannot leave her here. I do not trust this innkeeper and how he treats her."

"I can defend myself," said the girl. "I have now, for years. It is not through fear I ask you, but through a wish to see this land that my parents came from, and of which they spoke so happily."

"Why did they come south?" asked Mischka.

"The winters were hard up there, they said, especially one, when the wolves came down from the mountains and all their sheep were killed by the storms and by the wolves. So they came south with what they had and set up here in this village as weavers. They were good weavers. They thrived in the trade, but I cannot do it alone. When they died another took the shop. I have here a place to sleep. But no longer a home."

"In the morning then," said Mischka, "we will talk to the innkeeper and you may come with us."

Next morning, Mischka and Ferenth, after they had paid the innkeeper his due, told him that the girl would be traveling with them.

"You'll find her little help," said the innkeeper.

"It is not out of need of her services," Mischka said firmly, "but out of compassion for her that we ask her to go with us."

"Well, she's no cook, she's no server. I have little need of her. For all I am concerned take her if you wish."

"We will be glad to be rid of her," said his wife angrily, her eyes darting between Mischka and her husband. "She has been nothing but trouble ever since she came."

Then they went to the weaver's shop. As they entered and introduced themselves, he said: "Silvren says that she wishes to go with you. Who are you, strangers, and what do you seek of her. You look to me like ragged gypsies."

"Perhaps so," laughed Mischka, "but I was a shepherd, a smallholder far in the western mountains, and that's where I return. If she wishes to go with us, she may."

"I do not want to stay," protested Silvren. "I want to go back and see the mountains where my parents were born."

"If she wishes to come," said Ferenth, "then she's welcome. Continue to hold this shop in trust for her. If she wishes to return, when once she has seen the mountains, then when we bring the wool back to the southern cities we may come this way and bring her back here."

"I will never return," said Silvren. Her eyes were on Saschka as she said that, who looked at her with puzzlement in his eyes. Ferenth smiled.

"I see you have bewitched her," said the weaver. "If she wishes to go, I'll not keep her. She would only run off, I expect. But if I hear that you have done anything to hurt her, then I will seek you out, wherever you may be."

So Mischka and Ferenth welcomed Silvren into their family. As they headed north along the road, they sang a light song of the pleasure of traveling.

The road lies before me, the road at my feet.
Down every path I wander, people I'll meet.
They greet me with pleasure as I walk along,
And I greet them too as I sing them my song.

The road is for wandering, the road is free.
The road is the place where I must be.

Long I have wandered this road through the land.
Wandered everywhere, wonders on every hand,
Though I may wander, still I see as I roam,
The road ever goes onward, the road is my home.

The road is for wandering, the road is free.
The road is the place where I must be.

And so they traveled on by the smaller roads. Each night they found themselves near an inn or some small farmstead, and there they would beg shelter and a bit of food from the common pot. Even by poverty they were welcomed, though some looked askance at their foreign dress, and their accents that were strange to these southerners. They traveled on, across the length of Egeria.

As they traveled northward, they saw rising before them the great mountains: sharp peaks, like white teeth against the horizon, growing taller and taller as they plodded slowly towards them, rising as though drawn from the earth by the distance that Mischka and his family traveled. At last they stood near the foot of the mountains.

The ground was harder here and rockier, the grass sparser, the people hardier. Yet things were not so poor as they had been, as though the Baron's grasp had not yet reached so far. People who had so little were of little use to the Baron, so he left them for some later time.

At last they came to the house of Mischka's brother, Linar, and his wife Niëra. It was a house at once familiar to Mischka and yet strangely changed. Rooms had been added; flowers grew by the door. Most different, however, was the sense of long years of settled growth, evident in the five children who tumbled through the door and ran to greet them.

Strangest of all was the sense at once of being home and yet of this no longer being home. The house was strange to Mischka; this was where his brother lived and where he too had found shelter in the days of conflict with his own parents. Yet though it was still a sheltering place, it seemed that the threatening pall that hung over all of Egeria hung over this house too, in the lines in his brother's face and the gray in his hair.

"Welcome strangers," said his brother, coming forward. Then he stopped, hesitating, his two hands outstretched in a gesture of greeting.

"A stranger is it, Linar?" laughed Mischka.

"My brother!" said Linar, embracing him in a strong hug. "Last we heard you had left the continent, banished with wife and family, and our sister with you."

"So we had, yet we are returned, though not all of us, for Lutha is still beyond the sea. Yet I at least am back, with Ferenth and children, as you see."

Niëra came from the house: "Mischka!" she cried and put her arms about him. Mischka was surprised that her head came only to his shoulders, for when he left she had been as tall as he, those years before. Now he stood eye to eye with his brother who was, as men go, taller than most.

"Welcome, Ferenth," said Niëra. "And are these Saschka and Mirath? How you have grown!"

"Our gratitude for this welcome," replied Ferenth. "We hope that you might welcome us the more, for all the years we've been away."

"None can be dearer to my husband and to me than Mischka and his family. Come inside, all of you. Although we're crowded in this house with our own children, yet there's room enough for all."

"Misk," Niëra called to the tall boy who stood in the doorway, "come help us with these things of your uncle's."

The boy came forward and Mischka started in surprise. In the young man before him, he saw himself twenty years before, the same dark and silent air and a face as familiar as his own.

"Welcome, uncle," said Misk.

"My thanks to you, nephew" said Mischka as he took the boy's hands. "Glad I am to see again the son of my brother and his wife. Glad I am to find that he is such a son as I would be glad to call my own. Saschka, come forward! Mirath, greet your cousins."

So they did, and from the house came the boy's sister, Lutha, and she too was familiar, as though she was indeed Mischka's sister again, yet with something of Niëra in her too. The others were there as well: Lilath, Andor, and Mirim, all of them as dear to Mischka as his own. So they went inside and the house that night was filled with talk and stories and singing, as it hadn't been for many years.

Chapter 23

Families Reunited

Mischka and his family felt warmly welcomed by their relatives, and the brothers found much to talk about. His father, as Mischka had feared, had died years before. The house stood empty, and Linar offered it to them if Mischka wished. They could repair it and the two families live as neighbors.

For some time they considered this. The thought of being again where he had grown up attracted Mischka strongly: the mountains so tall in their majesty behind him, and the great rosy light upon the peaks in the morning; the cool, keen air; the rocky bones of the earth showing through the thin skin of grass that covered them. All of these things were dear, inexpressibly dear to him.

. He and Ferenth talked of it often. She was willing, and the children too, for Saschka and Mirath had found in young Misk and Lutha another brother and sister, as close to them as they to each other; Silvren too became like a sister to them all and the five became inseparable. Mischka was glad to hear their voices joined in laughter and song, to find his own son and daughter sharing in the tasks of the rest of the family.

Mirath was the youngest of the five who were so close, the rest all much of an age. But though occasionally they teased her, young Misk especially was very caring and was always careful to include her in whatever adventures they might have. Adventures they did have, for though Misk, like his father before him, was responsible for tending their sheep in the upper pastures and there protecting them from the wolves, yet in the summer at least the wolves stayed higher up in the mountains that gleamed white to the north and west of them. So the days, as they sat in the meadows, were full of laughter and song. There were days too, when Linar would give in to Misk's pleading and the five of them would go off into the mountains.

It was on one such day that young Misk asked his father if he, his cousins and their friend Silvren could take several days to travel up into the mountains. He wanted to show them the high meadows and to sleep in one of the caves that pocked the mountainside.

"Let them go," urged Niëra. "They've done plenty of work, and while you're away I will need their help the more. So let them play now."

Linar agreed. The five youths packed food and blankets, then left, talking excitedly left for their walk up into the mountains.

That night, the four parents sat around the fire, "Young Misk grows fond of our Mirath," said Ferenth to her sister-in-law. "It is early still. He sees in her and Saschka another brother and sister. Yet I think It may become more than that. Mirath's laughter, her stories of strange distant places, all of these are leading to feelings that he doesn't yet know he has."

"And Silvren," asked Mischka, "what of her and Saschka?"

"She has changed, I think," said Ferenth.

"So she has. Her face none would call beautiful, perhaps, yet it is full of strength. Saschka matters to her a great deal."

Though they flirted, those two, taking hands and lowering eyes, Saschka seemed unconscious still of the love that Silvren felt for him. But to the four sitting by the fire, it was clear what feelings the weaver's girl had for him.

"She's becoming like another daughter to me," said Niëra. "I am glad of her help, always. She has, I think, in her fingers, a skill that her parents must have had. She too is a weaver."

"But Saschka is no shepherd," Mischka replied.

"Perhaps he will be, if you will stop your wandering," argued Linar. "Could you not settle down with us?"

"Perhaps. Perhaps one day. But not yet."

"Why?" said Niëra.

Mischka looked into the fire. Then his eyes turned to Ferenth. "I am glad to be here again ," he said, "and that is the reason why we came: to see these places which are home to us, or at least to me."

"And to me," said his wife. "We visited them many times over the years of our travels, and they are as dear to me as to you, Niëra, and your brother: this is my home, too."

"Are you so drawn to the life of a wandering singer?" said Linar to his brother. "Can you still not rest, still not settle down?"

"It is not just that," said Mischka. "I feel I have some part of my tale still to live, and that it's not yet here in this place. When I left Antar, and we sailed south hoping to reach the Far Southern Lands, I promised Ferrar that I would one day return, if he could not, and bring justice on the Baron."

"Ferrar learned better," said Ferenth. "He cared no longer for revenge, only to be with Brethil and to stay on the island of the forest."

"So he did," Mischka agreed. "Nor did I come back seeking revenge. Yet now that I'm here, I see that he was right, and that the Baron is a great evil that we must strive against."

"There are places free of the Baron still," protested his brother.

"But for how long? How many suffer, as Silvren did, as do the people we saw in the hovels. I must do what I can. If all I can do is sing, then that I will do. But if Saschka wishes to stay here with you, then I'll gladly help build him a house."

"I don't think he is ready for that yet," said Niëra. "In some ways, our Misk has in him the same urge to wander that you had long ago, my brother. Perhaps even if he is not a singer, he might travel with you and Saschka stay here with us for a while."

"Perhaps," said Mischka, looking at Ferenth. "What do you think, my love? Perhaps both Saschka and Mirath could stay here?"

"We will see," Ferenth replied.

The five friends traveled far up into the mountains, following the path west from the village and then continued on into the foothills. In two days of walking they were among the high meadows. As they walked, Saschka and Mirath sang, and at times Misk would join them too.

Once, Saschka asked, "Silvren, won't you sing with us?"

She shook her head and replied: "I never have sung."

"Then try! You remember that song we sang as we walked earlier. Sing it with me."

So he began singing, and Silvren joined him. Her voice was very soft and light, not as true in pitch as Saschka's, who had for many years sung with his parents, but lovely nonetheless. Then Mirath joined in, Lutha and young Misk too. They sang louder and the five of them laughed with the joy of being alive, with the joy of the music that they felt.

Night came on, and they found themselves with light hearts, high up on the hillside, looking down over the plains lying far below them. Young Misk led them to a meadow where sometimes he pastured the sheep, but at this time of year was full of wildflowers. The grass was tall, grazed only by the goats and wild sheep of the high mountains, by deer and gembocks.

"I have dreamed of a place like this," said Saschka as they lay that night by the fire made of deadwood culled from the forest around them.

"Really dreamed of it?" asked Mirath.

"I don't know. Perhaps it was just stories that father and mother told. But it seems that I know that pasture and these hills. All our time on the Far Southern Lands seems only a dream. Now at last I'm awake, to be here with you, my cousins, and with you Silvren."

"Was I a part of your dream?" asked Silvren.

"It seems so, in a strange way. Though we never knew you before we came here, any more than we knew our cousins, yet now that we are here it seems that you have always been part of our life."

"I feel that too. I feel at home here."

She held out her hand to Saschka, and he took it and held it closely. "I am glad you're with us," he said.

"And I with you," said Silvren.

The next day they climbed higher and slept again in the high meadows. Then they returned home, much faster for going downhill, back to the stone cottage lying amid the pastures on the mountain slopes.

So the summer drew on toward the time of the great fall fairs, when Linar must take his wool south again in his cart to trade it for what they could not grow or make themselves. Mischka felt restless, that this was where he belonged, yet at the same time that there was something more for him to do. Songs came unbidden to him as he sat in the evenings at the door of the cottage and talked with Ferenth, Linar and Niëra, or when he saw the children walking the pastures and remembered his long years tending the sheep.

"Soon," said Linar," I'll take our wool south to Ravas. Other years, I've gone alone, or taken Misk with me. This year, brother, will you go with me?"

"I will," agreed Mischka, "but I'm not sure that when you come back, that I can come back with you."

"Where will you go?" asked Niëra. "Why not stay here with us or in your father's house?"

"Tell me, Linar," said Mischka. "How much of the wool you grow goes to the Baron?"

"Of what I have here, none," said Linar. "When it is in the hands of the merchants, they must give some of it into the hands of the Baron's collectors."

"How long will it be before his collectors come to these mountains and begin to demand their toll of you? When they do, how will you survive on half of what you now have?"

"Why should they come? I owe nothing to the Baron! He does nothing for me."

"You will have no choice. Do you remember, Ferenth, those hovels that we saw on the way here? What choice did they have when the Baron's soldiers came and took from them half of what they grew. They were people such as we and now they are little better than beggars."

"I have heard of the Baron," said Linar. "But his soldiers are too wise to come here, to the mountains. We will not succumb to his violence nor to the force of his arms."

"Did not others say that, even in the city? Did I tell you, Linar my brother, of how Ferenth's brother Ferrar was stripped of his home and exiled? Did we not tell you of how many people were driven from their homes to swell the coffers of this Baron?"

"We are far from his soldiers."

"Not far enough. The time will come when they will be at your door as well."

"What are you going to do?" asked Niëra.

"I don't know," Mischka replied. "But I think perhaps I'll begin with you and your journey."

"I'll go with you, father," said Saschka.

"And I too," said Misk.

"No," said Mischka. "I think you must stay here with Niëra while both your father and I are away."

"Many a time I've been alone before," said Niëra.

"The times are not the same," Mischka replied. "It would ease my heart if Saschka and Mirath were with you. Will you come with us, Ferenth?"

"What choice have I?" Ferenth laughed. "I'm not about to let you go alone."

"Then so be it," said Mischka. "Linar, Ferenth and I will go."

So it was that Mischka and Ferenth and Linar set off to the south, loaded with bales of wool, for the southern port of Ravas.

When they arrived in Ravas, Mischka and Ferenth found rooms in a tavern in one of the poorer quarters of the town, where the weavers and tailors had their shops. It was buzzing with the rumors of how the Baron had arrived in a rich coach, how he had spoken glowingly of the wealth of other cities and how by increasing trade the citizens of Ravas might grow the more rich. If the city would but grant him the right to trade, he would fill Ravas with treasures from other lands. There would be no longer be beggars in the city, not even poor men, for everyone would benefit from the wealth the Baron would bring. The men of the council had listened with greed glinting in their eyes.

"It has begun," Mischka said. "So we too must begin. This is what we must do."

That night they went from tavern to tavern, singing. But the songs they sang this time were not of the Far Southern Lands. They sang of their exile at the hands of this man. They sang of the Baron's greed and power. At each tavern, there were angry words, sometimes against Mischka and Ferenth, sometimes among those who listened, between those who supported the Baron and those who did not.

At the end of the night, Mischka and Ferenth returned to the inn where they were staying; and there, seated at the table with Linar, were two senior members of the council. As they came in, Mischka and Ferenth felt these two merchants glared at them as though they were thieves of the worst sort.

"We hear that you are spreading trouble," said the councilors.

"Not trouble, but the truth," Mischka replied.

"You are guests in our city. If you wish to stay here, you will refrain from this slander."

"Is this not a free city, still? One may be brought before a magistrate, but not before two councilmen."

"If you wish to stay in this city, and if your brother wishes to sell his wool here, then you will do as we say."

"Have you been so seduced by the promises of the Baron?" Mischka replied quietly.

"We are seduced by nothing. But we will not have you spreading dissension and revolt."

"When there are such lies and deceit, then criticism is necessary. Truth demands it."

"We've warned you all. If you value your trade," they warned Linar, "then silence your brother. If you would stay here longer, "they warned Mischka and Ferenth, "then silence your verse."

With that they left the tavern.

Chapter 24

Mischka Faces the Baron

"You have aroused their ire," said Linar.

"Not their ire. Their fear," replied Mischka. "As Ferrar said, long ago in Antar, the Baron rules with greed and destroys with fear."

"What would you have us do, brother?" asked Linar. "Do we stay?"

"We must have silver," Mischka replied. "We will sell your wool tomorrow, and tomorrow night we will see what must be done."

So Linar went out to the market in the morning. From stall to stall he went, from shop to shop, yet none would buy his wool. They said "Your wool is no longer welcome here, man from the north. Take it to some other city. Perhaps they will buy."

The answer was always the same. Even those with whom he dealt for years turned away and would not meet his eyes. When he returned to the inn at the dinner hour, he felt angry and troubled, yet convinced as well that something must be done. The two merchants were waiting.

""If your brother does not leave, then you will sell your wool to no one," they warned again.

"What you do here is wrong!" growled Linar. "My brother has the right of it. What the Baron forces you to do will destroy you all. If you will not buy my wool, then soon you too will be unable to sell your cloth."

"We do not need your wool," replied the merchants, turning to leave. "We do not need your custom nor your brother's songs. Both of you must leave. We will be glad to see you gone."

"And if we do not choose to leave?"

"Then you must leave this inn at least, for only patrons of the wool guild can stay here and that you are no longer."

"If we must leave, then we will leave," Mischka said calmly. "But the trouble you have seen so far, the songs you have heard, are nothing to what you will see if the Baron gains a foot-hold."

"Do you threaten us?" demanded the two merchants.

"No, I do not. The Baron is the threat and you are threatened already. You yourselves are a threat to your city. If you will not hear the truth, then you yourselves will destroy your city, and your families with you."

"We will listen to no more of this. Innkeeper, turn these people out."

"I am sorry," said the innkeeper. "But as the merchant says, this inn is only for the patrons of the wool guild."

"Then we will go," said Mischka. So they gathered their things and left. But at each inn they were recognized. No one would give them a room.

As Mischka and Ferenth, Linar went through the streets, they passed a beggar sitting in a doorway.

"Alms, alms for the poor," said the beggar in a whining voice.

"How do you come to be here?" Mischka asked.

"Masters, it is a long tale of misfortune and troubles. For a poor coin or two, gladly would I tell you of my life. Or for a coin or two you may have my silence."

"Your silence?" asked Mischka.

"Yes, I'll not afflict you with my woes as my woes have afflicted me."

"I see," Mischka replied, laughing. "Take this copper, put it in your bowl, and tell me of your life. Were you born here in this city?"

"Masters, this city has a side that you don't know, you who walk its streets so proudly. There is woe and sorrow here."

"As in every city " said Linar. "Why should this city be any different from all the others?"

"I see you are a man of wisdom. But the woe in this city is greater than in any other."

"Why is that?" asked Mischka, smiling at the beggar's taste for exaggeration.

"Because the joy in this city is greater, so that those who have less must sorrow the more, seeing what others have."

"Such envy is poisonous," said Ferenth, "to take from you what happiness there might otherwise be."

"But it becomes itself a kind of satisfaction. I was born in this city. My parents were poor artisans and I grew up expecting that I too would be a silversmith. But misfortune befell my family, oh wise ones. My father was accused of stealing from those for whom he made his jewels. As the law demanded, he was forbidden his trade and all that he had was taken from him to recompense the one who said my father had stolen from him."

"Could this have been the Baron?" asked Mischka

"The Baron? Rumor flies through these streets and comes to these gates first of all. I know that the Baron, the man who styles himself the Baron of Egeria, has arrived in the city. But it was not he who destroyed my father all those years ago. No, the merchant who destroyed my father is dead himself now. But while he lived he was as great a thief as this northern Baron. I hear you are from the north, by your voice?"

"So we are," acknowledged Mischka. "Your parents lost their shop?"

"Yes, and their lives soon afterward, for my father could not live with shame and my mother could not live without my father. I was left to beg a living on the streets, and have done so all the years since."

"None would take you in and shelter you?" asked Ferenth.

"What friends I had turned away when this accusation was levied against us. There is no provision in the city for those without family and friends. So I like others live on the streets."

"Come," said Linar, "we must be on our way to find somewhere to lodge."

"It is true," agreed Mischka, "but I see it is not the Baron who has brought greed to Ravas."

"Oh no," cackled the beggar. "There is greed enough in every man's heart. It needs no one to bring it to them. What are you greedy for?" he shouted as Mischka, Ferenth and Linar left.

Mischka looked back. "Greedy? Perhaps I do grow greedy for justice."

"Justice!" mocked the beggar again. "You will never find justice. Justice is a dream of fools. There is poverty and there is wealth. There is power and there is impotence. But justice? That you'll never find."

Mischka, Ferenth and Linar continued on their way. At last they came to an inn by the east gate. When Mischka asked for a room, the innkeeper looked them up and down and said, "if you have gold, then you can stay."

"We have no gold," said Mischka.

"Then I have no room," replied the innkeeper.

"Wait," said Ferenth, "this I have." She took from around her neck a locket that Ferrar had given her many years before. "If we have not gold for you tomorrow, then you may keep this treasure."

"What use have I for such a trinket?" said the innkeeper. "If I need such things I can buy them for myself. Yet perhaps in earnest of the coppers you must give me, I'll take it. If you do not bring me coin tomorrow this locket I will keep"

"So be it," agreed Ferenth.

Mischka looked at her with troubled eyes.

"We must find a place to stay. And if this is the only place, then we must pay what the innkeeper asks," she said.

That night, they again went from tavern to tavern. In each one, the crowd gathered as Mischka told how the merchants had driven them from the inn, how each of them, the tailors and weavers, the tanners and fruit-sellers, would be driven from their homes. The crowd pressed coins into his hands and began to speak against the Baron. "What can we do? What can we do?"

"Tomorrow," said Mischka, "we must go to the council when they hear the Baron's request for trade. There we must show them his treachery."

"What do you know of the Baron?" mocked a scornful voice from the corner. "You say you are but newly come from the

Far Southern Lands, and that it's many years since you left Antar. What do you know of the Baron and who he is now?"

"Does a man change so much in ten years?"

"A man may." The speaker stood, to reveal himself as a thin, sharp-looking man, lines of bitterness etched in the corners of his mouth. "A man may change greatly in ten years, though rarely, I admit, for the better."

"And you know the Baron, then?"

"As I know all men. Whatever goodness they profess, yet when their deeds are known, they are they like everyone else, their goodness a sham and mockery."

"It may be so," Mischka admitted. "It may be that you cannot trust me. But you can trust what I say. You can trust that the power that this man wields led him to dispossess many. The power that this man wields enabled him to gather the wealth of others into his own hands. The wealth of this man is a great evil for Antar."

"All this may be true. But there are other powers in this city."

Everyone was silent, looking from Mischka to the man.

"What powers are these?" Mischka asked.

The man reached into his pocket and drew out a gold coin. "For this coin, could I not buy all these in the tavern, make them my slaves, if not in name yet in fact, to what I wish. You there!" he said, calling to a rough man leaning against the counter, "if I gave you this gold and told you to strike down this stranger, would you do it?"

"Without a second thought."

"Strike down his own mother, he would," shouted another.

"If gold can appeal so to one, is any so different? There are those with wealth in this city, wealth not as great as the Baron's yet enough for these purposes."

"Yet," replied Mischka, "when the wealth becomes so great, then itself it leads to thirst for greater power and to the belief that one stands beyond the law. This is what the Baron has fallen to. The greed in the man is not just for money, but for power."

The man tossed the gold coin on the counter. "Well, stranger, you may be right. It may be that we must be wary of the Baron. But for now, my friends, slake your thirst with this, and treat this stranger well."

He left the tavern and the innkeeper set ale after ale on the counter. The patrons of the tavern swarmed forward to drink it. As they were drinking, the door was pushed open and a harsh voice said, "Stay where you are, in the name of the prince of the city!" Into the tavern rushed a squad of soldiers from the city, and behind them a troupe of the Baron's men.

The patrons shouted "The Guards!" and leapt for the doors and window. The newcomers began to lay about them, with clubs. The innkeeper took Mischka, Ferenth and Linar and rushed them out the back door. "Go quickly, or the Guards will capture you."

From the hall there came the sound of blows and shouts and breaking tables. "Don't come back," the innkeeper said.

"For this I'm sorry," said Mischka.

"The gold the prince left will more than pay for this damage," replied the innkeeper.

Mischka, who had already begun to walk down the alley, turned back to the innkeeper. "Was that the prince?"

"He will walk these streets occasionally. We all know him, for he speaks well, and bears the burden of rule. Go now. And again, do not come back."

Mischka, Ferenth and Linar returned to the inn by the eastern gates. They gave the innkeeper their coins and received back Ferenth's locket.

"What do you think to do tomorrow, then?" asked Linar as they sat again over their meal.

"I will speak before the council, as all have a right to do. If they can be swayed by anything that can be said, they may refuse the Baron. We must try. For unless the Baron is stopped, none will be safe; he tries now to reach too far."

So the morning came. Mischka, Ferenth and Linar joined the crowd streaming toward the council hall. It was full to bursting, but room was made for Mischka, the crowd recognizing him from the night before. When the council leader asked: "Before we make our decision, is there any who would speak on this matter?" voices went up, shouting "The stranger! Let the stranger speak!"

Mischka strode forward.

"Members of the council. What you are considering is treachery to the people of this city. To grant this man what he asks places a heavy toll on the town. What you give him will turn your city into another Antar and you into his servants and vassals. He speaks to you now and his greed strikes an answering response in your hearts. But I tell you, his greed is greater than yours. He will swallow you up as you seek to swallow your neighbors."

"What is this person saying? We will listen no longer to this slander!" someone shouted.

"It is your own law I invoke, that any may speak in the council."

"You may speak in the council, but the council may choose not to listen!" said another.

"You may choose so. But if you do, then your fate you yourselves have sealed."

"Why should we listen to this stranger," said one of the council members who had come to the inn, rising in from his bench. "We ask that he be silenced by vote of the council. If the council wishes they may silence any who comes before them."

"What say you my friends?" said Mischka, turning to the crowd at the back of the council room. "Will you let these councilors deny you? Will you let these councilors betray you? Let the Baron..."

"Let the Baron what?" called out the Baron himself in a cold voice that instantly silenced the room. He rose from his chair next to the council table, his expression of reasonableness at odds with the anger in his eyes.

"What would you ask the Baron, stranger? What do you do here? You are not a member of this town, are you?"

"Neither are you. What right have you to be here, when you are from Antar?"

"The right of trade, bringing wealth to these cities of the south. I am the guest of the city."

"Then have I not a right to be here? Am I not welcome?" Mischka replied, turning again to the crowd.

But not one answered.

"My friends," said the Baron, "I don't know what this man has told you. But look at him. I am a merchant, like you. What I offer, I offer out of the hope of a reasonable profit for all of us. I offer to share the wealth I gather and to bring into your houses the comforts that I have in mine. You've heard stories of other cities and how the markets are full of gorgeous stuffs, of jewels and gold. This is what I offer you. Will you deny yourselves this opportunity? The wealth I offer you is your right. Why do deny yourselves this wealth?. What does the stranger fear, that he would deny you your own due?"

Eyes began to look with suspicion at Mischka and Ferenth. They and Linar stepped closer together.

"My friends, what do you know of this stranger? But you know me. I have more to lose than any of you. It is true I have wealth,. Yet someday any of you may have as much. I have stolen from no one. I am no brigand, no bandit. I am a merchant, as you are, though your trade be tailor or fruit-monger. The opportunity is there for each. If I have been successful, then so may you be, and will be, with what I offer. This town may be no less rich than Antar itself. We may call it Antar of the south. I beg you friends, let me help you, and do not fall into fear of things that are different, nor succumb to the wiles of this stranger. What do you say, my friends. Are you with me?"

"Yes! Yes! Do what the Baron says," shouted the crowd.

"Why would you trust this man?" said the Baron. "Why does he spend his time in the taverns, not here in the council, if he is the leader he says he is. he is one of the brigands himself!"

Now all eyes looked with hostility at Mischka. "I am no brigand," he said quietly, "nor vagabond. But traveled I have, throughout Egeria and the Far Southern Lands."

"If you have been to the Far Southern Lands, then why have you come back but to cause trouble? That is your profession, is it not? To cause trouble! We do not need your help. I say, he must leave this council. He is no citizen of this town. I pray you, citizens, drive him forth."

A roar rose from the crowd. Mischka could not make himself heard above it. There was no more to be said. Soldiers on each side of Mischka took his arms and forced him from the chamber while the crowd jeered and the Baron grinned coldly.

Chapter 25

Mischka Captured

There was nothing to be done. Returning to the inn, Mischka, Ferenth and Linar loaded the cart with their unsold wool and drove out the eastern gate.

"There was little benefit in that," said Linar.

"Little benefit," agreed Mischka. "Perhaps there is nothing one can do to resist this Baron."

"Would it be different in Antar?"

"No, it would be the same," said Mischka in a discouraged voice.

"Do not blame yourself," Ferenth urged. "Their ears were closed to you before you began."

"The Baron is a stronger opponent than I realized. If we're to have a hope of disentangling Egeria from his clutches then it won't be done here."

"But we will do it," said Ferenth. "What is this but a small set-back?"

"It is not the set-back that troubles me," Mischka replied. "Nor the rejection by the council and the citizens. It is not the fate of the city at the Baron's hands. It is that I was not able to sway them, that the strength that I thought I had in voice and song failed me so when put to the test."

"You ask a lot of yourself." Ferenth took his hand in hers. "There are times when one succeeds and times when one does not, when the words well up of their own accord and speak with the authority of the Lady and times when they do not. If that greater gift wasn't there this time, then another time it will come."

"Another time?" asked Mischka bitterly. "Who is to say this is for certain?"

"No one," replied Ferenth. "But we cannot ask so much just of ourselves. Do you remember Firfal's tale of the storymaker?"

Mischka was silent, thinking back over the long years to when he and Ferenth, her brother Ferrar, and the great singer and musician Firfal had traveled the roads of Egeria.

"What tale is this?" asked Linar.

"There were many stories that Firfal told," said Ferenth, "stories not of himself nor of us, but of other times and places, other people. One story he told was this: that long ago there were no cities, there were no roads, but each family lived with only one or two others in a small village in the forest or at the edge of the sea."

"In those days, Firfal said, there were no stories. The people lived from moment to moment, and if they remembered such things as that the sun would rise the next day, yet there was no sense of the past, nor of the future."

"Among those who lived in a village, he'd said, in one village deep in the forest, there was a boy named Walk-alone, who often would go by himself for long walks into the forest. When his parents and his friends asked him what he did, he would say 'I walk alone', and they would laugh and call him 'Walk-alone', one who walked by himself."

"One day, as Walk-alone was in the forest, gathering berries for the village, watching the squirrels that leapt from tree to tree and chattered at him in mock seriousness, he came to a fallen oak, one of the monarchs of the forest, that had been toppled the night before by a great wind that whipped and swirled through the forest. The wind had lifted the tree by the roots and tossed it on its side to lie broken on the forest floor.

"As Walk-alone approached, the leaves, withering now that the tree was no longer rooted in earth, quivered and shook. In the rustle of those leaves he heard a voice, and the voice said to him: 'Come closer, my son. Come closer and listen to me. I have something I must say to you.'"

"Walk-alone drew closer, for though he had often heard the wind in the trees during his long walks by himself, yet never had he known that a tree could speak to him so. Never had he heard its voice in the rustle of the leaves. 'My son,' said the tree, 'come close so I can talk to you.' The boy drew closer and he put his two hands on the trunk of the tree."

"Then, in the words that the tree spoke, he saw all that it had seen over the long years of its life: the rising and falling of the sun; the turn of the seasons around it; the changes in the forest as the older trees fell to the earth and rotted away, as young saplings that spring up. He saw the tree itself grow and change. He saw the squirrels that ran along its branches, and the foxes that dug at its roots, the boar that trampled the ground and the deer that grazed on sapling leaves. He saw the lion that crouched in the under-brush. He saw the people who walked beneath its branches."

"All this the tree showed him, all the long years of its life in the forest. Then at last, when the boy knew the story of the tree, it said to him, 'Take this bough of mine that I have dropped. Take it and shape it into a great bow; across this bow string tightly these root strands. Tell your people what I have told you. Let them hear my voice and the whisper of music in my branches.'"

"The boy took the bough and carried it back to the village. There he strung it with the root fibers of the tree, tightening them so that they sang when plucked. That night, as he sat by the fire in their lodge, he said to his family, 'Listen, listen to what the tree told me today.' As he plucked lightly at the strings of his harp, he told the stories the stories the tree had told to him of the life of the forest, of the people who had walked beneath its branches."

"When he was done, one across the fire, the oldest of the family said, 'Listen, as I tell you of when I was young.' The old man spoke of his parents, of running through the forest. Another spoke, and another. As they spoke, the boy played his harp and when all had spoken, he said, 'This I call the storymaker, for from its music comes the stories that we tell.'"

"So it is that in music, said Firfal then, we set aside who we are, and come back to who we once were and might have been. From that past and future come our stories, drawn from us by the music of the storymaker."

All three were silent when Ferenth had finished her story. Then Mischka said, "One day there will be a story in all of this that we now endure."

"The music will find it," Ferenth agreed.

"What will you do, Linar?" Mischka asked his brother.

"The only thing I can do. I must go to another city and hope that there I can sell my wool. Though I fear," he said, looking sadly at the bags of wool, "that I will not get half their worth."

"We bring you ill-luck, my brother."

"What luck brought you here is good luck. None can take from me the pleasure of having you and your family restored to me."

"You have welcomed us and I am grateful for the welcome you gave us. Ferenth, we must go to Antar."

"I will join you there," said Linar, "when once I have sold this wool."

"Stay out of this quarrel," urged Mischka. " It is none of yours."

"You are a better singer than you know. Having seen now the Baron extending his reach, I begin to fear that what you say of his greed reaching out even to our mountains is too true. I will join you in Antar. Where can I find you?"

"At Ferrar's house, the house of Amerach."

"I'll look for you there." Linar. He turned away with his cart and set out to the west.

Ferenth and Mischka traveled north, once again taking the smaller roads. They came, as evening fell, to a small farmstead.

The couple who lived there welcomed them. Ferenth and Mischka sat down together with the farmer and his wife for a quiet meal of bread and cheese and water, all that the farmer had to offer. They added what they could from their packs: a bit of fruit and some bread as well.

Mischka and Ferenth told the farmer and his wife of the troubles in the great city, then the farmer talked of the years they had lived on the land and of their struggles to make a living from the land. They told of the death of their son, of the marriage of their daughter, who was now gone with her husband to another farm. Mischka and Ferenth heard in the story of these farmers something of their own history, Mischka especially, the story of his own years as a shepherd far in the western mountains and the difficult life he had lived there as a boy.

At last, Mischka said the farmer: "My friend, for this welcome you've given us, and the dinner you've afforded, let us repay you at least in part by giving you something of our music."

"That would be welcome. It is rare that we have music in this house."

So Ferenth and Mischka sang for them a song that Mischka had written once in the Far Southern Lands, thinking of his home far in the western mountains, a song of longing for what he had left behind.

Though this place I have come to know
No stranger, but welcome,
Still another place I see.
Where once I was at home.

There in the mountains, there on the hills
My brother gathers autumn sheaves.
Only I wander, only I roam,
Driven like autumn leaves.

Over the sea lies my home,
Over the surging foam.
Where is the boat to carry me,
Carry me back home?

Over the sea, over the land,
Blows the restless wind.
Over the sea, over the land,
Dark clouds are driven.

There in the mountains, there on the hills
There the heart is free.
There one day, though distant far,
There one day I'll be.

In the middle of the night there was a pounding on the door and a great many voices shouting. "Let us in! Open this door!"

The farmer and his wife ran to the door, but it was broken in before they reached it. Mischka was pulled roughly from his blanket. As the farmer and his wife looked on in fear, Mischka was bound, gagged and carried out, Ferenth struck to the floor as she tried to follow.

When Ferenth awoke, she was lying on a pallet by the fire, a damp cloth laid on her head, the farmer and his wife standing anxiously and angrily by. "Why have they done this? Why have the soldiers come? Why have they broken into our house?"

"Where is Mischka?" asked Ferenth.

"They've taken him away. You must go! We want no trouble in our house.

"Where have they taken him?"

"We don't know! We know nothing! You must leave, now, tonight! It is an ill return for our hospitality, to bring the soldiers down on us. Who knows what they may do now? They can destroy us as quickly as hurricane or a hailstorm. You must be gone before they come again."

By dawn, Ferenth was on the road. She returned to Ravas, hoping there to catch some word of Mischka. When she arrived, the town was buzzing with news. The Baron's request had been granted. He would distribute to each citizen in town one gold piece, in earnest of the wealth which they would soon have. He was returning back to his own city of Antar and would soon be sending shipments of goods to Ravas.

All day Ferenth went from tavern to tavern, from shop to shop, asking if any had news of her husband. Some scorned her angrily, others smugly, still others with fear. Yet no one had word, no one had heard of what had happened to Mischka.

As evening came, she returned to the inn by the gate and again gave the innkeeper coins for the night. It was late when there was a knock on the door.

"Who is it?" she asked.

A familiar voice replied, "Open!"

Ferenth went to the door. There was the stranger they had met when they landed in Ravas from the Far Southern Lands.

"Come in," she said, relieved that there was someone in the city to whom she might turn.

"I had hoped to be here before the Baron arrived," said the stranger. "But his ships are fleeter than my horse and so the deed is done. Your husband is taken by the Baron's men."

"How do you know that?" asked Ferenth.

"I have friends here in the city, some few who tell me things that they would not tell to you. Your husband is in the prisons of the city, to please the Baron: a small price he demands to so capture a city."

"Can we free Mischka?"

"There are but two ways. We might free the city of Ravas from the Baron. But the city does not even know yet that it is a captive! The other is to enter the prison ourselves and seek to bring him out."

"Can we do this? Do you know where my husband is imprisoned? "

"I do. If you would free your husband, we must do it tonight."

"I am willing to try."

"Come then. If you will trust me, we have a chance."

"A chance?"

"It may be that we will also end up sharing his prison."

"And if we do not help him?"

"I do not know, but I expect he will stay there until he dies. Under the Baron's tender care, that will not take long."

"Then we must leave tonight," said Ferenth, determination and fearlessness in her voice. "I'll go with you and trust you."

They went down the stairs and to the streets. There was a single light burning in the prison near the council chambers as the stranger led them in. The jailer looked up in surprise.

"So, are you back again? Do you seek lodging again here with us?"

"What guests have you?"

"We have no one here!"

"We will see for ourselves," said the stranger, advancing on the warder.

The man was edging toward the door.

"I would not call for help," warned the stranger.

"And if I shout?"

"You will shout never again," replied the stranger, drawing his dagger. "Take us to the prisoner."

The jailer took the keys from the wall and led the way back to the cells. Ferenth ran forward as the warder opened the door. There was Mischka, unconscious still, his head bloodied.

"If you please," said the stranger to the warder, "step into this cell. I'm afraid we must ask you to be quiet." He tied the warder to the cell door, then took a handkerchief from his pocket and tied the gag round his mouth. Then the stranger lifted up Mischka and carried him from the cell.

"We must be careful or the Baron's soldiers will see us." He led the way through the streets to the inn where Mischka, Ferenth and Linar had stayed.

"We have need of a private exit," said the stranger to the innkeeper.

"Go through the gate," scowled the innkeeper.

"Those at the gate would be glad to see us, but that would not be wise. You must let us out the other way."

"Why should I do that?"

"None but the fugitive knows what it is to run."

The innkeeper nodded. The stranger lifted Mischka again and the innkeeper led them to the stable, where he pulled back a section of the stable wall. The stranger and Ferenth slipped into the night landscape beyond the city walls.

"Our thanks," said the stranger.

"I ask only that you tell no man."

"I promise this."

"Make no promises."

Nodding the stranger lifted Mischka and strode off into the darkness.

Chapter 26

The Stranger Unveils

The stranger led them to a small farm. There were several horses in the barn and he mounted one, taking Mischka in front of him, while Ferenth took a second and led a third.

They traveled in silence, the stranger leading across fields and along small paths. There was no sound of pursuit behind. When the sun came up, the stranger brought them to a small hut amid the pastures. He climbed down from his horse and carried Mischka into the hut, spreading a blanket on the dirt floor for Mischka to lie on. Mischka's face was drawn and white.

"They will be searching for us," said the stranger. "We must rest here for the day, then quickly make our way to some safe haven."

"Where is that?" asked Ferenth. "Where is safe from the Baron?"

"Where you are from, perhaps, had you not tried to oppose the Baron. But now, it is safe no longer. There is, it is said, a band of those the Baron has displaced. While his allies gather like vultures at the remains of a slaughter, those he has injured live far north, at the foot of the mountains."

"Our children are there in the north. We would not draw the wrath of the Baron upon them."

"Then you must come with me," said the stranger. "The leader of that band they call Dalvar. I am he."

"It is a name I know," replied Ferenth. "There are stories of Dalvar the thief."

"Some say he is a thief, but you see I am not," said Dalvar. "There are brigands and brigands, the Baron most of all. Those who have been robbed may turn to robbery, or they may turn to avenging themselves on those who have stolen from them. If I steal, it is from those who steal from me. We have banded together, not in thievery, but in protection and strategy. If you wish, you may join us."

"Mischka cannot travel far. Tell us how we can find you."

"Do you journey to Antar?"

"That is the heart of the Baron's power, and our home."

"When will you be there?"

"As autumn turns to winter."

"I will meet you there."

"How will you find us?"

"Do not worry. I will find you. Or seek me, if you wish, in the northern mountains. Go to Lea, and ask at the inn of the Blue Boar. They will direct you to our camp."

And so he left again.

Mischka lay for a long time in fever. At times he would cry out and say things like: "Rakal, no!" remembering, it must have been, the time when Rakal had killed another man on the island of the forest. Or he would call out "Ferenth, Ferenth, help me!" and she would take his hand and talk to him: "Mischka my love, Mischka, I'm here," moistening a cloth and wiping his forehead, damp with sweat.

When he was most agitated, she would sing to comfort Mischka and still his anxious, wandering thoughts. Then he'd lie quietly and sleep for a while, until again the fever gripped him and he cried out and tossed on the straw.

When morning came, Mischka seemed better, sleeping quietly. As Ferenth watched over him, the door of the hut was pushed open. She sprang to her feet. A man dressed in roughly sewn sheepskins stopped in the doorway, puzzled.

"You are not sheep," he said.

"No," said Ferenth laughing, "we are not sheep. We are strangers, seeking shelter here for the night."

"Only sheep stay here," argued the shepherd, laboriously trying to understand what these strangers were doing in his sheepfold.

"Not only sheep," said Ferenth patiently. "We are strangers, and my husband is sick."

"Sheep get sick."

"Sheep do get sick," agreed Ferenth, "but my husband is not a sheep. He doesn't know where he is nor who I am. I don't know what to do."

The shepherd came in and took some bread from his wallet and placed it in Ferenth's hands. Then he knelt down beside Mischka, his rough hands on Mischka's brow. "When sheep are sick, I give them water to drink."

"I've given him water to drink."

"I give them heal-grass."

"What is heal-grass?"

The shepherd reached into his pack. He pulled out a handful of dry leaves, wrapped in an old cloth. He opened the cloth carefully and held it out to Ferenth. "Heal-grass I give to the sheep when they are sick."

Ferenth took one of the leaves between her fingers and rubbed it carefully. It smelled strongly aromatic, like thyme or dittany.

"It grows on mountains, on rocks," said the shepherd. "It helps sheep."

"Perhaps it will help Mischka as well." Ferenth tasted it carefully. It had a sharp, bitter taste, like willow bark, which she knew would help with fever.

The shepherd rose to his feet. "I make a fire." He gathered some scraps of wood from the corner of the cottage and went outside and made a fire. He heated some water in a clay pot, put some of the leaves into the pot, and then held it out to Ferenth.

"He drinks this, like the sheep."

Ferenth took the pot from the shepherd, held it in her hands with a questioning look in her eyes.

"It makes him better," the shepherd insisted. "He drinks this."

Ferenth, gently lifting Mischka, held the clay pot to his lips. He gagged on the tea, coughing. Some of it dribbled out the corners of his mouth. But it seemed to Ferenth that he lay more quietly.

As the morning went on, the fever began to leave him. The shepherd squatted on his haunches next to Mischka. Twice more went out to heat another pot of water and brew a few more pinches of the herb. When at last evening came, the fever was gone and Mischka lay sleeping quietly.

"He gets well," said the shepherd. "He was sick, he gets well. Like sheep."

"He will get well," agreed Ferenth. The shepherd again took out bread and cheese and gave it to Ferenth, who dipped the bread into the broth and placed it on Mischka's lips. They moved slightly, drawing the broth from the bread, taking the soft crust and swallowing it. It was nearly an hour before Mischka had swallowed all of the piece of bread that Ferenth held.

Tears fell from Ferenth's eyes, splashing down onto her gown.

"Sheep do not cry," said the shepherd.

"No," said Ferenth. "People cry."

"Crying hurts."

"It does, but not always. Sometimes it heals. I am crying because I am glad that he is better."

The shepherd gazed at her with a puzzled expression. "Sheep don't cry."

"Truly?" Ferenth replied. "You must go to your sheep. I will stay here and rest."

The shepherd took his staff from the door. "You stay here tonight."

"We will stay here tonight," she agreed. Then she too fell asleep.

When morning came, Mischka opened his eyes. "Ferenth?" he said in a puzzled voice, as he saw her sitting beside him. "Where are we?" So Ferenth told him how she and Dalvar had rescued him.

For two days longer, Mischka and Ferenth stayed in the hut, while Mischka slowly grew stronger. Then they set forth once more, taking again the smaller lanes and the empty bridle paths.

It was two weeks before they came again to Linar's home.

Niëra came to the door with a glad look on her face. But she faltered when she saw that Linar was not with them and that Mischka, looked gray and weary.

"Come in, my brother," she said. "What has happened? Where is Linar?"

"The Baron has taken the southern cities," Mischka replied. "Linar couldn't sell his wool there. I in my singing incurred the wrath of the merchants and he had to travel farther to find another town where he could sell his wool."

"When will he come back?"

"He will meet us in Antar."

"In Antar?"

"Yes. We will meet him there."

"But why, why?" asked Niëra.

"Ferenth's house is still there."

"And by now it is empty and derelict. There is nothing there for you."

"Niëra," said Mischka, "do you remember long ago when I said I would follow Lutha, when I grieved so that Linar had left the house? You said then the time would come when I would find what I needed to do."

"Yes, I remember," replied Niëra, "and so you did, when you left to find Lutha and found Firfal instead, and your wife Ferenth."

"I have found something else which I now must do. I thought I came back to Egeria to be again Mischka the shepherd, to live again here in these mountains with you and Linar and our children."

"So you may."

"I cannot. I am called now to another duty. The wounds the Baron has given our family are not to be forgotten."

"Are you so obsessed by this Baron that you must go to Antar and again be exiled?"

"They will not exile me this time. This time the struggle has grown more serious, the Baron more greedy in his power. He no longer cares what those who oppose him think. He no longer hides his actions under the cloak of law. When he imprisoned me, I knew that I must find a way to bring him down, and find it not for Ferrar's sake, nor even for our own, but for the sake of all the people of Egeria."

"You need not do this for us, said Niëra. "You need not prove yourself against the Baron."

"It is truly not to prove myself. The struggle that was Ferrar's is now mine. I cannot sing unless I witness to the evil that this Baron does. I have no choice. I must go to Antar."

"But what of our children?"

"They must stay here," said Ferenth.

"I will not," insisted Misk. "I am as old now as my uncle was when he left. I will go with you."

"And I!" said Saschka.

"No!" Mischka replied "None of you will come with us. Saschka, you must stay here, and Misk too, in case the Baron's soldiers come here and seek to harm your mother."

So it was decided that Ferenth and Mischka would go alone. But Misk made other plans.

Chapter 27

The Brigand Citadel

While they prepared for their journey to Antar, Mischka inquired of the neighbors for any news of the brigand Dalvar. Many had heard of him; some had heard that his camp was in the northern mountains, not far from the village of Lea. So when Mischka and Ferenth set off on their journey, they decided to take a northern route that would bring them through Lea, and perhaps give them news of Dalvar.

On the first night after they left Niëra and their families, as Mischka and Ferenth made their camp, they heard a sound from beyond the light of the fire. "Who is there?" shouted Mischka. "Show yourself !"

"I come not in peace," said the young voice beyond the fire, "but it is not you I fight with." Into the light of the fire stepped Misk.

"What are you doing here?" demanded his uncle. "You must go back to your mother and family!"

"She knows I am here," replied Misk. "Saschka is there and will take care of the family. But this is my fight too. If my father goes to Antar to meet you, then I go too."

"And what of your family, if you are imprisoned, or worse?"

"My father will return to them. Saschka will protect them. Understand me, uncle, I will not be turned aside. You feel you must go. So do I."

"Why?" asked Ferenth. "Why would you embrace this struggle as your own?"

Misk looked at Ferenth and Mischka with eyes dark in the firelight. "I am not a singer, like you or Saschka. Neither am I a shepherd. I tend the flocks, but my thoughts lie beyond these mountains. If I dare not go to Antar because of a Baron, a Baron who drove you and my aunt Lutha from this country, then where can I go? How can I believe that this greed that you describe so well, that drives him so fiercely, will not bring him to these western hills?"

"So it may," agreed Mischka, "as I said to your father."

"And I believe you. So it may, and it is best to go and face the Baron now."

"Are you sure," asked Ferenth, "that it is not just restlessness that drives you in this?"

"Perhaps that plays a part. But it is only a part. I feel I must confront this Baron and to do what I can to stop him."

"If you feel this need," said Ferenth slowly, "and feel it so strongly, then how can we deny you? Your mother knows you have come?"

"She knows and has given me her blessing."

"We must let him come with us," Ferenth said to her husband. "If it is that important to him, as searching for your sister Lutha was important to you, then we have no right to keep him from our company."

Mischka held out his hand to his nephew. "Then closer than nephew you will be to me. As Saschka is my son, and Mirath my daughter, so you are my son as well."

"I have a father. But I am glad to be so a part of this family too."

Ferenth took his face in her hands and kissed him. "As a son you will be to me. What I can do to protect you, I will do."

"It is I who seek to protect you."

"Then together," said Ferenth seriously, "we may indeed defeat the Baron."

Together they continued to the village of Lea. There they left the road, striking off on smaller tracks, and came at last to the brigands' citadel.

As they approached it, they heard from all sides the calls of the watchmen, telling each the other of the arrival of these strangers. The citadel stood high above the pass, on a stony hill, looking down over the valley and out over the ridges to the lowlands and beyond. There was no sign of farms, or orchards, or more settled and gentle occupations. It was a grim bastion and a hard group of men and women who lived there.

The brigands, for so they called themselves in defiance of the name the Baron had given them, had all good cause to hate the Baron. Some, like Dalvar, had been landowners whom the Baron had dispossessed, others poor farmers, merchants or artisans who had been broken and impoverished by the Baron's greed or that of his followers.

Dalvar met them at the gate, his chief lieutenant beside him. Arne was a hard-faced man. He eyed the m dourly as they came in.

"Who are these strangers?" he demanded. "What need have we of them?

"The time has come for a new strategy," replied Dalvar. "They will help us to achieve it."

"A new strategy?" scoffed Arne. "And what may that be?"

"It has not helped us to prey on the minions of the Baron. We must find a way to confront the Baron himself."

"Confront the Baron!" said Arne scornfully. "He is surrounded by wealth and riches. You intend to wage war on him?"

"A weakness he must have. That weakness we must find, though I don't know yet what it may be."

"This at least I can tell you," Mischka said. "He grows sensitive to criticism and insult, to anything spoken against him."

"What good are words against such as him?" retorted Arne.

"They will goad him to action that will betray him to his downfall."

"This is you strategy? What we need, "argued Arne, "is an army to march on Antar and capture the Baron and all his men, to drive them forth as we were driven from our homes."

"Those who have suffered from the Baron must drive him forth," Mischka replied. "The people of Antar will join us."

"What a fool you are!" Arne mocked. "Our only hope is to attack the Baron, to bring him down with the force of our arms."

"We will not settle this here at the gate," said Dalvar. "We will talk more of this tomorrow, with all our comrades."

Misk was very like Ferrar in his earnestness and his anger. The more he learned of the Baron, the more hotly burned the flame of his determination. That night as they sat together in the rooms allotted to them, Misk spoke to Ferenth and his uncle.

"What will we do, to drive the Baron forth? After what he inflicted on you, uncle, how can you sit so idly by and not strive to see an army raised against him?"

"I do not believe that an army will answer."

"Why not?"

"Who would you attack?"

"The Baron and his minions."

"For what cause?"

"For their greed, their robbery, their brigandage, worse than any that these men have done."

"It was all done within the law. What we do must also be within the law. We will speak of this tomorrow. It gains us little good to speak of it tonight."

"It seems to do us little good to speak of it at all," replied Misk bitterly.

With morning came the summons to Dalvar's counsel chamber. Dalvar rose to speak first. "I bring before you two who have suffered no less than we. Mischka, tell us of the Baron."

"Ten years ago, my wife, my brother, my sister and her husband were driven forth from this land at the command of the Baron. We were to be cast adrift, and only the mercies of the captain who carried us were enough to spare us from that fate. We were shipwrecked on the island of the forest. My brother, sister and her husband are there still with their children."

"At last we came back to Thallhiar with our two children to find a way to oppose this Baron who has so oppressed the land. I spoke against him in the great southern city of Ravas. There was I captured and beaten and freed only by the help of your Dalvar and my wife. We go now to Antar, there to oppose the Baron in whatever way we may. We ask your help in this."

"Our help?" called out Arne. "Have you thought of a plan then, you who oppose our idea of armed rebellion?"

"Not yet a plan. But I have an idea. How is it that the Baron has taken from others what they have?"

"By the twists and turnings of the law. The sharpest of thieves are his lawyers , and the sharpest greed is his tool," said Dalvar.

"Then what we must do is turn the law against him."

"How can you do that?" asked an old man who stood and came forward. "You know me, Mischka. Riman I was, when I lived in Antar. For long years I opposed the Baron in council and at last I too escaped only with my life to find my way to these mountains, stripped of everything I had. How would you oppose him?"

"Were there no ways in which what he did could be opposed?" asked Mischka.

"One way," replied Riman, "and yet I had not the strength to do it. The council in Antar is his puppet now, and only by disbanding the council have you a hope of capturing the Baron. But the suffering is great and perhaps there is a way, for under pressure the council may still succumb and there is a chance perhaps that those who spoke against the Baron might gain courage if a leader were among them. I was not that leader."

"But you understand the law."

"Understand it I do. Little good it did me."

"When I was captured in Ravas," said Mischka, "I found the folly of relying on the crowd and found how easily words may be turned against one. It was the Baron himself who turned the council against me. Yet I believe there is a way for words to overcome the Baron and his minions. This is what I counsel."

"Words!" said Arne scornfully. "You counsel words, that we go to Antar and try to overcome the Baron with words?"

"How does the Baron conquer but by words," argued Mischka.

"Others have tried that, including your brother Ferrar," replied Riman.

"Yet he spoke in anger, and only as one. How many of those in council must fear the greed of the Baron now, have seen how the Baron betrays those who follow him? If we can but find enough of those to oppose the Baron, might we not have a chance?"

"What would you do? Pass a law against the Baron?" scoffed Arne.

"Not against the Baron, but perhaps against his wealth, for it is his wealth that is his power, his wealth and his words. Now he moves beyond wealth and words to deeds; that may be how we can yet trap him. If once the wrongs that are truly the Baron's are proved against him, if once we can find some who are willing to oppose him. then we may be able to stand against his strength."

"That you will never find," declared Arne. "What you seek to do is hopeless."

"Perhaps," Dalvar replied, "perhaps not. "I heard the stories of how this man swayed the people of Ravas. Their voices rose against the Baron until he himself twisted again their thoughts with his words. If anyone may win with words against the Baron, I think it is this man who may do so."

"You trust words against one whose words have robbed all of us?" said Arne. "We'll trust no one, none but ourselves and our arms."

"Are you content, then, to go on living in these caves?"

"No! The time has come for us to scour the country and raise an army against the Baron. We can then advance on Antar, take it by force and drive the Baron forth."

"You are the fool," Dalvar replied. "None of you has traveled this country as I. None of you knows the web the Baron has spun. I believe in these people. I will go with them if none else will. Who will stand with me?"

Only Riman came forward. "I am old already and have little left to lose. If any may win against the Baron, and if what I know may help them, then I will come. But I tell you, I have little hope that this will succeed."

"Little hope?" laughed Arne. "None, I tell you! Go your way, old man, and you, Dalvar. Your travels have softened your brain. We will see your corpse hanging from the walls of Antar, the crows are pecking out your eyes and the vultures clawing at your liver, when we arrive with an army at our back."

"Are you all in like mind to Arne?" Dalvar asked the rest of the men.

"We will not go to Antar!" they shouted. "We will build an army to fight the Baron!"

"So be it," said Dalvar. "Then we four will go alone."

That night Arne to the room allocated to Mischka and Ferenth. "You take from us our leader, our greatest hope of raising an army. If you go, you will die in Antar."

"Perhaps," replied Mischka. "What you seek to do is even more hopeless."

"There is no hope but swords. I will not waste my life in your folly," Arne retorted angrily and stormed from the chamber.

It wasn't until the next evening that Dalvar came to their rooms to tell them that all was prepared. They would leave the next morning. He sat down with them by the fire. In the flickering shadows, Dalvar's features were stern, set in lines of anger and bitterness.

"Arne is very angry that you are leaving." said Mischka. "He believes only you can raise the army he seeks. How did you come to be one of these brigands and their leader?"

"I lived," Dalvar replied, "in the city called Sallas, on the eastern shore of Egeria. We welcomed the Baron into our city, and believed his promises of wealth and good fortune. But all too soon it became clear that all the fortune was flowing to the Baron and not to us."

"I was a farmer, raising fruit and grain in the fields to the west of Sallas. These were the only wealth that I had. The Baron's man came to me and said that if I would trade to him alone, then he would pay me such a price. It was less than I earned when I sold them in the city of Sallas. 'What reason have I to accept this proposal of yours', I said to his man, 'when it takes gold from my pocket and bread from my mouth?'"

"'You no longer need not worry about carting your produce into Sallas,' the man replied. 'The lower price that the Baron offers you is simply recognizes that you have less cost than if you must sell them yourself.'"

"'And yet,' I said to him, 'I enjoy those trips to Sallas. Why should I deny myself that pleasure?'"

"'Because if you don't, you will have no grain to trade, and no fruits in your orchard.'"

"'What do you mean,' I asked."

"'Your fruits and grains are less expensive than those the Baron would sell. If you take our proposal, then your goods will be the Baron's and he will sell them at a good price. But if you do not, then he cannot afford to let your goods drive down the value of his.'"

"'You mean, because you bring your grains and fruits from Antar to here, and therefore have the greater costs cartage, you seek to drive me out of trade?'"

"'Not out of trade, just to more profitable trade.'"

"'The profits go to the Baron, not to me.'"

"'You will do well enough.'"

"'For now, perhaps. But what happens when the Baron seeks a lower price from me? What happens if I have bad year? What happens if the Baron decides he does not want my fruit and grain at all? No, this proposal is too fraught with risk for me. If I am to bargain away my life, it will not be for such poor recompense as this.'"

"'Be warned: you'll get no better recompense. Perhaps worse!'"

"But I turned the man from the door. 'Tell the Baron from me that I stay here and that I will trade in Sallas.'

"The next week on market day, I again loaded the wagon with apples and with my last harvest of wheat. I left behind my wife there at our house near the fields, for she had come to join me from our house in Sallas while the harvesting was going on. She had decided, since I went to Sallas only for the market day, not to return with me to the city, but to stay and enjoy the late summer weather."

"I'd gone halfway to Sallas, was passing through the he woods when three men stepped onto the path in front of me. 'Well,' one said who appeared to be the leader, tall, broad, with black beard and blacker heart, 'what have we here?'"

"'Nothing of value to you,' I replied."

"'If not to us, then why should it be of value to anyone?' The brigand stroke to my cart. 'See my friends, what this man has brought us.'"

"He reached in and took an apple, then threw an apple to each of his two comrades.

"'The apples are not for you, nor the grain. I must sell them in Sallas.' I said."

"'Only if you have them,' laughed the brigand. 'You will not have these for much longer. Your barrel is leaking."'

"The brigand leapt into the cart and tipped over the barrel, spilling the apples out into the road."

"I seized my cudgel, and leapt upon him. Before he could draw his knife I'd felled him to the ground. His two men set upon me. I wielded the cudgel as fast and as hard as I could. They danced around me, but first one I hit and then the other. I left them lying on the road."

"Were they dead?" asked Mischka.

"I hope they were," replied Dalvar. "I don't know. I went into Sallas, sold the grain and what remained of my applies, telling everyone of the brigands. People shook their heads and said how bold the brigands were getting. Then I drove home. The brigands were gone from the road when I drove past the place they had ambushed me. When I reached home my house was gone as well, my wife kidnapped."

"I tracked them for four days and at last caught up with them. But I was too late. They had sold my wife to the slavers. In the years since, I have not found her."

Chapter 28

Amerach's House

The five set forth the next morning: Riman, Dalvar, Mischka, Ferenth and Misk, who rode at first in silence, angry with his uncle.

At last he said "You are wrong, uncle, to make this choice."

"Wrong I may be," replied Mischka. "But I think it is our only hope. When we arrive in Antar, we'll open your uncle's house. Whatever the Baron has done, he will not have taken the house of Amerach. From there, we may begin our search for those who might speak against the Baron, find those on the council who might speak against him, and so plan our campaign against him."

"There is one thing you must do," said Riman. "If you are going to seek to win the council to your side, you must have something more than this beating to which the Baron subjected you, something more deadly than what he has yet essayed."

"The Baron is a man of anger, and greed and pride," said Mischka. "If we speak against him, he will do something that will betray him."

"You do not know what it is?" asked Riman.

"Not yet," said Mischka. "Yet something there will be."

When they reached Antar at last, they went straight to Ferrar's house. It was rundown, if not derelict, showing the signs of having had no master for long years. The door was barred and bolted; a board nailed across it.

"What can have happened," said Ferenth. "Where is Imrach's old servant who lived here before?"

"Perhaps he has died after all these years," said Riman. "While I have not been here to protect him, who knows what may have happened to him."

Mischka and Ferenth stepped back into the street, Misk with them, looking up and down the road. As they did so an old man came around the corner of the house. He limped and stumbled, but as he saw Ferenth he started and ran to her, saying "Young mistress, then you've come back at last!"

It was their old servant, Bethor, who lived now in a shed out behind the house. There was no money any longer to keep the house open. The Baron had tried to have it torn down; but confiscation of property of one of the families of the town, at least that the council would not agree to. So the house had been kept through all the long years while Mischka and Ferenth were away.

"Oh mistress," said the old man. "Sorry I am to see that you have come back to such a scene of poverty and degradation."

"My old friend," replied Ferenth, holding him tightly. "Is this what my family has brought you after all those years of taking care of us?"

"It is nothing. I have a garden and my chickens, out in the back."

"Chickens," laughed Ferenth, "in the house of Amerach?"

"Yes," said the old man, as tears welled from his eyes. "It's all that I could do. I sell the eggs to buy a bit of bread and the vegetables see me through the winter. I had to live somehow."

"I don't reproach you for that," said Ferenth gently. "If turning the house into a chicken roost has helped you survive, then who am I to complain\?"

"Not the house!" protested Bethor. "It's just an old shed out behind the house that I keep the chickens in. Come and see."

He led them to the rear of the house. For years he had tended the garden, tending it as he had in the long years of Imrach's wandering, looking for his brother's children. The garden was now given over to vegetables and fruits, carefully tended, and with every sign of being lovingly taken care of. With winter starting, the beds were tamped down, the carrots and potatoes and squash harvested. All that the old servant could he had set aside for the winter.

He led them into the house through the back door. A small fire burned in the fireplace in the kitchen, where the old man camped to cook his meals. Mischka and Ferenth walked through the house, which was draped in cobwebs, furniture covered in cloth.

"Oh mistress," said the old man, "I could not keep it clean. I am only one person."

"It is enough that you survived," replied Ferenth. "Now that we are here, we will open the house again. Here," she said, giving the old man a coin, "go and buy us some food for supper."

"Food I have enough," protested Bethor, "if you don't mind eggs."

"We don't mind eggs," said Mischka, laughing. "Prepare us what you will. Misk", he said, turning to the boy, "would give the Bethor a hand with the meal?"

"Certainly. Do we go and look for my father then?"

"After supper we will," replied Mischka.

"Who is that you look for?" asked the old man.

"My brother Linar," Mischka replied. "He was to meet us here in Antar."

"He hasn't come to the house."

"Then we must go and look for him. Perhaps he too found the door barred and is waiting for us arrive.

"Then the first thing we must do," Dalvar suggested, "is to unbar the door." He returned to the front, took a hammer and one by one pulled the boards. "People of Antar," he said, "the daughter of Amerach has returned to her house here in Antar, where she belongs."

A lean, thin man called out, "Should we rejoice at that? It is ten years she have been away. Antar has changed in those years."

"We understand that," said Mischka, joining Dalvar at the door. "But where once we were at home we will be at home again. The heirs of Amerach will stay in this house forever."

"A bold claim! I have lived here fifty years and more, and in all that time rarely have any of the house of Amerach lived here. But still, you are welcome."

"Thank you, friend," Mischka replied.

So the house of Amerach came to life once more. That night they went through all the taverns, spreading word, asking if Linar had arrived anywhere. But there was no news of him in the taverns and Misk was angry and worried that his father was not yet there.

"He may be on the road to Antar now," Mischka said, "or perhaps he has decided to turn back to the mountains of the west."

"If he told you he would come to Antar, "Misk replied, "then to Antar he will come. I hope that the Baron has done nothing to hurt him."

"It was I who spoke against the Baron in Ravas, I whom he beat and imprisoned. I do not think that Linar will have been attacked. It is a long way from the western cities and he would not leave his cart behind. I think we will yet hear from him and see him here."

"I hope you are right," was all Misk would say.

Mischka went down to the docks next day There they found Rakal, who grinned when he saw Mischka.

"Have you come to claim your passage to the Far Southern Lands?" he asked.

"Not yet, old friend. We are come to twist the Baron's tail."

"His teeth be sharp. You best beware his bite."

"We will try. Can you join us for dinner tonight?"

"I will come," Rakal agreed.

That night, as Mischka, Ferenth, Misk, Dalvar and Rakal sat at dinner in the old house, there came a knock on the door. Mischka rose and opened and there at the door was Riman.

"Come in, old friend," said Mischka.

"Come in indeed," agreed Dalvar. "What have you found, in your visiting of the council members today?"

"Many are the fears that the council members have now of the Baron," Riman replied, sitting down at the table with them. "I'm not the only one who was exiled. Those who remain are afraid of him. But you are free to go to the council tomorrow, for Ferenth is of the ruling families, and she cannot be denied her seat even though her brother was banished. They bid you come and speak with them."

"And the Baron?" asked Mischka.

"The Baron is there most days, too, or at least his henchmen. They rule the council now. It is the Baron who calls the tune and the council that dances to his piping."

Rakal leaned back in chair. "Our little group be a small army for starting a revolution. You cannot sail the ship before the wind faster than the wind blows. The wind be not yet against the Baron, nor behind you."

"I see that," agreed Dalvar. "Now that I see Antar, I see that we may need my comrades, to have their backs against ours."

"Summon them," said Mischka, "if they will come."

That night, as Mischka and Ferenth lay in bed, he said to her, "Are you troubled about returning home, my love, to this house and this city?"

"It is an ill omen that the house was boarded up as though the family had died. There is an air of death and desolation about the city now, an air of despair." She paused, then said, "I dreamed last night."

"Did you, my love?"

"I dreamed that I looked down on my body on this bed and that it was still and cold. You stood next to my body, weeping, but couldn't hear my voice as I called to you, nor feel my touch when I reached out to you." Ferenth began to cry.

Mischka took her in his arms. She was cold, chilled by the loss of all that she loved.

"It is just a dream," he said gently. "Do not worry, my love. You and I can never be parted."

But while Ferenth was shaken by sobs, Mischka felt in himself the chill of her dream.

The rumor spread quickly through the city that the heirs of Amerach were back in Antar, for Ferenth, the daughter of Amerach, was now his heir and therefore had the right to a seat on the council. The word spread quickly through the city. Mischka and Ferenth spent days and often nights too in conversations with those in the city. Misk grew angrier and angrier, and his words grew hotter and hotter.

One evening, as they sat at dinner, Rakal said to Misk. "My young firebrand, you be stirring the populace to some considerable extent. You have your uncle Ferrar's tongue!"

"Should I not speak against this fat, treacherous spider", asked Misk angrily.

"Speak against him if you will. All the sooner will you need of my fast ship to take you from Antar as once I took your uncle.

There be rumor at the docks that the Baron grows angry at these words you speak against him. Walk warily my friend, or the Baron soon will spread his net for you."

"What would it take," Mischka asked, "for the ship captains to refuse to carry the Baron's merchandise?"

"More than your family could afford. The Baron pays well."

"There are stories of captains whose cargoes he has stolen," suggested Dalvar.

"Stories there be. Only a fool trusts the Baron. But none refuses him."

"Then there's nothing there that we may use to bring him down?" asked Misk.

"There is only one thing that matters more to the Baron than his wealth," said Dalvar. "His arrogance and pride. Those who speak against him rarely escape injury. They may be subject first to the rigors of suits and then to exile or even assassination. None can prove this against the Baron, but all know it is his doing. None will oppose him out of courage. Perhaps they will oppose him out of fear."

"Will they not oppose him out of conscience?" asked Misk.

"Out of conscience?" Dalvar laughed. "The rich have no conscience."

"But If we speak against the Baron and arouse him against us, would he not again seek to stop us, as he did before?"

"So he might," agreed Dalvar.

"Would he not in doing so, in moving against one of the houses of Antar, threaten the councilors whose support he has relied on?"

"It might be."

"Then if we are the bait, perhaps there are those who will help to save us from the jaws of the wolf."

"This is a dangerous plan that you consider," said Dalvar

Mischka looked at Ferenth. "Should we do this?" he asked her. "There's no hope from the council members. All are afraid when they speak of the Baron. Now that his reach stretches across Egeria, even as far as Ravas, there is little that any can do against him."

"It is dangerous for you," replied Ferenth.

"There must be a place for me in this!" Misk said suddenly.

"Are you so anxious to draw the Baron's wrath to yourself? I will be the bait," Mischka replied.

"Not alone," Misk said.

So they began their campaign. Antar hummed with the anger of Mischka and the anger of the Baron, which grew hotter and hotter as the days passed. The council grew more and more nervous. Day after day the creatures of the Baron rose in the council chamber. "These slanders that are spoken of the Baron among the populace, these must stop," they said. "These trouble-makers must be stopped!"

"What slanders are these?" Ferenth replied from her seat in the council chamber. "State them, that we may discuss them." Rakal stood behind her, his brawny arms crossed against his chest, looked with amusement at the rest of the council.

But the followers of the Baron refused to say anything except "These slanders must stop". The Baron's face as he sat in council grew more thunderous and his anger hotter still.

Then one night, as Misk sat in a tavern railing against the Baron, the guards or Antar came in and seized him by the arm.

"You must come with us!" they said. They took him to the council prisons and next day brought him before the council.

"This is the enemy of the people!" shouted the Baron's men. "This is one of those who spread lies and sedition."

"What lies have they told?" demanded Ferenth, rising from her place.

"That the Baron is a thief. This is their slander."

"Did they indeed say that? Where are your witnesses?"

The Baron rose from his place. "He must be banished," he said. "He has spoken lies, committed treason against Antar."

"There is no law against the truth," Ferenth replied.

"I say, he shall not go free!" the Baron demanded coldly. "He is as bad as Ferrar who was banished. He too must be banished. And he too," continued the Baron, pointing to Mischka, "he too is one who speaks lies."

"You speak easily of lies. They come easily to your mouth," Mischka retorted. "Members of the council, you must release this boy. He has done nothing to warrant his arrest. You are guilty under the laws of Antar if you do not release him, guilty yourselves of this false arrest. Is that not so, Riman?"

Riman stood up from his council seat. "It is so, for those who arrest falsely are themselves guilty of crimes before the council, and bearing witness falsely is the greatest of these crimes. Lesser only than physical injury is this injury by lying."

"I will bring witnesses," said Mischka, "that what we speak against the Baron is true. Does not the Baron own half the property in Antar? Does not the Baron own the greatest merchant house in the port city? Does not the Baron own the slave market?"

At that, everyone fell silent. The slave trade was forbidden in Antar, and to deal in slaves was punishable by exile or death.

"That," said the Baron even more coldly, "is slander."

"Is it? I call the trader, Freyth, to this chamber."

The council members stared at Mischka with frightened eyes, for all knew that Freyth was a slave trader.

"He will not come," laughed the Baron

"He will come," Mischka replied. "Rakal, bring him."

Rakal left the hall and returned immediately, pushing before him the hawk-faced man who ten years before had spoken against Ferrar.

"Who are you?" demanded Mischka.

"I am Preyth, the slave trader."

"And who is the owner of your trade?"

Preyth licked his lips. "It is he," he said, nodding his head with a quick nervous gesture, "the Baron."

Chapter 29

Fighting in the Streets

The council erupted with angry shouts and cries. The Baron pointed at Freyth. "Take away this creature!"

"Does anyone who speaks against you tell lies?" shouted Mischka.

"You will never prove this creature's lies," shouted the Baron in return.

"Is this so? There is one way to prove it. members of the council, in so serious a charge, we must see the records of the Baron."

All faces turned to the Baron, his face was red with anger.

"You dare!" said the Baron even more coldly. "You dare to believe this man's word against mine?"

"No man's word is enough," declared Mischka, "when the charge is so grave."

"What proof does anyone need that I do not engage in so heinous a crime as slavery?" demanded the Baron. "You must have better cause than the word of a self-condemned criminal before you expect that I will let you see the workings of my house and business."

"Cause enough we have," shouted Mischka. "If any man will swear against you, that is cause enough. In so grave a charge, no man may be trusted save by the truth of his records."

"I will not listen to this slander any longer! This council dare not so move against me." The Baron cast a scornful look around the chamber and then walked out, followed by many of those in the chamber.

"Members of the council," said Ferenth calmly, her voice cutting through the uproar in the chamber. "It is your right and your duty to pursue this charge, for so grave a crime cannot be left unexplored."

The council leader rose from his seat. "Fellow councilors, if there is a chance that this charge is true, then your duty is clear before you. As it was when you banished Ferrar, so you must find out the truth of this. I put it to the council that we must examine the Baron's records."

"Examine his records?" spoke one of the Baron's followers. "That is beyond the scope of this council, for there will be nothing there to find."

The Baron's men looked from one to another, exchanging grins.

"Nonetheless, it is the duty of the council," replied the council leader, who called for the vote. To Mischka's surprise, the vote passed and a commission was appointed to inspect the Baron's records.

"One more thing," said Ferenth. "This matter has nothing to do with my nephew's arrest. There is no charge against him that has been proven. He must be released."

Again the council leader looked from member to member. "No slander has been proven. But bear in mind," he said to Misk, "that next time the council may not be so lenient. Guard your tongue!"

Mischka, Ferenth and Misk returned to their home. No sooner had they gone inside than there was a knock on the door.

"I have come from the Baron," said the man who stood there.

"We'll offer you neither hospitality nor welcome," replied Mischka.

"I seek neither. I have only a message for you: the Baron wishes to speak to you."

"So he may anytime in council."

"That is not enough. You must come with me"

"One thing the fly knows who escapes from the spider's web, is not to blunder again so quickly into his snares. If the Baron wishes to speak with us, let him come here."

"You grow proud in your folly! Pride and folly will destroy you."

"It is not pride, but caution. I know the Baron, his violence and lawlessness."

"I will tell the Baron what you have said. He will be angry that you rejected his invitation."

That night, as the friends sat at dinner, the door was thrust open. Two armed men entered, followed by the Baron.

"You trouble me," he said. "This may not be. I tell you, if you do not leave Antar, I will crush you like the insects you are."

"We will not leave," Mischka replied. "If you seek to crush me, the very weight that you wield will rebound against you. You will be brought down, and destroyed."

"You think to prove this charge against me?" laughed the Baron harshly. "What do you think you can prove? That I have traded in slaves? What do think that these councilors will find? You are a fool and know nothing of the ways of power."

"Perhaps. But I know the truth of this and I will find a way to prove it."

"You will prove nothing. None will confess, no record will be found. Then I will crush you and your house."

"If you do, you will be caught in the destruction no less than we."

"I have never failed before. I will not fail in this." The Baron turned and stalked from the room. In silence the friends looked at each other.

"What now?" asked Ferenth.

"We must again take to the streets," Dalvar replied.

So they began again and Mischka's songs against the Baron were sung throughout the town. Tensions grew; arguments broke out in the council meetings. The commission could find nothing against the Baron in the records he provided; Mischka's supporters condemned the commission for being duped by the Baron.

As Mischka, Ferenth, Dalvar, Rakal and Misk sat before the fire one night, they heard a rumble in the street outside and then again a knock on the door. Dalvar and Rakal drew their knives as Mischka walked to the door.

"Will you let me in, brother?" asked the tall figure in the doorway.

"Linar!" shouted Mischka.

"Father," shouted Misk as he ran to the door.

It was Linar indeed whom Mischka led in, a Linar strong and well, though weary from long travel.

"How are you, my brother? Was your journey successful?" asked Mischka.

"The wool I sold and I have with me the silver that I got for it. Small enough; every city now feels the pinch of the Baron's greed. Many were the tolls I had to pay."

"Were you troubled on the road here by thieves or brigands?" asked Ferenth.

"Only by the Baron's soldiers, who are become little better than thieves. I brought the cart too, though there were many laughing looks as I trundled it through the streets of Antar. But it may prove of use for something, at least to carry us back to our holdings in the west, if we do not succeed here."

"We will succeed," declared Misk. "Now that you are here we are sure to succeed. Come in and tell us what has happened."

Linar looked at Dalvar. "So stranger, we meet again."

"So we do. My name I can give you now. I am Dalvar, an ally of your brother."

"I have heard of Dalvar the brigand."

"No more a brigand than you and I," replied Mischka.

"You surround yourself with a strange company," Linar said, shaking his head. "Ferenth, are you here too?"

"I am, as you see," she laughed, hugging her brother-in-law. "This is my home, now that Ferrar is here no longer; I am the one who must speak in council."

"And the children?"

"Safe with Niëra, except for your son, who would not stay behind."

"This is my fight too, father," said Misk. "Mother said I could come. My sisters and cousins are still back at the holding, safe there."

"Niëra is strong and brave," Linar replied. "But who guards our flocks from the wolves?"

"Saschka has become a good shepherd," Misk declared.

"Linar," Ferenth said to him, "if you feel you must return home without delay, then do so. I do not wish to keep you here against your will."

"While I have supper, tell me your plans. For the fight against the Baron is my fight too. If I can help here, then I must stay and do what I can."

Mischka led his brother to the table and all during the meal they talked of what had happened, of the council and of what chance there might be to defeat the Baron.

Antar continued to seethe with tension. But still Dalvar counseled patience. "Wait until my men get here."

So in council Ferenth was quiet, speaking occasionally against the depredations of the Baron when she could, but not yet challenging him further. Riman met with the council members to persuade them to oppose the Baron. But though everyone feared a crisis and saw that it was coming, none was ready to step forward.

On the streets of the city the tension between the two factions grew stronger. The supporters of the revolution began to wear blue armbands to show their support for the house of Amerach, whose banner was blue and white. Then the supporters of the Baron began to wear their armbands, and theirs were red, for the Baron's banner was red and gold.

One day, as Mischka and Dalvar walked the streets, he heard a sudden outcry in the streets behind him. A group of men with blue armbands and a group with red confronted each other.

The leader of the red-ribboned faction was a man that Mischka knew well from the times in the taverns. One of the Baron's supporters, named Haras, he'd often heckled Mischka. At times fights had broken out within the taverns, though usually quelled by the innkeepers and their men. But here, one of Mischka's own friends had met Haras in the streets, and the two groups faced each other with words and weapons.

"So the servants of the Baron walk on two feet, after all!" mocked Tenar, the leader of the blue-ribboned faction.

"Walk on two feet, yes, and have two hands free still to deal with those who speak slightingly of us!"

"Slightingly? Do we speak slightingly of you? We call you snakes, we call you spiders. But these are all honorable names. Who is wiser than a serpent? Who more industrious than a spider? We say that you have all the wealth of Antar in your pockets. Is that not honorable, that you should be known by all to be so rich and your pockets so well lined?"

"What we have we have earned!"

"Not for what you have earned, only for the manner in which you gained it. We ourselves strive to become better than we are. We are interested in virtue and right, and so are you. But our interest in virtue is to acquire it, while yours is to suppress it. Our interest in the right is to serve it, while yours is to suppress and subvert it."

"Your speak slander!" shouted Haras. "You are nothing but robbers, condemning those who have more than you."

"We don't condemn those who have more than us, only those who seek to take from us all that we have. Is the Baron so great a man, Is his life longer than ours? Are his friends more true, or his foes less fierce?"

"What foes the Baron has count for nothing," mocked Haras.

"In the Baron's eyes, perhaps in yours. But in our own eyes, we are true enough and worth as much as the Baron. Strip him of his rich clothes and would he not be like any man? Strip him of his followers, and would he not be weak?"

"The Baron is shrewd and clever. It is not just his riches that make him the man he is."

"On this we agree. None is shrewder than he or more clever for his own good. Yet is it not reasonable to ask that those who lead be as shrewd for the good of all as for their own? That instead of taking what wealth they have and keeping it for themselves, to share it among those who for whatever reason are not as shrewd as he?"

"You scum of the gutters, why should the Baron share wealth with you? What do you offer Antar?"

"What does the Baron offer?"

"Wise government, care for everyone..."

"Care, yes. He cares to acquire everything!"

Haras' followers were muttering among themselves. Haras silenced them with a sharp movement of his fist. "You are like your leader, the singer. You know nothing but lies and words. If you are so sure of the truth of what you say, then show it by your actions."

"Actions? You mean by fist and knife?"

"By fist and knife and cudgel," replied Haras as he drew his dagger from its sheath and whipped it at Tenar, who stumbled back into his followers. One leapt forward with a cudgel and in a moment both groups were fighting fiercely. Then Dalvar leapt forward. He grabbed the two leaders and pulled them apart. He thrust them at their followers, who fell back at the advent of this tall and angry man.

"Go to your homes, boys," he said, scornfully. "The game is over for today.. Go home before the watch comes and takes you all. Go home!"

He turned away, and the two groups broke apart. But Haras looked at Dalvar and Mischka with hatred in his eyes. "We will meet again," he growled. "When we do, look to your knife."

Three nights later, as Mischka, Ferenth, Misk and Linar were coming home from singing at one of the taverns, they were set upon by four figures with cudgels and knives. One struck Ferenth on the head and knocked her to the stones, while the others engaged Mischka, Misk and Linar. A glancing blow from one of the cudgels struck Mischka on the temple and he too fell to the ground. But Linar and Misk grabbed the cudgels and laid about them so fiercely that the attackers fled.

Chapter 30

Exile

The next day, the rumor spread through the town that the singer and council member Ferenth was dead, struck down by marauders. When Mischka entered the council chamber, his head still swathed in bandage, his face gray and set, the council members looked at him with fear in their eyes. The Baron's men looked at the Baron warily as Mischka walked forward to the front of the council chamber. Rakal leaned against the chamber door, which he had closed behind them.

"I accuse the Baron," declared Mischka, his voice ringing in the council chamber, "of the attempted murder of my wife, Ferenth, daughter of Amerach and member of this council."

"You have no voice here," said one of the Baron's men. "Leave this chamber and do not inflict these lies and slanders on us any longer."

"I accuse the Baron," Mischka repeated, his voice now rising in anger and power. He pointed his finger at the Baron, who sat stonily in his chair, "In such an accusation of injury against a fellow council member, the Baron must answer. I demand that this council indict the Baron and force him to answer this charge of murder attempted."

There was a shocked silence in the council chamber. Then the Baron stood.

"You have no proof that I was responsible for any attack on your wife, whatever the slanders you have said about me."

"I have proof enough."

"am not a violent man. I am not one who would stoop to violence."

"Rakal," said Mischka to his friend, "bring in the four witnesses."

Rakal thrust open the doors of the council chamber and beckoned to someone who waited outside. Dalvar came in, followed by four men with ropes bound about their wrists and hoods over their heads. Behind them were men in the uniforms of the city guards.

"Remove their hoods," said Mischka and Dalvar did so, to reveal four members of Dalvar's own brigands. Chief among them was Arne, who looked with hate equally at Dalvar and the Baron.

"What do these creatures have to do with me?" demanded the Baron.

"These creatures," replied Mischka, "are your creatures, and the death they intended is on your head. To seek the life of another is to lose all that you have. You must spend your life in payment for what you done."

"There is no proof of this," said the Baron indifferently. "You speak of payment, when I am innocent of what you charge."

"Members of the council," declared Mischka, "last night as my wife, my brother and I walked these streets, we were set upon by these four men."

"How do you know it was these four?" asked the Baron scornfully.

"Speak," said Dalvar to Arne.

"It was me, and I would do it as soon again." The other three prisoners looked in horror at their leader. "I despise you all. If I could, I'd destroy everyone in this room, the Baron and his enemies alike."

"You confess that you attempted to kill this man and his wife?" asked the leader of the council.

"I said I did, you fool," replied Arne.

"But why?" called out one of the council members.

"Because I was paid, that's why. The Baron paid me well. I would have done it, too, if it hadn't been for these weaklings I brought with me."

"This man is suborned," shouted one of the Baron's men.

"I do not lie," shouted Arne back at him. "I have the silver he paid us to do this deed."

"It's a lie!" shouted the Baron. "This is a tissue of lies!"

"This is no lie," repeated Arne. "I would have sooner struck down the Baron; but silver is silver and I hated the singer only a little less than the Baron himself."

"Silence, you dog!" said the Baron, striding forward and striking him. "This is no proper trial, my lords of the council. What right has this man to speak against me. He is no citizen."

"In this, he need not be a citizen," said the leader of the council. "In this, he need only be a witness."

"He is a liar," shouted the Baron.

"There are no lies here," replied Mischka, "but the lies you speak. You have brought my wife to the threshold of death. You are a wolf that ravages all of Egeria. Members of the council, do you need any more proof of the guilt of this man?"

Council members looked still uneasily at each other. The leader of the council stood and said: "A grave charge has been brought against one of our members. We must consider this question."

"You will not," said the Baron, turning to face the rest of the council. "You are nothing but puppets. Those who think otherwise will not leave this council room alive. I am the ruler of Antar, not you. Those who oppose me shall die. This council is dismissed. I have no need of you."

"Guards!" shouted the Baron. "Take these murderers to the prison. As for these councilors, escort them to their homes, for as long as I choose to let them stay there."

The guards did not move. Dalvar stepped forward from the door.

"These are not your men, but mine."

Dalvar's men took the Baron's arms.

"You have spoken treason in the hearing of all the council," Mischka said. "There is no need for further proof. Out of your own mouth, you has convicted yourself. Councilors, is this Baron to be banished or not? Treason has been spoken; you yourselves have voted banishment against those who speak treason."

The council members looked at each other and at the hard-faced men who stood around the council walls.

"What is your decision?" asked the leader of the council.

One after another, the council members said, "Banish him," they said, one after another, all but the Baron's men.

"It is the decision of the council that the Baron be banished. And for the murder that he has attempted to commit, this decision may not be revoked," said the council leader. "His wealth is to be stripped from him. He is exiled to the island of Baille, where we may guard him. So the council decides."

"I will break you all!" shouted the Baron. "I will break you all!" In the violence of his anger, he tore himself from the men who held him and threw himself upon Linar, who still stood among the guards at the door. But Linar knocked him to the floor. "You are lucky I do not have a staff in my hands now, snake," he said, standing over the Baron. "A serpent of such venom, I would crush it beneath my heel. You will not escape. You will kill and poison no longer."

Dalvar's men took the Baron and bore him out of the chamber to the docks of Antar, where Rakal's ship road at anchor. Rakal ferried the Baron to the small island beyond the harbor of Antar, there to remain for the rest of his life..

But Ferenth still lay unmoving, unspeaking. Mischka sent to Niëra, asking her to have Saschka and Mirath join him in Antar. Within two weeks they had arrived, and Saschka took his place on the city council, the head of the house of Amerach while Ferenth was ill. With him was Silvren, whom all acknowledged would become his wife. Misk and Linar too remained in the house in Antar.

Day by day Ferenth grew weaker. Mischka sent for the wise women and the doctors of the city. Then came and shook their heads. One prescribed this syrup, another that. One wished to bleed her, another to care her to the temple of the Lady.

But when Seneren, the best of them call, came to Ferenth's bedside, he gently touched the livid bruise on her skull that still showed where the cudgel had hit her. Then he turned to Mischka and said, "There is nothing I can do. The blood lies beneath the shattered bone. She will die soon."

"Can nothing be done? You must save her!" Mischka said in desperation, holding the doctor by the shoulders and shouting angrily into his face. "I don't care what you do, you must save her!"

"This is not a Baron you can defeat. It is Death herself who stands by the bed of your wife to welcomes her with gentle arms. Turn and look upon your wife, Mischka. Look upon her! You must see the truth of what I say."

Mischka saw with despair how Ferenth had withdrawn from life. In the imminence of her death, the flesh had shrunk from her bones. Yet she was infinitely precious, indescribably beautiful.

The doctor rested his hand on Mischka's shoulder. "I am sorry," he said, and left.

Mischka knelt by the bed. He took Ferenth's hand in his. "My love, if you die, I shall die. I have no voice without your voice. I have no life without your life. I have no joy without your joy. Do not leave me, beloved."

He wept and wept. Night came and still Mischka was there. "Go to bed," he said to Saschka and Silvren, Misk and Mirath.. "I must stay and watch."

"You must rest too," insisted Linar.

"I will not leave her. Give us this time alone."

In the early morning hours, as the candle flickered and failed, Mischka raised his eyes from Ferenth's face. Across the bed from him he saw a woman dressed all in white, her face calm and beautiful

"It is time. Come, child. Come with me." Ferenth opened her eyes and rose from the bed. As she turned for a last look at Mischka there was deep love and joy in her face.

"Do not despair my beloved," she said to him. "I promise you, we will meet again. I promise you, beloved, that this separation will not be forever."

Mischka couldn't move. He looked up at her, at the beauty that shown in the figure before him. She was the woman he had loved, the girl he had known, the mother of their children. All the times of her life were at once in her face and form. All the times that she didn't live to see were there as well, the serene old age that they had hoped to share.

Then she turned and the beautiful woman led her away, down a path that Mischka could not follow. It seemed to Mischka that the two figures walked a great distance, then at a last turning of the road, Ferenth looked back once again. In her eyes Mischka saw such joy that he could hardly breathe for the love he felt, the longing and the terrible sorrow.

When Saschka and Misk came in the next morning, they found him still kneeling by the bed, his head pillowed on Ferenth's cold hand. Gently they lifted him up. They placed him in bed and he slept all that day and the next while the news went through the town that Ferenth had died and that her son Saschka was now the head of the house of Amerach.

It was some two weeks later than Linar and Misk came to Mischka as he sat out in the garden. "My brother," said Linar, "it is time for us to return to Niëra. She must be told of these events."

"Yes, you must go. For your help in all these things, all Antar must thank you."

"Will you be well?"

"I am well. You will come back for Saschka's wedding?"

"We will all come," Linar promised. Then he left the garden and Misk was alone with his uncle.

"You return to the sheepfold?" asked Mischka.

"I have no place in these politics," replied his nephew. "I have learned that I am my father's son."

"That is all anyone could wish for you. But you are also are my son too, and Ferenth's. As she loved you, so I love you."

Misk knelt down by his uncle, taking him in his arms, then rose again to stand before him. "I must go," he said.

"Yes, you must," Mischka replied. "There is much to do back at the holding."

"Is there any message you wish me to take to my mother?"

"Only this: Tell Niëra that Linar my brother and Mischka her son are the bravest and truest men in all of Egeria."

So Misk and Linar left, returning back to the west. That night, as the sun settled to the western mountains and the stars came out over Antar, Mischka remembered the song that he and Ferenth had sung so many times together and wept again in love for her and in sorrow for what he had lost.

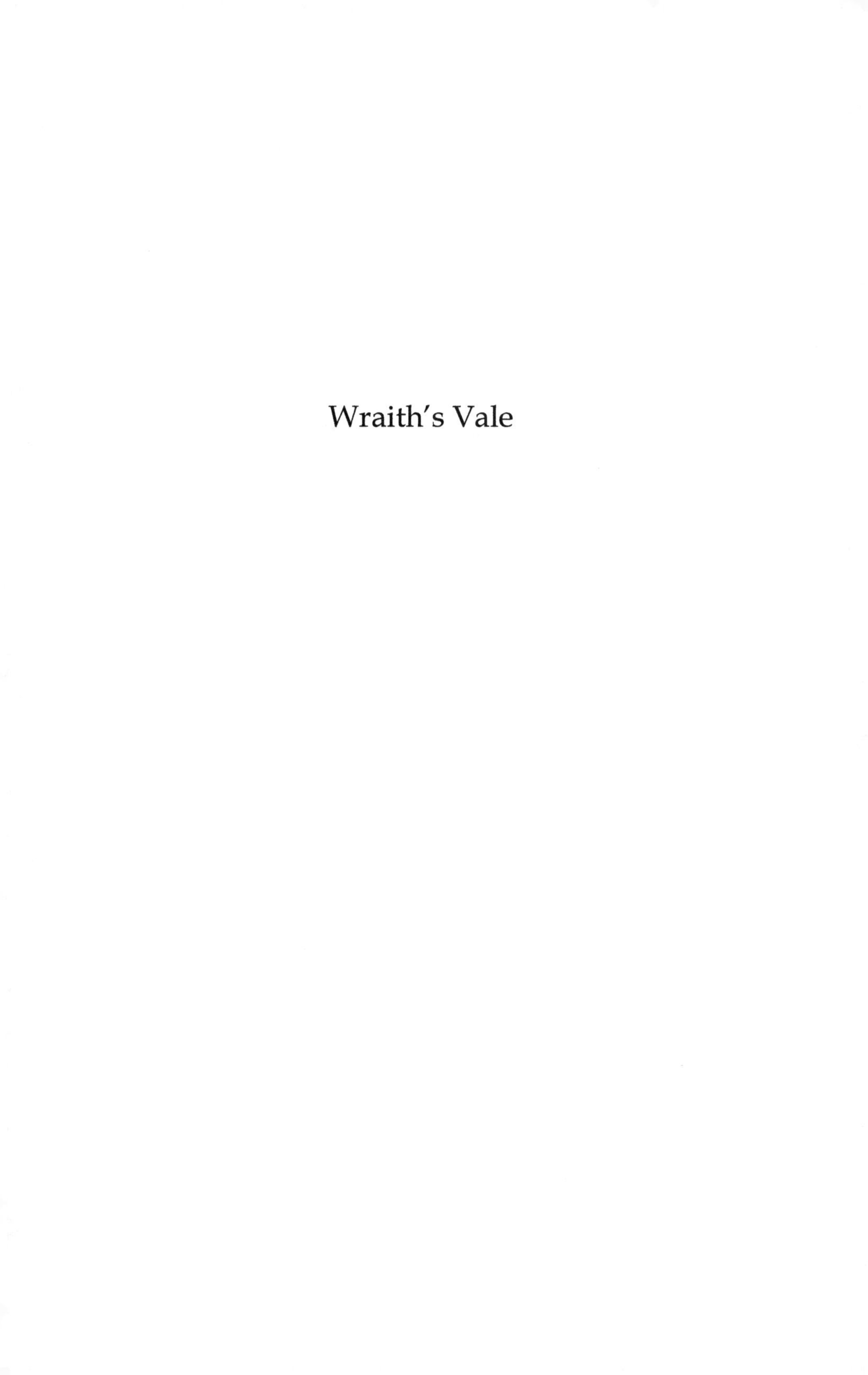

Wraith's Vale

I'll walk with you where night is long
And stars are dim, stayed in their course.
Where memory fades to emptiness,
I'll walk with you, follow the thread
Of love to find my way again.

Chapter 31

Mischka's Decision

In the aftermath of the banishment of the Baron, all Antar was in turmoil. Many of those on the council gave up their places, and a new set of councilors took their seats, those with no ties to the Baron, with long-standing interest in the welfare of Egeria. The Baron's estates were confiscated throughout Egeria and were distributed back to those from whom they had been taken. Dalvar's men were brought back from the mountain citadel and many of those were settled on the Baron's one-time estates. There was a feeling of liberation and optimism in Egeria.

Saschka took the leadership of the house in Antar and sat on the council as one of the younger members. Mischka was silent and withdrawn; as the days went by, the loss of Ferenth grew greater for him, not less. It was as though half of himself had been ripped away. He no longer sang, hardly even spoke. When he did speak, it was as though his mind were far away, on far distant things.

Saschka grew increasingly worried about him, as did Dalvar, who had stayed on in Antar at Mischka's house. At times he would go down to the dockyards to talk with Rakal about their old friend.

"What he needs," said the captain, "is to get away from here. I'll take him off to the island of the forest again, and there he can look up his sister."

"Or perhaps," Dalvar suggested, "I should take him back to the mountains of the west so that he could be with his brother and sister-in-law there."

They couldn't decide, and when Dalvar raised the subject with Mischka he just shook his head and said he had no desire to leave. So the days slipped on and fall turned to winter. Though early yet for snow, there was a chill bite in the wind at night and at times the voices of the winds that rounded the corners of

Amerach's house sounded like the voices of the wraiths in the vale that Mischka had escaped so many years before.

It was on one of those evenings, when the wind moaned around the house, tapping at the casement windows as though to be let in out of the cold, that Mischka first raised the question of traveling back to Wraith's Vale.

"To Wraith's Vale?" said Saschka, looking with troubled eyes at his father. "What would you seek there? Both you and Mother said that you barely escaped with your lives last time, and that Ferrar might not have had it not been for your singing."

"I seek word of your mother. If any might know, I think it might be the wraiths who are in the vale, or she might be among them, become one of them."

"Become one of the wraiths?" aske4d Saschka.

"You know the story of them," Mischka replied, "how those who die in grief or anger become wraiths and find their way to that vale. I fear that because your mother died in violence perhaps she is there with them."

"But they are treacherous," Saschka objected. "No one knows if they are indeed the lingering spirits of those who have died or something else that takes the form of those whose faces they have perceived in our thoughts."

"Even so. If her face can appear before me once more then it is worth whatever danger there might be."

Come my friend," said Dalvar, "this is morbid musing. What you need is to go and see Linar and Niëra. And if you want to go by way of Wraith's Vale, then I'll go with you there. But let our goal be your brother's; let our goal be the living, not the dead."

"For whatever reason we go, I will go to Wraith's Vale."

"Father, this is folly. If she is there, what would you do?"

"What I can. There is a story of at least one man who saved his wife from Wraith's Vale. His name was Plerach, or so Firfal said. Plerach's wife, Elena, had died in childbirth, and her child with her; distraught by her death, Plerach left his house and eventually found his way to Wraith's Vale. As he entered the vale, there among the faces to greet him was that of his wife."

"'Come, my wife,' he said, 'come and let us be again together.' He reached out his arms to her, and as he did the wraith stepped forward and placed her arms about him and he died."

"Do you seek your death?" asked his son. "Is that why you go Wraith's Vale, to embrace one who has died?"

"Better that than this half of a life," replied Mischka. "What is there before me, now that Ferenth is dead? Our voices were as one and our thoughts too, our dreams."

"What of us, father?" asked Mirath.

"You no longer have need of me. Saschka is an important member of the council and has duties here now. He and your cousins will care for you."

"Your place is with us," said Saschka.

"My place? Is it among the western mountains with my brother? Here with you? On the island of the forest with my sister? Or in the valley of the wraiths with my wife? Tell me, Saschka my son, where is the place I belong, whose life is joined to so many places?"

"As Dalvar says, Father, if you feel you must go back to where you grew up then we will come with you. We do not need to be here in Antar, do we, Silvren?"

"No, I would gladly go back and be with your cousins again," his betrothed replied.

"I, too," agreed Misk. "Yet I do think there is need for us here."

"So there is," said Mischka. "Though all are happy now and speak with praise of what we've done, yet the Baron's greed is a disease that can be hindered but never cured. He was not alone in his depredations. Now that he is gone, although the vultures are driven off for a time, yet they will come back. Then you must guard the city."

"You are better at that than I," Saschka protested. "It was you who spoke in the council and brought the Baron down."

"My work is done. Your voice is as strong as mine, and your vision clearer. No my son, the time has come to leave, whatever else I must do. And Dalvar, old friend, if you are of a mind to journey with me then I welcome your company. But I do not expect to see my brother and sister again."

"Rakal is waiting at the dock and would gladly take us to the island of the forest," said Dalvar. "Perhaps on the sea you might rediscover that same zest for life that once you had."

"No," Mischka replied. "When I left the island of the forest, I thought never to return. If Rakal would try to find again the island of the forest, then bid him take word to Ferenth's brother, Ferrar, of her death. For the two were close, and he must know of her death."

At last the day came when Saschka and Silvren were to be married in the temple of the Lady, above the city of Antar. On a day on the threshold of winter, when the air was bright with sun and yet edged with the chill of northern snows, Saschka and Silvren were wed. Mischka, though he could not sing, yet took out his harp and played one of Firfal's songs for them, a song of deep joy and hope. Everyone who was there wept to hear it and smiled as they wept, so great was the strength of Mischka's music. When it was done, Mischka bowed his head over his harp, and his tears fell too, as fast as the waters of the great river that flowed through Antar.

Saschka and Silvren became master and mistress of the great house in Antar. Dalvar and Misk stayed with them too, as chamberlain of the house and as speaker for the house of Amerach when Saschka could not be there in the council chambers.

As the days went on, news came from the island where the Baron had been exiled that he had killed himself. He had tied together his sheets, bound them about his neck, and hung himself. He had left a note, in which he blamed everything that had happened on Mischka. He had sworn that Antar would collapse without his leadership and that Mischka would be to blame for all. He had ended by saying that Mischka would be cursed even more than the Baron had been, that he, the Baron, cursed Mischka to a bitter and unhappy life, that he should know at last the same suffering that the Baron had felt.

Such was the news in the taverns. Mischka rarely stirred from the house, and none of those in the house thought that he would have heard of it. But one night at dinner Mischka said: "The Baron's curse is already at work. I have lost what I most care about, and can find no rest here. I don't know where to go or what to do, but I can no longer stay here. I will stay until after Souls' Night. But then I must leave."

Souls' Night is the great fall festival that celebrates all those who have passed into the darkness. It was said that at that holiday the dead again walked the earth. The people of the city set lights in their windows that burned all the night through, so that the dead might remain outside the houses. Before the dark had fully come, into the streets the children would go, dressed in costume, and would bear in their hands candles to walk the streets and in the innocence of their hearts bless the streets and protect them against the coming of the dead.

All those in the house of Amerach were now too old to take part in such a festival, except for Mirath. She decided to stay at home with them, so they placed candles in the windows and stood at the door as the children of Antar walked the streets. In a long procession they came down from the temple, where they had gathered. A thousand children, they walked down the street, the oldest in the lead, the youngest following, and at each house they passed they sang a small song.

Vale of death, do not open,
Shades of night, come not near.

All who passed into the night,
Remain far, far from here.

So they sang as they passed by, with neither flutes nor strings, nothing but the singing of the children, and the light of the candles winding down through the streets.

In the house of Amerach. they could see far up to the temple itself, which stood above all the houses, even above the grand house which the Baron had built for himself on the site of the old prince's palace. That had been the highest house below the temple; it now had been given to the temple as a place for pilgrims. Down the hill the children came, an endless procession of candles winding down the streets. At last they came past Amerach's house, passing one by one, some laughing, some serious, some taking the ceremony with the boredom of many years, others excited still with the mystery of their robes and candles.

As the procession came by, one child, a boy of nine or ten, stepped from the throng and came up to where Saschka, Mischka, Silvren, Misk, Mirath and Dalvar stood in the doorway. He was a stranger to them, this child, nor did he know them, it seems, yet he came to them and spoke.

"Sorrows be far from you this night, and ever, people of this house."

"And to you, child," said Mischka, looking at him with surprise.

Then the child returned to the throng as it continued weaving past them.

For almost an hour it went by, and then the last of the children, the one who had led the procession last year, passed them by and as he did his eyes, too, turned to them, his smile a benediction and a promise.

"Strange thing, that, that one of the children should have spoken so to us," Mischka remarked.

"Times change in Antar and customs too, I suppose," Saschka replied.

"Perhaps," said Mischka. But it seemed to him nonetheless something more than chance, something more than whim.

As they sat at supper, Saschka said, "It has been long since you sang, father, or played an instrument. Tonight will you not sing for us or with us?"

Mischka took his harp, old and battered from years of travel, and sang this song that had been much in his thoughts.

Dark my heart with all I've lost.
Dark my heart and cold.
All I've loved has passed away,
Weary am I and old.

Long the days since I have seen,
The ones I loved. Now
Darkness lies upon the sea
And sorrow on each brow.

Dark the nights and cold the winds
Silence all around.
When I dream, I dream of her
Her face, her voice, her shroud.

Alone I dream, at night alone,
Alone in night so chill,
In the darkness ever with me,
I dream still.

Saschka and Mirath could see that their father wept, flowing tears that stained his cheeks with long tracks.

"Good night, my children and friends. May the Lady keep you this night."

In his room he lit the candle and set in on the table by the bed. In defiance of all custom he opened the window wide to the cold night air, on this night when the air is filled with the sparks of all those who had died, the good and bad alike, for this night the gates of Death were opened.

He leaned out the window. The procession was gone now, the children returned to their homes. The city was silent and shuttered. From the temple high in the mountains, you could hear the faint chanting of hymns by those who lived dedicated of service of the Lady. On the river, the deep black of the sky was reflected, broken only rarely by the glitter from a star reflected in those waters.

The stars were beautiful. As he watched, suddenly a cascade of stars fell in the north, the direction that his window looked. It was silent; the wind barely stirred, as he lay down on the bed, his eyes still on the candle. As he lay there he fell into a deeper sleep, and then into his sleep stepped Ferenth.

"Oh, my love," she said, "how long are the days since we were together. I yearn for the day when we again will see each other. For all the times I forgot to say how I loved you, let this be the reminder."

She came close to the bed, and there was no sound to her step, to the tread to her feet. She leaned down and placed a kiss on his lips. Mischka reached up with his arms, crying, "Ferenth!" Between sleep and wakefulness, it seemed to him that she was there with him in the room, her eyes filled with longing and love. Then like breath in cold winter air, she thinned and vanished.

Mischka, sobbing, knelt at the window until Saschka came in, wakened by the cries, and gathered him in his arms.

The next day, Dalvar and Mischka gathered together supplies, bought horses, and set off for Wraith's Vale.

Chapter 32

Narad

The first night Mischka and Dalvar camped to the west of Antar on a spur of mountain looking down over the city and out to the ocean. The lights of the port formed a crescent of dim illumination along the line of the bay.

"My friend," said Dalvar, "this is folly. We should avoid the valley of the wraiths. Though you passed through it once, there is no guarantee that you can win through it again.

"I do not expect to pass through it."

"What do you mean? Do you think to find Ferenth in Wraith's Vale and return with her to Antar, to bring her back from the dead?"

"I do not know what I expect to find in Wraith's Vale, yet there is a voice within me that says that what I find there will not lead me back to the mountains of the west."

"Is it your death that you foresee for yourself, there in the vale of the wraiths? Do you see yourself as a wraith?"

"I have had no vision. I am neither a prophet nor a seer. But in my heart feel that this is true: that my fate lies there in Wraith's Vale and that I must go to meet it."

"Rather you should avoid that fate. Let's journey south, to the great port cities. Or skirt to the south around Wraith's Vale and go straight to the mountains of the west, there to visit your brother."

"Dalvar, my friend, there is nothing you can say that will dissuade me from taking this path. In my heart I feel I must do it. I offer neither reason nor wisdom, only necessity. And though I welcome your company, if there is aught that you must do, then do it and we'll part as friends and hope one day to see each other yet again."

Dalvar turned to him and laughed; "You'll not get rid of me so easily. If your heart is set on looking into the face of each wraith, then I'll go with you. If you find one to embrace, then I'll embrace it too. Your fate is mine, and where you go I will go as well."

"Your heart is true," Mischka replied, "a truer friend than I am to you. Then I ask you, have you no life of your own, have you no need of your own that you would follow and fulfill?"

Dalvar looked at Mischka with a quizzical expression on his face. "There are things I must do. But if you feel in your heart that Wraith's Vale must be your destination, then I feel in my heart that to be your companion is mine. Time will come when I must return to Sallas and assume charge of the estates that are mine. But meanwhile, Misk and Saschka will care for all our affairs. For now, your companion I will be and you must let me attend you. Tide life, tide death, I'll not be parted from you."

Mischka shook his head. "I have no right to ask this of you, nor have you reason to follow this path, yet I am glad of it, and welcome your company."

"How few," said Dalvar, pointing out to the east, "how few the lights that shine there, yet is there not a pattern that we can see? Have faith, my friend, though our way be dim at the moment, there will be a path, somewhere, somehow for us to follow."

On the next day, they reached the deep cleft in the mountains that led to Wraith's Vale. The sun, though now well past the strength of summer, still struck into the sheltered cleft with warmth, so as noon drew on they stopped to rest and eat. Sheltered as they were from the wind, they felt quiet and relaxed in the warmth.

All day, as they had climbed, the city Antar had fallen away beneath them, and the plains beyond that. The sea had sparkled in the distance, and the white sails of the ships heading south before the winter storms should come had gleamed like the wings of birds or butterflies in the light. The snowy peaks before them had beckoned. They wouldn't turn so far to the north, but follow the cleft until they reached the portal of the vale of the wraiths.

They rested in the cleft, had their meal of dried meat and bread and cheese, of wine, dried fruit. Then they resumed their walk, Mischka deep in thought and Dalvar ahead of him.

After an hour of following the path, Mischka called out to his friend: "Wait, Dalvar, I must rest for a moment." He turned aside to sit on a pile of rocks beside the path. As he did so, there was a quick rattle and hiss; from a niche in the rocks a snake reared its head, its tongue flickering.

"Mischka, look out!" shouted Dalvar, as he leapt forward, his knife in his hand, the snake weaving back and forth, its eyes cold and as calculating as it watched Mischka, who sat frozen into immobility. Side to side it swayed. Its tail shook with a dry rattling that warned of its intent. Dalvar picked up a stone and hurled it at the snake, which dodged to one side and darted forward at Mischka.

He shouted in alarm and leapt backward as Dalvar sprang forward. Dalvar grabbed the snake in one hand. Its tale lashed wildly, its body wrapped about his arm. Its mouth opened and closed, venom dripping from its fangs. Dalvar squeezed with both hands and then with a twist he broke the back of the snake. He tossed it to the ground.

"Are you alright, my friend?" asked Dalvar.

"Only winded. And you?"

"Untouched. You are careless with your life. But look: when the chance offered, you recoiled from death. Life is not something to throw away, my friend."

"I will not throw it away," Mischka replied. "When we walked through the vale of the wraiths before, we sang to protect ourselves from them. So I will do again. Though I've not sung for any other, I will sing for Ferenth. I'll sing to her of my longing and love, if she is there. The wraiths will not touch us."

"Then let us go on. The sooner we are there, the sooner will this be over." Onward up the valley they went.

Later that afternoon, while they rested against the rocks, Mischka said, "It is not the first time that I've encountered such a snake."

"For one who has seen them before, you are careless about walking in their haunts."

"There is much in my thoughts."

"When was this other time?"

"I was a boy," said Mischka "My brother Linar and I were high in the mountains, tending our sheep in a pasture that lay high up in the hills, a pasture that my brother's son Misk loves no less than we did, and to which he has taken my own son as Linar did me. Much like this, the north side of that pasture ends in a tumble of rocks, against a cliff that rises in jagged scree up to the mountain peaks."

"While Linar tended the sheep I went to scramble on the rocks, and as I scrambled up the scree, just as now, there was a rattle and a hiss and there on the rock facing me was a snake much like this one, diamonds on its back, its tongue flickering to taste my scent in the air. Linar shouted and I stood still, and the snake slowly subsided. Its rattle stopped. Its tongue flickered still, and its head darted in small jabs. Linar came close and I said 'No Linar, wait!' The snake lowered itself, stretched out in the sun on the rocks, in the warmth. A second lid came down over its eyes, and it lay there, quiet."

"It didn't strike you or Linar?"

"No. We stood and watched it for a long time, and then I stood slowly and walked back down the hill. I had intruded on it, after all, and it had no reason to attack me unless I attacked it. So it was when I was growing up: that though there might be dangers and threats in the world, yet they were no threat to me."

"There was unhappiness," Mischka continued, "and as my brother left and then my sister, I grew unhappy. My parents, I think, did not understand what it was in a boy to love his siblings. Did not understand, I think, how the harshness of the life that they had suffered had hurt them: the children they had lost, the long winters when there was barely food enough to feed the children and in which they gave up what they had that we might eat; days when brigands came from the hills."

"There was a time before I was born, when Father, as strong a man as Linar, stood before the house with his cudgel and defied men who sought to steal from him. The howling of the wolves in the winter, the winter wind that was fiercer than any wolf or brigand, striving more fiercely than any enemy to kill us all: these they had known and had in their suffering grown hard. But to me that world was full of wonder. When I left home to find my sister, the only thing that could have taken me from that land, it was at first an adventure. But now I know what I lost. Were it not for the happiness of loving Ferenth, then I would have been sad indeed. But with her, even exile was joyful."

Both men were silent for a moment. Then Dalvar said, "You have been a lucky man. One day I hope I may find my wife, find where the slavers have taken her, if she lives still. But for me that happiness was all too short and the Baron's evil all too great. Yet I too know the pleasure of the mountains and of family. My house along the coast to the south had been my father's, and my father's father before him, and so for as long as any could remember."

"For me there was the ocean below the clefts of the rocks. As for you the wind on the moors, so for me the waves that crashed against the shore were a source of mystery and wonder. There was a cave carved deep into the cliff by the undercutting waves, and there I would go, while my parents fretted and called for me to come back. There was a sandy beach inside it, and when the sun came in the cave was lit with deep green shadows and blue depths of water. Bands and bars of light played across the walls of the cave. It was a place of magic for me. But those days are gone. We face other journeys now."

"So we do," said Mischka. "and must go on. But when I am done with this search for her whom I love, then I promise you that if I can, I will come with you. Together we will look for your wife."

It was late the next afternoon when at last they drew near to the canyon leading into Wraith's Vale. Suddenly a voice called to them from the rocks at the north side of the canyon.

"You there! Whither are you bound?"

"Who is it who calls," shouted Dalvar. "Show yourself."

A ragged figure stepped from behind the rocks and came forward with his hands outstretched. His hair was long and matted. A beard long and straggly grew from his face. His clothes were dirty and tattered.

"I am but a poor man, escaped from the slavers and living in poverty among these rocks. I ask your help, strangers, for the weather grows cold and anyone who lives in these rocks so near to Wraith's Vale would soon be no better than the wraiths themselves without the comfort and care of others."

"An escaped slave, say you?" asked Dalvar.

"Yes, escaped with nothing but the clothes on my back, ragged and poor as they are."

"What is your name then?"

"I am called Narad, Narad the slave."

"Come forward. Let there be no tricks. Have you comrades hidden among these rocks?"

"No comrades, no companions, no consort. I am alone. That is the only way a slave can survive."

"There are no more slaves in Egeria," said Mischka quietly. "The Baron is defeated and his tyranny is ended. Slaves are now free men and the land the Baron stole is theirs for the asking."

"What do I know of land?" replied Narad with a shrug.

"What did you do then, as a slave?" asked Mischka.

Narad looked quickly from one to the other. "I was a horse tender. My skill is in crop and bridle, in saddle and spur, in stirrup and rein. I would be glad to tend your horses if I might go with you."

"You do not wish to go where we go," Mischka replied.

"Better to go with you than to starve here among these stones. Do you not return to Antar? Where are you going?"

"We go to Wraith's Vale," said Mischka.

"Wraith's vale! Few take that route, and of those who do, fewer still return. If you are going that way, then I think I will wait here for your return, if it may be. I do not wish to go with you into that danger."

"Then at least come and join us for a meal," offered Mischka.

"That I will do gladly and in recompense will do what I can to ease your journey. I am clever with my hands in tending horses."

"We will have no need of horses in the vale," Mischka replied. "If we leave them here with you, will you tend them carefully until our return?"

"Will we not pass straight through," asked Dalvar, "as you did so many years before?"

"The horses will not go into the vale," said Mischka. "We must go on foot. I will there ask the questions I must ask."

"Ask questions of wraiths?" Narad shook his head in dismay. "As the wise say, 'As soon think to get answers from a serpent as from the wraiths.' Why should they answer you? They have no need of the living, but only seek to wrap you in their arms and draw you among them."

"Answer I will have," Mischka replied, "however I may, answer I will have. But come, come and eat and then we will see what we must do. Where are you from and how did you come to be in these mountains."

"That is a long story. For many years, I don't know how long, was I a slave in a city to the north of here."

"What city is that?" asked Mischka, puzzled.

"There is no city in the mountains to the north of us," declared Dalvar. "There is nothing but rock, snow and wind. Everyone knows this."

"No, master, there is a city: the city of the wise, the city of the magicians."

"This I know nothing of," said Mischka.

"Nor should you, master," agreed Narad, "for they keep themselves close and say nothing to anyone. Yet a city there is, a weary journey on foot. Two months it took me, coming south, to find this place."

"Why did you leave?" asked Mischka.

"I was a slave there, as I have said. But now I have broken the shackle from my ankle. No, master, the city of the wizards is no place for me. Nor for anyone else who is not as powerful as they, if he would not be sold in the slave marts.

"Then how did you escape," asked Dalvar.

"My master grew old and careless. He was anxious to recover his youth, so he sent me forth from the city to find the water of life which it is said springs forth in the mountains. He put a compulsion on me that I should return within five days if I had not found the fountain by then."

"As the five days ended," Narad continued, "I felt the compulsion growing stronger. But then suddenly the compulsion vanished and I knew that my master had died and his spell with him. The shackle fell from my ankle and I was free. Having no desire to be slave to another, I kept what food I had and journeyed south. It has been a long trip through these mountains, but I have come nearly to the gates of Antar and but wait here to see what fortune may offer, and to whom I may pledge myself as a free man, and so gain protection in these troubled times. As the wise say, 'It is a clever servant who seeks a strong master."

"Go to Antar then," said Mischka. "If you speak well to those you see in the market anyone may hire you. If you are as good with horses as you say, then surely a place you will find in Antar, for the need for help is great."

"I will go, master. But what of your offer, that I tend the horses?"

"If, as Mischka says, we will return here, then you may tend the horses," said Dalvar. "But hear me: if you play us false, by the sword I carry I will seek you out and your head will have no place on your shoulders."

"Good master, do I speak you false? I tell you the truth of my captivity, with no false witness, and you would threaten me with injury I do not deserve?"

"As long as you do not deserve it, you need not fear it. But by my name, Dalvar, you will not live to profit from the fruits of any ill you may do."

Narad looked quickly from Dalvar to Mischka and back again. "Masters, poor Narad is a man of honesty and trust. If you leave your horses with him, then you will have nothing to fear."

"So be it," said Mischka. "If and when we return, we will discuss further what we may do. Perhaps we may return to Antar, and if so you may come with us. We will see. But for now, tend our horses well. Come Dalvar, if we are to face these wraiths, then let us do so." And Mischka strode forward, into the vale.

Chapter 33

Embrace of the Wraiths

"Wait, Mischka," said Dalvar, "wait. One last time I ask: are you so determined on this?"

"My friend," Mischka replied, turning back to him, "don't you see? If there is any chance that I can find her here any chance that a song might restore her to me, then I have to try."

"But last time you barely escaped with your lives. You were four people then. How will you survive with just one when the wraiths are so powerful and their song so cruel?"

"I must try. If I don't survive, it will be better than this half life I live."

"Is death by agony so much better than life? What of your son, your daughter? What of the children that will come from your children? Have you no wish to see them and care for them?"

"I wish to see them and care for them, but I can see nothing but Ferenth before me, can see nothing but her face in the faces that I meet, can hear nothing but her voice in the voices that I hear."

"This is folly! Let her go."

"I can't," said Mischka, "or she won't let go of me, I don't know which. But I know that half of myself has been ripped away, and what is left now is little better than one of the wraiths of this vale."

"Why master," protested Narad, "that is not true. Even to the far north the stories of this vale have come, how those who are here are consumed by a hunger for the life they can no longer have. Everyone knows how treacherous and dangerous are the wraiths of the vale."

"Treacherous and dangerous they are," agreed Mischka.

"No one knows that better than he," said Dalvar angrily. "Long ago he himself walked though this vale with the woman whom he now seeks to bring from it, and then the four of them were hard-pressed. And now, with but one? When their lives were nearly drawn from them even then in their singing?"

"Even so," Mischka replied. "All that you say is true. But I have no choice."

"You have every choice," said Dalvar impatiently. "Look at me. Friend, look at me! Come back with me to Antar, or to the mountains."

"No. Perhaps once this trial is done. But not until then. Are you afraid of seeing your wife among these wraiths?"

"If she is there, she is there. But I will not try to pull her from the vale. I will not try to lift the curse of this place from her. I know what is beyond my power and I know this is one of those things."

"Ah, my friend," said Mischka, "but you do understand how the longing for what you have lost may drive you to dangers even such as these."

"I do understand."

"Then, let me go! Do not hinder me any longer. If there is any chance that Ferenth may be among these wraiths and that I may win her from them and bring her back to life, then I must try."

Turning once more to Narad, Mischka said, "Take good care of our horses. If we do not return they are yours."

"I will guard them well," Narad replied. "Never fear for the horses."

"Do you come with me, Dalvar?" asked Mischka.

"I will come with you, though my heart says that this adventure is doomed and that what we will meet in the vale will not be your loving Ferenth. But I will go with you."

So Mischka turned and led the way into the vale.

Narad stood for a moment in thought, watching them walk into the tunnel that led to the vale. Then he turned to the horses. He checked their equipage. Then he said to them, "So we are to wait here are we? Wait here to see whether the wraiths let them go? What folly is this? The wraiths will release no one, least of all those who seek to take a wraith from among them. This is folly, and worse than folly. There is no need for us to wait. As the wise say, 'Opportunity has a long forelock, but is bald behind!" Why should I turn my back on what fate has offered? They'll never return, the poor fools."

"Or do you think," he continued as he rifled through the saddlebags, "do you think they may return? Do you think I should step to the portal of the valley and see what becomes of them? No, such a sight would haunt my sleep. I'll let them go, and lead you away from this desolate place. You're anxious to return back to the city, I'm sure. I'll take you back, we'll find new homes for you, and a new home for me, far from this desolation."

"Come, children, let us leave this place behind." Narad climbed onto Mischka's horse. Leading Dalvar's mount, he rode from the camp. Down the track he went, as quickly as he could. When he had gotten a league from the camp, he dismounted and rifled through the saddlebags. Pulling out the spare shirt and trous that Mischka had brought, he slipped off his rags and put on Mischka's clothes. The spare boots he took as well and pulled those on. Then he carefully searched the saddlebags for anything else he could find, especially gold. But the only gold was still in the pouch that Dalvar's wore, so there was no treasure for the thief to find.

"Well, children, so there is no gold?" he said to the horses. "Still, this is not a bad barter: a few idle tales for two good horses. Why should I not take advantage of what the Lady has placed in my hands? We will make our way to Antar and there find our fortunes."

So, with the two horses, he set off to the east.

As Mischka and Dalvar walked into the vale, before them stood a pillar of black marble on a plinth of gray granite, both of them roughly carved. As Dalvar drew closer he could feel, as though from a furnace, a glow of power from this black marble obelisk, as though with some sense other than sight he could see like waves of heat above a hot summer road the flickering and pulsing of its power. He could feel, the way in which it drew at them, and how, were they wraiths, it would draw them to it.

Even from this distance, as they looked into the vale, they could feel that drawing power, could feel the call that it made, the hunger that it aroused for life in the wraiths trapped in this vale, unable to escape, unable to cross beyond the stone, unable to leave the vale that gave them form and substance.

The stone had been placed long years before, no one knew by whom. On it were letters that said: "

Beyond this stone, stranger, do not seek to pass.
Into this valley, stranger, do not seek to come.
Here wait those whose life is done,
Drawn here to free the world of their hunger.
Do not enter, lest they feed on thee."

Mischka and Dalvar had no sooner passed through the entrance of the vale than before them the wraiths began to assemble. Beyond the sunlight, in the shadows of the cavern, the cleft in the mountain, they could see their shadowy forms and the rapacious eyes.

"What do you do now?" asked Dalvar

"Now," Mischka replied, "I must sing."

So Mischka began his song. A line, invisible yet potent, marked the boundary of the vale, a boundary fixed in the earth and air, present like the ridges of rock that thrust their way out of the sandy waste here and there. As they crossed over it, they knew they had passed into the vale, because suddenly what they saw was different: first the phantasms of the vale themselves, and then on the rocks around them, spires and pinnacles, and in the walls of the canyon, the blind walls of abandoned houses, the blind construction of a city long since abandoned and now given over wholly to the wraiths, who swarmed in its empty rooms, who gathered in its council chamber, who stood at the windows and looked out at these two intruders who dared enter the valley.

Mischka sang, and sang without ceasing, and Dalvar behind him walked warily. Around them the eyes of the wraiths gleamed in the darkness of the shadows. One by one the wraiths appeared on the path before them. A pitiful sight they were, and fearsome too, for they were dressed in clothes of all times and places. Yet one thing they had in common. As they looked at Mischka, he could see in their eyes a burning hunger, an anguish at their death in life, and a fierce desire to take from Mischka and Dalvar the life they brought to the vale.

The wraiths watched them closely as Mischka and Dalvar advanced, until at last the two men stood only a dozen paces from the nearest wraith, and could see the figure and face as clearly as one sees that of a friend on Restday morning.

Mischka began the song that he and Ferenth had sung so many years before when they first passed through the vale. There was a stirring among the wraiths. Among the forms, it seemed that this one had the form of the Baron, that one Mischka's father. Mischka sang still, and the wraiths came forward. Beyond the boundary of the vale they could not go. They came to the very edge of that boundary, and those who stepped past trembled and grew evanescent until they stepped back inside the vale. Some sorcery in the stones themselves gave them their shadowy embodiment.

Then among the rest, Mischka saw Ferenth, as shadowy as the rest.

Mischka stepped forward again and his song changed. He sang no longer of the world, but only of Ferenth, of her dark hair and her lovely eyes, of the children she had borne and the love she had carried for so many years. He stepped forward and the wraiths too pressed forward, their arms reaching out for him. But he sang still and the wraiths drew back from him.

Dalvar followed. As they walked forward, the wraiths fell back before them, yet their arms were outstretched and their voices seemed to whisper: "Come to us! Come to us! Let us place our arms about you. Come to us!"

Mischka still walked forward, the song was still on his lips. "Ferenth my love, return with me, come with me, leave this deathly place and come again." The shadowy forms swirled around him, drew back, and then in their midst stood Ferenth.

Her eyes were cast to the ground and her hair was long and black and her arms were at her side. "Ferenth, Ferenth, come with me away from this place," sang Mischka. But her eyes were still on the ground.

Still Mischka sang:

My heart is shattered by your death.
Come and take me to you.
Come my love, come to my arms.
Let me lead you from this death.
Let me lead you back into life,
Back into the light of the world.

My harp is shattered, my song is done.
Without you, my love, I cannot sing.
Without you, my love, there is no music.
Come to me, my love.
Then my heart will be whole again.
Then I too will live again.

Come to me, my love
Come to me now.
Take my hands.
Remember the vows that we spoke,
Each to the other,
And come to me, my love.
Come to me.

As he sang, she drew nearer. As he sang her arms reached towards him, until at last she stood no more than an arm's length from him, yet could not seem to come closer.

Mischka sang, "Ferenth, my love, come to me!" and the voices of the wraiths whispered, "Come to us! Leave your singing and come to us!"

Then Ferenth raised her eyes and looked into Mischka's eyes, and those eyes, so beautiful, so terrible, were filled with a terrifying hunger and a terrifying sorrow.

Mischka's voice faltered. The wraiths pressed forward about Mischka and Dalvar. Ferenth swiftly stepped across the short distance between them and her arms wrapped about Mischka .

Dalvar heard Mischka's voice rise in a cry of agony, and he shouted: "Mischka, no!" Then he began to sing in his rough, gravely voice, but his song was of hate, anger and fear.

"You shall not have him!" he sang. "Though your hunger be as great as the ocean, as great as the mountains around us, you shall not have him! Though your hunger is strong as night, strong as death, you shall not have him!"

The wraiths drew back from them again. But the wraith who was Ferenth held onto Mischka. He fell to the ground and the wraith knelt by him. Dalvar advanced, his song still cutting and slashing at the wraiths, but still the wraith of Ferenth looked at him with hate in her eyes. Dalvar's voice tore at the wraiths, driving back all but the one that crouched over his friend.

"You shall not have him! You shall not have this man! You shall not take the blood from his veins, you shall not take the heart from his chest, you shall not make him a wraith like you! For every pain you force on him, such pain I will force on you! Though you are fierce, I am fiercer! Though you are filled with hate, my hate is greater! I hate all who hurt him, and I will protect him! You shall not have him!"

With a snarl, the wraith that was Ferenth stood up from Mischka and retreated. Dalvar gathered Mischka in his arms and began backing toward the entrance to the valley. His throat ached with pain from his song, yet he sang still. He tripped and fell, his voice faltered and stopped, the wraiths advanced and knelt by him and their hands reached out to draw him to them. But with a great surge of anger and fear he burst out in song again. He struggled to his feet, Mischka still in his arms, and reached at last the black stone and the entrance to the valley.

The wraiths massed before him, their eyes hungry, their voices shrill: "Come back! Come to us, come to us!"

Dalvar stumbled from the vale, back through the portals to the clearing where he had left Narad and the horses. But Narad and the horses were gone.

Dalvar dropped to his knees and lay Mischka in the dust, cursing Narad. He cursed him with all the vehemence of his fear and despair. Then he collapsed across Mischka and was silent.

When he awoke, it was full night. The frost was on their clothes. Mischka's face was cold, his chest unmoving. But when Dalvar held his knife before Mischka's nostrils, a thin mist shadowed the blade. So he began chafing Mischka's hands and talking to him: "Mischka, wake up! We must go back to Antar."

Mischka didn't stir. There was no way to make a fire. There was no food. Dalvar took Mischka in his arms, wrapped their cloaks about them both. All that long cold night, they lay on the stony ground and Dalvar held his friend until the chill from Mischka entered into his bones. His dreams were filled with skeletal hands reaching out to him, with skeletal voices that said, over and over, "Come to us! Come to us!"

It was the deepest dark of the night, Dalvar woke from a troubled sleep to find Mischka was no longer in his arms. He looked about, and saw his friend stumbling toward the entrance to the vale. Dalvar leapt from the ground, his muscles aching with the cold and with the punishment of sleeping on the stony bed. He grabbed Mischka, and cried: "Mischka! Mischka, my brother, stay!"

Mischka struggled like a madman until at last Dalvar, not knowing what else to do, hit him as hard as he could, knocking Mischka to the ground, where he lay unconscious. Dalvar fell sobbing to his knees at his friend's side, his head bowed, his heart aching as those the wraiths held him in their cruel and cold embrace.

Chapter 34

The Search Begins

For the rest of the night, Dalvar sat with Mischka in his arms. At times again Mischka stirred and seemed about to struggle to rise, but Dalvar spoke to him, said "Mischka my brother, stay. Mischka, rest; rest Mischka." The movements would subside and Mischka would again lie quiet. At last the sun came up and struck through the gap to the east into the small clearing. Mischka grew quiet as the sun rested on his face, the chill of the night flowing out of him, drawn from him as the sun draws water from the earth.

Dalvar too, welcomed the sun, turning his face toward it gladly. "Lady, creator of all there is, guard this man and give me strength to bear him home." So when the sun was fairly up and hunger gnawed at Dalvar's stomach, he once again raised Mischka to his feet and speaking urgently to him, led him from the clearing, half carrying, half walking. Mischka stumbled forward, his eyes closed for the most part, yet now and again opening with a wild look, as though he had no recollection of where he was, or who he was, or where he might be going. They walked along the stony path over the edge of the mountains, down at last into the foothills to the north of Antar.

The next day was again hot and dry. Though the night had been cold, the sun beat down into the long cleft that led back to Antar and turned the stony path that coursed along the edge of the precipice to iron. The sweat poured from Dalvar's face as he walked down the path, half carrying Mischka, who seemed to weigh little more than a wraith to Dalvar, half carried still. When Dalvar set him down to rest, Mischka lay in the sun unmoving. Each time, Dalvar felt a shock of fear that Mischka had died. But when he held his knife blade before Mischka's nostrils, a slight misting of the blade, quickly dispersed by the sun, promised that Mischka yet lived.

Dalvar struggled on all that day along the stony paths in the mountains. When the day faded, he was still less than halfway back to Antar, his steps slowed by the burdens that he carried: the burden in his arms and the burden is his heart.

As he set Mischka down, to once again lie unmoving, unhearing, unspeaking, Dalvar said: "My friend, what folly was this, what madness? None can be brought back from the dead! Will you ever sing again, when your song has done such damage to you? Will you ever be well again, and happy?"

"In all the years since I lost my wife," Dalvar continued, "I promised myself only that I would find a way to destroy the Baron. I learned cruelty and hardness of heart at the hands of grief. But this grief too great. If you die, then I fear I will die also."

Mischka began to writhe and twist. "No," he cried out in agony, "no, Ferenth!" Dalvar knelt down to hold him as tightly as he could to keep him from flailing. "Ferenth!" Mischka called out in heart-breaking agony. "Ferenth!"

At last Mischka fell asleep. Dalvar sat and watched by him until at last he too fell asleep. But in the middle of the night Dalvar woke in panic to find that Mischka had risen and again was stumbling back along the path to the vale. Dalvar ran after Mischka and held him tightly. Mischka flailed wildly, until at last, pinned by Dalvar's fierce embrace, he collapsed and fell to the ground.

Dalvar again lay down to sleep, but twice more that night Mischka struggled to his feet and stumbled back along the path. Each time it was harder for Dalvar to get up. He such weariness and despair that he was tempted to lie down in the dust, amid the rocks. But each time he considered such a course, he forced himself to run after Mischka, to hold him close until the nightmare had passed.

The next morning they at last reached the road to Antar. Once again they began to meet people traveling to or from the cit7. Of each one they met, Dalvar asked: "Have you seen a man with two horses? Two black horses, with good bridle and gear?"

"No," the passersby said, "no such man have we seen. No, there has been no one this morning."

"And last night?" Dalvar asked.

"Man with horses? No, no one."

"I will find him!" Dalvar swore to himself as they continued. At last he met a man leading a horse, and said: "I have need of your animal."

"No more than I," replied the man.

"My need is the greater," said Dalvar, pulling out his purse. "My friend is under the shadow of the wraiths. We must seek help or he will die."

"Then what will you give me for my horse?"

Dalvar dug in his purse and found two gold pieces. "Take these. If you come to the house of Amerach in Antar, you will find your horses there. You may claim them and keep the gold."

Dalvar lifted Mischka to the horse's back and held him there. "Come, my dear friend," he said. "We will get ourselves as quickly as we can to Antar and hope that something can cure this fever."

They journeyed on, with no sign of a change in Mischka. Though he did not grow worse, yet he often was troubled still and grew no better. He gave no sign that he knew where he was, who he was or who he was with. As they traveled, Dalvar bought some poor food, bread and cheese, from another traveler to sustain them. Each night when darkness came down that night, again Dalvar spread their blankets on the earth, removed the horse's tack, hobbled it, and prepared their food for them to eat. Each day they continued on toward Antar, Mischka neither better nor worse. He said not a word, or at best unintelligible phrases in which only the cry "Ferenth! Ferenth!" was clearly spoken.

So they traveled back to Antar, Dalvar on foot and Mischka on a-horse, and came at last to Amerach's house.

Saschka, Silvren, Mirath and Misk came from the house at once. When they saw Mischka, his skin blanched, lying like a dead person on the horse, and Dalvar himself nearly dead with weariness and anguish, they feared the worse.

"Get him to bed," said Dalvar. "There is life in him still. But the wraiths hold him yet."

Saschka sent immediately for a doctor.

"Ah," the doctor said, "this is an interesting disease. What might be the cause of this coma?"

"We were hoping you would know," said Saschka dryly, "and know therefore a way in which to treat it."

"I know well enough what is wrong with him. This coma that he is in, is a coma of shock, a coma of pain not physical but emotional."

"He is Mischka, the singer," said Dalvar. "His song is silenced and without your help it may be silenced forever."

"For such an ill of the mind as this, one must go carefully, so as not to break more than is broken already. Keep him warm. I will send one of my medicines. That may help. But for such a case as this, there is little that a mere doctor can do."

"Then go," said Dalvar angrily. "If you cannot help, then we wish to see no more of you."

"Give him this elixir," said the doctor. "It is made of sovereign plants, good for strength and healing of wounds. Though it will not restore him by itself, yet it may give him the strength to heal."

They took it, and as the doctor had said they gave it to Mischka in small doses, sparingly, at regular intervals. But the medicine seemed to have no effect. Mischka continued unresponsive, lying unresponsive on his at the house of Amerach in Antar.

Dalvar, meanwhile, grew angrier and angrier at Narad's treachery.

"Have you seen our horses anywhere about the town?" he asked Saschka. "They were stolen from us there at the vale of the wraiths by a stranger we met. No sooner were our backs turned than he took our horses, so that there were not there when I needed them to carry your father back to Antar."

"No, I've seen no sign of them," Saschka replied.

"Then I will search for them."

While Saschka, Silvren and Mirath tended their father, Dalvar searched through the city for Narad and the horses. He started by going down to the docks to meet with Rakal.

"So," said Rakal, "be you returned to your estate? Be you once again in place as a man of property?"

"Not yet. There is more work to do on them than I have the heart for. The fields lie fallow, the house derelict. It may be that one day I will return to them, but for now Mischka needs our help."

"It were an ill-omened day that I brought them back to Egeria," said Rakal, shaking his head.

"You had no more choice in this than I in escorting Mischka to the wraiths' vale."

"True it is. What Mischka wanted, he always could get. His tongue was always silver and his words ever persuasive."

"No longer," said Dalvar. "He lies still unresponsive, in a coma. "

"He cannot long continue that way," Rakal said sadly. "Either he dies or he recovers and there be little that anyone can do."

"So I fear. But I'll stay and tend him as best I may."

"And visit friends, too?"

"So I will. But this is not just a visit. I search the town for one who stole our horses."

"Ah! You seek the one who betrayed you?"

"So I do," said Dalvar grimly. "If I once find him, it will go ill for him."

"There are others who will join you in this search if you wish."

"You?" asked Dalvar.

"I cannot. I must be again on my way and return to the south. I live by trade and cannot stay long in port. But before I go, I would see Mischka."

"The let us do so now."

Together the two men, much of a size, similar in their harsh, lined faces, strode through the streets. None greeted them, and they greeted none, but talked earnestly as they went. When they came to Amerach's house, and Mirath saw the burley captain standing on the threshold, she threw herself into his arms.

"I come to see your father," said Rakal gently.

"Is there anything you can do for him?" asked Mirath, her face buried in his shoulder.

"Not I. But it would do my heart good to see him."

"I hardly know him any longer. He is so ill!"

"I understand," Rakal replied. "I understand well how hard it be, how desperate the longing that he recover. Take me to him, little one."

Mirath led the way to the large chamber on the main floor where they had placed Mischka, so that they might easily care for him and visit with him. He lay still in his bed, not a movement of his hands or his face, except the slight rise and fall of his breathing.

Rakal stood at the side of the bed, placed his hand on Mischka's forehead. Then he sank to his knees, took Mischka's hand in his, clasping it tightly, and bowed his head over it.

"Old friend, forgive me that ever I brought you back to this place. What you did for Egeria was not worth the price that you had to pay. The evil the Baron did to others was unmatched by what he did to you and your wife. You must hear me, my friend! You must not give up! As we did in sailing to the Far Southern Lands, pull strongly at the oars, steer the boat to take advantage of every breath of wind, every gust that courses over this sea of darkness! Be strong, my friend. Return to us soon!"

Saschka and Mirath stepped forward and put their hands on Rakal's shoulders. When he stood, on his stern face there were tracks of tears. A knot of misery showed in the muscles of his forehead.

"I must go. But if you be ever needing help, send word. All I have is yours, if that is what you need. Care for your father well."

Then he turned to Dalvar and said, "You will stay by them?"

"I will not fail this trust, I promise," Dalvar replied.

Day after day, when he was not with Mischka, Dalvar stalked through the streets, searching for the one who betrayed them both and perhaps condemned Mischka to death in his betrayal. Then one day, in a stable near the eastern gate, he saw the two horses.

"Where did you get these horses?" Dalvar demanded.

The stable hand blanched. "A stranger brought them and my master bought them from him."

"Where is your master?"

"Inside, having a drink with that very stranger."

Dalvar entered the house and there seated at the table was Narad, wearing new clothes and sporting a pouch of silver.

"So, thief," said Dalvar, striding to the table, "I trust you have no longer need of your head."

Narad jumped up and backed against the wall. "Oh master, I am glad you are here again! I brought your horses and they are doing well! Come see them!"

"What does this man want?" asked the man who had been sitting with Narad.

"Nothing," protested Narad, "just to see the horses."

"The horses you have sold to me?"

"Well, sold in a manner of speaking, but..."

"What do you mean, in a manner of speaking. I have here a bill of sale, signed with your very name."

"Well not so much my name," replied Narad, "as something by which you might call me."

"I gave you good silver for those horses!"

"Silver enough," agreed Narad. "Yet I think perhaps, good merchant, I will not make the deal after all."

"They are my horses now!"

"No," said Dalvar. "They are not your horses, any more than they were this man's. They are the horses of the house of Amerach; any who seeks to cheat that house must suffer for it."

"Then I will take back my silver. You may have the horses again.":

"I have not all of the silver," said Narad, pouring out the silver from his pouch on the table. "What I have I will gladly give you."

"A quarter of it is missing!" the merchant said angrily.

"Clothes are so expensive!" Narad said placatingly. "And good is terribly dear!"

"Shall I give you his hand in payment?" asked Dalvar. "It is easy enough to cut it off."

"No, master! No! No!" protested Narad. "My hand would be of little use to the merchant without an arm attached to it, and a torso to that. I pray you, good merchant: I had need of the money to fill my empty belly and dress my bare back. If you but give me a few days, I will gladly repay you what is missing."

"What choice do I have? Your clothes are no good to me, nor the food in your belly. But I tell you this: Antar has a way of dealing with those who do not pay their debts. If you do not, you will be counted no better than a thief and will suffer the penalty that all thieves must suffer."

"And what is that?" asked Narad.

"The loss of both your hands," replied the merchant. "And I myself will prosecute the claim."

"Then your money will I return to you. Three days grace is all I ask, merchant."

"Three days it is. And then I will bring you before the law."

As Dalvar and Narad left the house and led the horses back to Saschka's house, Narad cast surreptitious glances at his companion. Finally he said, "I imagine you may be angry?"

"I am not angry. But if Mischka dies, then so will you for what you have done to my friend."

"I have done nothing! "

"You have killed him. Had we been able to bring him by horse, he might yet live. But your treachery has condemned him. So I condemn you.

"But master," pleaded Narad. "There are ways in which we might restore him even yet."

"If so, perhaps I might spare you. How will you heal him?"

"Do you not remember I told you of the great city to the north and the magicians who live there? If you and he were to go to that city, then surely you would find there that which would heal him."

"This is but another of your tricks. I'll not trust you again."

"This is no trick," Narad protested. "Let's go to your house, bring these horses back. Then I can tell you the route to the wizard's city so that you can save your friend."

"If I go, you will go with me."

"Go with you?" Narad protested again. "I dare not! If I return there, they will put me in chains, or worse, to death!"

"If you do not," said Dalvar, "I will put you to death."

"You leave me little choice!"

"None. Do not seek to escape. Or I will tie you up, to ensure that you do not."

When they reached the house, Narad told Saschka and Misk of the wizards' city to the north. The next day, Dalvar declared, he and Narad would head forth to the mountains, to find that city and a cure for Mischka.

Chapter 35

Into the Mountains

Early the next morning, when Narad awoke, the door of his room was locked. He had tested the windows thoroughly the night before, in hopes that he might get out, but the bars in them were as strong as when they were put in years before at the first sign of unrest in the city. There was no way for him to break through, at least not in a single night's lodging. He accepted his situation with humor and resolved to keep a clear eye for the chance to escape, which he was certain would come.

It was some hours later when Dalvar entered the room with Saschka. "So," he said. "Are you ready to begin the journey?"

"Any journey you wish, master," Narad agreed.

"I am not your master," Dalvar replied. "Consider me instead your jailer, and your executioner if you betray us again."

"I seek not to betray you, only to serve you well!"

"This you will do by guiding us to this city you speak of. You will first describe to us how to get there."

"When you say 'guiding us', master, do you mean that I am to go with you?"

"Yes, you and I."

"Not this young gentleman here?"

"This young gentleman is the son of the man you betrayed, who lies now so near to death.

"If he is the one who entered the Wraith's Vale with you, it is no wonder he is near death."

"You'll speak not so," Dalvar said angrily, slapping Narad across the face. "If he dies, know this: even if we find the city of the magicians, your life will be forfeit. So pray that they can help him."

"Oh, most assuredly they will, master. But I, a poor slave, I will delay you on the long journey there. Surely you would go faster by yourself."

"We will have horses."

"Horses will do no good on this journey. The path is narrow and rough. We must go by foot and by foot it will take us a long and weary time. Now that winter is coming in it will be a grave and dangerous journey too. The wise say, 'The fool walks when the snow flies.' The stone giants play in those mountains, seeking to capture unwary travelers. If they do, we have no hope of escape."

"We will leave today," said Dalvar firmly, "and travel as swift as we may to find this great city. Mischka's plight brooks no delay."

"I cannot go in these clothes, master!"

"Indeed you'll not," said Dalvar and put into Narad's hands thick boots and heavy clothes of durable cloth. "I've gathered all we need. Change into these and then we'll be on our way."

"Will the young master truly not come with us?"

"The young master stays here to care for his father," replied Saschka. "If you value your life then do as Dalvar says and return safe, for Antar has a short way with thieves."

"Speaking of thieves," said Narad, "there is a small matter of silver that I owe to one merchant. Though I am loathe to throw good money after bad, still he did speak of slicing off hands and such things. I pray you, if I have not the chance to earn the money myself, that you would at least send to the merchant the silver I owe him."

"It shall be done," Saschka replied. "You need have no fear of returning to Antar and so will have the better will to find this city of enchanters and the medicine to heal my father."

"I do it for you gladly," protested Narad. "But it is a dangerous journey for me. If I return there, I am sure to be made a slave once again. I would count on your good will, if by great good fortune I should return with this elixir?"

"You can count on my forbearance, at least," laughed Saschka. "And I undertake to gain that of our friend Dalvar as well."

"That will be no easy task," said Dalvar, "for the suffering that we have borne because of this one."

"If he holds to his word, then I charge you, Dalvar, that what is past must be past and not held to his account."

"One thing I will hold to his account, should it occur, is the death of Mischka. So pray to the Lady, slave that you are, that Mischka does not die before we return."

So they set off on their journey, Narad leaving in Saschka's hands the description he said would lead to the great city of the enchanters, although none had heard of it before and they were, Misk said, catching at straws to believe the word of a trickster. They set forth, Dalvar and Narad; and as Narad advised, they left the horses behind and set forth on foot.

The path that Narad had taken from the city of the wizards had led him to the vale of the wraiths. So it was to the vale that they went again. This time they had no horses. The only animals that might survive in the mountains were what he called Raffars, glimpsed sometimes by hunters from Antar who ventured into the mountains, but not known as a beast of burden.

By the evening of the first day they were on a ridge that looked back to the east, on a level with the temple of the Lady at the top of the city. The waterfall could still dimly be seen, a sheet of silver wrinkled and shimmering in the sun, though its roar was hidden. As Narad cooked the meal, Dalvar said, "You have a choice. Either you prove to me that you will not run away, or I will tie you up."

"Master, you can trust me," Narad protested. "Have I not given you my word that I will lead you to the city of the magicians and not try to escape?"

"I have little cause to trust in your word, when once already you have stolen our horses."

"I said I would take care of them, and so I did. Your friend himself said that, if you did not return, the horses were mine. Why then, when you went into that vale and I knew you could not possibly come out again, should I not take advantage of the daylight to lead them to Antar and to safety? As the wise say, the day for the journey, the night for repose. "

"Were we so long in the vale?" asked Dalvar ironically.

"It seemed long to me. You did not say how long I should stay await for your return."

"Mischka is too trusting! I knew we should not leave the horses with you! It has proved his undoing. Were it not for the promise you've made, my hand would lie heavy on you now."

"Master, please!" said Narad, "scuffling back from the fire, "If I'm to lead you I must be healthy and well. Lay not your hand heavy upon me, or we shall never make it to the city of the magicians."

"Do you think that we will make it even so?"

"Trust me, master."

"I have trusted too many times already. All too many times my trust was misplaced. It is better to doubt that to trust."

"Oh no, master. It is much better to trust. One who goes through life doubting, what has he to look forward to?"

"At least this: that he will not be a dupe of others, nor the butt of their jokes."

"Master, we are all the butt of jokes. The is the greatest of jokesters. Why, think you not that the Lady must be a being of great humor, to have created such ridiculous things as you and I? Here we are, two ill-matched persons if ever there were, traveling north together through mountains that might fall on us, in a season that might freeze us, among animals that might seek to eat us! Does not this seem comical to you?"

"Comical? Perhaps. But it will be no comedy for you if you have lied to me."

"I have not lied, master. But who knows truly what we may encounter on this journey."

"What do you mean?"

"Who knows what people we may encounter. There are rumors of villages far back in the hills. In the city of magicians, I saw strangers who were certainly not from Antar."

"Strangers may come from anywhere."

"True, master. And each of us is a stranger, to ourselves first, to friends second, and then to all the world. Even to those who know us best, we are still a stranger."

"Then is there none that we can trust."

"None but the Lady, say the wise."

"I trusted that the Lady would protect those who are love, as I and my wife loved," said Dalvar. "That trust was misplaced. I trusted that I understood those who followed me. That trust too was misplaced. The only trust which has not disappointed me is my trust in this man whom you have killed."

"Not killed, master. We will heal him, with the medicine we seek."

"I pray it be so. He is a man unlike others."

"I believe that, master, though I have met him only once. He did not berate me and mistrust me as you do."

"No, he is too good a man for that," laughed Dalvar. "I saw that even when I first met him, months ago, when he and his family arrived from the Far Southern Lands."

"Far Southern Lands? Is there such a place?"

"There is. When I first met him and heard his songs, his and those of his wife, I knew in him a person who was more true than anyone I had ever known."

"He is one who means a lot to you."

"More than you can know. If we do not find the elixir you have promised, you will regret this journey."

"How should I regret it when I may do service to your friend?"

"If you speak in jest, I will cut the tongue from your head. He is a better man than you know, or can know, you with your lies and thievery."

"But master, all men lie and steal. Have you never told a lie, nor stolen anything?"

"Stolen I have. Thief I was, when all I had was stolen from me. But I always dealt in honor with those who dealt in honor with me. My friend was never less than honorable. So it was that he brought down the Baron. So it was that he drew me from a life of banditry. Have you heard of Dalvar the bandit, slave?"

"No, master, no. I was from the city of enchanters and knew nothing of the land beyond the mountains."

"It is not a name I am proud of. But there was honor to it that neither baron nor slave will ever know."

"I do not dispute your words," replied Narad. "Yet I pray you, master, do not doubt that a slave, though without honor to some, may yet be honorable, and that a slave, though forced at times to deceive, may yet be truthful. I will be both honorable and truthful."

"Then I will trust you. But I warn you. I sleep on a knife edge. Should you seek to rise to do me injury or escape, I will hear you and bring you down before you have gone a step."

"Master, you speak as though I were treacherous! I have given my word that I will lead you into these mountains. What I have sworn I will do."

"See that you do," said Dalvar. He drew his cloak about him and soon fell asleep. Narad lay awake for hours into the night, pondering his chances to escape: whether here, closer to Antar where he might lose himself again in the city, or later in the mountains, where even a hunter such as Dalvar could not hope to find him. As the night drew on toward morning, Narad stood up, slowly and silently. But no sooner had he done so than Dalvar leapt from his blanket, knife in hand.

"What is it you do?" shouted Dalvar.

"But answer the call of nature," said Narad. "Nothing more! Nothing more."

"It is near dawn already. We may as well get up. When you return we will start. I grudge any minute we are not traveling."

"No breakfast, master?" asked Narad. "Those many years I went without food have trained me, never to relinquish a chance for sustenance."

"Cold bread and meat you may have as we walk. I will not stop except when we must, when Death stands so near to my friend."

The rocky path they followed led along the edge of the cliff, bare of vegetation, a strange desert in the midst of the greenness of Antar, watered everywhere else by the winds that blew from the sea and brought the clouds against the mountain.

"Master," panted Narad, as he stumbled along behind Dalvar, "can we not stop and get out of the sun?"

"There is no shade."

"At least let us stop for a rest and to take a drink."

"Drink as we go. We have a long journey ahead, you've said, and we must take advantage of every moment."

"But master, if we wear ourselves out so early in our travels, then we'll have no strength for the longer journey."

"We'll gain strength as we travel. The body hardens to ill use, little food and long marches."

"Master, I am not a strong man like you. My years of slavery sapped my strength. I have not yet grown into what might have been my rightful heritage of muscle and bone."

"Then you must grow into them as we walk. I begrudge every moment we spend resting and not moving forward toward your city of wizards."

"Your impatience is laudable, I'm sure. I will do my best. But my legs are weary and the breath catches in my throat."

"It is because you talk too much," said Dalvar dryly. "Save your breath for the path. Concentrate your thoughts on the end of our journey, that we may get there the sooner."

"As you wish, master," Narad sighed.

They went on in silence for the rest of the day, Dalvar leading, setting a swift pace, always checking behind him to make sure that Narad followed still.

That second night, they slept near to the end of the path to the vale, determined that next day they would go on to the small hollow at the entrance of the vale of the wraiths. From there, they would climb the stony slopes that led north, toward distant sharp-edged, snow-clad mountains that the people of Antar called the Great Wall of the North. Narad felt so weary from the forced march at Dalvar's pace that he stumbled blindly through dinner, chewing on dried meat and dried bread that they had brought for provisions for the trip, then falling asleep as someone dead to the world.

Dalvar sat looking up at the stars, his thoughts returning to Mischka . He wondered what had become of his friend, whether he would last long enough for them to bring medicine back to him, or whether all the journey would prove in vain. If it did prove in vain, what would he, Dalvar, do? At last, he too curled up in his blanket and went to sleep.

By late afternoon, they reached Wraith's Vale. They were about to turn north, into the rocks from which Narad had emerged, when they heard a horse clambering up the path behind them. It was Misk, his horse covered with a lather of foam. He began shouting, as soon as he came within earshot.

"Mischka has left the house. He has disappeared. You must come back and help us find him."

"What are you saying?" shouted Dalvar to him.

"Last night, he must have risen from his bed, made his way downstairs and out of the house. This morning, when we searched through the town for him he was nowhere to be found. The northern gate was open, and some felt he might have gone that way. Yet they who searched for tracks could find trace of him nowhere. We fear he is gone and will do himself injury if we do not find him."

"This is the madness of his illness," said Dalvar in frustration. "We must return."

"But if we do not continue our trip to the city of the enchanters, then we'll not have time to return before the snow starts," protested Narad.

"We have no choice. We must find Mischka. Misk, follow the road back to the city and then go north. We will east to try to intercept him. With luck, we will find him quickly. Come!"

Dalvar and Narad took a little-used path along the edge of the mountains while Misk road back to Antar. Two days later, as Misk, Saschka and Mirath rode north from Antar, they came upon Dalvar and Narad resting at the crossroad where the mountain path met the northern way. From the look on Saschka's face, Dalvar knew that they had no news of Mischka.

"Hopeless, is it?" he asked.

"We have searched everywhere we could. We fear that in his illness he collapsed somewhere and could not respond to our calls."

"Have you heard rumor that someone might have sought revenge against him for his defeat of the Baron?"

"None," Saschka replied.

"Then we must go further north, while you return to Antar."

"I will come with you," said Misk.

So Saschka and Mirath turned and rode back to town, taking with them Misk's horse, while Dalvar, Narad and Misk turned north once again.

Chapter 36

Following the Trail

When they camped that night, Narad said, "Master, is there no reason to expect your friend to have gone back toward Wraith's Vale? Should we not search that way rather than continue to the north? Surely in his fevered condition, the thought of returning again to the one he sought there would surely occur to him. It would draw him as strongly as the north draws adamant."

"He may be right," Misk said to Dalvar. "If my uncle is still alive, then surely his love for Ferenth will draw him back to the vale."

"We saw no sign of him there," Dalvar replied. "Nor did you see him when you returned to Antar."

"He may have hidden among the rocks and escaped my notice."

"Let us return to the vale, masters," urged Narad. "I will be keen of sight and sharp of eye. An eagle will have not the mastery of me!"

"Perhaps you are right. We cannot risk that he has returned there. It is decided then. Tomorrow we shall return to the vale."

As the approached the vale two days later, Dalvar saw signs that someone other than themselves had passed that way: a footstep scraped in the dust here, a branch broken off there. He felt a conviction that this must have been Mischka. Somehow Mischka must have slipped by them, to find his way back to Wraith's Vale. Perhaps he had already entered the vale and been captured by the wraiths.

But suddenly, Mischka stood before them. His eyes were clear and he greeted Dalvar by name.

"Dalvar, my friend. You knew where I would come."

"I feared it, feared that this mad desire to find Ferenth drives you still."

"That is not the reason I came. I sought you. In my fever, I heard this man speak of a city of magic to the north, where one might find an elixir of life. With that, I may perhaps bring Ferenth again from the dead."

"Uncle," cried Misk, "what madness is this? You are not well. And she is a wraith!"

"Not madness," Mischka replied, "unless it be madness to hope. Narad, did you not speak of a city of enchanters and of an elixir of life that might heal me?"

"So I did, great one. The city does indeed lie to the north and I can guide you there. But to bring back one from the dead, that is more than preserving life."

"More than preserving life," agreed Mischka. "But he who has no other hope must grasp at what hope there is. I tell you, I will go there, and will go alone if none will go with me."

"Are you determined on this course?" asked Dalvar.

"As determined as ever I have been."

"Then Narad will guide us there. Misk, you must return to the city to tell them where we are gone."

"I will not."

"What of the worry that Mirath and Saschka feel?"

"I am determined to come with you. Send the Narad back."

"That is an excellent plan!" urged Narad. "I can give you infallible directions to the city of the wise. The children will be glad to know that their father is safe. An excellent plan!"

"We need your guidance through these mountains," said Dalvar in a voice that brooked no disagreement.

Misk was silent for a moment. "I will go, then, to tell them that we have found my uncle. But I will return. If you have not waited for me, I will find the way that you take. If you do not mark the way, I will still follow you."

"I will mark our path," promised Dalvar. "We will wait here for two days. After that, we will travel north again. But I hope that Saschka may persuade you not to follow us."

Misk took off his pack, everything but the shoes on his feet and the clothes on his back, and ran off down the path.

"I would not have him come with us," said Dalvar to Mischka.

"Nor I," Mischka agreed. "But I do not think that Misk will be denied, any more than I."

"As stubborn a man and boy as ever I've seen," declared Dalvar.

"As the wise say, not even the Lady can cure an ass of its stubbornness," said Narad. "And no one shall be more stubborn than I in my faithfulness!"

"Do you mock us? If harm comes to this boy or this man, you will die at my hand."

"Master!" protested Narad. "Have you not learned by now that I am sworn to your service and will serve you as well as any man may?"

"See that you do," said Dalvar.

"But I must warn you all that the way will be difficult. None knows what mischance might meet us on the way."

"That risk we must take. But you will especial care of this man. His safety is your safety. His death will be your death."

"Let us make a fire," Dalvar continued, turning to Mischka. "Though this is an ill-omened place for us, we will wait here."

"Misk will return," Mischka quietly as he sat down on a rock to rest. "Almost it makes me forswear this journey. But I cannot relinquish the hope of reviving Ferenth."

"Good master," said Narad, "just think of how warm and comfortable a house you have in Antar. How glad all would be to see you there."

"I think of it often," Mischka. "But it's not warm and comfortable for me. It's empty and echoing, as empty and echoing as my heart is with the loss I've suffered. My heart will not let me rest until I have done what I can to recover she whom I loved."

"Master, even the greatest magicians are but as children before the power of Death. Her touch cannot be stopped by anyone."

"Not even by this elixir of life?"

"It is but of man's creation. It is strong enough to heal the wounds that men or nature inflict and which invite Death's touch. But I pray you, master, put not so high a value on it, lest when we find it, it works not and then you be disappointed."

"The value it has to me is the highest that it can have: not my life, but the life of one I love."

"Then I will bring you to it. No man will serve you as faithfully as I, master."

"Thank you, Narad," Mischka replied. He pulled his blanket over him and fell asleep.

The next day, as they waited for Misk to return, Mischka was very quiet.

"What is it, my friend?" said Dalvar at last.

"I am thinking that I must go once more into the vale of the wraiths."

"Remember what happened last time," warned Dalvar.

"I will not seek to go beyond the black stone. But I must look once again upon Ferenth."

"Why torment yourself like this?"

"The void she has left in my life, I have tried to fill with memories. It is not enough. If she will come to me, there in the vale, I may see her once again."

"You will not go alone. If we are to enter the vale, then all of us will go. Narad, you come with us.

"I have no desire to see wraiths! They may desire to see me, but I have no desire to see them."

"Yet see them you will. If we go in once more, I will not leave you this time alone, lest you vanish into the rocks and refuse to guide us."

"Master, you don't trust me," complained Narad.

"Trust you?" laughed Dalvar. "I trust that these rocks will not crumble beneath my feet. I trust that the sun will rise tomorrow in the sky. I trust that one day I will die. But trust you? Not yet, at least."

"Master, any man may make a mistake. That is all that happened, truly. I but made a mistake."

"I will not make the mistake," said Dalvar, "of letting you escape, when your help is all that we have."

"I will not try to escape."

"No, you will not.".

"Not try to escape?"

"No. You will not escape," said Dalvar coldly.

They walked through the arching tunnel of rock that formed the gateway to the vale of the wraiths. Soon they could see again the black stone pillar, the power that held the wraiths to this place, that drew them and gave them form and feature. Around them, the valley walls were bleached to a cold, harsh white in the vale, as though the wraiths had leached even the color from the stone. All was stark and staring in the sun.

Mischka, Narad and Dalvar advanced to the upthrust ridge that marked the edge of the stone's power. One by one, the wraiths appeared and stood before them. One by one, they reached out, called to Mischka, to Narad, to Dalvar. Suddenly Ferenth was there. Her eyes were pleading and anxious, and yet cruel and hungry too, tormented by the conflicting desires of her situation and her past.

"Oh my love," cried Mischka, "I dare not touch you again."

"Come to us," whispered the wraiths. "Come to us. Be with us. Let us hold you."

Narad, as though entranced, stepped forward. But Dalvar grabbed his arm and slapped him across the face. "Wake up!" he hissed. "Resist the enchantment of the vale."

"Oh, master," wailed Narad, "I am afraid! I must not stay here!"

"You will stay," said Dalvar, "until Mischka is done."

Mischka had again begun singing. But it was a different song this time from what he had sung before. Instead of asking her to come with him, he sang only of his longing for her, of his love for her.

Love has hurt me deeply, love.
Love holds me still in torment.
Love calls to me deeply, love,
Come stay with me a moment.

Love, I dream that we will
One day be one again.
Love, your voice to me is still,
Yet I hear it again.

Love I hear your voice, it calls me
In the night's deep stillness.
Love I see your face before me.
My thoughts your presence fills.

Love be near me, love be here,
Let your love be round me
While I dream that you and I
Hold each other closely.

As he sang, the wraiths whirled before them, the hunger in their eyes softened for a moment. The wraith who was Ferenth stood completely still, in her look such longing and love, such deep anguish of parting, that Mischka fell on his knees in the dust and cried, "Oh Ferenth! Oh, my love!"

But when the song ceased, the wraiths began to change again. Cold hunger returned to their eyes, all but those of the wraith who was Ferenth, who stood silent, her hands at her sides, and her eyes still filled with anguish.

"Come Mischka!" Dalvar cried. "Come my friend, we must leave this place now!"

He lifted Mischka in his arms and carried him from the valley. Behind them, the voices whispered: "Come, my love, to me! Come, my love."

Dalvar and Nard stumbled back through the narrow cave and out into the light. Dalvar lowered Mischka to the ground and knelt down beside him Slowly Mischka's sobs diminished and at last ceased altogether.

"Dalvar," he said, "are we fated never to have what we most want? I have lost her I love and yet she is there still."

"So she is," said Dalvar, in a troubled voice. He knew Ferenth too, after all, from the travels they had had together. He was no longer sure that the wraith was not Ferenth.

As it grew dark and they finished supper, Mischka curled up in his blanket near the wall of rock. Dalvar told Narad to take the first watch, to wake him if anything untoward happened -- and to remember that Dalvar slept very lightly! Then he cast himself to the ground, pulled his cloak up to his shoulder and was soon asleep.

To Mischka, as he lay there, half asleep and half awake, it seemed that Ferenth stepped through the gateway of the vale of the wraiths and came to his bedside. "My love," she said, "I can speak only a short time before I must return. You must not come again. You must stay far from this place. Do not come back!"

Then she vanished. It seemed he was back in the great pastures below the western mountains. He was there and the sheep were fine and gay in the long light of summer. But then one by one the sheep changed, became ravening wolves whose eyes looked at him with a fierce light. They gathered around him, snapping and snarling at him. He cried out for his brother Linar, for his father Andor, a for his sister Lutha. He cried out, again, for Ferenth. But the wolves advanced, and just as he saw that the one in the front was Ferenth, he awoke sobbing.

"Mischka! Mischka!" shouted Dalvar, who was shaking him. "Wake! Wake up!"

Mischka looked up at his friend. Dalvar's eyes were dark and bruised.

"You were dreaming some terrible dream," said Dalvar.

"So I was. It was desperately frightening."

"I will sit by you. Sleep again. You will need your strength tomorrow."

"And you."

"Strength enough I have. What I need," said Dalvar, "is hope." He leaned back against the wall and drew his cloak about him, settling in for the long watch of the night.

About noon the next day, they heard horses coming up the path. It was Saschka, Silvren, Misk and Mirath. Their horses were steaming with sweat, their legs trembling. Saschka jumped from his horse and threw his arms around his father.

"You'll come back with us, Father! Give up this idea you have of traveling into the north. Do not trust this man. What if the story he tells is nothing but a lie?"

"I must go."

"And if it is as disastrous as your attempt to find Mother in Wraith's Vale?"

"It was not disastrous. I found her there. Her touch was cold agony, but it gives me hope that I may find a way to restore her. Perhaps these magicians are but a fable. But they offer the only hope I have. I must seek them."

Saschka turned to Silvren and said: "My love, I must go with them."

"That you will not!" said Mischka.

"You have two to take care of," said Silvren quietly to her husband, "for I bear your child in my womb."

Saschka stood as one struck dumb.

"There is no choice here," Mischka said to his son. "You must do what you must do, as do I."

"Then I will go with you!" declared Mirath.

"You will not," replied Dalvar angrily. "You are not strong enough for this journey."

I am not a child anymore!"."

"Are you so grown up, then?"

"In this I am. With my cousin I learned to climb in the mountains, gained strength and stamina. But more than all else, Ferenth is my mother. If this journey is on her behalf, then I have the right to go with you. I am as old as my father was when he sought his sister. Have I not the more right to seek to free my mother?"

"Oh my child," said Mischka. "It is easier for the child to leave than for the parent to accept the leaving. I had hoped that you would find in Antar a place of rest, there with your brother. I did not wish to force you to this difficult journey."

"You have not. I go of my free will."

"This is foolish, mistress," objected Narad. "Your way here was difficult, but it was nothing to the journey that we take to the north. Who knows if we will find the city of the magicians at all? It is only once I've traveled this route. Perhaps I've forgotten the turnings. If you do not slow us down, our concern for you may make us falter if we face hard choices and difficult decisions."

"So may your concern for each other. I am no child, and have the right to make this journey. Is it not so, father? Is it not my right to go on this journey?"

Mischka looked at her with troubled eyes. "Mirath, this same strength your mother had, has still perhaps, if that be she in the vale of the wraiths. I cannot command you to stay in Antar, if your heart bids you go."

"I can forbid her", said Dalvar, "if you cannot."

"No, my friend. For my sake, if my daughter wishes to go with us, then accept her too as a comrade and let her come with us. There is danger for her, I know, as for us. But as she says, it is a choice that she is old enough now to make for herself."

"But she imperils the whole enterprise," protested Narad.

"She imperils nothing except herself," said Dalvar.

"Is this what you seek to prevent, my friend?" asked Mischka.

"And should I not? She is your daughter and therefore important to me? If I cannot dissuade you from this journey, yet I am right to dissuade her from coming."

Mischka shook his head. "Be guided in this by me. I feel we will have need of her before we are done, have need of her strength, the innocence of her courage. If she wishes to come with us, then so she shall."

"This is disastrous," moaned Narad.

"If it must be accepted," said Dalvar, "then you will accept it. But if you do not guide us true, if anything happens to her, accept as well that you will not survive."

"I think," protested Narad, "that I have little chance of surviving at all. First you punished me for the horses. Then you would punish me if we find not the city of the sorcerers. Then you would punish me if anything happens to Mischka. Then you would punish me if anything happens to his daughter. It would be better if I just sat down here on these rocks and refused to move."

"No, Narad," said Mischka, laughing for the first time since he had embraced the wraith. "There is need for you. If you lead us truly, we will repay you. You need not fear what lies before us. Mirath, one last time I ask you. Will you not stay with Saschka and Silvren?"

"Life or death," replied Mirath, "I will not leave you." But as she said this, her eyes turned to Dalvar.

"Come," he said.

Mischka embraced Saschka and Silvren, as did Misk and Mirath. Then Narad led them into the broken mountains of the north, as Saschka and Silvren watched them go, with sinking hearts.

Chapter 37

The Village in the Mountains

As they left behind the vale of the wraiths, the five travelers could see ahead of them the tall peaks of the great northern range that rose thousands of feet above the foothills to the south. Even those foothills to the south were white-capped already with the snows of late fall. As they journeyed north, the weather grew colder and the footing more treacherous.

It was an area little known by any and never mapped. The settlement of Egeria and Antar had been from the mountains and plains to the west. The mountains to the north had proved forbidding to any.

Before meeting Narad, Mischka had never heard of any people who lived among those peaks. So it was with surprise that he had heard Narad's story of a great city of wizards far off in the mountains. Dalvar still looked with doubt on the story. But Mischka needed to believe in it so strongly that he'd carried his friends with him, and at least one who was less than a friend, who called the others master.

They followed a river northward through the foothills. Each night, the cold of the wind and rocks struck into their bones. Each morning when they woke, there were skirts of ice around the rocks, even though the stream was fast-moving. The river grew smaller, dwindling to a stream as they climbed up out of the valley and onto a ridge. There before them, far closer than they'd realized, the great range of mountains.

"Where is this city of yours?" Dalvar asked Narad.

"We just go straight on. We head toward that great peak, the White Mountain it's called in the language of those who live there.

"How is it you speak our language?" Mischka asked.

"It is my language as well, the language of the city of wizards."

"Strange that none should have heard of these people, when you speak our language."

"Not so strange. It is from Egeria that the magicians came."

"This is a story of which there has been no rumor," said Dalvar. "Magicians in Egeria?"

"So it is said."

"Indeed, and who were they?"

"One was called Aluinír. The others I do not know. They carved a great city out of the living rock of the mountain and have lived there ever since."

"And you say that if we follow straight on towards that mountain we will come to the realm of these wizards?" asked Dalvar suspiciously.

"So it is, master. I am honorable and truthful. Just follow me and we'll arrive there soon enough, if we can outwit the storms of these mountains, and if we do not meet any stone giants, and if..."

"Enough!" shouted Dalvar.

But it was not enough, at least for Narad. Every night, he made plans for his escape. He did know the mountains. If he could escape from Dalvar, he might hope to get back to Antar, or to other cities of the south. That night, when it seemed everyone had fallen asleep, Narad gathered his cloak and his wallet of food, and stole away from the camp.

Dalvar watched him go. When Narad had left the camp, Dalvar wakened Misk. "Our guide has run away," he whispered. "I will follow. Wait here for me. I'll be back with our guide, willing or no. It lies in his hands which it will be."

He stole after Narad, who meanwhile first had scrambled back down the path they had come, then cut off abruptly at an angle to the west. Though he went as quietly as he could, there were still occasional slips, sliding on rocks, tumbles of shale that told Dalvar where the Narad had gone. When the sun came up, Narad threw himself to the ground to rest. No sooner had he done so, than Dalvar stepped forward.

"Is this the way we should go then?" he asked in a quiet, threatening voice.

Narad leapt to his feet and looked wildly about him. Catching sight of Dalvar, he turned to run. But Dalvar grabbed him by the scruff of his neck.

"What, in such a hurry? We've left behind our companions."

"I was scouting the way!" Narad protested. "I had thought perhaps we took a wrong turn and so came back this way to see."

"Indeed? And have you discovered our error?"

"Not yet. I think I should go a bit farther this way. If you would go back to the camp and bring the others..."

"I think we will both go back to the camp," said Dalvar, pushing Narad before him.

"If you wish! But really, I'm not sure we're on the right path. If we don't go back this way, I'm not sure..."

"I thought you said the city was straight to the north."

"Perhaps I have forgotten a little bit of the way. It has been, after all, some time since I made the journey."

"How long? One month? Two?"

"Oh, much longer. I stayed in these hills for quite a while."

"And perhaps you are thinking of staying in these hills again?"

"Oh no, master! I am looking forward to returning to Antar."

"If you wish to return to Antar, you will tell the truth now. Is there this city of magicians?"

"Oh indeed, indeed, indeed!" protested Narad. "We just have to find it and then you'll see it."

"And this elixir that you've promised to my friend?"

"I was told of it by the old magician. I'm sure it is there."

"If you have betrayed us, your life is forfeit and your end will be swift."

"Trust me, master" said Narad. "I am faithful unto death."

"Be true: or dead you will be," said Dalvar, as he shoved Narad down the path before him. When they arrived back at the camp, Mirath, Misk and Mischka were sitting by the fire, waiting for them.

"So, Narad," said Misk. "Have you decided to return?"

"I never thought otherwise," protested Narad. "Here I was, doing my best to scout out the path and then this great lump of a fellow comes and rudely buffets me forth. I tell you, I am little appreciated for all I am doing for you."

"That may well be," laughed Mischka. "Lead us to this city of magicians and you 'will be rewarded."

"Rewarded by being sold back into slavery, no doubt!"

"We will protect you from that if you lead us true."

"I'll not lead you false. But there are many paths, perhaps to remember clearly. But I will do my best. Surely we will find the city, as I have promised."

"Surely we will," agreed Mischka. "Now lead on. Or should we go back the way you went?"

"No, I think we are on the right path after all. We should go straight ahead. Of course, we may need to halt now and then so I can inspect alternate paths to make sure they are not the ones we should take. But do not worry. Narad will find the way. As the wise have said, he who would follow his nose need never look behind him!"

But there was no path at all, no trace of a path. They curved around knolls and up over ridges and down along streams. The landscape was all but barren, only a scattered tree, here and there, sculpted by the wind that blew harder and harder. Snow fell more and more often. Though the path was difficult, more difficult was the weight in their hearts.

"How much farther is it to this city?" asked Dalvar one morning when they woke up with three inches of snow on their blankets."

"Oh, not far now!" said Narad. "We should be there within two days, at this rate. We will soon reach that mountain that is the city of the magicians." But there was no sign, from where they stood at least, of any city.

"You cannot see it from here," Narad assured them. "It is a city inside the mountain."

"Then we will see it when we arrive," Dalvar replied. "Lead on!"

But the weather grew worse, the cold more bitter and the snow deeper.

"Master," Narad said, "We cannot go on. We will never make it to the city of the wizards. Let us go back and wait until Spring. Surely it will make no difference to wait that much longer? This journey will kill us all. What good will that do, if we are ourselves turned to wraiths? Do you seek your death in this way?"

"No," replied Mischka. "But we must go on."

"Father," asked Mirath, "why would Mother have come back as a wraith, someone as gentle as she, someone as loving as she? Surely she, if any, should have found rest and peace rather than this half-life of haunting and sorrow."

"Perhaps what we see in the vale are only the shadows of our own sorrows. But she whom I saw in the vale was in some part Ferenth; the violence of her death at the hands of the Baron's assassins brought her to this. I must try to free her."

"Uncle," said Misk, "there is truth in what Narad says, that this journey we take at this time of year is dangerous for all of us."

"So it is. I would be glad if you all returned home. I understand that you cannot, if I do not. For that I'm sorry. I need this man to lead me to his city. If I go, will the rest of you stay behind?"

"I will not," said Dalvar. "You know that well. Where you go, I must go."

"And we as well," said his daughter and nephew.

"Then we have no choice." Mischka turned and walked ahead, saying, "Come, Narad. Is this the way we must go?"

"It is the way to the city of the wizards," Narad agreed. "But I wish we were going another way."

Finally the climbed to the top of a final ridge. In front of them, a great escarpment that marked the fault at the edge of the range, soaring up in their path. A broken defile slanting up into the sheer cliff was to be their path forward.

"Lead on," said Mischka to Narad, "if this is the way we must go."

"So it is. You must be careful. The rocks are loose and treacherous."

"Show us how we should go. We will follow."

Narad went first, then Misk, Mirath, Mischka and Dalvar last of all. When one of those near the front slipped, a small shower of stones cascaded downwards. Those below put their arms over their heads to protect themselves from the stones. At last they came to the top of the cleft in the escarpment.

First they turned to look behind them, to the south.

They stood high above the foothills. They could see to the east a glitter and shimmer of sea, a full two weeks walk from them. Near the sea, though it was hard to tell from that distance, a distant flash of light might well have been the golden roof of the temple of the Lady in Antar.

They turned to the north, and there a massive storm loomed before them.

"Find us shelter!" shouted Dalvar to Narad. "We must not be caught in the open by that storm."

"Masters, there is no shelter here," shouted Narad.

"Let us back up against the cliff, "said Mischka. "At least it will give us some protection against the wind and snow."

They set their backs against the rocks and their cloaks about them. There was no wood for a fire. They had few provisions left. As the snow piled up around them, Mischka, worn out by the experiences in Wraiths' Vale and by the difficult, began to shiver uncontrollably.

"Father?" Mirath wrapped her arms around him. "Help him!" she cried to Dalvar.

Dalvar took off his cloak and wrapped it around his friend. "I must find wood for a fire!" he said.

"If you go out in this storm," warned Narad, "you'll never find your way back."

"You must stay with them," said Dalvar. "I will find my way. Though I do not know these mountains yet, yet mountains are no stranger to me."

He went off in to the darkness. It was nearly two hours later that he returned, carrying a small armful of wood tied up with his belt.

"You are lucky you did not lose your trous," said Narad seriously, but with a glint of mockery in his eye.

"It was the easiest way to carry it," said Dalvar shortly. "Come help me set this fire and find some way to warm water for Mischka."

They peeled back one of the sticks to get at the dry brittle wood inside. Dalvar made a pile of shavings, carefully coaxed a spark to light, and soon the fire was burning well, despite the snow and wind.

Narad took from his pack a small beaten metal pot. He filled it with snow and set it on the fire. When the snow had melted, he added to the water a pinch of herbs from his pouch.

"What is that you've adding in?" asked Dalvar.

"Just heal-all. I pray it may help your friend."

"What of the rest of you?" asked Mischka.

"You must take it first," said Narad, holding the pot out to him.

As Mischka drank, his shivering gradually subsided. His eyes grew weary and heavy-lidded. "Thank you, my friend," he said to Narad. "I trust there is enough for the rest."

"Water is one thing we have no dearth of," Narad replied, "even if it is frozen!"

"In the vale of the wraiths, there is not even water. So we have at least something here that we should be grateful for."

"I am not ungrateful," replied Narad. "But I would be more grateful if there were less ice water in my clothes!."

Everyone laughed at that.

The next day dawned sunny and dry. As they continued on their way, Dalvar was constantly at Mischka's side, supporting his arm, seeking to distract him from his dark thoughts by an occasional word of comfort and hope.

That night, there was a rustle in the darkness around them. Suddenly, they were surrounded by people gesturing threateningly without stone-tipped spears.

"Do nothing!" Narad said. "Stay calm!."

He spoke to the strangers in some other language. Then he said, "I have told them that we are pilgrims on a journey to the city of the wizards. They accept that and offer us a place to stay."

"Who are they?" asked Dalvar.

"They live in the deep valleys of these mountains and trade occasionally with those in the city of the wizards. That is all I know of them."

"I have never heard of them," said Mischka.

"Few have, only traders and slavers, for sometimes they buy slaves from the south."

"Is it safe for us to go with them?" asked Dalvar.

"Safe enough, I think," Narad replied. "And as the wise say…"

"What do the wise say?" asked Mirath.

"I don't know," Narad answered. "But in any case, we have no choice."

They went with their captors, following a long and winding path down into a rocky valley. A honeycomb of rooms facing to the south was carved into the mountain wall. The leader of their captors led them to one of these rooms. Others brought food and woven blankets of a strange coarse felt, as though from the hair of a horse or other heavy animal. Dalvar studied each one who came in, looking for any sign of weapons, any hint of a threat. But suddenly he stopped, staring across the room, and then called out in a loud voice: "Lethen!"

All the eyes in the chamber turned to him. He strode across the floor, to one of the women who now stood with her eyes raised to him, staring at him as he approached.

"Dalvar, is it you?" Her face was white with shock.

"Who is it?" called Mischka.

"This is my wife, Lethen," he called back. "What are you doing here?" asked her.

"I was sold as slave to these people. I have been here ever since."

"You shall be a slave here no longer," shouted Dalvar.

By this time all the hall was in an uproar. Narad tugged at Mischka's sleeve.

"What is happening?" Narad asked.

Mischka told him the story of Dalvar's wife being kidnapped and his search for her. Narad turned to the men around him, explaining as they watched with stony faces, then replied with harsh voice.

Narad turned back to Mischka. "They say the woman is theirs and may not leave."

Dalvar drew his dagger. "She will come with us, whether they will or no."

"Dalvar, what would you have me do?" said Lethen, her voice halting and uncertain. "Can I leave this place and return with you? Look at me. I am no longer the girl that you knew. My family is here. I have a daughter and two sons. I have a new husband. I cannot go with you."

"You must, I will not let you stay."

"Is this what you wish?" Mischka asked Lethen.

"I do not know who you are, stranger," she said to Mischka. "But if you can convince my husband that this is my will, then you do us both a great service."

"Narad," Mischka said, "explain to our hosts that we must have time to understand this." He took Dalvar by the arm and led him back out of the room.

All that day, he sat with Dalvar while his fried raged and cursed and said, "She must come with me!" At last Mischka asked Narad to bring Lethen to them again. She came, wariness in her eyes.

"I have come to know Dalvar, to know that his love for you is strong. Would you really stay here and not resume your life with him?" Mischka asked.

"When a parting comes, it comes," Lethen replied. "Years of sorrow have changed me from the woman that I was. I am no longer Lethen. I have a new name, a new life. I no longer seek to leave. Dalvar, my husband, your ring was taken from me. Though I see you now again, see again the man that you are and were, yet I cannot go with you."

She turned and ran from the room. Dalvar put his hands before his face and wept with all the pain of ten years of loss and loneliness.

Chapter 38

Narad's Confession

They spent the night in the village. When morning came and they prepared to go, Dalvar said, "These people have stolen from me more than anyone else, more than I ever took from anyone."

"Not stolen," Mischka replied. "When separation comes, it comes."

"You can say this?" Dalvar bitterly reproached his friend. "You, who drag us with you on this journey, unable to accept separation from Ferenth?"

"You know that Lethen is well and happy," said Mischka

"Happy? Well perhaps. But happy?"

"If not happy, at least accepting of where she is. She has a life among these people now and loves that are her own. However great your loneliness, you cannot tear her away from these things. You cannot ask of her what she cannot give."

Dalvar sat in stony silence.

"Is there such pain in this?" asked Mischka. "Is it because of her having found someone else, or is it because you love her still? "

Dalvar looked at Mirath with a fleeting expression of surprise. Then he said slowly, "I cannot tell."

"My friend, to have hope appear so suddenly and so suddenly be dashed, this is more than cruel. But believe me in this, that however much you may have suffered, however much you suffer now, yet what she has asked of you, you can and must give."

Mirath came and leaned her head on Dalvar's, put her arms around him. "My father has need of you still," she said. "Can you set aside this sorrow and come with us? What would you have done, had she said she would come? Bring her with us too, and her children?"

"They could have waited. I could return this way."

"Perhaps," agree Mirath. "But if you do not return, what then?"

Dalvar turned to Mischka. "Your daughter has inherited your silver tongue. I owe you a debt which I will repay by coming with you. But if we succeed in saving your wife, then I will return here again and take what is mine."

"Perhaps here among these people you might find a new life worth living. Or perhaps you will find it somewhere else."

"Masters," interrupted Narad, "if we must go, we should be on our way before the storms come again. We should not linger, if we are going. But would it not be better to stay here until winter has passed?"

"That may be so. But we have made the decision that we have made."

"Then we will go," agreed Narad with a shrug of the shoulders.

"Ask the people of the village if they will give us warmer clothes and for anything else we must have to survive the trek through these mountains."

"You speak wisely, master." Narad gathered warmer cloaks and stouter boots, a good supply of food to take them further in to the mountains, thick felt hats of the wool of their ungainly animals, the raffars.

As they left the village, Mischka looked back and saw Lethen with three small children, looking after them. With her was a man in whose features Mischka thought he could detect a resemblance to the children. Then he set his face once again toward the mountain where Narad had promised they would find the wizards.

Dalvar said little as they walked. But Mirath stayed by him, and as they walked it seemed to Mischka that Dalvar's anger and sorrow grew lighter.

"Had you no thought of leaving us there," Mischka asked Narad that night as they sat again in the cold and the dark.

"Leaving you, master?" Narad asked in his turn.

"There in the village you would be safe, free of dangers, free of us. How could we constrain you to go on?"

"But a stranger is always a stranger in such a village. Better to go with you than to be a stranger among those people. It is a harsh life they live, master, for the snows are cruel and the winters long and hard. And one would grow tired of eating nothing but raffar meat, morn and night, thirteen moons of the year."

"Do they have nothing else?" laughed Mischka. "Surely their beasts themselves must eat something!"

"Only the poor grass that grows on the valley floor in winter and the mountain alps in the summer. They have a few crops sturdy enough to survive in these high places and short summers. Berries they pick along the watercourses and roots that they dig where pockets of earth have collected. It is a harsh life."

` "You dream of something more?"

` "I have dreams enough, or I should never have come south in the first place.. Yet as we come north, it seems strange that everything here should seem so familiar and welcoming."

"Then it is true that you came from these mountains and there is such a city as you have said?"

Narad gave Mischka a sidelong glance. "Do you not trust me, master?"

"I follow you. Your story gives me the only hope that I have. I hope it may be true, and will follow you in that hope. But whether I trust you, that is a question I am not yet prepared to answer."

"There is little room for trust in the world. Where can one place trust when all things change?"

"Not all things," said Mischka, staring up into the night sky brilliant with stars. "Some things there are that endure: Love. Hope. Faith that there is beyond this vale in which we find ourselves, a vale in which joy and pain are so intermixed, something more enduring and free of sorrow."

"Beyond the stars, you think?".

"Perhaps," said Mischka. "Or perhaps it is here with us and we do not see it. When I think of what Ferenth and I shared, what one may share in love with another, then I believe that the Lady has given us a world good and true, that such a wonder as love will endure beyond it."

"I hope it may be so for your sake, master."

"It is my hope," said Mischka. And so he slept.

Narad lay awake for a long time. At last, when he thought everyone was asleep, he got up, gathered his things and crept out into the dark. Dalvar again rose behind him, and this time he woke Mirath, Misk, and Mischka: "Come we must follow this time. We dare not get separated in these mountains."

They could hear the stumbling steps of Narad ahead of them. There was a great cry, a sound of falling, and then silence. They continued forward cautiously, until they came to a cliff. Some twenty-five feet below, they could see Narad sprawled on the ground.

"I will go down and bring him back up," said Dalvar.

He got out the rope, went down, slung Narad over his shoulder, and with the aid of the rope climbed back up again.

"is he dead?" asked Mirath.

"No, more's the pity," said Dalvar. "He's deceived us from the start. We're nowhere near a city now."

Narad opened his eyes. "You're right, and now we will all die. I had hoped to escape, but there's no way forward and no way back."

"There is no city?" asked Mischka.

"No city. No elixir that heal you, that will bring back your wife. It is a story I made up. It's just a story."

"Not a story," said voice behind them. All four spun about, Dalvar drawing his sword as a tall man stepped forward, barely discernible in the starlight.

"There is an elixir," he said "for those who seek."

Chapter 39

The House of the Wise

Dalvar stepped forward. "Who are you?" he demanded, threatening the stranger with his sword.

"Put up your blade," said the man, whose face was lined and seamed with years, yet seemed rather ageless than old. "There are dangers enough in these mountains. You need not bring any more dangers into them."

"Who are you?" asked Mischka, looking with puzzlement and suspicion at the man's carefully woven clothes and guarded face.

"There is no city of magicians, and yet one magician there is. My name is Aluinír."

"So there is such a person?" said Misk. "Narad wasn't lying?"

"So there is, and he am I. This creature has been my servant."

"Master, I did not mean to run away," said Narad in a piteous voice.

"Strange that you did mean to run away and yet you've been gone for months? You will bear what penalty I see fit to levy."

"What you will, master. I have come back, after all. It was but youthful excitement and exuberance that led me astray. These people need your help and so I brought them to you."

"Sought rather to abandon them, I believe, something you are all too good at. But if they have sought my help, help they shall have. Come," he said, turning back to Mischka and the other, "you must be weary of your journey. Come with me and I'll find you comfort better than this rocky hillside and these barren rocks. You may tell me your story later. For now," he said to Narad, "bring these strangers to my house." With that, he turned and disappeared into the night.

"You must come," said Narad. "It is the only hope you have of finding what you are seeking."

"Little enough hope it seems," replied Dalvar, "yet what choice have we but to go with you or to starve in these mountains?"

"I do not trust this magician," said Mirath.

"No more you should," agreed Mischka. "But I do not think he means us harm."

Narad rose and led the way after the magician. They went among stones and rocks. At times it seemed a path, at times the random tumble of stone from the peaks surrounding them. For two hours they followed Narad. Then as the sun was just coming over the eastern peaks, they came into a small valley. Waterfalls cascaded down the mountain walls, rivers meandered across the valley floor, bright with flowers despite the snow on the mountains above them. Before them, carved into the north wall of the valley, was the wizard's house.

"Welcome," said the magician, standing at the doorway.

"What is this place?" asked Dalvar.

"This is my home. I have lived here many years. Once I lived among, watching the works of humankind, their follies and cruelties. I withdrew to this place to rest, to listen to the waterborne voice of the Lady. I have lived here for centuries now."

"Centuries?" asked Mirath in disbelief.

"Indeed, child." replied the magician. "I have lived here many hundred years."

"There was a story that Firfal told, of a great wizard who lived long ago and vanished suddenly," said Mischka. "I thought it was just a fable."

"It's true enough. Who but I could have lived that long and yet done so little? That is the first lesson that the wise learn, that all that we do is but little. Come, all is ready for you, and you are greatly welcome."

He led them into the hall. It was a great carved stone chamber with pillars along the side walls that radiated out at their capitals into fanned ribs of stone, crossing and re-crossing the ceiling. The room was carved into the rock of the mountain and the walls glittered with crystal and mica. In the center of the hall was a large table, with places set for six.

"Tonight you are my guests. You may have what you wish. Ask my servants and they will provide you. As for you, Narad, you may help serve."

Carefully, as though afraid a single move might annoy the magician, Narad bowed and went to kitchen, to begin helping with the serving and carrying.

"Now then," asked the magician as they sat down, "how can I help you? It is the same as all who come, is it not? You seek riches? gold and jewels?

"No," Mischka replied, "something more precious than gold and jewels."

"And what may that be?"

"My wife has become one of the wraiths of the Vale. I would have her restored to me, or if not restored, free of being a wraith."

"None may break the bonds the Lady has set on those who assume the forms of grace."

"Narad spoke of an elixir that could restore the sick to health. You yourself said there is such a treasure."

"This is true."

"Then all we ask is a vial of this liquid, that I may try using it to heal Ferenth."

The magician was silent for several minutes, looking at Mischka. Then he said: "The water of life is not mine to give or to keep. It is from a spring deep in the mountains. The water you drink now is leavened with a trace of it."

The guests looked down at their glasses in surprise. Indeed they were drinking something more than water, more satisfying and subtle.

"It is from the heart of the earth.. Those who drink of it find courage and strength."

"Will this then restore my Ferenth?" asked Mischka.

"It is potent, but who and what the wraiths are none can say. What effect the water of life will have on them is hidden from me. Still, I will take you to the spring."

He rose from the table and said "Come, let us sit by the fire. Bring us more water," he said to Narad.

As they sat by the fire, sipping the water their host gave them, Dalvar was silent and Mirath, weary with the journey and the worry, slept at her father's knee.

Chapter 40

Return to the Vale

When morning came, Mischka, Mirath, Misk and Dalvar rose together and found, in the great hall where they'd eaten the night before, the table set again and the old man waiting for them.

"You may come with me," he said, "to see the spring."

"Master, you would take these strangers there? " asked Narad, who had come to the table with a tray of fool.

"It is not mine, to deny to anyone. If you would take some with you," the magician said to Mischka, "come and we will get it together."

He led them up through a tunnel built through the rock onto the plateau behind them. Up still farther they went, where the great silver fang rose above them in its solitary splendor. Higher and higher they climbed, though folds in the rock and narrow passageways. As they climbed above the trees, the air was filled with the sharp, clean smell of rock and snow.

At last they came to an opening in the mountainside.

"We must enter here," said the old man.

"What is this place?" asked Dalvar.

"Enter and you will see."

In the grotto, in a pocket of sunlight, a small spring gushed from the wall of the cliff. It tumbled into a small pool, and yet the pool grew no bigger, draining back into the mountain from which the water sprang.

"None knows where this water goes. I believe it runs under the sea, to well forth again in some far distant land."

"That may be so," agreed Mischka. "I have knew water such as this once before, in an island far to the east."

"Then you know of its potency," said the old man. He took a small flask from the pocket of his robe, held it under the water pouring from the rock, then stoppered it firmly.

"It is precious and potent," he said, handing the vial to Mischka. "If you take it with you to the vale of the wraiths it may have the effect that you wish. Yet I know not truly what effect it may have and counsel you to have caution."

As they came back through the cleft, already the westering sun was dipping below the mountains. Narad lit a torch and the old man led them back down the mountainside, back to their rooms in his cliff dwelling.

"Tomorrow when you leave, I will give you a raffar to carry your provisions. You will need more than when you came, for the weather now will make the passes nearly impossible. Narad must go with you to guide you on the way and to bring the animal back."

"Do you not think he will try to escape again?" asked Mischka.

"Perhaps," replied the old man, smiling. "But he has had his taste of the world. He will come back and return to his fellows from the village. Some other one from the village will join me here, some other with dreams of something beyond these mountains. He too may leave for a while. But he too will return, as all do."

"Then Narad is from that village?" asked Dalvar.

"Of course, as have been all those who served me here."

"What are you?" Misk asked.

"As I have said, an old man, who has seen many things and known many people."

"Are you a magician?" Misk asked again.

"Magician?" replied the old man musingly, as he sipped his water. "There is a story that years ago the Lady sent wise ones to the world to tend it, to protect what needs protecting."

"Are you such a one?" asked Mischka

"If so, I am no longer wise," replied the old man. "It is time for sleep. You have an early start to make tomorrow. Narad!"

"Yes, master?"

"Guide them well. Do not stop at the village on the way south. But when you are done with your journey, return with the raffar back to the village and there bid them send me a new apprentice."

"You do not want me to help you any longer? " asked Narad.

"Narad, my friend, you have been anxious enough to leave. Are you regretful now that your time is done?"

"Master, it was only youthful spirits that led me to wander. Do not the wise ones say that youth has ever a restless leg?"

"If so, I have never heard it!" laughed the old man. "It is time to take those youthful spirits and apply them to some useful task. Go with them. Guide them safely back."

"I will, master," said Narad.

When morning came, the old man stood at the door of his castle to bid them farewell. "You must be on your way, for again storms grow close, and the way will be long and hard, as it was on the way here. Do not seek to find me again. Farewell!"

There were five of the sturdy animals for them. Narad led them back along the track swiftly. No sooner had they left the wizard's vale than the snow began again. The first night as they slept it piled up about them until, when they woke in the morning, each was to the others no more than a pile of snow. They stood and shook the snow from them, but the snow still fell

"We must take care not to get separated," said Narad, and tied a rope from one the next, and then led the way south. All day long they rode, and at times the snow blew so fiercely that they couldn't continue. It was like needles of ice carried by the wind, striking them in the face. The next day was the same, and on the third day as they rode south over the pass and saw below them the cleft that led south to the land of the wraiths, they heard on all sides a great thunder and booming.

"The stone giants!" said Narad, and indeed it seemed to be. From the moutains on either side of them great torrents of snow came pouring down. Then high above, they saw the giants themselves, tossing boulders at one another, the mountains shuddering under the impact. They hurried down the path until the tumult was far behind and at last it was silent and the earth still again.

They saw no sign of the mountain people and of their villages. When Mischka asked of them, Narad said, "None of the villages lie in this direction. They are mostly farther to the north and to the west. My own village lies in that direction."

"And will you return there when this journey is done."

"Yes, my time as a slave is done. Perhaps," he said sheepishly, "I should really say servant, or perhaps apprentice?"

"Who is that old man, your master," asked Misk.

"No one knows. He's been there as long as our stories can tell, and has always been an old man. Some say that when he is angry he causes earthquakes and avalanches. They say from his house he can look about across the wholeworld and know what events are happening. But the truth of all this no one knows."

"And yet you lived with him?" said Dalvar.

"For ten years I was his servant."

"And knew no more of him than anyone else?"

"Only him. It was a lonely house for a boy," said Narad quietly. "Except for the animals that I tended, months would go by when I would see no one else. But he taught me languages, took me up into the mountains, showed me many things."

"Why you? " asked Mischka.

"I have wondered that too. I thought perhaps he intended that I should become someone else, someone wiser, who might be a leader of his people."

"And will you be?" asked Misk.

"Not I," said Narad, laughing.

"Yet," said Mischka, "it seems to me you are not the same as on the journey north."

"Perhaps I'm not. Then I was running away, seeking to find my way in a larger world. Now I know that my home is here in the mountains. I return to your world only at the bidding of one I can now respect, not fear and resent. Perhaps I have changed."

"After you return to the village, will you ever again venture to Antar?"

"I don't know.. People of the mountains have long kept themselves aloof. Perhaps the time has come when we should involve ourselves with these southern lands. Perhaps you'll see me again."

So they continued until they reached the vale of the wraiths.

"Will you be alright in these snows?" Mischka asked as Narad repacked the raffars for his return journey.

"People of the mountains grow used to snow," Narad replied. "It may not be an easy journey, but I do not fear it. Farewell my friends -- friends now, and not masters. May the Lady guide and protect you!"

"And you too," they said as they watched Narad lead the beasts back into the mountains where the storm clouds had cleared and the sky shown a deep and brilliant blue.

As they climbed down the ridge, the air grew warmer. They reached the valley floor and there they slept. The next morning, when they rose, Mischka led the way into the Vale of the Wraiths.

"My friend," said Dalvar, "do not do this."

"I have made a long journey to come to this moment. This time I ask you all to wait here. Come no farther into the vale. Do not draw me from the arms of her who is my wife."

In one hand he carried the vial. Again as before, the wraiths began to gather from along the walls, to stretch across the eastern boundary of the vale. Their voices began to sing in his ears: "Come, come to us. Find rest in our arms, find peace in our arms."

With a grim face and his jaw set, Mischka stepped forward, past the stone pillar, as behind him Mirath, Misk and Dalvar waited at the entrance to the vale. They saw him step forward. They saw him reach out his hands and call "Ferenth". They saw her step forward, out of the crowd of wraiths. They saw Mischka take the vial and unstopper it. And they saw him pour some of the water on his hands and fling it upon Ferenth and the other wraiths.

There was a great scream from the wraiths. Mischka again poured water on his hands and again flung it on the wraiths.

Again a great scream came from them, a scream of dying souls dying again. Those nearest him fell to the ground. Again he flung the water on them. All but Ferenth fell before him. Only she stood. She reached out and put her hands into his, still wet from the water of life. Then she too fell to the ground, vanishing as she fell, and Mischka fell to the ground with her.

Mirath, Misk and Dalvar rushed forward. The ground was bare. Mischka lay alone. They lifted him up, and a faint pulse flickered in his wrist and neck.

Once again Dalvar carried Mischka out of Wraith's Vale, waiting there with him and Mirath while Misk set off to Antar to get horses for them all. For three days they waited, tending Mischka, talking quietly, eating what little they had left in their packs, until Misk came riding back with Saschka and two spare horses. Saschka took Mischka in front of him and they rode slowly back to Antar. All the way there, Dalvar rode next to Mirath and held her hand in his.

Chapter 41

End of the Journey

They came at last to Antar and to the house of Amerach. Silvren was there to open the door to her father-in-law and cousins. The signs of her pregnancy were easy to see now and the house was filled with the joy she felt.

They carried Mischka to bed, and took turns keeping watch. Although he did not wake, day by day he grew stronger.

Dalvar and Mirath often sat together at Mischka's bedside. On the day after they had brought Mischka home, as they watched at Mischka's bed, Mirath laid her hand on Dalvar's shoulder. "Does he matter so much to you?" she asked.

Dalvar's hand came up and rested on hers. "When first I knew him, I thought he was a dreamer and fool But I see now that his dreams are the dreams of truth, that his folly is better than wisdom. He is for me so dear a friend that I would sooner die than have him die."

"Why? What is it that you see in him?"

"I don't know, unless it is that in him there is a sense of the beauty of life and its possibilities that I had lost long ago."

"Was it not there in the laughter that you shared with my father and mother? Was it not there in the love that you gave him on these journeys? Is there nothing in your heart now but regret for what is lost?"

"What is in my heart," replied Dalvar, "I do not intend to speak."

"Then I'll speak it for you," Mirath said quietly. "You found your wife, but she is no longer the wife you knew. Though she lives, she is now a stranger to you."

"So I do feel."

"But it is more than that, is it not? You feel that you have no home, that you will forever be a stranger, condemned to be homeless, restless, forever a wanderer"

"So it is."

"But have you not found another that stirs your heart in the way that she once did? Is it not that you are afraid to acknowledge what you feel, and in acknowledging to ask whether she may feel the same?"

Dalvar stood and looked at Mirath. He took her two hands in his. "You are young still. You are the daughter of him whom I love more than myself and more than my own life. What have I to offer anyone? What have I to offer you?"

"What but who you are? What but the love you feel for my father and the love you feel for me. Is it not so, Dalvar?"

Dalvar, the man who had been for so many years an exile, bowed his head over his hands. "What you say is true."

"And this is true as well," continued Mirath. "As my mother loved my father, I love you. As you were true to my father, you will be true to me. As you have been faithful to him, you will be faithful to me."

"And your brother? What will he think of this?" asked Dalvar.

"He will think it the best of matches," said Saschka from the doorway, with a grin on his face.

"You know nothing of me," protested Dalvar.

"I know this much of you," replied Saschka. "I know that my sister loves you and that you love her."

"I cannot go back to the home I once had."

"Then we will sell it," Mirath said without a pause.

"We can decide nothing," said Dalvar, "until your father's fate is decided for death or for life."

"I am content to wait," Mirath replied.

They waited, two days, then three, and then on the fourth, Mischka stirred and opened his eyes. He looked in wonderment around the room.

"Was it all a dream then?" he said.

"Was what a dream?" asked Dalvar

"The wraiths, the magician?"

"None of it was dream."

"And are they all gone?".

"They are, and you a great hero, the one who freed the wraiths of Wraith's Vale."

"Not only the wraiths are free. I have freed myself too, my friend. Wherever Ferenth is, there I know I will one day be too."

From that day he grew quickly stronger. His friends and family were glad to see in him again something of the Mischka of old.

One day he asked Saschka to bring his harp to him. He played a melody they had heard before, but now re-shaped with deeper harmonies and simpler line, refined by the loss of what he held most dear, enriched by what he had gained in ending the torment of Wraith's Vale.

Dalvar was a great hero in the city for his role in freeing it from the Baron; and he had sold his estates and much of the money he had given to those who suffered from the Baron. When people asked where he would live, he smiled and shook his head and said that soon enough all would know.

In the temple high above Antar, with its high arching nave starkly furnished and yet filled with light, with a grace that drew the eyes upward as in a soaring beech forest of slender silver trunks -- in the wood-paneled sanctuary of this temple, Mirath and Dalvar knelt by each other. They pledged vows as Ferenth and Mischka had pledged long years before. The lines of grief that had been etched so deeply into Dalvar's face were smoothed away, until only lines of laughter and love remained.

Mischka stepped forward to lay his hand on their heads in blessing. Then he said to Mirath and Saschka: "I can no longer sing. Will you sing for me?" And they sang, and the tears ran down their cheeks, and Mischka's, and Dalvar's and everyone's.

So Dalvar and Mirath were married in the temple of the Lady, thronged with those who came to celebrate the wedding as the streets were thronged with crowds of revelers. If there were some dissenters from the happiness, they were discreet enough to remain indoors and not intrude on the joy of others.

That evening, as they sat together in the house that once had been Amerach's, then Ferrar's, and now Saschka's, Mischka said to Mirath: "Now my daughter, what will you and your husband do?"

"First, tell us what you have decided you will do," she replied.

"I will return to the Tabirnian Hills. I'll become again a shepherd."

"And we will return with you," said Mirath.

"Do you not wish to remain here with Saschka, in Antar?"

"No," said Dalvar, "Ever since I saw those western mountains I have been drawn to them. Though the life may be harsh, yet we have wealth enough to be free of the tyranny of weather and live in freedom from want. We wish to come with you, my friend, if you will have us."

"With all my heart," said Mischka. "And you, Misk, will you join us, too?"

"Perhaps one day," his nephew replied. "But for now, I will stay here in Antar, perhaps even take to the sea with Rakal."

Mischka, Mirath, and Dalvar stayed until Silvren was delivered of her daughter. Then they bid farewell to Saschka, Silvren and Misk, promising they would return soon to visit them, and set forth for the western mountains. There they restored the old home of Mischka's parents, not far from Linar and Niëra, and had soon settled in.

Though Mischka no longer traveled the roads singing, yet to him came many who loved to sing. And his house was always filled with laughter and music, with the deep gruff voice of Dalvar, the sweet voice of Mirath, and the many stories of Mischka's tale.

www.ingramcontent.com/pod-product-compliance
Lightning Source LLC
LaVergne TN
LVHW010051110826
845155LV00028B/284

* 9 7 8 1 8 8 9 3 1 4 3 3 4 *